THE BLOOD OF THE EMPIRE

BY XAVIER LEGGETT

To Jennifer!
Have fun.

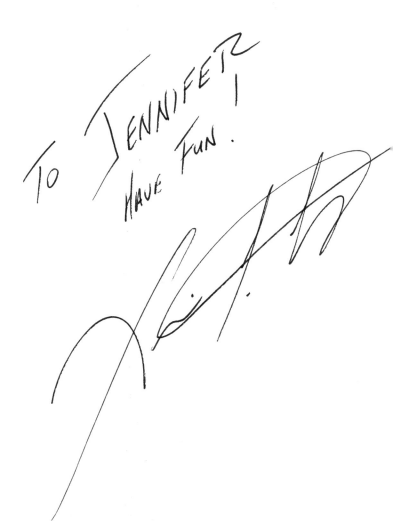

Acknowledgements

It would be impossible for me to thank all of the people who have had a positive influence on me and my writing. However, three people have made *The Blood of the Empire* a better novel than it would have been without their contributions: Francesca diStephano, Cynthia Kuns, Jillian Jurica, and Lisa Roberts-Traver. This book is dedicated to them.

PROLOGUE
Stardate: 4959.267:5. Between the orbits of Darmen and Vouther

DANNEN Leers thought he was going to die the moment the small starship decelerated from Warp; thought that his guts were going to be ripped from his body in surreal spaghettification just seconds before angry flame incinerated him. He bit his upper lip, eyes scanning the mutely lit forward hold as it thundered into a violent maelstrom of noise and mayhem.

An experienced pilot in his own right, he knew this wasn't a routine transition from Hyperspace back into normal space—*sweet bloody hell, it was anything but a normal deceleration* . . . and since he wasn't on the bridge flying this beast, he had no choice but to ride this thing out. The deck plates beneath his boots shuddered for several seconds, and then bounced and gyrated to such an extreme that he would have tumbled from his jump-station if he hadn't been securely fastened in. Flashing amber warning lights turned into angry red emergency strobes. The cover to one of the emergency electrical buffer panels shredded itself into a column of sparks several feet long.

And yet no alarms sounded to alert the crew to the danger. Then again, Leers didn't need shrilling alarms to tell him something was wrong and that he and everyone on this ship was about to die—not with the bulkheads protesting against the quantum tidal forces slamming against the hull. The human gripped the armrest of his seat, fingers digging in, straining to hear the computerized tocsin signifying the ship's doom. Waiting for that piercing shriek . . . *waiting* . . . the thunderous shuddering continued unabated. It made him wonder what was happening up on the bridge because his mission would have to be aborted if the damned Pulsarians detected this starship's Warp re-entry signal. It would be suicide for them to stick around. Not a thought Leers relished—*to come all this, after weeks in Hyperspace just to head back to the asteroid base empty handed.*

Despite his feelings, Leers knew that Captain Marksen and the crew of the *Renegade Runner* would do everything in their power to get him to the surface of the fourth planet of this star system. The *Renegade Runner* was a KR-91 Infiltrator, an extreme range, deep-space gunboat with speed—an insane amount of speed. As a starship, it was designed to get personnel from friendly territory or star systems into enemy space where they could carry out rescue missions, demolition duty, search and destroy missions, or a host of other missions—it really didn't matter—quickly and quietly, then get the hell out of the area before the Pulsarians even knew they were ever there.

The *Renegade Runner* was a small ship, barely four-thousand metric tons empty, made of sensor and scanner absorbing composites, with a compliment of thirty-seven officers and crew. Its deflector grid was questionable; it had no room for a stage II cloaking device, let alone a stage I—besides which, cloaking devices only made detection more difficult, not impossible. Thus, the design of the *Renegade Runner* was perfect for an operation of this nature. If you kept quiet, the Pulsarians could not track you. If they couldn't track you, they couldn't kill you. KR-91 Infiltrator ships were designed to cross vast distances of Hyperspace in record time, while keeping detectable Warp emissions to a minimum. That was the rub, as many Warp engineers would tell you. As a rule, engines that could cut through the billions of cubic parsecs of Hyperspace the quickest were among the 'loudest' engines ever built. They issued a normal space re-entry 'boom' that could be picked up on the most archaic sensor. All well and good if your intent was just to set speed records or to ferry passengers from one star system to the next in the quickest time possible—not so good during wartime, when you needed to sneak in and out of enemy star systems and complete missions undetected. By contrast, engines designed for low or null Warp reentry emissions—engines specifically designed to thwart detection—were some of the slowest ever built, thus, making Hyperspace travel time last for months, even years. Not an attractive alternative when the execution of sensitive missions needed a turn-around time of a few weeks, if not days. What military planners needed was a starship that was both quick and quiet—a damned near impossible combination. Yet the KR-91, while not completely solving the problem of incorporating both speed and stealth, came awfully close and was the best the navy had to offer, and was the only ship that Admiral Doss—

Leers felt relief washing over him when the gyrations suddenly ceased; the strobing red diminishing into warning amber, then to pale green; the bouncing finally subsiding into smooth space travel.

He hit the quick-release mechanism on his straps and pushed forward, floating above his jump-station; no artificial gravity onboard the *Renegade Runner.*

All around him a dozen personnel, both human and non-human, began assembling themselves to their mission stations. Leers had never worked with any of these individuals before, but admired their patient professionalism. They showed no signs of being lightyears behind enemy lines—in the Darmen System to be exact; territory that would threaten to burn them all alive if they weren't careful. Nor did they seem to be affected by the fact that their Warp deceleration hadn't been as smooth as it should've been. Leers reminded himself to focus on his part of the mission and let the skipper—and the rest of the crew, for that matter, worry about theirs.

"Hey, how are we doing, commander?" Leers asked one of *Runner's* personnel he immediately recognized. She was the *Renegade Runner's* executive officer, fierce looking with dark hair and brown predatory slits for eyes.

"Mr. Leers, I've got a sitrep for you," Lieutenant Commander Aria Glennis said. She grabbed onto the handholds above her head and pulled her way toward him. "Glad you survived the Warp re-entry—that was a rough one, but all systems are nominal."

"That shouldn't be considered a normal space re-entry in anyone's book, commander," Leers disagreed politely. "I thought we'd have to abort—what happened anyway?"

"Don't ask me, you're a pilot, so's I hear—maybe you can tell me," Glennis said. "The threat board is clear. The Pulsarians don't know we're here."

"But, ah, we both know that the Pulsarians can be sneaky bastards . . ." *Even if they did know, I doubt we'd abort* . . . "I wouldn't put it past them—"

"We've got the best passive sensors in the navy, Mr. Leers—if a Pulsarian general flushes a toilet a parsec away we'll be able to detect it."

Despite the hyperbole, Leers knew they'd have ample warning for a quick exit. He just hoped the warning would come *before* he reached the surface of Darmen. A lot could go wrong with this job and if worse came to worse, he'd most likely be facing the music alone, while the navy hauled ass.

"How're you feeling, Leers? The temperature on that planet is going to be . . ."

"Hot." Leers took a deep breath and exhaled slowly, considering the fact that there was no turning back now. "I feel good, tired, ready; all of the above. I've spent the last ten hours before the deceleration inside the desert environment simulator module trying to complete ten-thousand restrained sit-ups."

"Ten-thousand?" Glennis eyed him briefly, skeptically. Despite his braggadocio, she knew it to be true. These Omnitraus operators—Officers, whatever they called themselves—were always in what was called, 'beyond peak condition'. They could hold their breath for up to ten minutes while submerge under more than 200 meters of water; or hold off the debilitating effects of sustained brutal lateral G-forces for minutes on end—on top of all that, they could handle a vast array of side-arms and packet explosives . . . their field-craft was staggering.

"Don't worry I did and hour's worth of pushups as well and high-G leg-presses too." Leers shrugged. He couldn't quite turn off the boasting. *What more do you want?* "Could've done more—but ya'll kicked me out of the environment-sim module for that, er, hair-raising Warp decel."

"We have to shut down all non-essential functions for the deceleration, as you should know," Glennis said flatly, "even if you aren't navy."

Leers knew this, but said nothing as he and Glennis rotated up and floated to the aft section of the cargo hold. To his left and right were storage lockers, ammunition containers, an emergency EVA suit, laser rifles with across-the-spectrum targeting scopes, and a dozen Fleeter and Phiser PBX side-arms. He smiled. Useful weapons, yes, but if he found himself in a fight he trusted his Delnalt '44 holstered to his right leg more than either of these weapons. He wasn't going to the planet Darmen to pick a fight and show off how brave he was, he was going in—sneaking in—to steal vital information the Delrel Federated Republic needed, then get the hell out. And that was it. No heroics, no bragging. Just get in, then get out.

"Here's where I leave you. Keep your head on a swivel, Mr. Leers." They shook hands awkwardly.

Leers watched her disappear into an above hatch, then turned his attention to the four technicians in front of him who were making final checks on the small re-entry vehicle that would get him to the surface of Darmen. There was nothing remarkable about the Mission Atmospheric Injection Sphere (MA-IS). It was roughly spherical in shape, hence the name, and perhaps a meter and a half or more in diameter. To him it closely resembled some of the smaller escapepods found on many luxury liners or some of the larger military capital ships. The KR-91 only held a crew of forty and had no escapepods of her own; seeing one in the middle of the cargo hold with cables and fuel lines snaking away from it seemed strangely out of place.

The first aspect of the infiltration plan was to approach Darmen from the southern polar region and launch the MA-IS. The capsule would penetrate the outer-atmosphere at more than 25,000kpx. On a casual scanner sweep, the capsule would appear to be nothing more than a small meteor, one of hundreds that crashed through the atmosphere daily—perhaps larger than most, but a meteor nonetheless—and would be ignored. Drogue chutes would deploy as the capsule dropped through the stratosphere, followed by the deployment of the main parasails when the capsule was a scant kilometer from the surface. Once on the ground he would—

"Let's get you suited up, Captain Leers," one of the female technicians said to him, looking up from her work on the capsule. She grimaced at calling him 'captain'. In the navy, a captain was a grizzled veteran with more than twenty years of service. This guy wasn't with the navy and he definitely was younger than she. He was an Omnitraus Officer, one of those secretive special-mission operatives she'd heard so much about, but had never met until this mission. They were fighter pilots who were also supposedly commandos, weapons experts, and covert agents. They had a formidable reputation as being highly skilled and dangerous. This one though—this *human*, of all beings—was a little too cavalier and easygoing; he didn't fit the mold. He smiled too much, joked around without a care in the galaxy. He could be serious at times, but in her mind, he just didn't look like one of those trained killers she'd always imagined.

"Twenty-three minutes to launch," another technician said, moving up from behind him. "All systems are nominal. The skipper reports that the threat board is clear."

"Bet ya'll be glad to get rid of me," Leers said to the first technician, "if only for a few hours."

"Don't worry, captain, you'll be back in no time . . . and we'll get to enjoy your company and your war stories for another two weeks in Hyperspace." Somehow she couldn't keep the sarcasm out of her voice. "And we'll also get to enjoy your two cases of beer."

"Wait a sec—how did ya'll find out about the beer? That was a secret bet between me and the skipper."

"There aren't any secrets on a navy ship, captain," she said curtly. "Do you really think you could hide two cases of bitter on a tin-can this small?"

"Ah, reckon not." Leers floated upright and held his arms out. He was already attired in a desert environment uniform. The planet that he was going to be working on was a hostile world of vast desert regions with barely twelve percent surface water. The suit was a triple layered khaki uniform with cooling cells snaking through it like arteries. The coolant even flowed into his boots and the skullcap he wore beneath his helmet. Of course, the fabric was made of breathable material, allowing heat and moisture he produced to escape while keeping the desert heat from poaching him. The technicians began strapping an ATAC module to his back. It didn't weigh anything now, but once he hit the surface it would probably feel like a ton. As much as he wanted to leave this piece of equipment behind, he knew he couldn't. It contained items needed for mission survival: five liters of water, a medical supply kit, tools, protein and carbohydrate bars, concussion grenades, detachable and remotely operable sensor jamming pods, as well as a small tactical sub-space radio with multi-mode scrambler and low-probability-of-intercept shielding, which he'd use to contact the loitering KR-91 once his assignment was complete. The only items in the ATAC module he didn't mind carrying were extra ammunition magazines for the Delnalt '44 energy pistol—although he hoped that he would not be forced to use them.

"On the way back, though," the tech continued, interrupting Leers' thoughts, "you're going to have to tell some better stories—flying serpents and alligator men, come on now."

"We're gonna be drinking so much beer ya'll won't even care," Leers whispered. He stomach quivered slightly. "And those reptiles almost killed me."

"Well, you survived, right? But tell me this captain; there are about forty of us on this ship and only two cases of beer. All some of us are going to be drinking is recycled water."

"I hadn't thought on that," Leers lied.

"No, sir, I guess you hadn't."

She, as well as the other tech, was Dracterian, one of the allied races within the DFR. After a few moments of sardonic laughter, she and the others returned to their work methodically, going down their checklist. His survival depended on her, whether she liked him or not. He was only joking, couldn't she see that. He smiled. She didn't smile back. Instead, she ran a small medical sensor over his body.

"Your bone density is down point zero-two percent. Immune system stable, muscle density is—"she blinked, then shook the device, reading the indicators again—"better than when we set out from port."

"How did you manage that?" the other tech asked absently, not expecting an answer.

"There, you're all set," she said after finishing her scan.

Leers nodded a 'thank-you' and gave her a 'thumbs-up'. He moved up and settled himself into the capsule, thankful for the zero-g sensation. Without it—well—he'd have managed to wedge himself inside, but it would've required cursing in several languages during the entire process.

The Dracterians, and now an Aracrayderian began securing him into the cramped capsule using their steel-shod boots against his shoulders to anchor themselves as they roughly cinched up his restraints. In spite of himself, Leers found that he was grunting with each pull. Flat on his back, he looked up. These females were enjoying their task. Did they actually hate him that much?

"Sixty seconds to launch," a voice echoed in the hold. "All lights are green, all indications operational, and the threat board is clear. The Pulsarians still don't know we're here."

If they did, we'd be dead by now, Leers thought.

"Roger that," the Aracrayderian technician barked. "We are ready to launch."

"Stowing all loose gear."

The Dracterian dipped inside the capsule, her face scant centimeters from Leers'. "Good luck," she whispered. This time she managed a slight smile.

The human merely nodded. He didn't believe in luck—it was the last thing he needed. For the first time, Leers became aware of his ragged breathing, and swallowed. He could actually feel his heart pounding in his chest. *Didn't an operative get killed in one of these spheres several months ago? Yeah, they called it a glitch. The poor officer got roasted alive during entry into atmosphere—a glitch? Hell of a time to be thinking about that now.*

"Sealing hatch," it was the last thing he'd ever hear from her again.

Stardate: 4959.265:1. Rohabagrah Wildlife Preserve, Murmansk

Rook stood on the desolate beach alone; those were the orders passed from one professional to another. He'd never been to this planet before, Murmansk—*what an odd name for a world bordering on the galactic Frontier.* Once he'd been briefed about this mission, he studied this world and its inhabitants and knew more about Murmansk than he really cared to—for instance, directly above him was the moon, Prometheus, nearly 400,000 kilometers away and needing only twenty days to orbit around her parent. There was also the smaller moon, Ellelexius, conforming to an orbit a mere 57,000 kilometers overhead and racing through another three-day cycle against the eastern horizon. *Two moons*, Rook thought, *how quaint*; on his homeworld there were more than fifty natural satellites.

It didn't diminish this planet's importance or the reason why he was here. He could die on this world and no one would know how it happened. On reflex, his hand reached down toward the gun-belt that wasn't there. No weapons, no packet explosives, he couldn't even bring a military grade sensor scrambler, nothing—unarmed meant exactly that. He wore light-weight mountaineering clothing, low-profile hiking boots, and a small rucksack filled with water canisters, salt tablets, and three days' rations. No knife. He could see not taking the energy weapons and the packet explosive—but no knives? Again, orders were orders. Which was why he'd been waiting here for three hours, feigning interest in the tidal waves slamming against the jagged rocks, the sudden gusts of moist air that smelled strangely of nutmeg and jungle rot . . . *waiting.* The cragged shoreline stretched for at least five-hundred kilometers to the north and south and bore no signs of sentient transformation. This beach, this shoreline, the mountains and forest behind him had been protected for more than 3,000 years by conservationists many lightyears away, who probably had only read about the igneous extrusions and the abundance of life that feed on each other beneath the waves. It was a shame, a neo-conservationist himself, Rook wouldn't be able to really appreciate the beauty of Murmansk's Rohabagrah Preserve, dawn was still several hours away and blind meets were always dangerous. *Waiting. . .*

For a split second, Rook thought that his ears had deceived him—no, there was definitely a sound, metal on metal—behind him and to the left. There it was again; this time he knew he wasn't mistaken. Two hundred meters away, loud enough to be heard above the wind and the crash of water against rock—Rook doubted that a human could've picked up those sounds. Now, he heard a third and final 'thump' followed by a bit of cursing.

The Aracrayderian resisted the urge to face the direction of the arrivals. Mist ticklishly feathering his nose and whiskers, he strained instead to concentrate on their conversation. A bit too far away to make out individual words—even still, they were relatively loud. They were whispering now and complaining as they traversed over gullies and shoots. Bad form, not very professional, despite previous assurances to the contrary. And they were carrying weapons. Not good. How many were there? The contact on Narterium said that there'd be two humans on Murmansk to meet him. By the sound of the jabbering, there were at least three of them. Two were bickering about weapons and driving, the third telling them to shut-up. Now a fourth voice chimed in—obviously the youngest of the group from the vocal pitch. Rook smiled briefly, they were all humans and hadn't spotted him yet. Supposedly, they were here to help him book passage off-world and would provide him with a passport—not to kill him, or conversely do something so stupid that he'd be forced to kill them.

One never knew with blind meets. He had enough money in his rucksack that any group of thugs or mercenaries would gladly cut out his guts for a tenth of what he carried. And here he was on a beach, alone, with no weapons, no back-up, thousands of kilometers from the nearest town, and several dozen lightyears from any allied planet. *What the hell was he doing here?*

Rook glanced to his left, the conversations had suddenly ceased—he'd been spotted, finally. There were five of them, cautiously moving through the darkness, stumbling over the calcified teeth of the beach. They weren't carrying any torches, which meant that they were trying their best not to be spotted too early; yet, they weren't spread out as they approached, indicating to Rook that they hadn't any military experience either. From the sound of their ragged breathing, they were out of condition too. Two of the men might find better use out of their weapons by using them as walking sticks instead of the laser-rifles that they were.

What Rook found unsettling was that they had approached the wildlife preserve in an aircar. Rook hadn't heard its engines, only the thumps of the slamming doors. Perhaps these men weren't as unprofessional as they acted and had an engine that—

"Greetings," one of the arrivals called out, clearly the leader. He was heavy-set, built low to the ground, and didn't appear to have any weapons. "Mr. Tyndak is that you?"

"Who else would it be," Rook called back. Turning to the five, he could really smell them now. One of them was wearing cologne.

"Yes, who else exactly," said the leader, his grizzled appearance unmistakable now. The man had to be half a century older than Rook. The others varied in age and disposition. The one wearing the cologne looked constipated.

"This would be a nice spot to bring the family for a camping holiday, no?" Rook inquired with a toothy grin.

"It would be nice at that," the human shrugged, scratching his beard. "However, this land is protected. It's a wildlife preserve and sanctuary, so to speak, for various indigenous lower lifeforms and, er . . . people in our business."

"Exactly." *Well, he didn't mangle the counter sign too badly,* Rook thought.

"We'd thought you'd be late."

"Who lost the bet, I'm never late."

"Is that so." The old man smiled. He turned to his compatriots. "Checking the rendezvous-point early and all that, eh? You see, clowns, I told you he was true professional."

"Are we supposed to be impressed," the cologne man said, "we've done this before." He kept his rifle leveled at Rook's chest. "Hold your arms out."

One of the other humans slung his weapon over his shoulder and proceeded to give Rook a pat-down.

"The arrangement stated not to carry weapons," Rook said.

"I know," answered the leader. "It's just good business to always check. No, I'll correct myself; it's good for survival."

Rook was about to supply his own comment when he saw a flash of metal out of the corner of his eye. A knife. One of the men had suddenly darted at him from the right. Rook ducked under the blade and delivered two quick punches to the man's mid-section, while rotating around to catch the man who had been giving him the pat-down in the throat with his boot.

Cologne man threw his rifle aside and launched his own attack, screaming guttural rubbish the Aracrayderian had never heard before.

Rook sidestepped, then ran his knee into the human's groin. The man folded under the brutal shock of his smashed testicles, his fists flailing into the air uselessly. Rook heeled the man's calf and finished him with a well-placed chop to the trapezius.

A fourth man raised his laser-rifle—

"That's enough!" The old man shouted. He shoved the barrel of the weapon down. "Enough. I told you he'd be good and that he could take you clowns."

Rook whirled again, slightly confused.

"Sorry, friend," the old man said. He gestured toward his team who'd all been beaten in less than two seconds. "You see, he doesn't need a weapon because he *is* a weapon. Now get up you fools." He turned toward Rook, his face an easy-going, business-like smile. "I'm Claude. This is Renn, Keither, and the one who smells like cheap whore is Arn." He began helping them up from the rocks. "This young one, next to me, is my son, Brno. Welcome to Murmansk."

Rook helped Claude bring Keither to his feet, who looked at Rook with dazed astonishment. Rook reached over to Arn, who had taken the knee to the groin. Arn slapped his hand away and began cursing. Rook unceremoniously stepped over and away from him. He knew what the human was saying and didn't appreciate any of it.

"Father, I would've gotten him."

"No, you would've killed one of your own men," Rook said. "If you're going to attack me from behind, make damned sure you know what you're doing—and make sure that your heart isn't beating like a—whatever you call those percussion instruments—"

"A drum?" Renn said.

"You could hear his heartbeat?" Claude asked. "Amazing."

"Only at the last second—maybe half a second."

Claude roared with laughter and bent over Arn, who was still writhing. "Arn, you hear that you cheap smelling rascal; you should be grateful for the lesson our friend here taught you."

"Always willing to oblige, only next time try to give me a little more warning," Rook said. "I could've killed—"

"Ah, but we gave you warning," countered Claude. "You just said so yourself."

"But it would've been a lot easier on your men."

"Easier on my men? Ha."

"Yes."

"Strange, you say that. My men have had it easy for a long time—maybe too long, eh? Brno, Renn, help Arn." Claude slowly reached into his jacket—Rook didn't flinch, something Claude took immediate note of. He slowly pulled out a laser pistol. "This is for you."

Rook took the weapon and tested its heft and feel. "Excellent, thank-you." Rook had used a Hellington Snub-nose before. Some operators called it a 'twenty-one'—*but how did Claude*—never mind, he didn't need an answer.

"The money?"

"In my rucksack."

Claude merely pointed and Keither limped over and picked up the payment. Keither had a little bit of difficulty lifting the rucksack, to which Claude turned to Rook and said, "that's way too much money."

"How do you know, you haven't counted it."

Claude pulled back the Velcro roughly and peaked inside, *tsking* to himself. "Too much."

"The job's that important."

"Alright, we'll get you off-world and through customs; no problem at all. You'll get to Nijimegan in a day or so."

"A day or so. . . You have nothing more precise than that?"

"I'm afraid not."

"Maybe you're right. Maybe you are getting paid more than what's necessary."

Claude's face began to darken.

"A mild joke, friend Claude—I meant no offense." He knew humans well enough to know that you could never tell if you were humoring them or truly insulting them. "After you get me through customs—with this," Rook gestured with the snub-nose, "you'll never see me again."

"That's unfortunate," Claude said. "My men could use the chance to learn more of those hand-to-hand combat techniques."

"Father, it's getting late."

"You mean early."

Rook knew Brno was right, they had to get moving. "I'm going to need some better clothes. Designer clothing—at least two business suits and an overcoat."

"Not a problem."

"And shoes," Rook quickly added. "These boots I'm wearing won't look convincing with any suit."

"Yes, I've already surmised that. Anything else?"

"Breakfast."

Claude stared at Rook for a moment then roared in laughter again. "Not extra magazines for the weapon, or the names of my ghost contacts on Nijimegan, or a duplicate passport? Friend, for what you're paying us, I think we can manage something civilized for you to eat."

Stardate: 4959.267:3. Klipsker Spaceport, Elst

"My body is *not* for sale," N'ckshell Slayton warned, her voice as meek and panicky as she could make it. It didn't work. One of the new arrivals, a Mr. Thorne by the look of him, greeted her words with an angry shove. N'ckshell went spinning toward the forward bulkhead of the freighter, smashing her face against the blackened metal.

"Kiss that bulkhead, sweetie," Thorne ordered, "and don't move."

Cowering, N'ckshell did as she was told—just on the edge of her peripheral vision she could see that in his right hand was a Comcack-497 laser pistol, activated and aimed at her head. Now her back was to the captain and his four crewmen, and most problematic of all, the two armed merchants who had just boarded the freighter not more than thirty seconds ago. Thorne, one of the merchants, kicked her feet apart forcing her to spread her legs; he leaned against her, forcing her palms against the cold metal.

"Stay up against the wall," he said. "That's it . . . nice girl."

N'ckshell could smell the stale whiskey on his breathe, her will alone kept her from puking. A small sob escaped her mouth as she let her body sag.

"Everything has a price in this star system, especially foreign women," the chief merchant said, patting the thick breast pockets of his parka. He stood at the center of the primary cargo hold, slowly surveying the liquid containers to his left and right, the power loader above him, and perhaps most importantly, Captain Cairn and his crew. All of them kept their line of sight away from his probing glare.

"Mr. Havelock, this really isn't necessary, you don't have to harm her—there's been a terrible mistake," Captain Cairn stammered finally, his voice cracking. His eyes darted crazily from Havelock to Thorne. He hit the lever to close the boarding ramp. More snow and ice raged inward before the ramp sealed itself to the hull. "I don't know what happened or how things got so fouled up—"

Dear God, shut up you idiot, N'ckshell's mind raged. *We can make it out of this mess if you keep quiet . . .*

"All I know is, I sent a couple of my boys to collect on the lease of this freighter—you know, back on Karaline," Havelock said, "and I don't hear from them again. I hail your ship, but you blast out of orbit and Warp into Hyperspace without answering. So Thorne and myself hop aboard my corvette and land here on Elst." He stood in front of the freighter's captain now, his face just centimeters from Captain Cairn's face. "You know I have to keep an eye on all my captains who ship freight for me. Then we find a woman on your ship, a woman I've never seen before, a woman I don't even know."

"She's the newest member of my crew," Cairn mumbled, looking at Havelock's boots.

"You get your crew from me, captain," Havelock snarled. "You get your trade agreements from me, your manifests from me—do you understand?"

"Yes."

"I don't think you do, otherwise this woman wouldn't be here."

"A friend strongly recommended that I take her where she needed to go—and I took the money and—"*Shut-up*, N'ckshell screamed at him from her mind.

"You took the money and you still haven't paid me."

N'ckshell managed to crane her head around slightly, her eyes straining to see what the opposition was composed of. She had Thorne holding her against the bulkhead, with Havelock standing behind him. Meanwhile Captain Cairn and his crewmen were to her left—rooted in place, not willing to take any action in her defense. They looked like men who were beaten;

they looked like defeated souls preparing themselves to die. Havelock spun and looked at her, their eyes meeting for a moment.

"What do you think, eh, Thorne? Maybe she's more than just a member of the good captain's crew, eh?" Havelock tapped Thorne on the shoulder so that he could get a better study of the woman's posterior. Even through the dual layered, olive-drab jumpsuit she wore, he could clearly see the outlines of her more than generous rump. Dracterian females weren't supposed to pack so much flesh. A rarity indeed, this one could easily fetch what Captain Cairn owed him for the year and then some. "Be that as it may, I'm taking her with me as payment for the next two quarters."

Captain Cairn stumbled back as the words hit him with the force of a lead pipe. "But, Mr. Havelock—how will I be able to—"

"That's your problem." Havelock turned to Thorne. "Be careful with her my friend, otherwise we won't get as much as we could from the Pulsarians. Frisk her—and let me know how firm that ass is."

"*Go and shite,*" N'ckshell hissed.

"I can't let you sell her to the Pulsarians—she's a citizen of the Delrel Federated Republic," Cairn managed to say. "The Pulsarians will kill her after they've—"

"I don't care what they do," Havelock said, reaching in his pockets for his pack of cigarettes.

N'ckshell flinched as Thorne began patting her up. He started with her calves then moved up to her thighs. She shut down a startled cry of rage and revulsion as Thorne took his time massaging her.

"You freak," she snarled.

"Shut-up, bitch." Thorne slapped the back of her head, knocking her face against the bulkhead. She could taste the blood after biting the inside of her lip. He punched her in the small of the back and shoved her to the grating of the deck. He quickly picked her up by the arm then shoved her against the bulkhead again. With Havelock clearly amused, Thorne began exploring her buttocks and breasts.

Captain Cairn wanted to turn away but couldn't. What could he do? Nothing. Not a damned thing. If he dared to intervene he'd lose his ship, or worse, Havelock might have Thorne execute a member of his crew, as an example to his other captains. Havelock could do any number of things, he had the power to change contracts, raise the price of his lease, even make people disappear.

N'ckshell knew what the captain was thinking. She could see him struggling with his mental paralysis through the tangles of her hair. She knew what had to be done.

"I think we should party, have a little fun with 'er before we sell 'er to the Pulsarians, no?" Thorne ventured. "She's a good piece of meat—sturdy too."

"You can't do that," Cairn pleaded.

"Oh, 'er hair smells good," Thorne said. "Turn around, love." He roughly spun her around so that they were now face-to-face. Thorne stared into her eyes, never before seeing such beauty, such calm. "Alright sweetie, let's have a taste."

Thorne never saw the elbow that struck him just below his left eye. He stumbled a half step back, more in shock than in actual pain—the bitch hit him. She was going to pay. Another fist caught him beneath the jaw forcing his teeth to snap down hard on his tongue. He tripped into Havelock, his laser pistol teetered from his grasp . . .

"*No, no, no,*" the captain was shouting at her.

In a whirlwind, N'ckshell launched herself against Thorne's body and snatched up the laser pistol as it clattered against the deck.

Thorne was already reaching for his hold-out piece when a triple-tap from his primary weapon—in the hands of that woman—caught him in the chest. In a nanosecond, his heart and lungs were flash seared. Thorne crunched to the deck grating dead. Havelock caught a single shot to his stomach causing him to crumple to his knees in agony. He began clawing at his ruined abdominals through his parka, spittle and mucus frothing from his mouth and nose.

N'ckshell strolled over to him—

"No," the captain screamed, "don't do it."

N'ckshell fired another laser through Havelock's forehead.

"My, God, what have you done?"

"Something you should've done five years ago."

Captain Cairn settled against the bulkhead, his breathing harsh, and began rubbing his chin. "But what am I supposed to do with their bodies?" His eyes were blinking furiously.

Slayton looked at him. "If you don't want them stinking up your ship, dump them outside in the snow."

"But, I . . ." Despite the chill, sweat began to bead on his forehead.

N'ckshell Slayton stepped up to him in slow, carefully measured steps; she placed her hands on both sides of his face and leaned in close to him, looking directly into his eyes. "Look, captain, calm down, okay. I know all of this is happening rather suddenly. I wasn't expecting it either. But you have to stay calm, okay? I just need five hours to complete my mission, then I'll be back. My government will pay you well for having to put up with all of this shit and I'm sorry." *What the fuck else do you want me to say?*

Slayton released him and activated the loading ramp. Snow and ice whipped up around her legs as she trudged into the whiteness without a word.

CHAPTER I
STRATAGEMS AT DAWN

DARMEN. A hot, dirty little planet; a remote rock tormented by the intense rays of a dispassionate yellow-giant sun. For six billion years, the blistering rays hammered the planet relentlessly, beating it into submission, drying oceans, killing vegetation, and tearing down mountains. Darmen was a planet embracing death, a planet dominated by the geological features of a vast desert. From the Gulf of Aracan where mountainous crags jutted out of the dunes like rotting teeth, to the towering wall of blood-colored rock shielding the Marwa Polar region, and the exquisitely layered shelves of the Garsum continental plate; Darmen was a world of hostility and beauty.

It was here, to this world of contrasting beauty and death, that the Pulsarian war-machine had come and established a base of operations. The base had been constructed on the eastern flats of the Tarrisaum Sand Ocean, ninety kilometers off the southwestern shoulder of the Sasmentar mountain range, and was relatively small. At the start of the war, this was where all the frantic action took place, the prepping and staging; the logistics of conquest ran through Darmen first. With the invasion of the Delrel Federated Republic, hundreds of warships Warped into the sector to load or off load equipment, weapons, ammunition; billions of metric tonnage moved on a daily basis, millions of Pulsarians trained in the desert. Darmen had been the prime port, the operational epicenter of the Imperial war-machine.

Now, after seven years of the bloodiest warfare the galaxy had ever known, the activity on Darmen was greatly diminished; loading docks, warehouses, hangars, bunkers, all deserted, all unused. Pulsarians still trained here, but it was nothing like the magnitude of the past.

At the center of the base was the monstrous Darmen Regional Operational Center (DROC). A dome of metal and duracreete eight-hundred meters in diameter, the DROC was the actual location where the admirals and generals had formulated stratagems for the invasion of Federation space more than seven years ago. The operations had taken place dozens of parsecs away, but the orders had been cut and signed here. The personnel who existed within the labyrinthine corridors and went about their daily assignments knew nothing of the grandeur of the past. Activities now, except for various weapon exercises, were routine and predictable. All that would change in a matter of hours.

A fact that would weigh most heavily on the shoulders of Major Haast Gheretti. He always enjoyed reporting for duty before all the others; especially Colonel Urethagon, who wouldn't get here for another three hours. There were more than two thousand rooms within the DROC. Gheretti was in control of just a dozen, but the personnel within them were the base's highest trained and most important individuals. Gheretti strolled down the long row of consoles, equipment, workstations, and empty chairs. His uniform, though faded, was sharp and crisp and wasn't sticky with sweat, yet. Like all Pulsarians, his once rich blue-grey skin had become somewhat lighter since his tour began on Darmen more than two years ago.

He sat at a desk cluttered with work that should have been completed yesterday if not the week before; life on an Outland Base. There was none of that front line urgency here. No Delrels loitering on the outskirts of the system ready to commence bombing runs. No commando teams preparing to carry out acts of sabotage, tactical demolition, or assassination. The only thing important being played out here was the presence of the vaunted *Ghelk-Vhech* Straaka mechanized-infantry Legion. The entire legion should be moving out to the Tarrisaum by now, to the combat ranges; where 10,000 infantry soldiers would exercise against the Outland Base's very own defense Legion. The *Ghelk-Vhech* had traveled a dozen parsecs just to engage in mock warfare with two cohorts of Straaka garrisoned here. The simulated siege of the base would prove rather interesting. Major Haast Gheretti was looking forward to it; if nothing else it would give everyone something exciting to do for the next several days.

"Major, I have something rather curious developing here, sir," a Straaka sergeant said from a nearby workstation.

"What is it, then?" Gheretti moved up behind the sergeant's workstation. Gheretti suddenly looked around. "Where's the night duty officer?"

"The leftennant's at the weather relay station, sir." The sergeant frowned. "This you should look at. About a quarter hour ago, I began picking up faint Warp re-entry signals near the orbit of the fourth planet. I was about to report—"

"Was about to report it—why didn't you?"

"I'm reporting it now, sir, because regulation demands that I provide you with something better than trace readings. So far, that's all that I'm getting."

The major ignored the sergeant's tone—most Straaka trained peasants were like that. "Anything from the other control centers?"

"Nothing, sir."

"We're not scheduled for any visits from the Imperial Armada," Gheretti fumed, he didn't like any of this. "By the Bloody Pit, this is a restricted system. If they want to pass, they have to go through the network first. Hell, those vacuum eating scum established the protocols."

"I've sent a dispatch to communications but the Armada hasn't answered our repeated inquiries," the sergeant said flatly.

Gheretti leaned forward. "Do you think this could be a—"

"No, out of the question." The sergeant knew what his superior was thinking. "The Federation wouldn't alert us to their presence—they would arrive without warning, then start bombing."

Gheretti felt a trace of a grim smile form on his face. The Straaka Sergeant was correct in his analysis. So many years out of action made him a touch nervous at such occurrences. The Delrels would come without warning; they'd jam everything that they could, commence their bombing attacks, then leave quicker than they arrived. Fortunately, Darmen was so far behind the forward edge of the battle area that the Delrels wouldn't risk bombers just to blow up a few hundred buildings on a base that lost its significance more than five years ago. But it was rather close to the Frontier, Gheretti reminded himself, and the Delrels were unpredictable at best. You think you have them cornered and they pull some surprise maneuver to completely disrupt what you're trying to accomplish. As much as Gheretti disliked the sergeant's appraisal of the situation, it did have merit. He glanced at the monitor. With readings like that, it had to be the Armada and not the Federation. However, as an officer, Gheretti had to consider the remote no matter how improbable. Good officers had to be able to analyze the situation and quickly move on to items that mattered.

Placing his fists on his hips, he nodded slowly, his mouth twisted in consternation. This was the Imperial Armada and not the Federation. They came as they pleased, disregarding protocols as they saw fit, then left without a word. They had done so last week and the week before. You don't hear from them in months, then they just show up, fly circuits through the system, then leave. But why? This angered Gheretti more than simply troubling him.

The only reason identity protocols and warnings were established was to keep ground commanders, like him, from thinking that every Warp re-entry signature was an indication of an impending bombing or invasion. Perhaps the power of jumping from one star system to the next at speeds that exceeded light enlarged their already turgid egos.

"Very well, let's keep an eye on them," Gheretti said finally. "Angle all of your scans on them. If the 'admiral' or whomever the hell else is commanding that ship has a bowel movement, I want to be able to record it and play it back to him before he leaves."

****

As the fingers of the morning sun felt their way through the crags of the Sasmentar Mountains, the Outland Base began to slowly awaken. Ventilation systems whirled to life among the roof-works of many buildings; sub-space communication dishes clanked into position and pointed their arrays skyward. Small single-seat sky planes buzzed through the air like frenzied mosquitoes as Armored Personnel Carriers, surface skimmers, cargo-transfer sleds, and Mechanized Aerial Targeting Ion Guns sped down the unpaved roads on their way to the exercise ranges in the deep desert.

Leers swore as he edged further back into the shadow cast by a water reclamation building made of steel and crumbling laser-cut basalt. He should've been done with his mission by now and on his way out of here well before dawn . . . but he was just now getting started. And with the activity on the base increasing, it was going to be difficult to complete his mission unnoticed. He knew something had gone wrong with that Warp deceleration and that it would lead to more bad luck. Mission parameters allowed for a certain amount of so-called 'non-lateral mayhem,' but this—a surface skimmer streaked by a mere ten meters in front of him, its engines yowling through the swirling desert dirt and sand.

Leers fanned the smog from his face as the skimmer roared around a far corner and cursed his predicament again. If only the blasted skipper—the near calamitous deceleration wasn't entirely his fault—he couldn't blame that on him, those things happened, they couldn't be controlled or predicted. But he could blame the captain of the *Renegade Runner* for dropping him twenty kilometers from his pre-briefed landing zone. Twenty kilometers! He was supposed to have landed five kilometers from the outer marker of the Outland Base—at the most—not twenty. The capsule had landed a little over twenty-five kilometers from the actual base. He was forced to cross the open desert in the dark of night; more than six hours of alternately jogging and walking through the desert, hiding behind brush, darting around rocky out-croppings. More than six hours of tripping and stumbling over rocks, sinking shin-deep in sand, his heart banging like mad whenever he thought he heard something: a wild animal, a grenade being thrown through the air, the whine of a laser about to cut him in two. At night, in the middle of hostile territory, on a planet he'd never been on before—despite his training, despite his solid professionalism, his mind still played tricks on him. Training only made you press on with your mission and stay alert, it didn't eliminate the fear.

Press on Leers did; he did have an operational time-line of eight hours for mission completion; but nowhere in the plan did it call for a trek across the desert, an act that pushed mission parameters to the extreme. Adding to the madness of the situation was the fact that he'd spent two weeks in a weightless environment. Yes, he'd trained in the *Renegade Runner's* environment module—but it robbed the ship of power and he certainly couldn't stay inside of it indefinitely; he eventually had to return to the zero-g environment of the *Renegade Runner.* The ship was meant to be fast, not comfortable. Once he did return to the cabin area, his muscles would begin their march toward atrophy. For two weeks, it'd been a constant battle with the effects of gravity then non-gravity and back again, just to keep in shape so that he could be fit enough to carry out his mission. Add to that the harrowing trip through the upper-atmosphere of Darmen inside the shell of that capsule, pulling between nine and twelve times the force of gravity. The parachutes of the capsule deployed on schedule, giving him about five seconds to catch his breath before slamming into the ground so hard he thought he'd cracked his incisors. On top of all of that, he had to suffer the indignity of crossing the desert with the ATAC strapped to his back, weighing him down. If mission parameters had been pushed to the limits, it didn't take much imagination for Leers to draw on how he felt. His thighs burned with lactic acid, his ankles and knees felt brittle, his lungs protested with every other draw of air. His back felt fine, strange, but his shoulders stung to the touch.

He would press on with his mission—had to. He was too damned close to surrender to fatigue now. Too damned close to just radio the *Renegade Runner* for extraction. He could go on, the most difficult segment, in his mind, was done. He had managed to successfully infiltrate the base without using a single stealth technique. The energy gates surrounding the base, which would have needed coded access to bypass, had been deactivated . . . after all, this base was dozens of lightyears behind the front lines, why would they need to be activated? And even if they had been activated, the ATAC module he wore on his back contained nearly a million codes to bring the gate down for a second, long enough for him to pass through, then pop it back up without the most discriminating Pulsarian technician being able to pick it up on his security monitor. There was that and the fact that the Pulsarians hadn't even bothered with their anti-personnel sensors either. So the jamming features of his ATAC went unused as well. Leers groaned inwardly, his nostrils hissing in the bitter heat. What angered him was the fact that he had to haul that damned ATAC pack across twenty-five kilometers of desert—twenty-five kilometers he should not have had to cross in the first place only to find that the energy gates were already down, to find out that the damned Pugs weren't even running their anti-personnel sensor sweeps. He didn't get a chance to use a single one of its features like he had on previous missions—the damned thing was useless to him now and it was even more useless when he had landed on this rock six hours ago. But it did carry five liters of water, of which two he'd already drank. If that was all it was good for, he would've preferred a canteen.

Still, shoving all nonessential thoughts aside, Leers admitted that base security hadn't been nearly as tight as he'd thought it would be. It was an Outland Base, to be sure, but even their aerial reconnaissance had been predictable, and thus, easily avoided. The base's infrared scans were active, somewhat . . . but a preschooler playing hopscotch could've dodged those. At least the faint infrared scans was there, but the material in his poncho all but 'ate' those scans . . . with all the things that had gone wrong with his mission thus far, he should've been jumping for joy at the prospect of low infrared scans, but he wasn't, things were going a bit . . . a bit too easily.

Leers ran from building to building, using the shade as much as possible. His destination was one of the base's computer sub-control stations. His progress was deliberate, and within an expanse of fifteen square kilometers containing more than ten thousand structures, it was also slow. He was looking for one building in particular, one he could enter without setting off an alarm, one where he could steal the one thing the Pulsarians treasured more than weapons or blood . . . information. Leers had to retrieve that information before the base came fully to life, and with the sun rising on the southwestern horizon, he didn't have much time. He paused as he stood in the shadow of a crumbling, domed sub-space relay station, breathing too heavily for only having just run two-hundred meters stop-and-go. Just now scrapping morning and the broiling air was almost too much to take. Quite different from the frozen mist he breathed the night before. He looked around to get his bearings, checking the compass feature on his chronogram. He figured that the control center was to the north, even though he couldn't see it. To the east were the tracking domes, that meant he was still within the southwestern quadrant of the base . . . good. For a moment he thought he'd overshot his destination and had wandered onto the extreme southern panhandle of the base. The Pulsarians didn't make their bases to conform to human logic. Not that it mattered, he wasn't here to conduct a survey.

Leers edged around a wall of duracreete and froze. The Pulsarians called their infantry Straaka and a squad of twelve was no more than fifty meters in front him now, marching in cadence across an intersection; their armor glinting, *Vgamh CR* laser rifles slung over their shoulders. Straaka were perhaps the most feared elements of the Empire because the Pulsarians placed every aspect of combat around these soldiers. In an era where staggering technology enabled space superiority fighters to fight for control over the high-orbits of planets, where massive weapons platforms could lay a hundred kilometers off the edge of a burning city and blast it into oblivion—

despite all that and after centuries of warfare, the Pulsarians knew—perhaps better than any other race in the galaxy, that battles were still won on the surface of a planet, on the ground and in the dirt where infantry soldiers fought and died. Space fighters and starships were good, they had their uses; but they couldn't hold territory—this was the key to Pulsarian doctrine, the essence of conquest. Territory had to be held or the very act of taking the territory itself was useless.

Leers raised his glare shields just long enough to wipe the mixture of sand and sweat from his forehead and set them back into place. From his position, they looked even more threatening than their reputation demanded. Fifty meters was too damned close. He exhaled slowly and watched the Straaka disappear from view around a distant avenue.

Leers turned to his right and moved quickly down an alley *away* from the Straaka. He peered around the corner, confused; he couldn't see any of the markers he'd familiarized himself with while onboard the *Renegade Runner.* The damned computer sub-station should be around here somewhere. He moved out of the protection of the shade and the sun's rays battered him. Even though it was low on the horizon, the heat was almost too much to take. *Damn, I should've done twelve-thousand sit-ups.*

There wasn't anything he could do about it now and—there! The computer station was thirty meters in front of him, to the left; if it had been any bigger he would've walked right past it.

He felt his heart pounding, adrenaline coursing through his body. His throat tightened, his fingers twitched. Tension bit into him, stiffening his gut. He'd been on ground assignments before but usually not alone. He ran up to the thick metal door, his breathing labored. Leers drew the Delnalt '44 energy pistol from his holster and flipped aside the safety, the weapon suddenly hot in his grip. With his left hand he reached up slowly, hesitating—he activated the door, hearing his heart thud loudly in his ears. Would someone be waiting for him, or would the building be empty? The door slid aside with a hiss, the human leaped inside, automatically assuming a firing stance. The station was dimly lit and surprisingly cool. Computer terminals, monitors, retrieval systems, and storage lockers were arranged in a rather haphazard fashion along the station's six walls.

As the doors closed behind Leers, three startled and unarmed computer technicians turned from their work to face the unannounced intrusion.

"Hands in the air," Leers barked. He was fluent in eight primary forms of the Pulsarian tongue and—

The Pulsarians simply stared at him in a peculiar manner bordering on disbelief and impertinence . . .

"Get your hands up," Leers barked again.

He knew they understood; they just stared at him, their eyes glazed; perhaps observing, as Leers often did, that Pulsarians and humans were nearly identical in appearance, disregarding skin pigmentation. Perhaps they were wondering what the hell he was doing there and what they could do about it.

Leers gestured with his weapon, his fingers twitching nervously. "Hey, listen to me, I don't—" His right hand began to shake. Sweat dribbled into his eyes stinging them, he blinked uncontrollably. One of the techs began to—

"No."

Leers fired. The energy bolt speared into the tech's chest and exploded out his back, splashing a nearby storage locker with burning bits of flesh, bone, and a greasy black spray of blood. Without hesitating, Leers turned toward the other two as they panicked and dove for cover—there wasn't any. Leers fired twice. The second Pulsarian was hit in the face, the right side of his head disappeared in a ghastly cloud of flame and blood. The last Pulsarian clutched at his destroyed throat, gagging insanely for several seconds then died in a steaming pool of bloody gristle.

"Damn." Leers grabbed his stomach, horrified at what he had done. He loathed Pulsarians; he didn't mind killing—he'd seen what they had done to others—but to kill them like this . . . not like this, not this close. *All they had to do was listen to me.* None of his victims had a weapon, and he burned them down on reflex alone, like they were dogs. *Why didn't they listen? They should have listened to me.* He wasn't going to kill them, he hadn't planned on it—not unless it was necessary—only if they were trying to escape. Were they trying to escape?

Leers locked the door, not wanting to be surprised the way those techs had been. Ignoring the wounds his weapon had created, he dragged the grisly corpses to the back of the room, away from where he would be working. He didn't want to be tripping over them and he certainly didn't want to look at them.

Why didn't they listen to me? "Goddamnit."

Reaching underneath his poncho, he hit the quick-release catches on his ATAC pack and set it aside. He shut off the cooling cells to his uniform, separated the watering canister from the ATAC and took a long drink from it, feeling the liquid soothe his parched throat. He thought about taking off his poncho but decided against it. Pulling a chair up to a computer terminal, he typed in the commands to gain access to the restricted data-base. A flood of colors danced on the monitor then it went black. Leers stayed alert and waited. The machine chirped then presented him with a menu. Good, a few more minutes of this and his mission would be complete; he'd signal the *Renegade Runner* and get the hell out of here—then figure out what to put in his report about killing three unarmed Pugs . . .

****

All semblance of a routine day were rapidly deteriorating into something

Major Gheretti didn't like. First, the damned Armada was streaking across the system without permission and now this.

"Someone has gained unauthorized access to the 'special mission projects' directory," the security technician said from his station.

Gheretti felt the muscles at the base of his skull knot with tension. "Where? In this building?"

"No, one of the computer control sub-stations."

The major straightened. Why did this deserve his attention any more than the Armada?

"Could this be a part of the exercise?" the sergeant asked hopefully, looking on from his station.

The major didn't respond immediately, trying to remember the closing comments of yesterday's war-games briefing. "No, this isn't a part of the exercise. The latitudes of operation call for battlefield tactics and deployments for today only. Nothing was mentioned about covert operations within the base." Gheretti moved to get a better view of the data on the screens. "And the morning crews haven't reported in yet . . . Damn. I don't like this—there hasn't been Federation activity in this sector ever. And yet everything that has transpired during the last hour is beginning to smell like a Delrel operation."

The sergeant didn't consider this. "Why does it have to be the Delrels? It could be anything."

"Sergeant, you're the one who alerted me to this situation. Besides, the Delrels may be losing the war but they are quite keen on this sort of operation. With half the base participating in exercises out on the sandoceans—but you could be right in stating that it could be anything."

Gheretti exhaled slowly, he didn't want to be known as an alarmist, still he felt his balance faltering. He gestured down the aisle at a bored looking private. "You there, get a squad of Straaka down to that station and have them investigate." He turned back to the sergeant. "It might be nothing; as you say, sergeant, but let's get a squad down there at any rate. It could be a tech trying to catch up on some work. But we can't take that chance. Not this close to the Frontier. There's highly classified information and then there's this type of information." He pointed at the screens. "*This* information could prove to be too damaging to just let it go ignored—and I'm not going to be shot for doing nothing. See if you can cancel his access."

"Right, sir." The sergeant tapped at his keyboard, frowned then typed in more commands. "He has me locked out."

"Why would one of our techs have us locked out?" Gheretti didn't like where his out-loud train of thought was leading him. "None of the visiting Straaka has the clearance to—put the base on silent alert. That *has* to be a Federationer trying to steal our information. And wake the colonel."

"Major, I think you should have a look at this," a leftenant yelled from a long bank of scanner and sensor equipment five meters away.

Now what? Gheretti had to stop himself from throwing up his arms in exasperation. The major marched up to the scanner-sensor station, he didn't have time for this, not with an enemy agent loose on base—he stopped. The look on the young leftenant's face was one of shock and dread.

"Someone just Warped out of Hyperspace in sector five." The officer was scared. Gheretti could actually see beads of sweat pop out of his forehead. "Target track is having a difficult time with this one—but they're heading right for Darmen, right for us."

"We're not supposed to have visitors today," Gheretti thundered. "The Imperial Armada is supposed to check with space clearance and control before they—"

"I don't think it's the Armada, sir. I think it's worse." The officer was shaking. "Look at these Warp signatures."

Gheretti, the blood draining from his face, stared with abject horror at the screens.

****

Leers sat troubled as the crystal copied the restricted files, his fingers tapping at the console. Why had it been so difficult to kill a trio of—Pugs. Even if they were unarmed, it shouldn't have mattered, right? The Pugs—Pulsarians—were butchers, the betrayers of worlds; they made slaves out of the millions they didn't kill. And the Pulsarians didn't give a damn how you felt about it either: Don't like it—fuck you, you're dead. *Yeah, you keep thinking on that, if it'll make ya feel better about killing unarmed men.* Leers shook his head at his uncanny ability to mock himself while still on a mission. Yet the thought of billions of intelligent, independently thinking individuals obsessed with the notion of manifest destiny, of planet grabbing, often times drove him crazy. *How could civilized beings drive themselves to enslave others, how did the Pulsarians just grant themselves that right?* Leers had difficulty grasping it and strangely, he wanted so desperately to make sense of it all.

Leers was shocked out of his reverie as the CPU chirped next to him. The job was done. Well, almost done. There was still the matter of leaving this planet, with body parts intact. What he had come here for was now stored onto the data storage container. He slid the metallic and crystalline octagonal out of the slot. He turned it around in his fingers, watched the glitter along the edges, saw his face reflected in the metal. An hour ago the octagonal was worthless, but now he held the secrets, the restricted information, worth more than all of the galaxy's treasures combined; a treasure with the potential to save the Delrel Federation from the brutality of the Pulsarians. He hoped this disk, whatever intelligence it contained, *could* turn the whole bloody thing around. Most conservative estimates stated the Federation was only a few months away from defeat . . . maybe even a year at best. It didn't take genius to realize that with Minerva and a majority of the human star systems firmly in Pulsarian hands, Shiborium and Narterium within the Dracterian Systems would be the next to fall . . . No, they all had to fight. The Pulsarians had killed a billion of his fellow citizens, had enslaved tens of millions more. Leers felt his heart racing. If it all started with the octagonal, so be it. Let it be the flame that would sear the Pulsarian soul. It was time that they started killing Pulsarians instead of allowing themselves to be *killed* by the Pulsarians.

Out of the corner of his eye, Leers caught sight of the mangled corpses. *To hell with them.* He stood and spat on the floor. *Vile, murdering bastards, you don't deserve my sympathy—or my understanding.*

He slipped the disk into an anti-shock container and sealed it into his breast pocket. Good. Now, all he had to do was contact the patrol ship. Leers activated the sub-space instruments on the ATAC. Even being inside an enclosed duracreete structure, he knew he could achieve a secured com-lock with the patrolship in its 25,000 kilometer orbit. The best part was that the Pulsarians wouldn't even know he was calling down a ship for immediate dust-off. To any Pulsarian tapping into his communications channel, his request would sound like spatial distortion, or interference from the sun, anything but a coherent communications link.

"Red King, this is Green Knight," he said into the pick-up. He waited, checking the power-band, then repeated his call. Nothing. "Red King, Green Knight is requesting recovery."

Still nothing.

Leers cursed. If they were making him 'sweat-it-out' a little, this wasn't the time. They could play their little navy games later. Now was not the time—

Loud banging thundered through the entrance door. Leers' heart jumped. He picked up his Delnalt '44. There was a pause then more banging.

"Attention, individual inside," the voice rasped in the Pulsarian tongue. "Come out now or be killed."

This time the voice was in Delrel Standard: "You only have five seconds to comply or we'll burn our way through." There was a pause. "Open this door now!"

Despite his training, Leers swallowed hard and felt trapped, helpless. *Damn.* He hunted for a way out realizing the door was the control room's only exit. He turned frantically, hearing that familiar *click-snap* of charging bolts being pulled back, followed by the chilling whine of lasers and energy bolts striking the thick door with explosive force. They were burning through, shit; he wanted to fight them, not get burned down like some stupid animal. There was no cover in the control room. As soon as they broke in, they'd kill him. Maybe he'd get one or two of them before he fell, but the outcome would still be the same. Even worse still, the intelligence he had come to steal would be lost. There'd be no hope for the future, no hope for the millions still fighting Pulsarians. He had to get out of here.

Looking for an escape, Leers felt acid eat at his stomach, could hear the panicked drumming of his heart. He noticed the hatch above him leading to the roof—but it was locked. Leers had an answer for that as he pointed his Delnalt '44 at it, shielded his eyes, and fired. Molten fragments of metal and stone exploded in all directions, sparks rained down on him. He looked up, fanning away the blue-green smoke. The cavity was still too small for an escape. He fired again. Meanwhile, the door began to heave, buckle, and smolder as energy continued to hammer it. It was only seconds away from giving. His escape was two meters above his head. Leers strapped on his ATAC and without hesitating, he jumped up into the burning cavity still ringed with crackling flame and lava. Struggling to pull himself through, he screamed. The goddamn lava was burning through his gloves. He wrestled his way through to the roof.

Inside, the doorway finally gave way. Ejecta from the obliterated door and wall erupted into the room. Two Straaka burst into the room firing from the hip, blasting away at CPUs and monitors, but the human was gone. One of the armored forms spotted the bodies of the techs and yelled over his shoulder, "forget them, they're dead. Where's the Delrel?"

"Check outside," a third Straaka barked, scanning the room. He looked up. "The roof; check the roof."

Leers scrambled away from the burning hole and flipped his glare shields down to protect his eyes when a jolt of pain shot through his left hand. He could smell the stink of burnt skin and fabric. He looked at his hand—*Universe!*—the glove, all blackened and crispy, had melted onto his fingers. He struggled to suppress the urge to cry out again.

Two energy bolts screamed up from his escape hole. Forgetting about the pain, Leers sprang up and ran across the roof knowing that in any second a Straaka could shoot him in the back—if that happened, he wouldn't have to worry about the pain in his hand anymore. He was nearing the edge of the roof—he'd either have to jump down onto the street below or across to the adjacent building. It was twelve meters to the next building at least, and he could take cover behind those bulky air-recirculation units. Twelve meters. Easy. He leaped, sailing through the air, legs pumping through the air, arms swimming—*CRACK!* His ribs smashed against the ledge of the building. Air exploded from his mouth in a spray of spit and blood. Hitting the ground at an awkward angle. He couldn't stop from crying out this time and doing so made the pain worse. Knives stabbed through his body. His lungs felt almost like they were being gouged apart by invisible claws. He tried to draw in a breath—his ribs felt cracked. *Oh, God, help me.*

The Pulsarians were coming. *Move or die where you sit. You will die on your ass if you don't move.* Leers willed himself to stand, the effort enormous. *Move now or die. Move!* He felt like vomiting, the heat pressing against him. He felt his strength slipping away. He took a step, pain jolting him to a stop. *Move!* He took another step. *Universe.* He took another step and another, trying to ignore the pain, saliva dangling from one corner of his mouth. *That's it. Keep moving,* he had to get away from the danger. But the act of moving, let alone breathing, was agony. He wiped his mouth and—

A glint of light bounced off his glare shields. He turned to face the source of the reflection, laser bolts shot past him or exploded craters into the ground at his feet. A surface skimmer, an armored attack sled with a crew of two and four gunners in back sped toward him. The aerodynamic body of the skimmer floated about half a meter off the ground and was supported by two thick skis allowing it to move over the desert sand with ease.

Leers weakly raised his weapon and fired. The pilots panicked behind the thin canopy as one of the wild shots caught a gunner in the face. His lifeless body bounced off the skimmer and onto the desert floor. Another burst pierced the canopy to strike the pilot in the chest.

The skimmer fishtailed, throwing two of the hapless gunners onto the road like discarded trash. Leers could hear screams as the vehicle blurred past him and plowed into a building fifty meters down the road. There was a loud crackling smack and an explosion. Leers turned to see Pulsarians caught in the twisted metal bleeding and moaning.

Leers turned away and scrambled up a nearby alley moving quickly, rasping for air and wondering what the hell he was going to do. His mission now looked hopeless but it was far from being completely smashed. He still had the stolen data, but how was he going to make it off the planet alive? The first thing he had to do was quit letting panic dictate his actions and act like the well-trained individual he was. An easy thought when one was carrying out an op with comrades. But he was alone. He had to deal with his emotions alone, had to face his fear alone, had to face death alone.

He could remember his training, could localize his fear and shut it aside. He had to make it. But he was so busted up—it was difficult to shut out fear when pain demanded your attention from every region of your body.

He activated the ATAC's communications system again.

"Red King, this is Green Knight, I'm in trouble—need recovery ASAP." Nothing. "Do you copy?" Nothing. "Goddamnit, where the hell are you?"

What was he going to do? He couldn't reach the ship. He damned well couldn't lurch around the base indefinitely. If he hadn't tried to leap across to the other building. If only . . . . He tried to scream but couldn't make any sound, his mouth parched, dry heat baking down his throat, cutting off his desperate cries. He felt frantically around him looking for water. He couldn't find his canister. Then he realized that he'd separated it from the ATAC module and had left it behind in that damned computer station. He had no water, the patrolship wasn't responding, half the base was probably after him by now.

Why had things gone so terribly wrong? He'd done his part. Nearly exhausted himself running thirty kilometers through the desert. His fingers were all burnt up, his shoulders burned, his ribs were cracked, he could barely breathe. He'd been on seemingly hopeless operations before, but not quite this bad, and never had he been alone. He had to keep his head. Maybe . . . okay, perhaps the ATAC wasn't sending out a signal for some bizarre reason; whatever it was he couldn't analyze it now. He could make use of the base's communications. The base had communication relay stations scattered about, if he could reach one, he could call for help—he didn't even need to talk, all he had to do was key in the guard frequency and scream. Help would come, it had to. He was so tired, so thirsty.

Something up ahead caught his vision as he burst into a courtyard. Without confirming first what his target was, Leers fired his '44. A half dozen Straaka dove for cover as one of their number disappeared in a raging ball of flame. Two Straaka returned fire as their target dashed into another alley. Collecting themselves, the Straaka sprinted cautiously after their agile quarry. They knew they had him trapped.

Leers realized the same as he ran into the alley with a dead-end less than twenty meters away. There was no way out of here except the way he had come. He had only two choices: make a suicide charge at the Straaka or wait for them to bring the fight to him. Either way he was going to die but he would kill as many of them as he could. Damn, he was only twenty-two years old and it was going to end like this. *It's not fair.*

Leers lurched down the alley, stumbling over weak legs that didn't want to move anymore. He turned to face his enemy as a hell-flower blossomed next to him. Angrily he dropped the first Pulsarian around the corner. *Here I am you murdering Pugs, take a shot at me!* He was squeezing the trigger again, his mind screaming, cursing, all pain forgotten. Another Straaka fell, his chest a mass of flaming metal, skin, and bone.

A shadow passed overhead and a tremendous blast of wind knocked the Straaka and the Omnitraus Officer to the ground, hard. The shock wave ripped through the air like thunder, flattening anything that stood. Sand and debris brewed around the scrambling figures.

Leers looked up to see a massive starship hovering just ten meters above them. If was far too big to be the patrol craft; it was a Gladatraus Rhoderium warship! And not just any Rhoderium warship, this was the *Mekadore Traveler*—easy to spot compared to other Gladatraus warships. *What is it doing here?*

Leers blinked against the blast of sand, disoriented. *Why are they here?* No one in Gladatraus Command knew he was on a mission to Darmen.

The massive starship dipped closer into the alley, trying to land, smashing into the duracrete structures which gave way like mounds of dirt under the pressure exerted from the vessel. The *Mekadore Traveler* was thickly armored and shaped exactly like the much smaller ocean dwelling animal from which it was modeled—it was a sight made all the more awesome since the desert would be the last place one would expect to see a crab, much less a starship shaped like one. Constructed from advanced metals and composites, the

Mekadore Traveler looked more like a living entity than a starship, fluid in motion instead of mechanical and clumsy. Five metallic legs dug into the sandy ground, twin pincers began snapping at the Straaka, holding them at bay, sending them to the depths of tortured panic for those pincers could rip them apart with little effort. With their resolve and discipline evaporating, the Straaka retreated from the freakish monster.

The *Mekadore Traveler*, like all Gladatraus Command warships, was among the most powerful star vehicles in the galaxy employed by the Delrel Federation. From the standpoint of firepower alone, the Pulsarian Dreadnought Destroyer Advancer came close—but then Dreadnought Destroyers didn't have the maneuverability of strategic bombers or the speed of an interceptor.

The landing ramp lowered and Leers stumbled toward it. Everything was a painful blur to him now. The heat, the whine of the Rhoderium's engines, the incredible smell of its vertical climbers' exhaust, the swirling sand. Leers reached the ramp and started up, sweat coming down in sheets across his face, stinging his eyes. Just a few more steps and he'd be safe; exhaustion slowing him, pain searing through his torso. He tried to move forward feeling the starship lift off. Or were his senses just fooling him? Somehow the question seemed damned important—more important than breathing. He collapsed before he could reach the yawning air-lock, darkness sweeping over him.

CHAPTER II
ICE

N'CKSHELL Slayton only had seconds to live. With pain raking her body, the young Dracterian stumbled out into the frozen courtyard, dizziness enveloping her. Shards of snow and ice stabbed at her face, her eyes; the cold ripping through her thin layered arctic suit. Blood was smeared on one side of her face—not her blood; the mephitic smear had belonged to one of the Pugs she'd killed just minutes ago.

Thrashing through knee-deep snow, stumbling and slipping on ice, she needed a weapon—or a place to hide—more than she needed balance. After killing two computer technicians with her Phiser PBX, the laser pistol had jammed. It was her assault knife that had allowed her to kill the third Pulsarian. She lost it while fleeing the building when two Straaka suddenly burst into the bunker and starting shooting at her. Even if the knife hadn't been wrenched from her grip, it was useless against the *Vgamh CR* laser rifles they carried.

The only thing she could do was run—get out of the computer bunker, explosions from near misses ringing her body—get out before they killed her. If only her Phiser PBX hadn't jammed she might have had a chance. *What caused the malfunction? Was it the firing safety lock, the intercooling gas pump?* She didn't know. The two Straaka were nearly on top of her.

Slayton tensed as she heard the scream of a rifle. An angry bolt of green light exploded the ground to her right. The searing heat of the beam washed over her; ozone burned through her nostrils, traveled down her windpipe, cooking her lungs. Fighting dizziness and fatigue, Slayton pulled herself around the concrete corner of a building before the Straaka could fire off another shot. She needed a weapon. The futility of her situation angered her; they were going to kill her and she couldn't fight back—*how could things turn to shit so quickly?*

Her eyes glazing with hate; weapon or not, she decided she was going to kill them. Like the technicians before, neither of them saw fit to raise the alarm; a mistake that both pleased and angered her. Pleasing because the mountain-top fortress hadn't yet been alerted to her presence—yet—drawing her ire because these two thought that she was some weak female that they could easily take. They were going to pay for their incompetence.

One of the Straaka sprinted around the corner. Cold hands reached out, fingers like hooks digging into the Pulsarian's throat. Slayton swung the Pulsarian around, using his momentum against him, viciously slamming his head into the stone wall. He tried to bring his weapon up as his head struck stone again and again. The Pulsarian dropped his weapon at the moment his partner rounded the corner. Instinctively, Slayton spun on her heel and kicked the second guard in the face, knocking him off his feet. In a blur, Slayton grabbed the rifle that had fallen out of the grip of her first victim and fired it at the second just as he was bringing his own weapon around. The second guard hit the ground dead, his skull shattered by a beam of energy.

Slayton turned toward the first Pulsarian and pumped two lasers into his body. Only then did she relax, her chest heaving from exertion. She quickly looked around, there might be more. The fortress was still asleep. Good. She gently set the weapon aside, ripped the gloves off one of the Straaka and put them on. The warmth felt good, reassuring. She rolled the armored corpse over and grabbed extra ammunition clips from the dead enemy's belt, slipping them into the hip pockets on her arctic suit.

With a functioning weapon with which to defend herself, she could now address the problem of escaping the fortress followed by blasting off the planet. She felt in her breast pocket; the data crystal was still there with the restricted data she had stolen—without it there'd be no 'blast-off.'

Slayton gathered herself for action; hearing her knees creak from the cold turned determination into anger. Perhaps if she would have pushed the mission planners harder, she could've been given the assignment to Darmen instead of Dannen Leers getting it—Dannen loved snow. But there had been no altering the personnel placements of their respective assignments, even if they were nearly identical. The only difference was that she had Captain Cairn's freighter and a 'cover' and had set out four days earlier from the

Frontier, while Leers traveled with the navy and had set out directly from base. If she had Dannen's mission, she'd be on her way back home by now, instead of being stuck here.

The wind whistled around her. *Damn this place.*

****

Elst was a remote world that glowed like the insignificant sun that it revolved around. Cold, icy fangs of light stretched out from the dying white-dwarf sun in a futile attempt to warm its only satellite before its light was extinguished forever. Elst circled the cold-burning orb to bask, as it were, in a continuous flood of radiation that permitted the existence of small lichens and mosses that gave the planet an oxygen-based atmosphere. Even with sparse vegetation and small mammals, Elst was chiefly a planet of massive continents of ice and frozen whitewashed rock.

The Pulsarians had established two Outland Bases on Elst; one near the northern arctic and the other near the southern pole.

The Outland Base of vital concern to N'ckshell Slayton was constructed along the peaks of the Triscerin Mountains which rose more than 8,000 meters above mean surface level in the northern arctic. Although labeled an Outland Base, its primary missions were scientific in nature, with geo-thermo experiments, glaciation and counter glaciation observations; military applications were secondary. The base was seeded with testing facilities, massive fifteen acre experimental blocks, sub-space relay antennae, a few hangars literally crumbling from disuse situated next to a small vertical take-off-and-landing platform, and a space traffic control tower constructed among a hundred snow-covered bunkers and polarcrete buildings. Make no mistake, however, Straaka ran the programs and experiments here. The threat here was real, the danger real.

Slayton dragged the two corpses into one of those buildings, a storage-equipment shed, the wind howling madly outside. God they were heavy, the process nearly wiped her out. With night approaching though, N'ckshell had to make her escape while she still had a chance. The Pulsarians were bound to discover her bloody work in the computer control room. She had to make her escape quickly, before the falling temperature made movement all but impossible, before the alarm could be sounded; and most definitely now, because the longer she stayed here the greater her chances of getting fried rose. Adding to her urgency was the fact that hours before her mission at the Outland Base, hours before she killed the Pulsarian technicians in the station, before she killed the Straaka; she had killed Havelock and Thorne on board Captain Cairn's freighter. Even though she was well within parameters, she had to move now . . . make her move before Cairn lost his nerve and left the planet without her.

"Okay, Ms. Slayton, quit standing around—you've got to find a way to the township at the base of the mountain—then you've got to get to that spaceport." Her voice was crisp and smooth. She stood to her full height and tried to run a gloved hand through her thick, velvet mat of black hair. Dried blood and ice held fast and kept her from freeing the tangles. Like all Dracterians, she had pale skin, more stark than the swirling snow outside. Large eyes framed a long rapier thin nose above her thin lips. She had sharply pointed ears that pointed away from the temporal bone of her skull and a deep streak of crimson colored hair above the left ear—not the blood of the Pulsarian, but rather, an indicator of ethnicity as far as Dracterians were concerned. Her ears twitched anxiously in the cold; every creak of metal, every whistle of wind could signal approaching death.

N'ckshell had dealt with violence and death from infancy—it was nothing new to her, or to her people, whom humans called Dracterians. The natives of Shiborium were a tribal race of intelligent humanoids—again, 'humanoid,' another label humans slapped on any race they 'discovered' that resembled them—thought by some to be more savage in warfare than the Pulsarians. The fact remained though, that the Dracterians were indeed brutal and it took extreme measures from the early human missionaries to save the billions from themselves. Many revisionists would state that the Dracterians weren't rescued by the humans, that they had ended the violence on their own accord. Yet proof against this lay in the fact that a majority of Dracterians possessed human names. 'Slayton' was of human origin, a name given to her after her parents were slain in the massacre of her village by a rival faction of Dracterians. The village contained more than 40,000 people, and all of them were butchered, save for several hundred children. Slayton, her sisters and twin brother survived and were desperately close to dying from starvation when human missionaries rescued them weeks after the massacre. With the absence of food and water, at three seasons of age, N'ckshell had to be nursed by her eldest sister to avoid death.

Not a wholly unusual tale when one considered the history of violence that marked the Dracterian people. For thousands of years, the Dracterians carried out acts of murder and mayhem that made human history look tame by comparison. There was the infamous two-year *Rhens du Meer*, where more than 75 million Dracterians were killed and more than 300 million were made into wandering refugees. In the three years that followed the intra-planetary war, a hundred million more had died from disease and starvation. The *Rhens du Meer* was only one example of the tribal hatred that marked the Dracterian race. For the Dracterians, the shape of one's ears, and the direction those ears pointed, in relation to the colored-wave pattern of their hair, determined whether that individual would be a welcomed guest or a mortal enemy. For instance, individuals with crimson streaked hair and ears pointing out, the *Mhaga' Gerst*, sought to rip the throats out of those with violet streaks and whose ears also pointed out, the *Hegra' Vom*—the ears matched, but the color streaks of the hair, the *D'erdrea*, didn't. Another example would be the *Dinda'*

Hirks, Dracterian artisans whose identifying markers were their sage *D'crdrea*, and smallish and quite straight *Hegra' Vom*. The *Dinda' Hirks* were at violent odds with the *Tranga' Noren*, whom also possessed smallish ears of a perpendicular nature, but the steaks of their hair were richly flaxen. That was the root beneath Dracterian madness, they went after each other, bent on killing. For more than 200,000 years, they practiced ethnic and racial warfare, garnered slavery, supported genocidal slaughter. The formation of the Tertiary Alliance mandated peace between the tribes; demanded Dracterian racial inclusion and de-emphasized exclusion; supported melting, not mere mixing; it acknowledged their common heritage, common ancestry—no claims of superiority. And yet, despite a decade of peace, many felt that all it would take was a hostile whisper and the peace would be shattered. What held the Dracterians together now—perhaps more than anything—was the Federation's war against the Pulsarians. The Pulsarians saw all Dracterians as viable military targets—it didn't matter if they were *Hegra' Vom*, or *Mesc'Crait*, or the *Mhaga 'Grest*, or which *kageh*, or clan, lay claim to the throne, or who had the biggest treasury.

Slayton knew that as grotesque and pathetic as the natives of Shiborium, it was minuscule in comparison to Pulsarian outrages. Her people, when left alone, confided their outrages among themselves; the Pulsarians however, took Dracterian violence, refined it, then spread it across the cosmos. Compared to Pulsarian military might, and their will to employ that might on a galactic scale, the Dracterians were children—their racial hatred illogical, infantile.

Slayton shut the door and surveyed the dark interior of the equipment shed, her Dracterian vision easily piercing the darkness. There were tools scattered here and there, several parkas, gauntlets, mountain boots, discarded armor, engine parts and, of course, the two corpses.

"Can't go back the way I came," she whispered. Meaning, going back through the computer control room, down into the long-abandoned command bunker and back onto the cargo-tram. All of those areas would be watched now. There were twohundred Pulsarians stationed at the Outland Base according to most conservative estimates. The base could take in more than 10,000, so there were many places for her to hide but there were many places for the Pulsarians to ambush her too.

In one corner were about two dozen pairs of mountain skis with bindings already mounted into them. Now if she could just find—Slayton looked frantically about the shed . . . boots. *Good.* She lifted one of them and examined it closely. Rear-entry with five locking clasps and heel and toe tension controls. Not bad, but they were in rough shape—they'd have to do. Skiing down the face of the mountain wasn't something she'd ever envisioned, but she needed to get to the spaceport and get off this frozen rock. There were only about a thousand Pulsarians on the entire planet and a mere fraction of them were stationed at this base, she'd have a better than decent chance for escape.

Slayton set the boots aside and shifted through the skis. It took only seconds to pick a pair that seemed suited for this task.

She grabbed an extra parka and put it over her thin arctic suit. She activated the parka's heat controller and—*blast!*—it didn't work. Well, at least the material would provide her with a little more protection.

"Don't need these anymore," she said, discarding her own mountain boots and sliding her feet into the pair of stiff ski boots. Despite her arctic training, Slayton felt the tension bubbling in her stomach. *Settle down, settle down. You've been in far worse situations than this.* She slapped the locking clasps and set the tensioners so tight that her feet began to hurt. "Shit, why do Pulsarians have such small fucking feet?" She stood up and lurched around—if the Pulsarians burst in here now—

She grabbed the skis, tucked them under her left armpit and hefted the *Vgamb CR* laser rifle in her right hand. Roughly she kicked the door of the shed out. All was clear and deathly quiet, buy for the mournful howl of the wind. The snow was falling much harder now. She set out cautiously, forgetting to grab a pair of vision enhancement goggles. Too bad—she'd need them.

****

"The trouble is," the lightly armored leftenant was saying as he handed the report to the company commander, and the highest ranking Pulsarian stationed at the Outland Base, "that this base is too big and we're grossly understaffed. This base was meant to hold tenthousand personnel in the surface complex alone and another seventeenthousand within the underground command sections. Current strength is less than a hundred. The spy could be hiding anywhere."

The Outland Base commander, Straaka Keptein Meitgon, glanced at the report dispassionately and handed it back to the subordinate. "What about the sensor probes—haven't they turned up anything yet?"

"The personnel sensors aren't functioning. The cold."

"Hasn't Leftenant Hertagon solved that problem yet?"

Immediately the leftenant thought, *well, obviously he hasn't repaired the damned sensors yet,* but kept his bearing and simply stated, "No, sir."

"Very well." Meitgon dismissed the leftenant and hurried into the crowded operations room, agitation burning in his stomach, making his movements stiff, almost robotic. He'd known of the arrival of the Delrel spy for two days. By his command, he even allowed the Delrel's dilapidated merchant star-ship to land at the spaceport in the township at the base of the mountain. Such action wasn't at all unusual. Elst was located just within the galactic Frontier and played host to Vassillian merchants, Tragonii traders . . . even Dracterians with the assumed cover of wildlife photographers. Yes,

Meitgon knew the Dracterian was a spy, he even knew the Federationer's name. Not that it was important; all information furnished to him via secured sub-space radio transmitted from unknown elements of the SSK and the Imperial Armada. The Imperial Armada cooperating with the fanatics of the SSK? The thought of it troubled him more than allowing the Dracterian to land did. Meitgon didn't like it. However his feelings, his orders were specific. Observe the movements of the Delrel, make reports, and nothing more. Observe what? Observe the Delrel scum break into his command post, steal valuable data, murder his men? What kind of asinine orders were those? What did the terrorist in the SSK hope to accomplish with their covert activities, their plots, their paranoia?

Gaming and plots and counter-plots. It was too much for Meitgon to take . . . not while his men were being killed; and with some SSK officer issuing the orders lightyears away, safe in some sterilized, computerized cubicle. No, orders or not, he was going to find that Delrel spy and kill her.

Meitgon took off his battlehelm and set it on a credenza. Straaka in heavily weathered battle armor filled the room. Some sat before CPUs and monitors, communications systems, and scanners, while others moved from station to station irritated by the fact that they hadn't been able to locate the Delrel.

"Straaka Sergeant." Meitgon had a moment of inspiration. A crusty blue-skinned noncom moved up to his superior. "We're wasting our time searching the base for this Delrel. She won't hide. She can't afford to. She has to get off this planet. Besides, Dracterians despise the cold more than each other."

The Straaka Sergeant considered this. "I understand, sir. We have search squads broken into two- and three-man teams. We can make a sweep of the base much more effectively—"

"It is effective, true. But we have to realize that this Omnitraus Officer would relish encounters with two- or three-man search teams. Terminate the search."

"Omnitraus? Sir, that hasn't been established yet."

"Who else would the DFR send?" Meitgon didn't try to keep the sting out of his voice. "We should concentrate our efforts on the spaceport and place guards around the freighter. We mustn't underestimate the Omnitraus, they can be most formidable at times . . . Also, keep an eye on the freelancers and other merchants. She may try to slip aboard one of their freighters. Finally, notify space traffic control and have them cancel all outbound traffic."

"They won't like that," the sergeant said.

"They won't like facing a lasering-squad either."

After relaying orders to nearby Straaka, the sergeant said, "all is in readiness, Keptein."

"Good." Meitgon began pacing. It was about options and knowing what your enemy could do and what he wouldn't do. The only avenue off-world was via the spaceport in the township at the base of the mountain. With the temperature dropping rapidly, with night approaching, no one could survive the severe arctic conditions. Not even the best-trained and best-equipped Straaka could survive alone in the wilderness. Meitgon didn't care whether Straaka lasers killed her or the cold finished her; just as long as she didn't escape. Escape. That was the vital factor. He'd never dealt with Omnitraus before, but from what he'd read in official reports, their ability to thwart death was uncanny. Acid began to burn in his stomach again. He looked around the room, his actions frantic. "How far away is the spaceport from here?"

"A little more than five kilometers," the sergeant replied.

Options. What were the Delrel's options? "We already have guards at key exits to the command bunker and the cargo-tram. So, what are we missing? What's the fastest way off this mountain?"

"The tram, which is being guarded—"

"And the second?"

"I don't understand what you mean."

Meitgon began pacing. "Do you think she'd dare to ski down the mountain?"

"Insanity," the Straaka barked, "she'll freeze before she can reach the forest."

"Perhaps. But she can't take the tram down because she'll know it'll be guarded. And she won't venture into the command bunker either, there's too many places for us to set up traps for her. Skiing, while dangerous, would get her to safety faster." The burning in his stomach began to ease. "Get a team in place on the double!"

"Yes, sir."

****

Slayton snapped her boots into the skies and tried to study the mountain below her. "I can't see a damned thing." She slapped the skis against the snow. It was hard packed, crusty, and probably had a layer of ice five to six centimeters beneath the surface. *It shouldn't be too difficult to make it to the town and the spaceport below, should it?*

She took one last look around again, and nothing. She didn't even know how steep the mountain face was—skiing down could be a good way to mort herself. But the town was down there, through the wilderness, the spaceport a couple of kilometers beyond. She had to do this, it was the only way.

Slayton took a deep breath and pushed off, picking up speed immediately. Tucking, she doubted she had the ability to stay in this position for very long, her thighs were already burning. Her eyes began to sting and water furiously. Common sense screamed at her to slow, the pain in her eyes a warning.

Goggles would be nice. She dug in the skis' edges, bleeding off speed, and began traversing calmly to the left and right; still traveling fast but under more control.

She thought she heard an alarm over the howl of the wind. Her ears twitched. No, it couldn't be. Could it? "They can't stop me now." She glanced over her left shoulder and couldn't see anything; turning back—snow and ice exploded in her face.

Slayton screamed as her face went numb. She wiped desperately at her eyes and strained to see what was happening.

"Goddamnit." More snow and ice geysered around her. Through blurred vision, she could see the flashes of red and blue light reflecting wildly off the swirling mass of whiteness.

They were shooting at her! *Where, blast it, where?* Were they behind her? Slayton tucked and picked up speed. More snow and ice exploded to the left and behind her. Then a dark shape loomed out of nowhere moving straight for her incredibly fast. Slayton bent down low and sprang up violently to crack the startled Straaka under the chin. The Pulsarian grunted and tumbled down the steep slope in a tangle of skis, equipment, and the snapping of bone.

Slayton tottered onward, struggling to keep her balance, arms punching at air. If she lost control, the Pulsarians would have her. With her right knee scraping against the snow and ice, her left leg high in the air, kicking, trying to get that ski back onto snow; she tried to spring back up, arms batting wildly. Her knee struck a shard of ice sending sharp needles of pain shooting through her body. "*No!*" But hitting the ice popped her upright again. Saliva gushed from her mouth. She looked down to see a wicked gash in her arctic suit and blood splatters covering her thigh and leg. She screamed again. It felt like her knee had been ripped off.

She tucked again as tears began to warm her cheeks. She had to get away. More explosions burst around her. Some so close her teeth chattered. She dug in her edges and began skiing a mad zigzagging course. All of a sudden the slope disappeared from beneath her. Slayton felt her heart surge. She kept her ski tips up knowing that if she hit wrong she'd lose control and would tumble. She hit the ground hard, air venting violently from her lungs, her right knee exploding in agony. She cried out again, her voice a signal the Straaka locked in on. They fired. An explosion flared near her left foot taking the ski and pieces of her boot with it. New waves of pain shot through her. Her foot felt as if it were on fire and numb at the same time. Miraculously maintaining her balance on one ski, Slayton raced on. But now she was veering sharply to the right and moving incredibly fast. Her remaining ski bounced over patches of ice, slipped over the tops of boulders, catapulting her into the air again. This time she knew that she wouldn't land. She had skied off the face of the mountain, the forest a thousand bone-shattering meters below her—

With sudden, jarring force, she landed on something hard and metallic, her left leg splintering on impact. Pain throbbed throughout her body as she looked around, vision dancing, trying to focus. Blood ran from her nose. She tried to raise her body off the metal skin that was surprisingly warm, but her muscles failed her. Darkness clouding her vision, N'ckshell Slayton couldn't tell if it was actually Dannen Leers dragging her inside of the Gladatraus warship or someone else.

CHAPTER III
PAWNS, BISHOPS, AND ROOK

THUNDER crackled in a vengeful crescendo during the early dawn on the eastern hemisphere of the planet Nijimegan. Not the thunder of nature, this was an organically engineered hell storm of lasers and energy weapons. The small computer station, located just on the outskirts of the capital city of Rhaudurian was burning from the inside out as a result of this thunder. Bright flashes of crazed light exploded wall monitors, memory storage systems, sub-space systems, communication relay panels, conduits, and the bodies of several Pulsarians.

The uniformed Pulsarian computer technicians shrieked as red and blue beams riddled them. Some of the computer techs, though not soldiers by nature, reached for their weapons and returned the murderous fire with all the dexterity and lethality of professional Straaka. New screams of agony flooded the morning as the charging killers, battle-dressed SSK agents, began to drop, their faces contorted in confusion. The SSK had charged into the computer station looking for traitors; their plan to kill as many of them as possible before forcing the survivors and their leader to surrender. This preamble of tactics was torn asunder as utter chaos reigned; for the computer techs, now returning their fire, did so with withering accuracy. In seconds the battle, which had started out as a one-sided slaughter, turned into a bloody stalemate; a desperate fight for survival on both sides.

SSK Major Bblaes Netergon entered the building and ducked behind a narrow bank of computer boards as energy raced his way. *The reports were right.* An explosion screamed next to him. *Of course they were, why shouldn't they be?* These weren't comp-techs. They looked and dressed as such—but their weapons employment resembled that of trained Straaka. The Pulsarians killing his men were members of one of the most fanatical cells of the *Crhira Mosxk* (the Pulsarian Underground), traitors who aided the Delrel Federation. *Damn.* The real computer technicians who reported to this station were most likely dead, their bodies disposed of.

"Surrender immediately! There is no escape!" Netergon ordered over the destruction about him. "Put down your weapons and surrender now. There is no way out of here."

He knew he was wasting breath—these fanatics would rather die for their idiotic causes than be captured alive. His SSK might have to pull out and level the building from the outside to survive this.

"Leftenant," Netergon barked toward his second in command. "Leftenant Whargon." He needed to form a plan and take these traitors while he still had SSK left—all around him were the dead and dying. These fanatics were well armed, their accuracy so keen that—no, he wouldn't call the base for Straaka help.

"Sir," came Whargon's determined reply.

"To me!" Netergon waved urgently as circuit cards and metal sparked and splintered around him.

"Yes, sir." Whargon ran from his cover toward the major. He never made it. A meter from where Netergon hid, Whargon was hit. His head exploded in a meaty cloud of bone, brain tissue, and flame.

"Damnit." Netergon was enraged more than disgusted as the gruesome corpse fell next to him. He wiped sweat from his forehead and looked around. "Leftenant Tienette, report." No response. "Tienette, where are you? Answer."

"Dead," someone barked over the carnage.

Netergon felt the rage brewing in his chest; his plan crumbling around him, his men dying.

An SSK sergeant, his steaming armor splattered with gore, rushed to Netergon. "Sir, what in the name of the Unholy is happening? Both of our leftenants are down, Sergeant Casktergon is hit. These traitors weren't supposed to be this well armed."

Netergon simply glared at him, and then flinched as fresh sparks danced around him and the sergeant. "Sergeant, I want you to—"

"We can't match their firepower, Major." The sergeant was shaking his head furiously.

"What?"

"Maybe we should pull back, Major. Get our wounded out of here and call for Straaka support—"

"Wait just a damned minute, Sergeant." Netergon was furious now. What the sergeant had said was logical, it confirmed his own feelings. But to do so; to beg the Straaka for help, to crawl back to headquarters and—no, he would not do it. "Do you think I'm going to let these traitors kill half my men then ask the rest of them to retreat? No, we're going to get them. Now, Sergeant, I want you to take three of your men, draw their fire—hit them hard on the left," Netergon ordered. "I'm going around to the right—the rest of you lay down a wall of fire to keep their heads down."

The sergeant ran to a knot of SSK hiding behind a bank of computers to the left. Netergon risked a quick glance around his cover. He could see that four of the traitors were alive, one of them female—she was their leader. Netergon had nine men remaining of the eighteen who had charged into the building. Two of whom were seriously injured, they would need immediate medical attention. The others were beyond help, their bodies ripped in half at the waist, decapitated, or worse. This had to end, this madness had to end now.

To his left, the sergeant indicated that he and his men were ready. Netergon nodded and pulled back the charging hammer on his service laser, feeling his body slacken with numbness. *Steady yourself, oldman, steady.* Netergon gritted his teeth.

Without warning the sergeant and his team rushed up from their cover and charged the traitors, guns blazing.

"Cover, fire! Cover, fire quick!" Netergon screamed as he charged the right.

The traitors responded quickly, killing one of the sergeant's men and wounding another. A wild burst of energy exploded near the sergeant's feet sending him missiling through the air into a bank of monitors. Meanwhile, Netergon rushed to the right undetected. One of the traitors panicked and began to flee toward the back of the room. Too late. Netergon cut him down with robot-like precision. Hopelessly cornered, one comp-tech threw his weapon aside to surrender as his partner screamed then fell over dead, cut down by those covering Netergon.

"Weapon down now," Netergon roared at the woman who had suddenly spun to confront him.

She froze looking at the SSK to the right and left of her. Even with the *Vgamh CR* type 3 in her hands, she knew she could only take one before she too was killed. With her jaw set, she glared at the SSK and the fool who had surrendered standing next to her—if only he hadn't surrendered, there might be a chance. There wasn't any chance and she knew it.

Netergon wasn't ready for what happened next. The woman turned her weapon on her confederate and fired at point blank range. Reflexively, Netergon released several bursts from his weapon killing her.

With the sound of her remains hitting the floor, the fight was over.

Netergon stumbled back, mind raging, he threw his weapon aside. The air in the computer station was thick with smoke and the choking rank of charred flesh and metal.

Netergon felt anxiety sweeping through him. The operation should have gone smoother than this. With half his team dead—the room began spinning around him—he needed air. He rushed out of the station, stumbling, loosening his chest plate, and undoing his collar. He bent next to his hovering command car, gagging—

"Are you alright, sir?" a private asked, his blue face streaked with dirt and sweat.

"No." Netergon tried to straighten, couldn't, and vomited violently on the ground. He wiped his mouth and glanced at the private. "I just need a moment to myself if you don't mind." Breathing heavily, Netergon looked at the dawn sky. How strangely beautiful it was, indifferent to the carnage that had just taken place. Beautiful, yes, but he knew there was a storm coming.

****

Omnitraus Officer Rook leaned against the thin balcony railing and scanned the horizon. A quick glance at his silver timepiece chained to his vest confirmed what he already knew. It was time. Yes, this was what star-travelers from all over the galaxy came to experience, the awakening dawn on the planet of Nijimegan. In seconds the dark sky shimmered, blues, vermilions and crimsons danced overhead, then sparked into golden flakes of light. Rook found himself gasping. He had seen ion storms, novae devastate entire star systems, but nothing prepared him for this. A smile formed on a face quite unaccustomed to smiling, as Nijimegan's twin moons hung gracefully in the morning sky. A cool breeze drifted in. The sun a fiery bead, a hungry pearl on the horizon.

With keen inhuman eyes, Rook swallowed the view. This moment of peace felt good—and it was good. In a galaxy torn apart by war, this moment meant more to him than anything else—to let his guard down, to relax, and not worry about the possibility of facing down death. His gaze shifted to the great city of Rhaudurian below him, which, he knew, stretched for dozens of kilometers in all directions. The city was just waking up. Its inhabitants cared nothing about the dawn and scoffed at the tourists who came from lightyears away to view it. Rook smiled. He wasn't a tourist, but his mission to Nijimegan and to this very city itself, dictated that he act as one. Following procedure, Rook had acquired a room on the 97th floor of the opulent and majestic triple towers of the Rhaudurian-Ithaca Resort Hotel. He had to be careful, the SSK were always watching. Suspicion would be aroused if he'd requested a room in the Carion Palace—only tramps, merchantmen, and those wishing to conceal themselves stayed there. As much as he disliked it, it was better to endure the luxury, and the overbearing and overpriced room service attendants, than to get involved in a gun-battle with the SSK. Hiding in plain sight was the best camouflage.

Rook continued to scan the horizon, seeing hundreds of hover cars racing along the magnetic freeways, and if he concentrated hard enough, he could even see their registration numbers. The freeways were to the north. To the east he could easily see the Sea of Greerfleck. Along its shoreline were the massive shipyards, loading docks and the Nijimegan Prime Spaceport, the eighth largest land-based spaceport in the galaxy, where overworked traffic controllers handled well over two-thousand space vehicles of all classes and sizes each day. To the west was the gambling district, literally a city within a city; a district of Rhaudurian that the tourists flocked to but the natives avoided.

Nijimegan was the fourth world within a stupendous sixteen planet star system that existed in a sector of space without a *traditional* name. Perhaps that wasn't entirely true, the sector had a dozen names, none, Rook knew, were officially listed within the registries of either the Delrel Federated Republic or the Pulsarian Empire. He knew that many within the DFR simply called it the Frontier; a thick band of space literally thousands of cubic lightyears in volume, nearly rivaling the size and depth of the entire Federation. In terms of the numbers of both charted and habitable worlds, both were nearly identical. There were hundreds of star systems of worlds within the Frontier; there lived billions of humans here, Ugrahms from the Advantier Regions, the mysterious people who called themselves Xerxes, Pulsarians who had fled the Homesystems more than five-thousand years ago. Trade in exotic goods ran wild through the Frontier. The region was rife with slavers, illegal pharmacists, renegade bio-engineers, weapons merchants, gamblers, and other 'entrepreneurs' both dangerous and harmless—at least that's how they saw themselves. If a coed disappeared from a college campus on Ruby-Royale, Minerva, or some other populous world within the Federation, you could make a sure bet that she'd been abducted and her captors were heading for the Frontier—outside of Federation jurisdiction—where the woman would be sold into prostitution. You could also bet that her family would never see her alive again; thus, illustrating the lawlessness and economic brutality of the Frontier in singular exactness. Not all abductees ended up this way, Rook reminded himself; there were 'happy endings' to be sure. The Aracrayderian just didn't know of any, for him they all seemed to end up the same way. Yet, there was some good to be found within the Frontier. There were Warp engineers here building better and faster starships, non-enhanced professional athletes, schoolteachers, artists, architects . . . billions of law-supporting beings living on the fractured crust of dignity and civility.

The Pulsarian Empire began occupying many of the worlds of the Frontier and used them as processing stations for Straaka heading to the frontlines. Nijimegan, while not a major processing center for the Pulsarians, was the principal location of operational information storage and retrieval. To keep the Nijimeganese in line, nearly a million of her people were conscripted into concentration camps. They'd 'serve' in the camp for a year, perhaps two, then were released to be replaced by another million or so natives. The only way out of the camps was to buy your way out, inform on your neighbors, or testify against captured insurgents. Nijimegan was a beautiful planet, but like many worlds within the Frontier, the beauty was gossamer sheen struggling to cover up the Pulsarian rot which lay beneath.

Rook folded his arms, *so much for beauty and independence.* He wasn't sure about how he felt about the Frontier. It was an enigma, a region that fought for its own identity. *Yes, you should feel bad for people living under the yoke of Pulsarian oppression—but then again, what were these people doing before 4952? They had this knack of looking the other way while innocent people were being kidnapped and murdered. How do you quantify a million people enduring a death camp all at once or a million people being put to death over the period of a decade or two on planets such as Proximus-Parr, Eagle-Centaur, Chinattii, Xornez, and of course, Nijimegan—perhaps you don't even try.*

Rook tried to remain dispassionate about such matters as he unfolded his arms, suddenly annoyed that he caught himself mimicking human gestures yet again. He had too many friends who were human, worked with humans, seen humans die trying to protect him. Perhaps it wasn't so unusual to act as them. His pride wouldn't permit it.

Yes, Aracrayderians were different than humans—vastly different—to the uneducated eye Aracrayderians resembled the quadrupedal mammals that ranged on many of the planets where humans had evolved. Even though Paranhoor, the home of all Aracrayderians, was hundreds of lightyears from Minerva or Ruby-Royale; it was as if nature was determined to make these 'animals'—to human eyes—walk upright, giving them two feet and two arms with hands that possessed fully articulated fingers and an opposable thumb. A Leopard Aracrayderian would have the head of a leopard, the spotted coat of a leopard, the claws and teeth, the predator's instinct—but it would also have unseen characteristics that would scream human . . . a similar chromosome count, the same number of red blood cells, the same hip, thigh and leg structure of humans—yet, one would swear that they were looking at a leopard, a leopard capable of speech, with clear enunciation and the ability to think outside of himself and ponder his place in the universe. Rook didn't like the comparison—and it was one that humans always made. It would never occur to them—the humans—that the ignorant mammals they were used to sprang from Aracrayderians 'models' and not the other way around.

The array of Aracrayderians was considerably more dense than those mammals. There were Starvaxyarian Lions, Strovaaga Lions, Arctic Lions, Desert Lions, Notovah Camel-lions, Obsidian Lions, Ridge Lions, Czardian-Cats . . . then there were the apes, the wolves, the jackals, the bears. . . millions of them. Ocelots, cerbal cats, panthers, bighorns, pilot-caribou,

Abbsyidan-caribou . . .

Rook was a Fenoothra-cheetah Aracrayderian, a distant cousin of the Fanoothra-gale leopards. Beneath his business suit, Rook had the black spots over a golden coat much like that of a leopard. That's where the similarity ended—cheetahs were much smarter than any leopard by far. And unlike any leopard, cheetahs had a slighter frame and possessed non-retractable claws. Rook was no exception to either rule and it didn't pose a problem. Non-retractable claws were as natural to him as retractable claws were to a lynx, or a lion, or an ocelot. And as for his slight frame—any Helen Ridger business suit along with a pair of Calidory wing-tips on his feet could hide that fact from the rest of the galaxy.

Rook moved away from the moving postcard morning and entered a suite that was as decadent as all the other rooms in the Rhaudurian-Ithaca. The lavatory was hidden behind a 'wall' of holographic projections, which could be programmed to suit the occupant's tastes. Right now the projection revealed the twin moons of Nijimegan in a delicate cosmic waltz. It could also be programmed to project weather conditions over any city on Nijimegan, breaking news stories, entertainment events—all just to hide a room where sentient beings primarily went to dispose of simple biological wastes. Rook snorted at the thought; Nijimeganese were a strange people. Then again, they weren't all that stranger than humans who made waste-room jokes at every opportunity—at least they didn't consider themselves to be at the center of the universe. Rook walked past the anter room where he had several more suits hanging—he originally asked Claude for two, but his contact on *Murmansk* had provided him with six—past the small but functional dining room where there were always places set for two. He entered his bedroom and quickly took note of the modestly sized bed that had not been slept in and the small library along the walls containing authentic hardbound books.

It was difficult to ignore the suite's many amenities, the opulence, the atmosphere. What demanded Rook's attention were the only items not part of the room's décor, two portable Roth & Stern CX-2000 tactical computers hooked into the suite's interplanetary communications network and a wicked looking Hellington Standard inter-cooled energy pistol (SN-90) with exclusive under-mounted laser range-finder and signature heat scan.

Rook ran clawed fingers over the casings of the computers as they sent jamming signals over the network to cover the fact that he was stealing Pulsarian secrets. There was nothing they could do about it because they couldn't trace the patch back to him. Besides, Nuera Algetti and her team had taken over a computer sub-station just on the outskirts of the city and were doing the actual transfer, and were also making doubly sure that the patch couldn't be traced back to Rook. It was an operation much more risky for her and her team than for him. His presence on Nijimegan had been one of low visibility, low Pulsarian contact. Algetti was the only Pulsarian he came in contact with and she was deadly serious in her work against the Imperials. All Rook had to do was make sure the tactical computers did their jobs and during his nocturnal excursions in the city, try not to look too bored with his assignment. Low visibility also meant he wouldn't get a chance to ski at the Mount Ningen Resort or take a three-day desert trek across the Rottervort Wastes. Too bad, maybe some other time.

Rook yawned and looked at his chronogram. He needed to eat and hadn't done so in nearly fourteen hours. Being a cheetah, he could go for much longer but why do so when it was not necessary? His mission was nearing an end, in fact all he had to do was wait for Algetti's signal, then he could disengage his equipment and hail a limousine to the spaceport. He looked at his chronogram again. Breakfast wouldn't be out of order. He had time. And no one prepared a five star meal like the Rhaudurian-Ithaca.

****

"Fantastic. So this is the infamous Nuera Algetti?" an SSK sergeant said, looking at the mangled corpse as it was hauled out of the computer station. "Commander of section 78, *Crhira Mosxk*? She doesn't look so infamous now."

SSK from department two were pouring through the rubble of the station, officers were giving orders and privates were digging through the debris or lifting bodies away. There were three APCs parked next to the burned out building which was still smoking from the aftermath of the firefight that had ended only fifty minutes ago.

"Interesting. She was observed with a Federation agent yesterday." The leftenant from department two moved the toe of his boot through a glob of greasy blood and gazed at the exhausted looking sergeant. "Why didn't we take them then?"

The sergeant shrugged, he hated explaining things to anyone from a different department. "Orders were to—"

"Do not discuss any of this outside of the facility, sergeant," Major Netergon boomed as he approached the two. "This is not a secure area—there are Straaka here."

"With respects, major. I was just asking the sergeant—"

"Leftenant, two of my officers with your rank were killed today. Leftenants are in very short supply. So I suggest that if you value your life, you'll occupy yourself with something or I'll have to task you with something that will leave you just as dead as the others. Understood?"

The leftenant saluted and moved off.

Netergon watched him leave and grunted in disdain. "Madness, that's what this is," he said to his sergeant. "I've got the section chief screaming at me about the dead. I've got Nijimegan security wanting answers—*'Why did this happen?' 'Why wasn't I notified?' 'Why is the communications grid nonfunctional?'*.

. . Straaka moving in to investigate, to clean up. And now I find out that the Imperial Armada is to arrive shortly to coordinate their own investigation."

"What does the Armada have to do with this operation? This is strictly a matter for the department." The sergeant gestured at the moving Straaka. "Perhaps their involvement is necessary as well. We can always use the Straaka to clear away remains. But I think you're right. There are too many hands moving in."

Netergon silently agreed; he didn't like any of this. He had been assigned the task of clearing out traitors and keeping an eye on a possible Delrel agent by the SSK Theatre of Operations Commander, Delgarada Sector, Colonel Trentergon. But a nagging rumor persisted that Marshal Admiral Rouldran Petti was behind all of this—unconfirmed, naturally. Though it would probably explain why the Imperial Armada was involved. Something big was on the horizon and Netergon didn't have a clue as to what it all meant or what his small part in all of it was. Everything was compartmentalized, made all the more complicated by rumors and distorted facts. Actually, when the major looked at things objectively, he didn't care, just as long as he survived it all with his career and life intact.

A thought came to him causing him to shudder. It had been like this weeks and days before the Minerva invasion. Netergon remembered secrets wrapped around orders and counter orders, there had been 'replacement' assignments where entire Straaka Legions had been purged of their senior field officers. Netergon could feel the strings pulling him in too many directions at once. All he could do was dance his disjointed dance and execute the orders given him to the best of his abilities. Infuriating Netergon more was the fact that Colonel Trentergon, who was on the other side of the galaxy, could recruit him at any time and at his convenience to perform any task he wanted and without first notifying Netergon's on-site section chief, Colonel Rahetti. It was an excellent arrangement for Trentergon, it was a confusing, rotten situation for Netergon.

Again, Netergon thought about saying something but thought better of it. Instead, he watched Straaka strut around in over-sized armor, displaying weapons that could blow a person apart from half a kilometer away—no style in that, no grace. Straaka were no more than uneducated beasts. *Useful beasts at times*, Netergon reminded himself. If he commanded a cohort of them, things on Nijimegan would be vastly different. He moved to his command car when another agent rushed up to him.

"Sir, I've word from one of our contacts." The private's voice had an urgent edge to it that Netergon didn't like.

"Yes? Continue."

"It's from Kiasar. He says that he's spotted our target and is preparing to make contact—"

Too many hands getting involved. "No, he isn't," Netergon boomed. "He'll blow this thing wide open. Where is he?"

"The Rhaudurian-Ithaca."

"Let's go," Netergon said. "Sergeant, gather your men; the Straaka can handle matters here." Netergon felt his heart pounding; things were moving very fast, his palms started to sweat. "We'll take two command cars and one APC—let's move."

"Sir, what about the orders to wait for the Imperial Armada?"

"Fine, sergeant, you can wait for them," Netergon directed. "I'm going to the Rhaudurian-Ithaca before Kiasar buggers everything up!"

****

Rook strolled into Rhaudurian-Ithaca's restaurant. The delectable smells of breakfast being served filled his feline nostrils. This restaurant was intergalactically renowned for its ability to prepare millions of off-world dishes with the ease and speed that it demonstrated with native Nijimeganese dishes. That's what tourists wanted more than anything else: a large selection of dishes and speed of service—if they wanted to wait, there was the Nikatus-Imperial Palace more than sixty lightyears away.

"Ah, Mr. Tyndak," the sharply dressed maitre d' said to the cheetah. "I trust your stay here is very pleasurable. The comfort of our guest is our number one concern."

'Mr. Tyndak', Rook, smiled pleasantly. He'd used the cover name for more than four days now and it almost sounded as natural as his real name. "I'm having a rather enjoyable time, yes," Rook lied. "I shall not forget your service." He handed the maitre d' a silver coin—on Nijimegan the custom of voluntary taxation took place before the service, not after.

"Did you see the dawn?"

"Yes, it was most exquisite," Rook answered pleasantly.

The maitre d' smiled as if she'd been directly responsible for its creation herself. "Breakfast then, sir? I trust that you'll want your usual seating arrangement?"

"Yes."

"Is the young woman going to be joining?"

"No, I'm afraid not today."

"Oh, a pity." The maitre d' smiled politely. The fact didn't escape her that the woman was Pulsarian and Mr. Tyndak was Aracrayderian, the deadliest of enemies. . . supposedly. Then again, Nijimegan was a Frontier planet and strange alliances formed all the time. "Very well. This way please, sir."

Rook followed her through the large, spacious, brightly lit restaurant. Antiques of Nijimegan and alien design decorated the triple layered dining area. Red, green, and orange Cesstessian ferns spiraled up thick, wood stained spires leading to the transparent ceiling thirty meters above. As usual the restaurant was crowded, bodies shifted in chairs, utensils dug into exotic entrees, the conversation a polite, intimate buzz.

He was seated at a booth that gave him a clear field of fire that covered 90% of the dining area. If trouble arose, he needed to be ready to kill and needed to have an unobtrusive view of those he was killing. He gave the outward appearance of the relaxed traveler, enjoying himself, while his senses stayed alert, ready for any sign of trouble: a sudden movement of a fork, a voice that suddenly rose then lowered to a whisper, anything that could be interpreted as an aggressive act.

Even with his sidearm hidden beneath his black Helen Ridger sport coat (a signed original), Rook knew he could draw, fire, and take-cover before an aggressor could bring his weapon to bear.

The maitre d' handed him a menu datacard and strolled off politely to intercept more arriving guests.

Peering intently at the menu datacard Rook wondered if he should choose something native or an off-world dish. The Greerfleck swordfish immediately caught his eye and was said to be the best in the galaxy. If it's the best, why not enjoy it for breakfast.

He placed his order to the overly polite waiter and sipped at the complementary wine. Then it happened! Nothing sudden or violent, he became acutely aware that he was being watched, studied. Rook remained relaxed, calm, as if nothing were transpiring—although his insides began to quiver and thrash. The action was subtle, subdued. The watcher wasn't sure of himself, yet. Rook caught a scent. It wasn't familiar. But then again it was. It was distant, from his past. He couldn't place it. In a few seconds he wouldn't have to.

A human male with thick ropes of blond hair slowly walked in his direction. Blue-grey eyes sharp and intelligent. Instantly Rook was flooded with recognition. Logan Kiasar—*Goddamnit!*—a wanted criminal within the borders of the DFR, which was probably why he was operating in the Frontier now. He was an 'operator', a weapons man, a slave-trader who sold human 'comfort' females to the Pulsarians returning from the front lines, he was a pirate who raided merchant ships in deep space leaving the crews stranded parsecs from the nearest planet. An all around murderous bastard—a twisted, violent snot with all the grace of pubic lice. Before Kiasar's infamous career began within the frontier territories, he'd been a student at the Bastian Academy on Minerva. Disgraced, he was, and discharged for a number of violations against the Honor Code. He was even accused of murder but vanished long before official charges could be registered. Oh yes, Rook was acquainted with the dossier on this scum. However, training and professionalism demanded his expression remain impassive.

Recognition was a danger all agents faced while in the field. For his part, Rook never lived with the fear of having his cover blown, simply because the galaxy was too damned big to be too concerned about bumping into someone whom might recognize him. He had a better chance of flying into a black hole, or getting ripped apart by an ion storm before he was likely to be recognized by someone while on assignment. There was no need to compute the odds because they were infinitesimal.

If recognition ever occurred, he'd simply tell the individual they'd made a mistake and press on with his business. But here he was trapped. Here he was seated, relaxed, had breakfast on the way. He just couldn't stand up and walk away. Such hasty action would be a sure tip-off. There was no escape.

And Logan's eyes! It was always in the eyes. The eyes knew. He'd already been made. Should he lie? He couldn't compromise his cover—but what could he do? Too late to think now, all he could do was act.

"Rook, my good fellow," Logan said, standing over the table, a wicked smile extended from ear to ear. "What brings you to this part of the galaxy?"

Rook eyed Logan keenly. *Would a lie work?*

"I'm afraid that you have me mistaken for someone else, friend," Rook said, his expression carefully relaxed and confused.

"I don't think so," Logan said. "May I have a seat?"

"Now is not a good time, my dear fellow," Rook said with a charming flourish. "I have a business associate arriving shortly and we have about a dozen things to—I'm afraid that he doesn't like uninvited guests."

"Uninvited or unwanted?" Kiasar smirked.

"The choice is yours."

"Very well. So, it's going to be like this." The smirk disappeared.

"It's not going to be like anything."

"Come on, Rook. I know you know who I am. Let's not trifle here. You and I both know Minerva can no longer train Omnitraus Officers to kill Pulsarians."

The words 'Omnitraus Officers' stung like hot needles through Rook's heart. But he maintained the mask of confusion.

"No effect, eh? You must commend your teachers of Gladatraus Command. Perhaps they were able to train you after all."

"*Who* are you?" Rook leaned forward, all business now—*don't overdo it.* "Do you work for Arcadia IBT?"

"You know who I am."

Rook acted exasperated and exhaled. "All I know about you is the way you're ruining my appetite with your rude confrontational behavior and accusations centering on suspicious loyalties. Will you please grant me the peace I need for dining or must I notify the authorities?"

"Why the hell would you want to do that, Rook?"

"And stop calling me that. The name's Tyndak."

"Tyndak? 'The name's Tyndak'—not, my name *is* Tyndak."

"I was adopted by humans after my birth," Rook supplied. Then his eyes narrowed and his nostrils flared. "Why am I telling you this? Get out of here. This conversation is terminated. If you don't leave I *will* notify the authorities or I'll take care of the matter myself." Rook pulled his lapel back to reveal the nasty looking SN-90.

"This isn't a very private place for a murder, now, is it?"

"The situation can change at any time."

"Now I know I have the right cheetah. At first I wasn't sure. But now I am. You see, I know more about you than you realize. I can help you. I can help you get off this planet."

"I don't need your help. I already have a starship—"

"The *Icarus Dawn*," Logan said. "The Pulsarians have already taken possession of it."

How did Logan know the name of his starship? *My God! What else does he know?*

"You're working with the *Crhira Mosxk*—"

In a blur, Rook grabbed the human by the throat and jerked him down, his face millimeters away from his own. Logan winced as he felt the SN-90 stick into his ribs. Such speed. He knew beyond a doubt that this was indeed his cheetah.

"Look, friend, I don't know who you are or where you come from. But you are this close to becoming a smoking stain on this table."

Despite his cool, Logan felt his heart rattle around in his chest. "Like I said Rook, this isn't a very private place for a murder."

Rook shoved the human aside like a rag doll and replaced his weapon. Several patrons turned to regard the two. Rook ignored them, his attention on Logan. "I'm leaving now. If you follow me, you will be killed," Rook hissed. "And it will be a private matter."

Rook whirled and moved rapidly toward the exit. The maitre d' intercepted him. Time to play important tourist again. "Mr. Tyndak, is everything okay? Is that individual bothering you? Should I notify the authorities?"

"No, that will not be necessary," Rook said. "But do have my meal sent to my room please with a bottle of your best Cordon-Adrian."

"As you wish, sir."

Rook moved quickly through the lobby and into a waiting elevator.

****

Logan Kiasar watched Rook leave and wondered why he was still alive. Rook should have killed him, he should've made a move instead of talking about it. Now, it would cost him. Kiasar moved out of the restaurant and stood next to a hideous form waiting in a darkened corner of the lobby. A stout humanoid joined them reading the data from a delicate instrument he held in his hand.

"Well?" Logan said to the Nijimeganese.

"Nothing, Logan. He kept his emotions in check. An' according to this, he wasn't ev'n lying or under any kind o' duress when he said that he didn't know you. And when he said his name was Tyndak, that registered as being truthful as well. He only got angry when you mentioned the *Crbira Mosxk*."

"What about when I mentioned his affiliation with Omnitraus Command?"

"Nothing, no emotion."

Logan smiled. "You see. I told you he was good. If he wasn't Omnitraus don't you think he would have shown a *little* reaction? Panic, maybe? This is a long way from Federation space. He would have reacted in some way."

The Nijimeganese nodded in agreement.

"Tell our friends, the SSK, that we have their man netted." Logan looked casually around the lobby. No one was paying them any heed. They were vacationers and walleyed types going about their business. "But tell them to hurry. He might be on to us."

A nasty grin came across the Nijimeganese's face as he hurried off. Logan turned toward the grotesque alien next to him. "The hunt begins."

CHAPTER IV
NIJIMEGAN INTELLIGENCE

ROOK bolted into his room, his SN-90 drawn and ready to disintegrate anything threatening. He made a quick sweep of the room, his heart pounding, muscles tensing. Nothing. He jumped through the holocramatic wall and surveyed the lavatory. Again nothing—no targets. He entered his room again, looking for something to shoot, something to kill. But all was clear. Still, he felt uneasy. *That damned Logan; of all the people in the galaxy to run into,* Rook thought. *I should have killed him when I had the chance.*

Rook knew that he'd meet up with Kiasar again. The human wasn't one to let him leave the planet without another confrontation—Kiasar's reputation demanded such. What surprised Rook was the fact that he made it out of the restaurant without a fight. Kiasar wasn't the only danger. Rook knew Kiasar wasn't acting alone. His senses told him that there was a male Nijimeganese who apparently hadn't bathed in days and something—some *creature*—Rook's senses could not identify, some unimaginable horror. Yes, there'd be a second encounter with Kiasar and his cohorts. The second time around, he'd make certain to kill Kiasar.

However, there were other matters pressing for his attention; he had to get out of his room and out of the hotel. There were probably Straaka and SSK agents already on the way. If Kiasar knew what he knew, then the Pulsarians wouldn't be much further than a step behind.

His hotel personal communicator chirped to life interrupting his train of thought. *Maybe the Straaka are here already.*

"Yes, what is it?" he asked without hesitation. If it was Straaka, let them think he didn't suspect them, act the tourist.

The female voice on the line spoke Nijimeganese; the monitor shut off to thwart efforts of the caller's identification. It didn't matter because everything had been pre-arranged. The call confirmed what he had been fearing—someone was coming up for him; it was a warning.

It was time to get out of here. He retrieved two encrypted disks, slid them into a small anti-shock container and inserted that into his breast pocket. He didn't have time to tear down his computer systems and take them with him—he only had a few minutes or less before the corridor outside his room turned into a blaze of laser fire. With a second's hesitation, he pointed the SN-90 pistol at the tactical computers and blew them all into a flaming mass of plastic and micro-chip lava. Earlier he had taken the precaution of removing his room's fire alarm system. If his room alarm sounded, other alarms throughout the triple towers would also be triggered. The corridors would be filled with panic-stricken civilians trying to escape in a choking chaos that would imperil them. The Pulsarians would cut them down in their efforts to snare an Omnitraus. Rook couldn't allow that to happen.

The cheetah bolted into the corridor and dropped to a knee sniffing the air. No danger here. He jogged up the corridor, keeping his senses tuned for danger and his pistol readied to fry anything hostile. With emphasis and concentration, he could hear a heartbeat a dozen meters away. He could sense panic, anticipation, and nervousness. And that was just employing the traits he was born with. When applying these traits to his Omnitraus training, he was a formidable weapon.

Rook avoided the elevators, they'd be covered first. He headed for the stairs, knowing they'd be covered as well. But only the approach from the lobby—they shouldn't have the roof covered—Straaka weren't that smart.

Rook had many escape contingencies. There was an AEM-9 rocket-pack stashed in one of the storage lockers on the roof, next to the heating and cooling units. But in the remote possibility Straaka were swarming the roof, Rook would make his escape through the basement, where he had scuba gear hidden, and would swim through the city's aqueducts to the spaceport. Again, only if necessary—the thought of making a fifty kilometer swim horrified him.

He accessed the door which led to the stairway, keying in his senses for danger. All clear. He sprinted up the stairwell. Racing along at nearly 90kpx, he was only six seconds away from the roof, maybe less. His breathing was smooth, dense chords of muscle pumping in his legs, filling up with blood, increasing power and speed. Up, around, and up again. He could see the access hatch to the roof. All he had to do was open the door and—

No! Rook careened to one side as lasers tore long gashes in the wall and stairs. The door above him had slid aside before he reached it, the plain-clothes Pulsarian appeared, weapon in hand, his intent deadly. His reaction was better than the cheetah's—his reflexes like lightning; his aim, however—and this was the only thing that saved Rook—was deplorable. And it would cost the agent his life, because Rook didn't miss. A thin beam of light speared into the Pulsarian's throat and exploded out the other side. Black blood expanded in a vaporized cloud of steam as the agent fell back gurgling in a spasm of death.

Rook leaped over the dying waste and through the doorway, assuming a firing stance as more lasers streaked by overhead. He returned the fire and dropped the Pulsarian who had been standing next to a hovering dual-engine air-car. The cheetah raced to the car and incinerated the face of the driver, who was too slow in readying his own weapon. The driver had fired once, the laser cut into the flight controls in a fury of sparks and flying metal.

Rook pulled the smoking corpse out of the aircar and was about to ascertain the damage to the flight controls when he noticed something peculiar. There was an opened security document container on the passenger's seat; it had restricted reporting markers and limited-handling caveats all over it. His whiskers flickered with curiosity. He looked around—shouldn't he be getting out of here? He tore into the thick envelope. Immediately he felt like throwing up; the sickness welling up in his stomach struggling to burn up through his esophagus.

They knew!

From the very beginning, they had known. His feline eyes burned with disbelief as he scanned through the documents. There was a schedule of his every move, his meetings with the *Crhira Mosxk*, pictures of his arrival at the space port, when he ate, slept. *God, it was all there. Every bit of it. They knew!* He continued reading . . . his plans of escape, contacts—damnit, everything! *Rhahun oc Mhar!* They knew exactly what he was going to do even before he landed.

Madness! The Pulsarians he had killed weren't Straaka, they were SSK, members of the most feared counter intelligence and special operations organization in the Pulsarian Empire.

Someone was going to pay for this. All this time they knew!

Rook's mind screamed at him; a strange exhaustion froze his legs, made his arms feel heavy. They could have killed him at any time and yet they hadn't. Why had they let him live? They'd identified him as an Omnitraus Officer and yet they did nothing. When Pulsarians dealt with the Omnitraus—especially the fanatical SSK—the action taken was violent, swift and immediate. They didn't record your movements. They didn't wait to see what action the Omnitraus was going take. No, the traditional Pulsarian reaction would be one of immediate, deadly violence. *Unless . . . my God!* They were using him, tracking him to get to Nuera Algetti. And the receptionist at the front desk could be killed now too. An entire cell of *Crhira Mosxk* operatives could be destroyed by now.

Rook raced for the equipment lockers. If everyone he had come in contact with over the last several days was dead or about to die, then he had to make it off-world and back to—*Rhom Vohgraks um Hiere!* His rocket pack was gone. Those Pulsarian devils! Their surveillance of him was indeed complete. What was he going to do now? Rook turned away, frantic. Should he fight his way to the basement? How long did he have before more units arrived on the roof? He had to think, construct a way out of the enveloping trap.

He raced back to the air-car and searched through its cargo compartment. Nothing of value here—yes, there were tools, equipment and safety gear but none of it would help him escape. Rook returned to the cockpit and wished that the pilot hadn't blown out the flight controls when he tried to return fire. Rook continued searching the cockpit, not knowing what he was looking for, completely aware that the longer he stayed in one spot the sooner he was likely to be discovered.

These air machines had ejection systems. Could he disassemble the parachute rig from the ejection seat, strap it on and just leap off the roof of the *Rhuadurian-Ithaca*? Why not? He examined the pilot and co-pilot's seats, making sure they were both safetied before he proceeded. He didn't want the seat to explode in his face as he removed the parachute.

Rook examined the seat, quickly identifying the archaic escape system. There was the ejection handle—he made sure he didn't touch it—the guillotine cartridge; leg restraint release handle; the canopy initiator firing links—again, another item he didn't dare touch—and finally, the canopy and seat interlock block. He'd have to remove the rig without removing the canopy and seat interlock block. If he removed the 'block,' the ejector seat would fire in his face. But the ejector seat should be in the 'safe' position, so it shouldn't fire, right? Rook didn't know, didn't want to risk it. He felt his heart thudding loudly in his chest. It was a tricky operation for someone who had never done this before. A skilled technician could perform this task in less than forty seconds—too bad there wasn't one around. If he mishandled one component, no matter how unimportant its function, it could cause a series of events that might be fatal.

He examined the setup for a minute, then carefully removed the parachute assembly from the ejector seat and eased away from the vehicle with a long exhale. He quickly strapped the shoulder harnesses around his chest and snapped the fasteners and connectors. The chute felt awkward—but then again it wasn't designed for this particular use. He secured his Hellington SN-90 and held the drogue chute in his left hand. The drogue would be the only mechanism to deploy the main chute since there wasn't a 'D' ring to pull.

Rook took a deep breath, then sprinted for the edge of the building and leaped. He felt his stomach leap into his throat, the cold air blasting into his face. He held the drogue tightly, wind howling in his ears; he could see the ground rushing up, concrete and steel. Now. He released the drogue and felt the reassuring tug against his shoulder harness as the main chute deployed with a rippling bang.

****

Major Netergon studied the burned corpses near the aircar and shook his head. Two dead here and a third without a throat at the entrance to the stairway. SSK agents were just finishing their sweep of the Towers' roofs.

"Any sign of him?" Netergon asked; he already knew the answer.

"None, sir."

"Sir, I think you should take a look at this."

Netergon walked over to the vehicle. "What is it?"

"Sir, this Delrel spy is clever," the SSK sergeant said. "I've never seen anything like this. He disassembled the parachute harness to the aircar's ejection system. He discovered his rocket pack had been removed and improvised another method of escape. He removed the parachute assembly from the ejector seat and floated to the ground. I'm surprised that the seat didn't explode in his face; escape systems are delicate and he didn't have proper tools with which to work. Clever."

"I'm glad you like it," Netergon snorted.

More SSK gathered around the car.

"Anything?" Netergon asked them.

"Nothing, sir."

"Where's Kiasar? I thought he said he had our spy cornered."

"We haven't heard from him, sir," said the SSK sergeant with a dried patch of blood on his forehead. "He isn't anywhere in the hotel. He made his initial report and nothing. And now I'm getting reports that Straaka units are moving toward the spaceport."

An SSK staff sergeant walked up, his face grim. "The spaceport? He couldn't have covered that distance in this short amount of time."

"Should we call off the search?" the sergeant asked.

"No." Netergon motioned for his sergeants to follow him away from the vehicle. "The Nijimeganese have their own security force there and with the Straaka moving in—damnit I can't believe the Omnitraus is going to be captured by them. Blast it. From the very beginning, this was my investigation, my case. They have him and I have nothing."

"Why would the Delrel go to the spaceport?" asked the staff sergeant.

"Why wouldn't he?"

"It plays too closely to *our* rules. Earlier, you said he was clever. He's not going to go to the spaceport and walk into a trap." He looked at Netergon. "We may still have him, sir."

Netergon pursed his lips. "Perhaps. Let's have a look at that list of possible safehouses."

****

"What about a safehouse?" Logan Kiasar asked, running his fingers through his blonde hair. "Any safehouse."

"We know of only two locations in this city," the crusty buck-toothed Nijimeganese said. "We have the *Crhira Mosxk* to thank for that."

Kiasar didn't say anything, gloved fingers stroked his chin, considering. Yes, the *Crhira Mosxk* had its share of traitors.

"Do you think he'll lie low for a while or will he make a move for the spaceport?"

They were on the roof of the *Wyvern-Astoria* eyeing the Pulsarians on the roof of the Rhaudurian-Ithaca eight-hundred meters away. It looked as if they were giving up their search.

"They haven't found him, idiots," Kiasar said peering through binoculars.

"Well, where is he then?"

"Not at the spaceport. He isn't stupid. He's Omnitraus—never underestimate the Omnitraus. He knows it's too dangerous to make a run for the spaceport now. His starship could have been taken by now—once more, he had to *assume* it's been taken by now. There are a number of things he can do on a planet as populous as this. He could hi-jack his way off-world—but he isn't that desperate yet. Or he could take a shuttle to the other side of the planet and buy passage on one of the merchant liners."

"If he does that . . ."

"Then we'll lose him. And the Pulsarians will lose him too."

"And the safehouses?"

"Well, most buildings in this city are shielded from sensor scans. That damned privacy act, if only—" Kiasar suddenly slammed his hand down on the hood of his aircar. "Right then, here's what we'll do . . ."

****

Rook hadn't paid the hotel innkeeper when he requested the room. Payment wasn't necessary. Survival was. For this was one of several safehouses scattered throughout the city. Rook had paid visits to two of those houses earlier in the week. Now, because the Pulsarians had his every move diagrammed, those safehouses were compromised. So Rook explored a safehouse that he had never visited before, *ever*, a safehouse with a location not known to the *Crhira Mosxk*. Only a few individuals within Intelligence

Commands Operation and Special Strategic Plans and Activities (STRATPLAN) knew of its existence and no one from that department was present during his pre-mission briefing. Arguably, the location shouldn't be known by the Pulsarians. Could there be a leak in STRATPLAN? Maybe, but what in the universe was he going to do about it—nothing while he was still on Nijimegan. And there were probably a few traitors within the *Crhira Mosxk* as well—a silly observation since the probability of SSK infiltration into the *Crhira Mosxk* was somewhat high at any rate. Rook could accept that, had planned on it. What he couldn't accept was the gnawing uneasiness he felt as he lay on the bed—he should be dead now . . .

What if the Pulsarians knew about this safehouse? No. He dismissed that thought. The SSK were good. But they weren't that good. *Still* . . .

Rook felt his limbs tightening, his guts cinching and knotting. He had to get off-world. There was no point in rushing to the spaceport . . . even if what Kiasar had said was false. To do so from the standpoint of his tactical analysis would be suicide. Hence the need for another escape contingency in the form of Star Fleet.

The brothers who ran the Inn had a ship. But it would take six hours to fuel and prep it. As a general rule, one just couldn't own a starship and have it fully fueled and ready to go at any given moment. Besides breaking a dozen or more regulations regarding the safe handling and storage of hazardous materials, one had to remember that the fuels utilized by most starships went beyond simple 'gas' or liquid-nitrogen mixtures. There were secondary, tertiary, and quadrantal chemicals that could be highly lethal to planetary populations if said starship had a leak. Not to mention atomic booster packs, tachyon containment pods, matter/anti-matter injectors . . . the list was as long as the possible dangers. The only environment where starships were ready to go was on military bases and Rhaudurian wasn't a base, it was a city with several million inhabitants.

Even when Rook landed at the spaceport, ground regulations mandated that the unused or spent fuel be removed from his ship and placed in a well-shielded and secure storage container. An exorbitant fee had to be paid to by-pass the restrictions; it also meant that his ship would have a safety monitor onboard at all times to make sure that his ship didn't have any leaks, spikes in power, or any other emergency that must be dealt with in an immediate manner.

Of course, none of that mattered now; current circumstance made it moot. He would've loved to see the face of the safety tech when he kicked him off the ship and then taken off without clearance. Now, he'd have to wait for the Nijimeganese of the safehouse to get him off-world. There were hundreds of auxiliary landing and take-off fields within a fifty-kilometer radius of the city. The Pulsarians couldn't have them all covered. Six hours to wait . . . the slower the better. Best to go through the procedures methodically than to rush through and attract attention. In the overall scheme of things, it was best to take it slow, but it was killing his nerves. Every splatter of rain against the window, every creak of wood was a potential threat . . .

There was nothing for him to do but wait. He was protected here. After all, he was in a shielded room and this was a safehouse. Sensors wouldn't be able to detect him. This was due in part to the security and privacy act passed nearly three centuries ago, enabling civilian and privately owned structures to afford the same protection from unwanted scans as military structures had.

He was safe from intruding sensor probes—if, that is, this building had been constructed with the security act in mind. Yes, Pulsarian structures had shielding as did the Federation. But Nijimegan was neither Imperial nor Federal and as such didn't necessarily have to abide by their building codes. But the Nijimeganese had constructed one of the biggest and most modern planet-based spaceports in the galaxy, and after mastering such a feat, they had to abide by something. Nijimegan was a neutral planet under the 'neighborly' occupation of the Pulsarians.

Rook turned to face the doorway. He was safe from intruding scans, and if for some reason the Pulsarians could scan into the room, his wrinkled business suit could absorb much of the radiation. And if his suit couldn't function as designed . . . he had his Hellington snub-nose pointing at the door—it would function as designed.

It was the waiting that made this situation intolerable. Forget about the SSK having infiltrated the *Crhira Mosxk*, forget about Nuera Algetti—nothing could bring her back. The waiting was digging into him like a parasite.

Six hours. He kept telling himself that mobility was the key to survival; staying ahead of the Pulsarians, even if it was just a step, would be beneficial. However, there was logic in staying put. If the Pulsarians were scouring the city, staying put was to his advantage. Provided of course, they didn't know the location of this hotel. *Oh, stop thinking about it.* He felt his limbs tighten up again.

Rook looked around the room. It was quite a contrast from the ostentatious accommodations found in the *Rhaudurian-Ithaca.* Well, this was the way missions turned out sometimes. He fished through his pockets and retrieved the octagonal. "I hope you're worth it."

He placed it back into his breast pocket. Six hours. Too long to stay awake and fret about exigencies and contingencies. He should rest. Good idea. He would need to be alert when zero hour arrived and not fatigued with apprehension.

He drifted into a troubled sleep, never once considering . . .

****

The rain began to come down in sheets as Dannen Leers calmly ducked under the awning leading to the entrance of the *Spaceport Voyagers Inn.* He had never been to Nijimegan before and as far as he was concerned, it had to be the wettest planet in the galaxy. If the dampness wasn't enough, the languages were tough to master, everything damned near impossible to pronounce . . . like this city, Rhaudurian.

With the rain pounding the sidewalk and streets, Leers studied the entrance to the motel. He cursed when he realized that he had to actually articulate a brass handle in order for the weather treated hardwood door to move aside and allow him entrance into the establishment. Leers only had the use of one arm; his left was immobilized in a sling. The tendons and muscles from elbow to shoulder were severely pulled, while several striations had been ripped altogether. Add to this the four cracked ribs on the left of his body, the look of fatigue clouding an unshaven face couldn't mask the pain Leers was in.

Leers reached for the handle, heard a metallic clicking and pushed the door inward. It was much easier than he thought. He entered the small dimly lit lobby. There was a massive rug of unknown origin on the floor, a fan above circulating the smell of wilderness, two sofas flanked by intricately carved end tables, probably antique by Nijimeganese standards—but Leers didn't know antique from post-renaissance or even if there was such a thing. To his left was a dark hall leading to the first floor rooms, straight on was a large wooden staircase leading to the second story rooms. Everything looked old, rustic, adding to the mystique of the Frontier; of it being wild, flavored by the untamed, the uncharted. But there was nothing antique or wild about the computers lining the Inn's registration and reservation counter. They were quite new, quite modern. Leers couldn't say the same thing about the scruffy Nijimeganese male standing behind the counter, eyeing the human's every move.

"My I be of assistance?" the greasy faced innkeeper rasped into a translator. He licked his lips nervously as the human approached the counter. His eyes darted around, taking in the threatening form, wondering why he was wearing a battle helmet in the middle of the city—and what was he hiding underneath that poncho? Weapons no doubt.

Seeing the innkeeper's discomfort, Leers held up a gloved hand. "Don't fear, friend," he said in rough Nijimeganese Standard. It was the best he could do since he only had twelve hours to study the language. "Maybe you can help me."

"A room then?"

"No, no rooms." Leers shook the beads of water from his poncho. "I'm looking for an old friend of mine, understand?"

"The galaxy is full of friends and enemies alike," the innkeeper responded, unaware of the nervous twitch in his jaw.

Leers blinked. If he could've scratched his head he would have. "No, you're not reading me correctly. I'm looking for someone."

"Keep looking."

What, is this sonofabitch actually trying to be rude? "Hey, look friend, this is no game . . . we're running out of time. I'm running out of time."

"Move on, human." The nervousness was gone, the dangerous tone unmistakable. "What you're looking for is not here."

"You don't know what I'm looking for."

"Don't care either," he said in perfect Delrel Standard.

Leers felt his thoughts stumble. He leaned closer to the counter, the computers chirping in his ears. "Well, now that we've pierced the barrier of language, let me state for the final time that I'm looking for a friend. The question is simple. Have you seen him? His name's Rook, but he could be going by a different name such as Tyndak or . . ."

The Nijimeganese began shaking his head. "I don't know what you're talking about."

"Why the hell do people say 'I don't know what you're talking about' when they know good and goddamned well what you're talking about?"

"Why don't you move on please, sir."

"His name's Rook, friend. I don't know if you and he set up recognition codes or duress codes—I don't care. I need to know where I can find him."

"Can't help you."

"Maybe you think you can reach a weapon you've got hidden beneath the counter here." Leers tapped the dusty surface with his knuckles. His eyes narrowed. "Believe me when I tell you friend that if you try to make a reach for it, I'll burn you down before you get the chance. I'm not here to kill you or Rook, but if you so much as—"

"Then why the boast, human?"

Leers fished for a retort but never found one, the creaking of footsteps on wooden stairs caught his attention. Leers whirled and snatched the Delnalt '44 from his holster. The Nijimeganese who had been trying to creep down the stairway heaved the heavy *Vgamh CR* laser rifle around in hands unaccustomed to the task. Leers released a burst from his '44. The stairs in front of the man erupted into a shower of splinters, dust, and sparking cords of wood. He screamed as the shockwave sent him over what remained of the banister. He landed on his face and chest in a sickening thud of lacerated skin and broken teeth.

Leers didn't want to kill these Nijimeganese, he had to rescue Rook—he turned back to the innkeeper behind the counter—no. Leers launched himself away from the counter firing his '44 as he sailed through the air—the idiot was actually reaching for a weapon. Leers' shots missed the innkeeper but blew apart the computers, the translator, and most of the counter. The Nijimeganese twisted away in agony as the shockwaves tore at him, the flashes blinded him, the noise deafened him.

Leers came down hard on one of the antique end-tables. The damned thing was stout, unwilling to collapse under his weight and tumbled him over the edge onto the rug. Leers sensed the cascade of pain coming seconds before he felt it. When it arrived, it was unlike anything he'd ever experienced before in his life; numbing cold ripped through his stomach, past his lungs to stop behind his ears, tears splashed around the corners of his eyes and it was all he could do to keep from crying out. He rolled to a knee and fired off two more bursts to keep the Nijimeganese at bay.

Universe, the Delnalt felt too damned heavy to carry. Leers wiped the tears away, feeling the pain seep down his neck, to his shoulders. He screamed and fired again. Damn, he had to find Rook.

****

An explosion snapped Rook to wakefulness accompanied by a throbbing heart and a ringing in his ears. For a moment, the cheetah thought he had accidently fired off his laser pistol while he slept. But it couldn't have happened, for the laser weapon wouldn't cause the door to explode since, obviously, it was still intact less than two meters in front of him. And if he had fired the snub-nose, it would've produced a shrill whine as the energy bore through the metal instead of the sound of something being blown apart.

Rook struggled to yank the grogginess from his head—how long had he been asleep? An hour, two, perhaps? He was on his feet as more explosions carried through the air around him. The Pulsarians. They had come for him, and the innkeeper and his brother were fighting them back.

Rook forced the door aside and stepped into a corridor strobed by explosions and weapons fire. "Damnit, no." He turned and raced for the rear exit. The safehouse had been compromised, as he had feared. The innkeeper and his brother were on their own—they knew the risks, they knew what they had gotten themselves into and Rook couldn't do a damned thing about it. Yes, he would've preferred to stay and fight, but he couldn't risk losing the information he had in his breast pocket.

Rook reached the exit and readied himself as it slid aside. Rain cascaded in as he forced a quick glance out, the skies of Nijimegan dark and angry above him. More explosions crackled behind him. "Damnit. Damn this mission." Without looking back he sprinted down the alley, his legs driving hard, boots splashing in puddles. He didn't know where to run to, but he had to escape. Madness was all around him; the Pulsarians everywhere, death around every corner waiting to embrace him, killers behind shielded windows—looking, hunting.

Then he heard it. A faint scraping sound above the rain. It came from somewhere above him. Then a familiar and deadly smell brewed up into his nostrils—*ozone!* Someone had a weapon activated, tracking him. He had to find cover—too late. A force beam struck him at the exact center of his back, knocking the cheetah off his feet. He tumbled down the alley, sliding and skidding for thirty meters, kicking and screaming on the wet pavement.

The pain spread fast, traveling from his back to his rib cage, down his abdominal wall to his crotch. It felt as if he were being beat up. Every muscle in his body ached.

Force beams, sometimes inappropriately called piledrivers, didn't pack the destructive energy found in the majority of hand guns: Phiser PBXs and PVXs, Delnalts, or Graagas, or even Fleeters. Force beam weapons, like the widely used KR-7V assault rifle, were employed chiefly by law enforcement officials as a non-lethal way of subduing suspects—there were stun rays as well, but these were a different class and seldom used. Getting hit by a force beam was like getting hit by a sledgehammer a dozen times all at once. Instead of disintegrating a target, force beams were used to batter, to hammer, to beat it into submission—these 'non-lethal' weapons, as they were euphemistically called, could be employed with devastating effect.

The impact of the force beam had nearly knocked him unconscious. He rolled over onto his stomach, his lungs emptied, saliva gushing out of the corners of his mouth. He tried to stand on weak knees, tried to draw in desperately needed air when he was struck again.

This time it was a low angle deflection shot that sent him into the air like a rocket. He smashed into the side of a building and dropped down into a bin of reeking garbage. Blood began to flow out of one nostril. He wiped the blood away as a voice sounded in his ears.

"Rook, fancy meeting you again. What are you doing in a garbage bin?"

Along with the sickness flooding his senses, Rook felt a surge of anger. Where was his weapon? It fell from his grip when the first force beam hit him. *Rook, you novice, you should have*—But that voice . . . no, it couldn't be.

"You, what do you want?" Rook croaked weakly.

"To kill you and to collect a sizeable reward, mate. You should've done the same to me back at that restaurant, no? Now it will cost you. I must say that we had a hard time tracking you down. You gave us quite a chase. Your problem is that you're an Aracrayderian—not many of you on this planet. All it took, really, was some asking around, a small bribe and . . . Well, you're witnessing the rest of it."

Rook moaned and tumbled out of the trash bin. Rotted food stained his brand new sports coat—it wasn't new anymore.

"Do you have anything to say?"

"Yeah, you've ruined my suit . . . scum."

"That's not an answer." Kiasar kicked Rook in the face. Blood exploded from the cheetah's mouth and he sprawled down the alley too weak to defend himself.

Two others joined Logan. The first was a grotesque abomination of evolutionary law: an Insectrovoidpod with large glistening orbs for eyes set against a huge, black, pock-marked skull of fine, even fur. It was a quadruped, its four scaly, hooked appendages were attached to the upper thorax, one held a Ran'Phil & Hoffensten KH-77 laser pike. The beast, as hideous as it was, could only be manufactured from the tangled fabric of a nightmare. It hissed and whizzed as it approached, spittle dripping from its mouth.

The second was the short greasy-faced Nijimeganese male. Crooked, stained teeth framed his mouth. He spat on Rook as he stood over him holding a KR-7V force beam rifle.

"Stop lying, you filthy animal and give the boss what he wants and there'll be no trouble," crocked-tooth said, kicking Rook in the ribs and then the stomach.

Kiasar joined in with another kick to the face, then waved off crooked-tooth.

"Rook, you're behaving like a stubborn idiot," Kiasar said. "Just tell us what we need to know and I promise you that we'll kill you quick." Kiasar lied. He had no intention of killing Rook. He was going to hand him over to the Pulsarians. The Pulsarians always had trouble capturing Omnitraus Offices alive, his reward would be great. But only after he had that disk. With it he could bargain for an even bigger reward. The Pulsarians wouldn't like it, but that was too bad; those were the rules and this was his game.

"So, which is it, Rook? Did you leave it in your motel room? Or is it on your person?" Kiasar grinned and nodded toward crooked-tooth. "Search him."

What sounded like a warning came from the audio chords of the Insectrovoidpod as it whirled around. A beam of red light struck its head first, splattering Kiasar and crooked-tooth with cyst fragments, bone, and boiling mucus.

"Bloody hell. What is—"

Another bolt of energy tore the Insectrovoidpod's upper torso from its lower portion. What was left of the creature crumbled into a burning mass of bone fur and ruptured organs. Kiasar hunted frantically for the source of the attack. A lone figure stood in the middle of the alley, weapon in hand. The rain, mixed with steam and smoke from the burning insect creature produced an eerie scene. The man advanced, looking like a wraith.

"Step away from Rook, so's you don't fall on him when I kill you both."

The figure moved closer.

"Leers! Dannen Leers." At the moment of recognition, Kiasar and his partner raised their weapons. They were both too slow and screamed as their bodies were torn apart by superheated energy.

CHAPTER V
GLADATRAUS ESCAPE PROFILE

"ROOK!" Leers screamed, running over to his fallen friend. *No—he's not moving.* Leers knelt down beside the cheetah's inert body. "Rook, no . . . don't die now. Not now." But the cheetah didn't show any lifesigns.

Leers felt panic gripping him, felt the heat biting down. His hands began to tremble. *No. Not here . . . not now, damnit think.* He looked around, irises dancing, pupils dilating. Do something.

He activated the communications disk in his helmet and brought the thin mouthpiece down. "N'ckshell, get down here quick. Rook's been hit."

"Say again, who?"

"Rook. Get down here now."

Great! You were supposed to use call signs; what an idiot you are Dannen! Calling N'ckshell by her real name—bad form. Get a hold of yourself.

"Roger, on my way," came a crisp, immediate reply.

Leers looked down at Rook, the rain seeping into the cheetah's nostrils. Rook moaned, a pasty pink tongue hanging grotesquely out of one corner of his mouth. He didn't know anything about Aracrayderian physiology—he knew how to kill, but he didn't know how to revive, how to give aid. Leers checked his pulse, weak; his breathing also weak. Then Rook began gasping for air, his arms flaying around helplessly. Rook's chest began heaving as he fought to sit himself upright; Leers helped, relief sweeping through him. Rook had always been a fighter—he never gave up—probably sensed the human's indecision and decided that if anyone was going to save him it had better be himself.

"Easy partner, easy," Leers said easing him to a seated position, wondering if it was a wise thing to do. What if his back was broken? He held his old friend tightly, letting Rook know that he wouldn't have to deal with his ordeal alone.

"Where am I?" Rook breathed heavily trying to bring his surroundings into focus.

"You're still on Nijimegan."

Rook tried to move but Leers held him fast.

"Easy friend, easy. You ain't in no condition to move around, so don't try."

"Dannen? Leers, is that you?" He brought a hand to his eyes rubbing the rain out of them. "I can't see. Gods, I can't see."

"You got hit by force beams, you're synapses aren't on full burner yet. You have to relax, help is on the way."

Rook pushed weakly at him, heaved over, and began vomiting violently. Pulpy blood surging out of his nose and mouth.

"Rook," Leers screamed, horrified. "N'ckshell, move it, move it. I think we're losing him."

Rook curled up and began coughing and wheezing.

Leers looked up as a mechanical scream cut through the rain-saturated air. The Gladatraus Rhoderium Skiff probed its power, decreased feed to the vertical climbers, and began a fast but controlled descent to the street below. From Leers' position, the Rhoderium Skiff looked smaller than it actually was. The sub-orbital machine was roughly four meters long, perhaps five, shaped like a torpedo with stubby wings near its aft section and razor thin canards near the cockpit forward. It had one engine; a mammoth thrust-vectoring absurdity too big for the armored spaceframe built around it. Though thinly shielded, the Rhoderium Skiff could protect itself with its single propellant-cooled 9mmx pulse laser gun, used chiefly to strafe infantry, and the twin 22mmx thorium blasters, employed to take out tanks or armored personnel carriers.

The Skiff landed about five meters away, kicking up debris in a wake of steam and swirling rain. Even through the gloom of the storm and the dim cockpit lighting, Leers could see N'ckshell Slayton smirking as she busily shut systems down.

"Hold on for a second while I angle in the deflectors to keep the rain out of the cockpit," the Dracterian's high-pitched voice crackled over Leers' headsets. "If I can find where the fucking things are."

"Hurry."

****

"Hurrying," Slayton mumbled back as she flipped several switches to get the shields in the proper alignment. She fought off the urge to supply a stronger retort to Dannen's order. Who the hell did he think he was ordering her around like that. *Go and shite, mister.* It was bad enough that she hadn't completely healed from her ordeal on Elst—now she was here, on Nijimegan, trying to rescue another Omnitraus Officer—whom, no one was saying. But it sounded as if Dannen knew; from the sound in the human's voice, it was someone *he* knew but hadn't told her about.

She paused for a moment to grab a better look at the downed Omnitraus Officer Leers was guarding. A few moments ago it sounded as if the human had said that it was Rook. But it couldn't be; Rook was on the other side of the galaxy on Narterium or Nikatus. Slayton peered harder. No, that couldn't be Rook. She felt her heart flare . . . if it was . . .

Slayton popped the canopy and undid her harnesses. Snatching the edge of the spaceframe, she pulled herself out of the cockpit. Gods! It was Rook. "Leave his ass here—let's go!"

All Leers could say was, "What?"

"I said leave him," Slayton snarled. "To come all this way to rescue that piece of shite—"

"Help me get him to the Skiff."

"Do it yourself."

Without thinking, Leers whirled toward Slayton, the Delnalt pointing at the Dracterian's chest. "Help me get him on board, now."

Slayton met the human's gaze for a second then spat, "You and the damned Gladatraus didn't tell me who it was we were picking up on this planet. You should've told me; you should've said something. Everyone knows how I hate Aracrayderians—*that* one in particular."

"That's why we didn't tell you."

"Oh, so now you're in the betrayal business too."

"N'ckshell, please, we ain't got time for this." Leers holstered the weapon, swallowing hard, trying to control his own racing emotions. He glanced around. There might be more bounty killers lining them up right now. Lingering here was dangerous. "Help me please. I can't do this alone."

"You should've said something."

"I'm sorry."

"Dannen, he was responsible for killing the woman I loved before the invasion. And that whore Theri Tissuard is just as guilty as he—they killed her right in front of me. They just shot her down." Her stomach seized for a moment causing her chest to draw inward. For a few moments she couldn't breathe, the ripe feeling of infidelity suffocating her. She searched the human's expression for an answer. "How would you feel if you were lied to—then find yourself face to face with an enemy you hate more than the damned Pulsarians?"

Leers stood silently, the rain pelting his poncho, his face. His shoulders sagged slightly. "I don't know, N'ckshell. I suppose I'd be madder than hell."

"Exactly."

"But now's not the time. . ."

"I know, to discuss this." Slayton climbed down and gingerly limped toward human and the Aracrayderian, her hand firmly on the pommel of a combat knife. "I may kill him before we get back to base."

"We'll worry about that later." Leers ignored the knife, focusing instead on N'ckshell. Her hair was a wet, tangled mass framing her eyes and face. "I'm sorry for lying to you. I didn't want to but—"

"Whatever." She helped Leers load Rook into one of the four ejection seats of the cockpit, she closed her eyes tightly, feeling her heart racing. Rook had been a close friend once, had saved her life on more than one occasion. But all that was nothing compared to the betrayal she felt. "Are you sure he isn't dead?" Slayton asked. The cheetah looked like a corpse. His fur was wet and reeked of stale cologne, mucus swung from his nose and mouth. Slayton felt her insides knot.

Leers paused to look the Dracterian in the eyes; he could see the hatred flaring. "N'ckshell, snap out of it, please. We have a job to do. We'll sort through this later."

Slayton finished with Rook's harnesses, her eyes burning through the Aracrayderian and mechanically looked at the corpses down the alley. "Who were they?"

"Bounty killers," Leers said flatly.

"Wha?"

"One recognized me."

"Who? Oh, this 'ne here looks like Logan Kiasar—or what's left of him."

"How do you know that?" Leers didn't expect an answer; sometimes her mind worked in ways Leers dared not think of. "Well forget about them, let's get the hell out of here before more arrive," he said, climbing into the seat next to Rook's.

Slayton climbed slowly into the front seat in a trance, her eyes glazed. She didn't know what to make of all this. The events of the past few days had been like a whirlwind—she had difficulty trying to wrap her mind around all of it. She'd nearly been killed trying to complete her mission on Elst; had snapped one of her legs, and thanks to Gladatraus medicine it was now healing. Now to see Rook like this—this was something she wasn't quite ready for. Something was definitely wrong here—not just seeing Rook, but everything. Everything felt so surreal, so hurried, so rushed, so blurred. It didn't take much mind wrapping to convince her that someone was tipping off their enemy; someone was telling the Pulsarians about highly classified Federation operations. From Darmen, where Dannen had to be pulled out of his op by the Gladatraus, Elst, dozens of lightyears away where she'd almost bought it—now here on Nijimegan. The distances between all three planets were too enormous to be mere coincidence. For it to happen to one of them—*tough shite, it just wasn't your day.* Two, was simply beyond belief—but now three? How in the hell could bounty killers, the scum of the galaxy, know about an Omnitraus Officer on a high-priority assignment with a double cover? *It's insane—who gave a damn if that Officer was Rook.* Something or someone was behind this madness and they would pay for involving her.

Slayton pushed the thoughts from her mind, concentrating on the here and the now, and getting the three of them to the *Mekadore Traveler,* loitering in a low orbital position—*since the tower officials in the Nijimegan Prime Spaceport hadn't given it clearance to land—as if the Pulsarians hadn't already broken it.* Putting those thoughts away, she concentrated on flying one of the most unyielding and least forgiving spacecraft she had ever flown.

"Stand-by while I try to put this beast into orbit," Slayton chirped, punching at inputs.

"Yeah, well, don't auger us into the *Royal Towers*—" Leers was suddenly cut off as an armored personnel carrier screamed up the alley toward them. The menacing black hulk careened to a stop about twenty meters away, the 45mmx thorium blaster turning, starting to track them. "Straaka!"

Leers drew his weapon even though he knew it wouldn't dent the dense armor of the APC. "N'ckshell, the shields."

Her eyes widening in shock, Slayton began fastening her harnesses, fingers frantic—then stopped. She started stabbing at the keys on the deflector shield/screen operations panel.

The APC fired, explosive force striking the shield the *instant* Slayton had it aligned. Strobing light dazzled the Omnitraus Officers as sparks and jagged shards exploded away from them in a welter of noise and flame. The Rhoderium Skiff rocked, the sound making her ears ring.

Rain began to pour into the cockpit. Unwittingly, Slayton had removed the shield that had been above them.

"The canopy, N'ckshell, close the canopy!"

Slayton hit another switch and the canopy came down agonizingly slow. Water continued to gush in.

"Let's get out of here," Leers screamed.

Another explosion rocked the Skiff as Slayton powered up the engine. At that moment, armored Pulsarians began jumping out of the back of the APC, firing their service rifles from the hip and more explosions danced against the phototropic shielding. Several bolts of energy pierced the shielding and shrieked past the canopy. The Skiff lurched awkwardly, then shuddered madly.

"C'mon N'ckshell, let's go, let's go." Leers felt like he was going to vomit.

"I have power. But we aren't moving—ah, shite."

Indeed, they had full power but the Skiff bounced, straining to lift off; the landing skids were stuck to the ground, like claws digging in.

"It must be the rain," Slayton said desperately, trying to figure out which button to push next.

Leers leaned forward in his seat looking over Slayton's shoulder—*damnit!*

"You idiot, you got the vertical climbers on as well as the descending thrusters—turn the damn things off!"

In her mind Slayton mumbled a curse and moved the control yoke to yaw the Skiff around one hundred and eighty degrees and shut the descending thrusters off. The Skiff responded immediately blasting down the narrow alley, away from the APC and advancing Straaka. Slayton notched the throttles forward two clicks, and was knocked back in her ejection seat by a quick burst of positive G's. She pulled the control column back and the Skiff pitched into the dark sky, the leading edges of its wings biting into the air and accelerating to 300kpx in under ten seconds. Slayton shut down the climbers, she didn't need them now; with the main engine screaming in fury, anti-grav flight systems weren't necessary.

"Stop screaming at me," she shouted over her shoulder, her face burning with embarrassment.

She didn't care if the human was disgusted with her—*his problem*—but why can't he just hold his tongue for a few minutes—besides could he do better with one arm immobilized—*no, I don't think so.*

The Skiff powered by buildings shaped like domes and pyramids, and ninety story spires of metallic glass. In seconds, they had reached the standard aircar cruising altitude. Slayton checked the inertial dampeners and was satisfied by the readings. She was about to say something to Leers when the craft was buffeted by fierce gusts forcing her to keep her silence and study the readouts demanding her attention. Slayton loathed flying in foul weather, but had to remind herself that this was nothing like being caught in an ion storm, lightyears from the nearest star system where a slight miscalculation for just a split second meant certain death.

Slayton leaned back in her seat as she leveled the Skiff off and brought it around. Another invisible fist smashed into the Skiff. *Damn, this storm could stretch around us for hundreds of kilometers*, the Dracterian thought sourly.

A sudden gust of wind slammed the tiny craft to the left, Slayton struggled to correct it. The Skiff was traveling fast and bucking around so fiercely that if she lost control for a second, she'd kill herself and her passengers—ion storms notwithstanding. With sweat beading on her forehead and her mouth suddenly dry, the Dracterian brought the mouth piece to her headset communicator down to her thin lips and keyed the transmitter. "Ah, *Mekadore Traveler*, this is Team one. *Mekadore Traveler*, this is Team one, do you copy?"

"Copy. I have you five-by-five, go," a strong feminine voice acknowledged.

"We have—" Slayton couldn't bear to say his name. "—the *subject* secured. His condition is critical. I say again, his condition is critical. We are going to need immediate medical."

"Roger, that. Say position please."

"We're currently at angels five, course is two-seven-one, fifteen kilometers from ground coordinate two-three-seven. Speed increasing to four-two-niner, copy?"

"Roger, copy all. Squawk three-seven-eight, please," the woman ordered. Both Slayton and Leers knew the voice belonged to Gladatraus Guardian Jasmine, pilot of the *Mekadore Traveler*. Thus far, this had been the most that Slayton had ever heard her say. *The Mekadore Traveler* was crewed by two Gladatraus Guardians. One was Jasmine, the other—

"Roger." Slayton tapped the transponder knobs until she was transmitting at three-seven-eight.

"I have you on my short range scan," Jasmine informed her. "Continue your climb at pilot's discretion, then level off at flight level two-nine, please. Maintain course and speed and we'll initiate rendezvous."

Updrafts surging at 90kpx slammed into the Skiff, ear-splitting thunderclaps buffeted them.

"Can't you keep us steady?" Leers barked.

"Piss off!" Slayton didn't like the tone of his voice at al. Every time he spoke, every time he exhaled—the very sound of it just grated on her already frayed nerves. "Just shut it. I'm trying to concentrate up here. This may not be an ion storm or a temporal vortex but if you keep distracting me, I'll mort all three of us."

"Hell, you'll probably do it anyway just ta' spite me."

"Don't give me any ideas."

"Fine, then, fly—you've got control."

"What the hell do you think I'm trying to do?" Slayton returned to her controls. Rain streaked by on all sides of the canopy; visibility nil. Her unease began to build and Dannen's constant harassment didn't help matters—or was he just trying to take her mind off of Rook?

"I can't see a thing through all of this rain," Slayton spat.

"Try your radar, ace."

"Wha—and get smoked once we light up? Those APCs have surface-to-air weaponry."

"N'ckshell, we're at least fifty kilometers downrange of that goddamned APC. I doubt they can track us."

"What if there's more than one APC down there? What if there's a Spark Racer waiting for us in orbit?" *He is trying to distract me from Rook.*

"What if, my ass," Leers said flatly. He stared vacantly at the swirling blackness beyond the canopy. "Team one, this is *Mekadore Traveler*,"

Jasmine's voice said in Slayton's ear piece. "We're right above you."

Slayton looked up. She could see a blurred shape in the darkness but that was it.

"I have visual, I think," Slayton said into the mouthpiece. "Standing by to shut down. You can lock-on the tractor beam at any time. I can barely see your anti-collision lights. Visibility is nil."

"Standby one."

Slayton glanced at Dannen. The human remained silent, staring straight ahead as if he was oblivious to what was going on.

The Skiff jolted.

"Tractor beam engaged, cut your power."

"Roger, cutting power," Slayton acknowledged, pulling the throttles back and killing the engine.

Another jolt rocked the Skiff as the invisible power beam pulled them up to the blurred outlines of the Rhoderium Crab. Moments passed and for the first time Slayton could see the anti-collision strobes dancing brilliantly along the outer hull, or thorax of the warship. She felt a chill jolt through her lungs and stomach. To be held fast by the most awesome warship in the galaxy was an unnerving experience—now she knew how Pulsarians felt when they had to fight Gladatraus. If Slayton decided to go to full burner on the Skiff, there'd be no way she could escape the tractor beam of the *Mekadore Traveler*. The only way they could escape would be in pieces. Gladatraus Rhoderium Crabs were warships, not simple starships with speed and fitted with weapons as an afterthought. They were weapons platforms flown by prime pilots with the ability to engage multiple targets from all aspects and all angles with cold, lethal precision. The body of the *Mekadore Traveler*, Slayton knew, was roughly twenty-five meters long and forty meters wide—the same dimensions of the twenty or so other Rhoderium Crabs in the Gladatraus inventory—some were bigger, others smaller and were as individually unique as the Gladatraus who flew them.

As they were being pulled closer and closer, the overall dimensions of the *Mekadore Traveler* seemed to double with the addition of its fully mechanized and functional legs and pincers, which, could be used as weapons by rending and tearing at the metal skin of any enemy craft. Perhaps even more impressive than that was the fact that Gladatraus Rhoderium Crabs hid their weapons; the offensive weapons, the starship killers, the weapons that you'd think should be displayed were hidden. Beneath the castellated hull were concealed scanner and sensor probes, weapons control arrays, threat and target warning receivers, along with proton, ion and photon weapon launchers, energy weapons, laser weapons, and Quartzmark missiles. In an era where warships boldly displayed weapons, Gladatraus Rhoderium Crabs kept their lethality hidden and in check.

The docking bay door slid smoothly aside on the thorax of the warship, harsh docking bay lights poured down onto the Skiff. Slayton turned away before her retinas flared, blinking out the dancing silvery specks clouding her vision.

Slayton hit a button and the wings of the Skiff folded into the locked upright position. Necessary because the craft wouldn't fit into the hangar otherwise.

In seconds they were inside, thick clasps held the nose and tail, locking the vehicle in place; the docking bay doors closed beneath it with a whispered hiss, the lighting dimmed to more tolerable levels. The hangar was small, perhaps eight to ten meters down each of the four walls with a ceiling not more than three meters above them; strobing flashers made it appear even smaller. The docking bay was just large enough to hold the Rhoderium Skiff, the Rhoderium Orbitor to the left of it, and the Rhoderium Skimmer, all suspended half a meter above the deck/docking bay doors. The forward bulkhead was lined with storage lockers containing armored space suits, propulsion/vectoring packs, medical aid kits, tools, and various types of survival gear. The left bulkhead was the armament section. Here was stored photon rifles, a plasma cannon, 20mmx pulse laser guns, ammunition, magazines and clips, power generators and reaction units for use on the weapon stores on board the nearby Skiff, Skimmer, and Orbitor. The rear bulkhead held fueling apparatus, fuel storage containers, fire extinguishers, and CO2 explosive cartridges. The right bulkhead was heavily shielded and contained the only access to the rest of the *Mekadore Traveler*.

"Pressure equalizing. Docking bay doors sealed," a voice sounded on hidden hangar speakers.

Slayton popped the quick release circuit on the canopy, exhaling loudly as she took off her headset. And then it hit her. The air smelled of lubricants and fuel, or stale ozone and polished metal, the smell of a Gladatraus Rhoderium Crab. It was a smell that didn't hide anything, it let you know exactly where you were, onboard one of the deadliest, most sophisticated warships in the galaxy.

"Hey, let's get him out of here," Leers ordered.

At that moment, the bulkhead doors slid aside with the sound of a rushing waterfall announcing the arrival of Gladatraus Guardian Jasmine. She was a physical contradiction of sorts. While appearing rather tall and slender in the hips, her shoulders and thighs looked to be borrowed from a mesomorphic statue. Like all Gladatraus, she wore thin, light-weight armor which covered her entire body. Even her head was completely hidden beneath a highly polished battlehelm that reflected the docking bay landing strobes crazily. Yet, even with her face masked, one could sense that her eyes were narrowed in concentration, her jaw set in determination—and her body, while projecting a camouflaging contradiction, was as equally impressive as it was powerful. Small breasts above a chiseled torso, all resting on thick legs of corded muscle; legs which could propel her through a marathon in under two hours, or launch her over a wall four meters high. Even more impressive than her physical prowess was a mind that could absorb dozens of humanoid languages as if born to them; the ability to support the boast of being able to fly the singular most lethal starship in the galaxy, a Gladatraus Rhoderium Crab.

Guardian Jasmine had been a member of the Gladatraus for more than twenty years. She had served aboard the *Magika*, the *Fallembersky*, and commanded the ill-fated *Illustrious*. Now she was pilot of the *Mekadore Traveler* and had been thus for nearly five years.

She rushed to the Skiff carrying a small medical kit. Without a word, she held an instrument above Rook's right eye, her battlehelm leaning close.

"I'm not going back . . . . I'm not going," the cheetah said. "We mustn't go back—they'll kill us all!"

He grabbed an armored arm and held it tight, as if pleading with her to listen. He was in pain, his eyes told the tale.

"We're not going back," she assured him, her voice soothing, yet even. "You're with friends now. We're going to help you. Rook, please trust me."

"Looked like he got hit by force beams," Leers said. "They were beating him up pretty badly down there. I almost didn't make it in time."

Jasmine said nothing. Instead, she pulled out another instrument from the kit and pressed it against the cheetah's neck, just beneath the jaw bone. She looked at Leers. "Hold him still." The human obeyed as she squeezed a tiny trigger on the device. "Rook, this will ease your pain."

"Force beams," Slayton turned away, seeing Rook's disorientation, his pain, it made her feel ashamed for wishing he were dead. She couldn't hold it back any longer, the sobs came in a hushed whisper, then raged coughs. "I have to leave."

Jasmine watched her flee the hangar then held a medical sensor over Rook. "Massive internal bleeding, a ruptured kidney and maybe an exploded pancreas—I don't know." She turned toward Leers. "Goddamnit, who did this to him?"

"Bounty killers, I think. Nicky said one was Logan Kiasar."

The name meant nothing to Jasmine. "Did you settle the matter?"

"Yeah, I took care of them," Leers said, wondering if he should start after Slayton.

"All right then, let's get him to medical." Jasmine gestured toward her helm's communication link. "Draystar, Rook is in a bad way. We're moving him to medical—let's not make planetary escape until I have him stabilized." Jasmine snapped her metal-clad fingers and a hovering gurney entered the hangar and pulled up next to her.

"Copy that," a voice echoed over the docking bay comm system.

She and Leers gently placed Rook onto the cushions of the levitating tumbrel and proceeded with urgent haste to the warship's infirmary.

****

While Jasmine and the Omnitraus moved Rook into the sickbay, Gladatraus Guardian Draystar adroitly operated the complex flight controls systems of the *Mekadore Traveler* with the ease and confidence of a seasoned veteran. The flight deck of the *Traveler* bristled with systems melding fluidly with other systems subjugating sub-systems; not in a display of turgidity, but in the absolute reliance of performance dominating form. There were four independent weapon control systems; dual control drive systems with shared engine control and navigational inputs for both pilot and commander; dedicated electronic warfare and spectrum arrayed (EWSA) instrument controls; hostile warning and threat indicator displays, and a host of other primary and sub-system instruments—this was truly a flight deck and not a cockpit. To Draystar's reasoning, a cockpit was an archaic term used to describe a bubble surrounding a pilot wedged into an ejection seat with barely enough room to breathe. No, what we had here was a flight deck—better still, a command deck—he relished the sound of that much more.

Despite its complexity, the flight deck was divided into four stations. To the left and forward was the commander's station, the seat that Draystar occupied; to the right of him was the pilot's seat—Jasmine's primary station. There wasn't the traditional pilot/co-pilot seating arrangement, the legendary arrogance of the Gladatraus forbade such an arrangement because *all* Guardians were considered pilots and therefore equal. The Guardian in the commander's seat was in charge of the operational aspects of the warship; while the pilot simply took the ship where it need to go and performed all of the combat maneuvering—all under the direction of the commander or lead Gladatraus Guardian. In this regard, piloting the *Mekadore Traveler* was Guardian Jasmine's job, as was weapons employment. Some would observe that she got to do all the fun stuff while Draystar just sat there with his armored arms crossed analyzing system functionality and power setting. Draystar wouldn't give such an infantile observation any dignity because he knew that *all* Gladatraus would rather be in the left-hand seat giving orders and directing the battle—and taking a chunk out of someone's ass if they didn't listen to every goddamned word said. At any rate, Draystar dealt with the defensive systems during a battle through the alignment of shields and screens, the analysis of scanner and sensor returns, and the jamming and disruption of enemy scanners and sensors. Draystar and Jasmine worked as a team, coordinating their efforts and sometimes performing double, sometimes triple duty. However, the *Mekadore Traveler* had been designed to be operated by a crew of four. Behind Draystar's seat was the weapons control station and to the right of that was the navigation and defense station. At the start of the war with the Pulsarians, many Gladatraus warships had an operational compliment of Gladatraus Guardians and nearly three times the number of Omnitraus Officers. After seven years of bloody warfare, the presence of a single Omnitraus Officer serving fulltime on a Rhoderium Crab was non-existent; while the numbers of Gladatraus crewing these ships had been dwindled to only two, sometimes only one. Draystar considered himself lucky that he had Jasmine as his pilot. She was a damned good pilot—better than most Gladatraus. When she managed to keep her temper in check, her weapons deployment skill was second to none. She was also highly proficient in others areas as well.

Although Draystar had been a Gladatraus Guardian for just over nine years, he had been in the Omnitraus ranks for more than a dozen. He started out flying experimental space vehicles. Like many Omnitraus during that time, he thought he'd enter advanced flight and weapons school and pick up the expertise he needed to pilot space superiority fighters; from there fly combat missions, go on strafing and bombing runs and the like, before moving on to Rhoderium Crabs. Many Omnitraus Officers thought this as a logical progression. You acquired a certain skill, you moved up the ladder, you acquired more skills, you moved further up the ladder. But Gladatraus Command had different plans for Omnitraus Officer and Star Force Lieutenant Derek Draystar. They sent him off to the Omnitraus test pilot school immediately after his graduation from the Bastian Academy. Feeling he was better suited toward punching holes in Hyperspace, blazing along the event horizons of serpent snares and Infernia instead of making the jump into Rhoderium Crabs and getting to fly combat missions.

Draystar was good at what he did, going from lowly lieutenant to major in three years—it usually took pilots eight to ten years to reach major. As much as he had hated thinking about it at that time, it had dawned on Draystar that he might remain an Omnitraus test pilot until he made general or advanced age determined that he was no longer fit to fly. Then something wonderful happened—the war, Pulsarian aggression, call it what you will, but it propelled Draystar out of the Omnitraus ranks and into the elite of the Gladatraus. Unlike many of his comrades, Draystar saw the war as a good thing. His career was heading nowhere—flight-testing was serious, challenging, but it wasn't what he had endured four years at the academy to do. He wanted to do something that advanced military astro-navigation, not supply the civilian travel industry with more data on the dangers of flying through ion storms—or being an instructor pilot—hell, there were thousands of instructor pilots in the galaxy. Jasmine had been an instructor pilot during her academy years, a capable professional who had washed out more cadets than she graduated. Trouble was, Draystar wasn't Jasmine. He couldn't allow himself to be used up in such an ignoble manner, as he saw it. No, his greatest chance for self-actualization lay in the war and his involvement in it. It was the war, always the war; he couldn't divorce himself from it. The war had given him the chance to fly the galaxy's supreme killing machine. And he pushed it, Jasmine, and himself to the limits of their respective capabilities, because by God, this was what he was meant to do.

The war was a rotten thing, of that Draystar was quite sure. Yes, it had propelled him out of the ranks of the Omnitraus, but the thought of all the millions who had died, the utter, tragic waste of it all . . . sometimes when he thought of these things it . . .it made him feel ashamed. Yes, ashamed that he relished nearly any opportunity to fight. He had to remember that he was a pilot/warrior tasked to defend the Delrel Federated Republic, and that meant killing enough Pulsarians until they were convinced that expansion into the DFR was too costly. And whatever Gladatraus Supreme told him to do, he'd do it—he'd fire at their Fleet or civilian targets—trouble was he'd never been told to purposely kill Pulsarian civilians. Too bad, for the vermin Pulsarians felt no revulsion when they killed Federation citizens. Why not fly into Pulsarian space and bomb a few of their cities and kill a thousand civilians, maybe even ten-thousand, or a hundred-thousand—and the Gladatraus could do it easily too. Perhaps it would bring the war to a speedier end. *The hell it would.* The politics and execution of war were much more complex than that—not even considering the moral and ethical considerations which shackled Federation war-time doctrine.

"Guardian Draystar, I'm picking up transmissions coming from the spaceport again," the flight computer informed him, waking him out of his reverie. "Shall I continue to ignore them or do you wish to speak with them."

The flight computer spoke in an authoritative, feminine voice. Nancy, as the computer called herself, could be augmented in a secondary pilot role. In circumstances where one or both of the Gladatraus found themselves on the surface of a planet participating in a commando raid or rescue operation, Nancy could operate the *Mekadore Traveler* in their stead.

"No," Draystar said, "I'm not going to waste any more time with them."

Draystar shut off the transmission, annoyance easing. The space traffic controllers at the Nijimegan Prime Spaceport had been hounding him since he made orbit. Draystar had no illusions. Just because he was Gladatraus didn't mean that he could do whatever the hell he wanted to do. There were Nijimeganese civilians to consider. And Nijimegan was, technically, a neutral world despite their client/whore relationship with the Pulsarians.

"Jasmine has Rook in the infirmary now," Nancy informed him. "His vital signs are stable."

"And Jasmine?"

"She's on her way forward."

Draystar shook his head sourly; his expression masked by armor in much the same fashion as Jasmine. "What a mess . . . who would send these Omnitraus—these kids, on missions without adequate support like this?" But Draystar already knew the answer. *The same individual that sent you across the galaxy to rescue them.*

"I beg your pardon, sir?"

"Nothing." Draystar couldn't let it go. "When I was in the Omnitraus ranks, we were told to fly and that's it. That's all we ever did. Now these kids are thrown into the inferno before they're ready."

Draystar leaned forward, scanned the power readings near the throttle controls, and brought the main engines on-line. He thought about prepping for immediate planetary escape and bringing defensive systems on-line as well—no, not until Jasmine was on deck and the Omnitraus were secured. Besides, all threat indicators were clear. There were Pulsarians out there—potentially dangerous, yes—but they were no match for the *Mekadore Traveler* and they weren't currently scorching space with their scanner and sensor probes.

Jasmine entered the flight deck with Leers tractor beamed behind her. She dropped into the pilot's seat and turned to the youngster behind her.

"Strap yourself in and keep quiet, please," she said, sounding like a mother warning her child to behave in the backseat of a hover-car. "You might learn something today if you pay attention."

Leers did what he was told.

Jasmine turned back to her flight systems. "Alright, everything's on-line and looking good." Her helm tilted toward Draystar. "Switch over."

"Switching over," Draystar acknowledged. Jasmine was now in control of the warship; all he had to do was monitor the threat indicators and provide her with the inputs she needed. "Where's the other one?"

"N'ckshell's in her berthing space right now," Leers mumbled. "Not telling her about Rook was a mistake, I think."

Draystar merely nodded.

"Switch-over confirmed," Nancy replied. "Engine and drive systems are go."

"Stratospheric drive holding steady," Jasmine said, scanning her instruments. She always talked while going through her in-flight procedures—it didn't have a damned thing to do with the presence of Leers sitting behind her—it was just her style. "Yeah, power output is nominal. Cabin pressure equalized; altimeter looking good. All lights *are* green. Thank-you, Nancy."

Jasmine pulled back on the control column until they were at ninety degrees then brought the throttles up to maxpower, full mach capability. The G-forces began to press her and everyone against their seats. It was invigorating, relaxing to a point, compared to the violent thrashing of high-G engagements with the enemy, making a simple planetary escape was . . . routine.

Leers glanced at the mach indicator. Mach three, five, seven . . . nine, twelve, they were burning through the sky and the flight deck didn't shudder, didn't gyrate . . . the smoothness of the ride was disconcerting to a man accustomed to claustrophobic cockpits and vomit inducing shearing and torquing.

"We're passing through Nijimegan's exosphere," Draystar said as they pierced the atmospheric shroud and plunged into the blackness of space.

"Navigational computer is working and our destination is already programmed in. Very good, Nancy, you're always ahead of the game."

"Roger that," the flight computer replied.

"Switching engine configuration now," Jasmine said as she flipped several switches next to the throttle and pulled back another lever; going from escape-drive to star-drive.

Leers watched their activity and forced himself to stop grinning. Seeing two Gladatraus going about their routine in the Federation's most awesome warship was a thrill he couldn't describe. Planetary escapes were easy, second nature for any pilot, but they were going about their duty as if there was a risk—slim—of blowing apart at the seams if they weren't vigilant and professional.

Leers felt a tremendous jolt and felt a moment of uncertainty as the Rhoderium Crab powered away from the planet with renewed vigor. Their speed was 70,000kpx and increasing. On a secondary monitor, the sapphire hulk of Nijimegan began shrinking rapidly. Leers felt a nervous tingle fill his gut. *Would there be Pulsarians out here waiting to kill them?* Upon arriving to Nijimegan just hours ago, they had detected what appeared to be a small Pulsarian force near the outer marker of the Nijimegan star system.

"Do you think we'll run into any trouble?" Leers asked.

A warbling alarm sounded in the flight deck. Jasmine glared at the human, *just how did he know—*

"I'm picking up several targets at extreme range," Nancy informed them. "Targets bearing two-three-niner-point-zero-one."

"Cross referencing now." Draystar typed in commands next to one of his monitors. "You're quite the clairvoyant, Mr. Leers." A picture flipped up on the screen. "Okay, looks like a single Battlecruiser Advancer—Drocokal class, I believe. And a squadron of Slave Racers, old DDX models—no problem there, probably only armed with Dirks, on an intercept course. The Slave DDXs are in the lead, ten-thousand mega-meters in front of the Advancer." Something troubled him. "Nancy, do you see any carriers?"

"Negative, Draystar."

"What the hell are those Slave DDXs doing out here?" Jasmine wondered.

The Slave Racer DDX was one of the oldest fighter-type weapons in the Pulsarian inventory, fifty years older than the newer Spark Racers and twenty years older than the Slave Racer LLR. The Slaves, as Draystar called them, were often regarded as slow; clumsy fighters with an egg shell for armor and speed that would make a turtle jealous. In combat with second generation Federation fighters (the VF-95 Valkyrie, the VF-97 Vision or the VF-98 Vigilante), it was a coffin for the Pulsarian crews who flew them—and engaging a Gladatraus Rhoderium Crab was certain death. Carrying their conventional munitions, the fifty-year-old Slave Racer DDXs couldn't hurt the Gladatraus. But if they were armed with the heavy stuff, plasma and anti-matter weapons, they were a threat to any heavily shielded combat ship, including a Gladatraus Rhoderium Crab.

From a head-on angle, the Slave Racer resembled the severed head of a vampire bat which functioned as the basic spaceframe containing the cockpit where an armor-suited pilot was strapped to an ejector seat that seldom worked, flight computers, weapons generators, kinetic kill cannons, engines, and two external pylons for additional weapons. Beneath the 'bat-head' were two inverted wings, each about seven meters long and could also be fitted with external weapons and fuel stores.

Fifty years ago, the Slave Racer rocked the galaxy with its awesome firepower, speed, and unsurpassed maneuverability. Now it was a joke; a bitter lesson the pilots would learn as they engaged the Gladatraus warship.

"The Slaves do not have us within range of their weapons yet," Draystar said. "And I'm not getting any scanner emissions from that battlecruiser. They must be getting vectors here from Nijimegan Prime."

"The spaceport?" Leers asked.

"Why not?" Jasmine fired back. "What would you do if the Pulsarians showed up in your star system with a battlecruiser and the Universe only knows what else? And if you hadn't noticed by now, the Pugs are winning the war."

"But Nijimegan's supposed to be neutral," Leers said drily. "Why don't we light that battlecruiser up and in the process teach the Nijimeganese a lesson in what proper neutrality is."

"Love to," Jasmine said. "Look at Draystar's primary monitor, Mr. Leers. See all those green dots? That's civilian and commercial shipping, more than ten-thousand bogies that could get caught in the crossfire."

"You can track that many?"

"Child's play."

"Then you should be able to control where your munitions land—right?"

"But we can't control explosions or flying shrapnel. All it takes is for one piece of metal the size of a coin to breach the hull of a starliner . . ." Jasmine regarded her own flight systems. "I think it's time we got out of here."

"I agree," Draystar said, shooting her a thumbs up.

"Commencing Warp Run." She flipped several switches and moved a different set of throttles forward and the warship rattled and jumped ahead, surging with power. "Ten seconds."

In order for them to make the jump into Hyperspace, and in-turn travel at faster-than-light (FTL) speeds, the ship had to execute what was commonly known as a Warp Run. Starships couldn't leap into Hyperspace from a standstill. Draystar knew this from his flight-testing years and had literally ripped the guts out of four experimental spacecraft just to prove the theory. No, starships had to build up power, speed, and the running room necessary to Warp through normal space into Hyperspace with as much violence and force as possible. From there, attaining and maintaining relativistic momentum through Hyperspace was simplicity in itself: raw power coupled with mind-shattering speed. Trying to accomplish the same effect in normal space was—

"The Slave Racers are firing at us," Nancy said. "Wide range, no coherent pattern."

Nearly a hundred thousand kilometers away from Nijimegan, the ship's speed increased exponentially with every passing second.

"Yeah, I guess the Pulsarians ain't too concerned about flying shrapnel."

Leers looked around—it was starting, all around him it was starting: the miracle of FTL travel . . . the engines, the navi-shields; more than two-thousand years of *human* galactic traveling down to this moment . . .

The Slave Racers increased their speed as well, or tried to; their quarry was escaping and there wasn't much they could do to prevent it. Any starship Warping into Hyperspace couldn't be tracked or safely pursued. The speeds were too great, the dimensions too many. Scanning beams would lock-on to a target momentarily then would splinter into a billion scintilla.

"They just don't want us to Warp," Draystar said. "Three seconds till we cross the threshold."

Through the main viewer, billions of points of light turned into streaks of red, blue, and yellow. The sight sent a shudder down Leer's spine. The power around him, humbling, awesome; he and all on board the *Mekadore Traveler* were now traveling at speeds that could outstrip a beam of light.

CHAPTER VI
COMBINED ADVANCER FLEET WEST

THE Pulsarian MI-349 Fleet Courier ripped an opening into normal space, rapidly decelerating from Warp, closing the verge of Hyperspace. Bubbles of raw energy danced against the tiny vessel's deflector screening for several seconds before evaporating into infinitesimal oblivion. The MI-349 shuddered briefly as it changed course with the agility and guile that belayed its hull design.

The Fleet Courier continued its graceful deceleration, reversing thrusters glowing orange, coruscating anti-collision beacons came to life along leading edges of the wings and spaceframe. The hawk-shaped vehicle yawed gently into another minor course correction then decreased speed to point-zero-five sub-light, a blistering pace in normal space, yes, but a snail's crawl when compared to the time-shredding speeds it had just endured within the eternal void of Hyperspace. Sensor probes reached out from the MI-349, navigational figures sampling the void in the shuttle's flight path; at current speed, it'd reach the assembling Pulsarian fleet in ten minutes.

Marshal Admiral Rouldran Petti sat silently in the forward cabin area of the MI-349, ignoring the noise and commotion behind him, ignoring his wife and her half dozen attendants as they fussed over her ceremonial gown. The pomp, the ceaseless chattering could have been a distraction, but Petti refused to let such activity interfere with his thoughts. He had a busy day ahead and letting thoughts of the upcoming ceremony or his wife's infidelities cloud his mood wouldn't be to his advantage. Clearing his throat, he glanced behind him. She and her attendants wouldn't be going through all this effort for a mere changing of the guard. How many of these functions had she attended with him? Several dozen, by all accounts—amnemonic numbers lumbering between twenty and thirty. And it was always when she was planning a rendezvous when the commotion toward the rear of the cabin was at its most intense.

Perhaps he couldn't completely shut away the barest essence of his marital problems—after all, he still loved her. He was Admiralty through his being and couldn't shower her with the attention she wanted, hungered. Being from one of the noblest houses of the Stratrealm, the *Aklear do Shar*, it was her right to have whatever she found pleasing; there were so many other things—important things—that demanded Petti's attention. He couldn't keep track of her lovers any more than she could keep track of her diamonds. Lord knows the MI-349 had a difficult time traversing Hyperspace from the sheer weight of her decorative artifacts. Petti rubbed a brow; having to sort through hundreds of intelligence reports, field reports, after-action reports; his demanding schedule, the strain of battle, all of it competed with his desire to attain stability with his wife. And because of it, he too had to look elsewhere as well. He had his own 'comfort wives' consisting of captured—no, not captured, employed he reminded himself—human females, and the selectively bred Pulsarian harlots who had the talent to make him forget his 'command fatigue' when his mood was at its darkest.

His thoughts turned forward again. There would be time enough in the future for mending to take place. Now he had a plan to carry out in the coming weeks that would dominate his full attention.

After more than seven years of bitter, savage, utterly bloody warfare, the Delrel Federated Republic was beaten. They didn't know it, wouldn't acknowledge it . . . but they were dying . . . their armies crushed, their fleets scattered. The Pulsarian Empire was the most formidable force in the galaxy. What angered Petti was the enemy's refusal to see this. Why continue to resist? The end was all but absolute. Didn't they realize that the more they resisted, the grimmer their future?

It all had to end, Petti mused; to continue to fight meant the systematic eradication of all Federation life. Needless to say, there were those within the Houses of the Stratrealm, within the Senate—Gods, even the capricious Emperor, himself—who wanted to destroy the Federation utterly. Nonsense. You could not rule over flaming rubble and heaped corpses. To rule an Empire, you needed subjects to dominate and resources to exploit—without those you had nothing—instead of creating opportunity, you created waste. No spoils, no victory . . . just waste. There had to be another way, and there was; Petti would exploit it. The key would lay in convincing the damned Delrels. He knew that the DFR, despite being composed of many different sentient entities—chief among them being the Aracrayderians, the Humans, and the Dracterians—weren't suicidal. Perhaps the most troubling aspect of this unique teaming of disparate sentients was how they managed to store away their differences and unite under a common banner. Petti had seen firsthand how they could turn the tide of many a hopeless battle, how they often counter-attacked where he and his Pulsarian brethren didn't expect them. Even when strategy failed them, when sheer determination had dissolved into a pool of futility, the Delrels could muster a frenzied determination that defied all reason. Reports of battlefield tenacity would reach the Senate and the cries for Federation extermination would resound anew. The problem was that the Senate, the Emperor, and all the others were so far away from the actual field of battle that their sense of Federation behavior was grossly exaggerated. Their cries made shrill by the fact that they wanted immediate results; they weren't strategic thinkers, they couldn't—or refused to see grander issues.

Getting the Federation to surrender would require considerable resources; pressure was needed now to break them. No easy task, when he considered the fact that the war should've been over three years ago. But the damned Delrels were virtual masters of trading space for time, then exchanging time for space. They'd hold onto a besieged star system for as long as possible—drawing out battles, spending lives, and wasting material—until Petti and other commanders like him were forced to bring more numbers and heavier machines into the contest—then the Delrels would retreat to the next star system . . . and the whole bloody mess would start all over again.

Petti fumed. The simple fact remained that the Delrels were clever in the defense of their territory. From a strategic point of view, they were far from being defeated. As a unified fighting force, they had the means to drag the war out for a decade; with their mechanisms of war and their uncanny ability to industrialize the most primitive of worlds. However, when calculating the tremendous losses of their civilian populations and property, the Federation could hardly hope to hold out for another year. They would lose at least a billion of their citizens, their soldiers, pilots, and sailors. *And traitors*, Petti reminded himself. Meanwhile Pulsarian losses during that period would stretch into the hundreds of millions. Many Senators and Families would lose sons, and again, many would call for the systematic extermination of the Delrels—as if that would equalize the losses they suffered. Fools. Didn't that realize that ruling over torched planets and mutilated corpses wasn't ruling, it was performing an autopsy with *finger and bone.*

"We're on approach for final, Admiral," the chief pilot said, waking Petti out of his musings.

Petti barely acknowledged. He clasped his fingers together. Yes, it would all be over in a matter of weeks. He'd annihilate the Tertiary Alliance as a fighting force, have the Dracterian capital occupied and have the Aracrayderians suing for peace. Even as he sat in his recliner on board the MI-349, plans and activities were already set in motion, the machine was moving, gears dozens of lightyears away were torquing, grinding with well-lubricated intent. All he had to do was wait and monitor the unfolding events—perhaps the hardest thing for anyone to do.

"This is Fleet Courier *Thgav Taseriel* passing through first security checkpoint," the operative pilot declared.

"Task Force acknowledges your insertion into security zone, *Thgav Taseriel*," the sterilized voice crackled over the communication system.

Petti tapped the controls on the viewer in front of him and sighed a silent curse. He had to think about other matters than plots, strategy, and scenarios. Sometimes it could become all too exhausting. Relaxation was the key. The picture on the viewer immediately solidified into the same image the pilots were monitoring.

"This is security control," another robotic voice echoed over the speakers. "We have you in position for final approach."

"Final approach, will comply," the chief pilot said.

"Your pattern is clear for landing, out."

"Acknowledged."

Escardeir Petti moved forward and stood next to her husband. The admiral nodded his approval as she looked down into his eyes. *Such beauty, such grace. She desires more than a mere sailor for a husband . . . so much more.* He took her right hand into his left. *Soon enough, she will have it.*

"You are truly magnificent, my darling," Petti whispered. "You will be the envy of the ceremony."

Escardeir curtsied, smiled, but remained silent.

Through the viewports, the Pulsarian Fleet increased in size, opaque geometric shapes dominating the heavens. Within seconds they were streaking past battlecruisers, destroyers, and frigates. Light danced off smooth surfaces creating a prismatic strobe arcing between armored hull and deflector shields, to finally careen into space. And on the MI-349 raced, plowing through the web of color, passing a dozen Advancers . . . then a hundred, two hundred, until it reached the heart of the fleet where the Capital Mothership Advancer *Nryevae* waited. Petti felt his heart racing faster. He centimetered forward in his recliner, excitement building within him. For a moment, it felt as if they were going to ram into the gargantuan warship. But the pilots bled off speed so expertly that neither he nor his wife felt the minute changes in inertia. A constant sensation of one gravitational unit maintained throughout the landing.

As the MI-349 taxied to the holding area, Escardeir's attendants began fussing over her gown and hair again. Annoyed, Petti stood and said, "She is the Marshall Admiral's wife, not some concubine of the Senator-elect from the planet Ajax. Be gone, all of you. Come, my dear. The officers and wives of the Fleet await."

****

The MI-349 Fleet Courier rested on the deck of the leviathan Capital Mothership Advancer which stretched for kilometers in every direction. The CMS Advancers were the largest Advancers in the Imperial Armada, nearly eight times the size of the fleet's Battlecruiser Advancers and four times the size of the Dreadnought Destroyer Advancers—with more than ten times the firepower of either. In addition to sheer volume in size and weapon's magnitude, the CMS Advancer possessed carrier capability and could hold an entire division of tactical spacecraft (Slave Racers, Spark Racers, Stressta Racers) and low-orbital to surface-attack platforms (Malactites, Battlebarges, Invasionbarges). Within its spaceframe were more than 100,000 controllers and technicians, combat teams, pilots, engineers, officers, and crewmen.

The marshal admiral and his wife started down the main ramp of the Fleet Courier. Escardeir squeezed his left hand fiercely. He reassured her with a confident smile. Every fiber of her body told her that walking onto the surface of a ship in space would require one to do so with the protection of an environment suit. And she was correct. However, the CMS Advancer, like all carrier-type warships of the Armada, had the ability to shield off the vacuum of space and pressurize the local surface area. Thus providing a comfortable, breathable one-G environment for individuals to work in, or on certain occasions, to allow for pre-functionary ceremonies to take place. It took a lot of mental training to get used to the sensation where the eyes and mind said that you should be dying or dead, but the body felt nothing. Escardeir would probably cling to him until they were safely inside the hull of the great Advancer with more than a million tons of metal to separate her from space.

Petti paused at the base of the ramp as trumpeters announced his arrival. Before him, on both sides of the polished blue and black deck, were a thousand of the Advancer's key personnel, all wearing crisp uniforms and crisper expressions. Stationed in front of them were the admirals and captains of the Armada and the generals and colonels of the Straaka. In unison, the assemblage saluted thunderously and Petti return the gesture with warming pride.

He started down the valley of men, saluting officers he recognized, merely nodding to those he did not. Out of the corner of his eye stood Admiral Aldar Dehyhitte. Ah, Dehyhitte, he came from a good family, a modest family with holdings on several planets. Dehyhitte could be trusted; he wouldn't allow greed to cloud battlefield judgment in an effort to acquire larger, more robust holdings. He was the commander of the *Kr'andoc-Threatta V'hriam* Carrier Task Force; professional, steadfast, lean of body, not afraid to take the occasional risk. Then again, he wouldn't be a task force commander if he hadn't allowed risk to enter his tactical train of thought from time to time.

Dehyhitte's dossier was impressive; he had never been defeated in battle and had earned the rank of admiral in twenty years. He hadn't graduated at the top of his class (he was at the bottom fifth to be painfully precise) but he had accomplished more on the battlefield, killed more of the enemy, than any of his classmates who had graduated ahead of him—Petti knew this because he was one of them. Dehyhitte's weakness was that he lacked the foresight of strategic thinking; ferocious in the heat of battle, but long-range planning eluded him. He was practical, concrete in his approach to an operation. His focus, matched by steely fortitude, couldn't be questioned. He didn't waste energy on the grandeur of the Pulsarian Empire or its right for moral dominion above the other races of the galaxy. Strategic matrix indexing had no place when he put his Advancers over the surface of a hostile planet in preparation for a bombing run.

Admiral Aldar Dehyhitte had his purpose; his focus like that of a laser, his actions quick and decisive. Petti smiled as he passed him. Dehyhitte could be trusted when it came to tactical brilliance, but Petti knew he'd have a difficult time trying to get him to think comprehensively within long-term stratagems.

The marshal admiral moved down the line saluting Admiral Sagan Thravagon. Not much of interest there. Competent, but on the whole rather talkative and boring. He wouldn't take too many undo risks, unless there was no other alternative. His battlefield philosophy called for elimination of actionable threats coupled with insertions of strategic thought processes. In this manner, he was more flexible than Dehyhitte, but not as savvy when the killing started. On the whole, he too could be trusted.

Petti moved on. So far Combined Advancer Fleet West was shaping into a venture with its own set of niceties and complexities. He would need trusting commanders; he'd need individuals who wouldn't question his every order, those who would stay the course, those he could keep in line.

Admiral Steiner Merwinette loomed ahead.

He didn't need him! Petti saluted and Merwinette returned the gesture briskly and with an enthusiasm Petti didn't trust. Merwinette was the tactically thinking opposite of Thravagon and Dehyhitte. Merwinette loved risk, it was a drug to him. Merwinette drove himself, his crews, his machines to the point of breaking—he'd push them, demand from them their best efforts, and just when they thought they had nothing more to give, he'd demand more. If they had nothing more to give, if they refused absolute commitment, absolute loyalty when he needed it the most, they were simply discarded—executed on the spot. Merwinette often performing the duty himself—why let the punishment officer enjoy the kill?

Merwinette was tall and handsome; he looked anything unlike his ruthless and brutal nature signified. His hair, perhaps his most distinguishing feature, was stark white, brilliant to the point of being obtrusive. To human eyes, his alabaster hair would be a symbol of frailty, of advanced age, but Merwinette was years younger than Thravagon and twenty years younger than Dehyhitte or Petti. His fleet uniform was immaculate, much like everyone else's. Yet, somehow, his uniform seemed to fit him better.

Petti continued onward, glancing left and right. The Admiralty was full of Merwinettes. Individuals who traded tactical thought for blind battlefield brutality; whose arrogance and bloodthirsty nature pushed them to kill their own officers and men with as much relish as they killed the enemy. They called it discipline. Petti called it savage. . . it had no place among officers of honor and true discipline.

He'd have to keep an eye on the young Merwinette; but perhaps not as much as he needed to on the officer standing next to him, Star General Preafect Sergon.

So here he was, the Emperor's Hand, the legend who rode in tanks beside his men. Sergon. Barrel-chested, ruggedly angular features, he was the personification of a Straaka general. His uniform and posture rigid and untiring. Sergon saluted him and Petti returned it. The admiral thought he could actually hear it whip through the sterilized air. Sergon was a warrior, a fact that he wouldn't let anyone forget; not the infantry in his command, not the Advancer captains who ferried his men and equipment to points of invasion, and certainly not those few individuals who, through matters of pure circumstance, if not luck, just happen to hold more rank than he. Sergon didn't toss about theories on political doctrine and its standards in battlefield execution. Conjecture was for theorists. His doctrine was simple: Identify your enemy, deprive him the means to fight, then destroy him. When Sergon saw combat, it was up close, it was all around him; he was always in the thick of it, in the blood, the vomit, the damning stink of it. Petti thought that only fools directly led their men into battle—Sergon was no fool. Those that thought he was, those who underestimated him, regretted it. A point Petti reminded himself not to forget.

He paused in front of Sergon. What was he thinking behind those cold steely eyes? That he was invincible? That he was beyond censure, reproach. Whatever he thought, Petti was convinced that the aura of Sergon was indeed a living entity, a force that no other Pulsarian could create. Sergon would be dangerous. But like all dangers, if one knew of its existence, then one could avoid its trap.

"So good to have you in my command, General," Petti said, keeping his tone even.

Sergon said nothing. Protocol forbade him from uttering a sound.

"We'll see if your reputation commands as much respect as seeing you in person does," the Admiral added before moving off.

Sergon allowed his eyes to follow Petti as he joined Marshal Admiral Rennoc Genthatorn. The faint etchings of a dangerous smile may have formed on Sergon's face. If it had, no one noticed.

****

Marshal Admiral Rouldran Petti saluted Marshal Admiral Rennoc Genthatorn, Commander Taszerite Imperial Fleet South, then followed him through the immense bulkhead doors into the sun-lit corridors of the Capital Mothership Advancer. It took a moment for Petti's eyes to adjust to the dazzling light, but when they did, he noticed that standing on either side of them were more than a hundred Imperial Marines, the Fetraaka-Starkerum. Armed with gleaming, ceremonial *Vgamb-4CR* heavy laser rifles, and decked in full-armor battle uniforms and capes, they were an impressive, if not intimidating sight. Despite the display, Petti ignored them, his mind busily trying to sort through ways on handling both Merwinette and Sergon. To have one man in the fleet consumed with ambition and guile was bad enough—but two? How had Genthatorn handled them? Petti wasn't going to ask. To do so would mean that he wasn't fit to command Combined Advancer Fleet West.

Genthatorn led him into a spacious Wardroom and stood behind a massive desk made of wood and brass.

"Welcome onboard, Admiral Rouldran Petti," Genthatorn's voice boomed as he brought his hand up in salute. "I now give you command of Taszerite Imperial Fleet."

Petti returned the salute. "For the service of the Emperor, the Houses of the Stratrealm, and for the peoples of the Pulsarian Empire, I do gladly assume command of the Taszerite Imperial Fleet."

Two youngish officers of the fleet entered the room from behind Petti. He quickly skimmed over the information on the tablet that was handed to him. Petti took the stylis from the other ensign and said, "I am now hereby signing the order to command this fleet." He handed the tablet across the desk to Genthatorn who also signed. When that was done, both ensigns quietly added their own signatures and fled, rather than exited the room, colossal metal bulkhead doors closing behind them.

"Now that the formalities are over," Genthatorn grunted as he undid the top buttons on his fleet coat, "come on over here and have a seat. This desk is now yours." He removed his fleet cap and tossed it on the desk. "And before I forget—congratulations." He extended his hand and Petti took it.

Petti removed his fleet cap but refused to loosen the noose about his neck. There'd be plenty of time to worry about that later; for now, he took the chair behind the desk while Genthatorn reclined rather lazily in one of the wardroom's recliners. Petti briefly thought about his wife then quickly shut it away. She was probably in the officer's lounge with the other wives, well on her third glass of wine by now.

"So, with this fleet merging with your own, makes you officially commander of Combined Advancer Fleet West," Genthatorn said. "What do you intend to do with a thousand Advancers?"

Petti was ready to venture a well-rehearsed reply when Genthatorn cut him off saying, "invade Shiborium, the Dracterian Homeworld."

"By the devil, why not?" Petti's face darkened.

Genthatorn chuckled lightly. "You might need more than a thousand Advancers, my friend."

"Do you really believe that?"

"I've been fighting these damned Dracterian savages for the better part of two years, Rouldran. They don't yield easily."

"Nor should they. Would you yield if they were attacking the star systems surrounding your Homeworld?"

"I think you know the answer to that," Genthatorn mused. "But they're fighting style is so much different than the humans'—fiercer. Their tactics—from defending entire star systems to singular planets is vastly different than the way humans put up a defense. I know the Tertiary Alliance is a fully integrated fighting force. But the more Dracterian worlds we capture, the more savage they get."

"Yes, one could go insane thinking about it."

"Friend, I'm already there." Genthatorn let out an exasperated breath.

"Don't worry about the Dracterians. I think I have something for them. When they hear of my approach, they will know what it means to go up against the greatest force in the galaxy . . ."

"And if they refuse to listen?"

"Believe me, sir, they won't," Petti said. "They won't."

Genthatorn lifted a dubious eyebrow. "You *must* elaborate, friend."

"Oh, I intend to." Petti let his gloved hand glide over the smooth surface of the desk. *Hmm, not a hint of dust.* "You're thinking of Shiborium, I'm thinking of Shiborium. By the devil, the entire Imperial Armada—everyone is thinking of Shiborium. Even the damned Dracterians know we'll hit their Homeworld soon. Frankly, I can see no other course that will lead us to victory."

"I truly hope so. This blasted war has dragged on for far too long and from all indications—intelligent indications, mind you, and *not* the poisonous ranting from the Imperium—this war shows no sign of relenting in the near future. I fear that we may face a decade of more fighting."

"I've the same feeling. I've fought the humans when they tried to defend their precious Minerva. Sometimes they retreated at the first sign of Advancer activity; other times they threw themselves at us in suicidal waves. And as our fleets spread throughout their territory, human reaction to us was unpredictable at best."

"Indeed. And as I've stated earlier about the Dracterians—they will come at you with a fanaticism only hinted at by the humans." Genthatorn clasped his fingers together. "If you are seriously contemplating invading

Shiborium, may God be with you."

"Bah! Admiral, we both know that now is the time to take the Dracterian capital. The Imperium is impatient for action. Oh—they won't come out and issue official orders—but they will sit behind their desks and wave their arms around, they will push little colored markers around on a strategic battlemap, and they will strategize. But they refuse to make anything official. They will just debate where it's safe for them to debate."

"Now may not be the time."

"If not now, when?"

"You don't understand the Dracterians. They will defend their planet—"

"You've said that already, Admiral. And I have listened. There is risk in it, yes. But I've studied the Dracterians for two years now. I've had special action teams capture their soldiers and have interrogated them myself. We've dissected dozens of them—cut into their skulls and pulled out pieces of their brains to discover what drives them. They will not surprise me."

"We may lose close to five million Pulsarians if we invade Shiborium. Dracterians may damned well sacrifice fifty million of their own people before they even consider signing peace terms."

Petti stood suddenly, walked to the front of the desk. He folded his arms, his face darkening in concentration. "Fifty million did you say?"

"You arrogant fool," Genthatorn raged. "You'll destroy yourself and this beautiful fleet if you invade now."

"Perhaps, Admiral, perhaps—that is, if I indeed employ conventional means . . ."

"What are you talking about?"

"To pit our Advancers against their starships, our Straaka against their infantry will indeed net the disastrous outcome you predict . . . what was it? Five million Pulsarians to take one planet—or a system of planets." Petti shook his head. "No, we have to think beyond so-called normal battlefield conventions when dealing with Shiborium."

"Damnit, the Dracterians will counter. And if they have help from those Gladatraus devils, the results—" Genthatorn stopped when he noticed a serpentine smile slithering on Petti's face. Genthatorn felt his stomach turn to ice. "My God, what are you thinking?"

Petti said nothing, the smile disappeared.

"Rouldran, what are you thinking?" Genthatorn boomed. "Tell me."

Petti regarded his elder, his eyes focusing not on him, but through him, through the bulkhead, through the billion cubic parsecs of space. When he finally spoke his tone was even, malevolent. "Admiral, I will destroy Gladatraus Command, and in doing so, the Dracterians will hand their goddamned planet over to me."

"My God, what are you—"

"You will see. The entire Empire will see."

****

The conversations taking place in the Grand-Armada Hall were thunderous as Marshal Admiral Rennoc Genthatorn, once of the Taszerite Imperial Fleet, stormed by with his Fetraaka and sub-commanders in tow. He paid no heed to the curious glances rising up from the two-hundred-meter long ceremonial dining table. The admirals, captains, and generals making up the newly formed Combined Advancer Fleet West sat at the whitened, gleaming table feasting on various dinner entrees from around conquered space. They had their choice of peppered waterfowl from Inon, seasoned wilderness beast and steamed vegetables from Minerva, sweet-wines from the low-equatorial regions of Yanattii, hotly buttered spice-breads from the Frontier. All of it served on gold and pewter platters and dining ware. The selection of food and beverage was so vast in fact that it would take an individual more than twenty hours to sample all of it.

Genthatorn increased his pace as he and his entourage stepped past the section containing Admirals Dehyhitte, Merwinette, Thravagon and General Sergon.

Preafect Sergon set his fork down and barely acknowledged the admiral's passing behind him. More honor should've been accorded to the Pulsarian who had won so many battles against the vile Dracterians. He was being shuffled aside so that this new marshal admiral—Rouldran Petti could replace him. As much as Sergon didn't like it, he knew that it was the ebb and flow of the Admiralty. The war was taking too long to conclude and changes had to be made.

". . . As I was saying," Admiral Sagan Thravagon continued after clearing his throat, "our enemy is extraordinarily good at imitating industry, but doesn't have the skill to duplicate our war machine."

Aldar Dehyhitte ignored him. Sitting across the table from Sergon, he watched quietly as his former commander strolled by without so much as a nod. Dehyhitte, finally clearing his throat said, "We just lost the finest marshal admiral the Admiralty has ever produced and yet you continue to prattle on about the Dracterian economy."

Thravagon glanced over his meal insolently and shrugged. "I know that I speak for many when I say this: he's good, our former commander, but the Dracterians have put a fear into him that he hasn't quite recovered from. Strategies have been late, he's been too slow to mobilize, and when he finally made a move, we took horrendous losses."

"True," General Sergon said after a sip from his goblet. "But I don't trust this Petti any more than I trusted Genthatorn."

Seated next to Sergon was Merwinette. He remained silent, tearing off a piece of flesh from the bone of some beast and shoving it into his mouth. One of the servers reached politely over his right shoulder and re-filled his wine. Merwinette looked up. The server was human, a captive, obviously from one of the human worlds. Although the human wore the uniform of a yeoman, the wearer was thin to the point of looking like a corpse. His head was shaved, his jawbone jutted out from the sides of his face, his eyes were sunken, almost hollow; he looked like an exhausted corpse. His hands and fingers, although clean, were badly bruised. Merwinette studied the human for a few moments as if the man were a test subject in a laboratory, then returned to his meal. He felt no mercy for the humanoid shell as it continued its duties waiting on their superiors with the other uniformed humanoid shells; shells both male and female.

"So, you say we're losing a great commander," Thravagon continued on, pointing an accusing fork toward Dehyhitte.

"Not exactly," Dehyhitte countered. "I was merely stating that he was a competent leader of the fleet."

"I feel that we're getting a Pulsarian who knows how to deal with an enemy who continues to defy us despite their apparent lack of technical sophistication."

Dehyhitte took the bait and said, "What the Dracterians lack in perceived technical skill, they more than make up for in tenacity."

"Tenacity?" Thravagon almost choked. "When in a battle, which would you take, tenacity or technology?"

"It'd be nice to have both," Sergon said.

Thravagon was undeterred. "A collection of fools attacking a taskforce of Advancers in unshielded gunboats can be handled quite easily enough, my friend. Do they call it bravery? Let them. I call it stupidity. Tenacity, bah—you both can take your tenacity. When used by a fool, it'll only net him a quicker death."

"And when it isn't in the hands of a fool?" Sergon asked. "As is so often the case with our adversary, the results can be quite disastrous."

"You overestimate them. Grossly, I might add."

"To *underestimate* your foe—"

"Dangerous, indeed, my friend," Thravagon finished.

Sergon suddenly stood and backed away from the table. "Please excuse me, my brethren. I have matters to look into. I'd like to finish our discussion about the Dracterians when the matter isn't quite so theoretical."

Merwinette watched the general disappear beyond the throng of servers and attendants. He glared at the malnourished humans.

"I'm somewhat dubious with so many human servers on this flagship," he spat.

"Chattel is chattel," Thravagon said, "no matter the race."

"I prefer my indentured servants to have Pulsarian origins," Dehyhitte mused. "At least you know where their loyalty lies."

"No such worries seem to concern our newly appointed Rouldran Petti," Thravagon noted.

"None concerned the late Admiral Terkodetti either," Dehyhitte interjected. "Until last year when one of his 'servants'—an amply feed female human, I believe—sawed his head from his body whilst he was in a drunken stupor."

"At least he didn't wake with a morning migraine," Thravagon bellowed, then erupted into laughter.

Dehyhitte laughed as well. Merwinette followed suit, then stopped short, rubbing unconsciously at his neck for a few seconds.

"Tell me, Sagan, what do you know of our Rouldran Petti?" Merwinette asked, hedging onto a different subject.

"Not much, unfortunately," Thravagon answered. "Only that he's not to be trifled with. He executed a commodore for pulling his Advancers back during a battle, by his own hand. In front of the commodore's battlestaff—shot him through the head. I know he has a lovely wife, a woman half his age, from a well-established family. I think he has three daughters—from the previous marriage—they're the same age as his current wife. He lost his only son some, er, a few years ago. And perhaps most importantly, he has never lost a battle."

"Sounds like you know quite a deal," Dehyhitte said. "What of his wife? I hear she's quite a tart."

"That's putting it mildly," Thravagon snorted. "As I said, she's his second, nearly eighty seasons younger than he, and financially secure."

"Twenty years?"

"Yes, and as rumor has it, she's known to keep company, from time to time. If you get my meaning."

Dehyhitte raised an eyebrow and cupped his chin behind index finger and thumb. "So he's never lost a battle?"

"No."

"Nor has our recently departed General Sergon," Merwinette noted absently. He tasted the fowl. The breaded meat was dry, how disappointing. He looked a Thravagon. "I couldn't help but notice he wears the medallion of the *Thraaga 'Rhone Ordgoth*, 'The Emperor's Hand'."

"Yes, and proudly," Dehyhitte added. "But there's no one better to have with you on the battlefield when you're killing Dracterians, or Aracrayderians, or even humans for that matter."

"He's attached to your fleet is he not?"

"Yes and despite his skill, it's an attachment I'd like to sever someday," Dehyhitte finished. He stood suddenly. "I must be excused. Petti is going to be giving a briefing in five hours; I must make preparations. Hope to see you on the battlefield in the weeks ahead."

"I'll accompany you to your shuttle," Thravagon said, also backing away from the table.

Dehyhitte shrugged. He couldn't get away from Thravagon and his combative conversations if he had the ability to walk through walls. Merwinette watched them go then eased his way into the conversations of the officers sitting next to him.

It took several minutes to reach the great doors at end of the hall, all the while Thravagon prattle about stratagems and how best to kill a harried enemy. The Grand Armada Hall was connected to a corridor which, in turn, led to the main hangar where the fleet commanders had their shuttles parked. Dehyhitte and Thravagon walked past several lines of Fetraaka and heavy-weapon Straaka in ceremonial armor and capes. Marines and infantry saluted as the two flag officers left the noise and commotion of the change-of-command behind them. Down another corridor and yet another, the two entered the grossly understated 'auxiliary hangar' where twenty MI-349 Fleet Couriers and MI-347 Command Shuttles were parked. In the mutely lighted hangar, the ships looked like huge metallic vultures, hunched over and sleeping.

Admiral Merwinette's shuttle was the first ship the Pulsarians walked by. Looking up Dehyhitte could see the pilots and flight-engineer in the cockpit going over several check-lists. It would seem that Merwinette was on his way to his flagship as well, he just didn't want to walk to his shuttle in their company. Dehyhitte nodded and looked at Thravagon. Who could blame him the way Thravagon continued to talk. He hadn't taken a break since they saluted the Straaka a few hundred meters back.

Dehyhitte thought he could hear—he paused, motioning for Thravagon to cease.

"What is it?" Thravagon wanted to know.

"Thought I heard something," Dehyhitte said. "A female."

"Couldn't be."

They walked slowly beneath Merwinette's shuttle, creeping slowly around the starboard landing gear. Then Dehyhitte saw it. Despite all his years in service, Dehyhitte's breath caught in his throat. Barely twenty meters in front of him, underneath the hull of another shuttle was the Lady Escardeir Petti with General Preafect Sergon. Escardeir had her ceremonial gown pulled up around her waist. Sergon had his trousers down around his boot tops . . . both, locked in ecstasy.

CHAPTER VII
PHASE ONE PLANNING

FIRST Lieutenant Maiko Arashi Greysen kept a firm hand on the control yoke as she guided the FB-25D Poltergeist over the surface of an asteroid the size of a city. The Poltergeist bucked slightly in the gravitational wake of the larger body but held true to Greysen's steering inputs no matter how subtle or violent. Greysen dipped the nose of the bomber 'down', held her breath for three seconds, then brought the nose up again, exhaling. The sensation made her stomach flutter, nothing compared to the unrestrained groans coming from the mouth of her copilot.

"You're enjoying yourself, aren't you lieutenant?" the copilot accused.

"Not in the least, *lieutenant*," Greysen said mildly, as she pointed the bomber toward another city-sized asteroid. "Just trying to keep us alive."

"I think you could manage it without—" He stopped, staring in horror at the onrushing boulder filling up the canopy. With one hand, he gripped the instrument panel in front of him, the other took firm hold of the edge of his ejection seat next to his right thigh. "Without taking so many chances," he finished breathlessly.

Greysen ignored his comments and twisted the Poltergeist around another asteroid and another. Space around the bomber was teeming with the tumbling masses. But she didn't mind. As long as she remained focused, the 'Blackghost' would not let them down. Besides, this was how you flew 'asteroid patrol.' You had to dive in close to the larger bodies, get in there as close as your nerves dared, then slingshot around toward the next large asteroid you found. And by and large, Greysen was always looking for something the size of a stadium, a city, or small continent.

The FB-25 Poltergeist, called the 'Blackghost' by the pilots who flew it, was one of the oldest weapons platforms in the Delrel Federated Republic's arsenal. Manufactured by Starhawk International, the mainstay of the Star Force and with a spaceframe more than fifty years old—more than twice the age of the crewmembers flying it—it showed no signs of nearing retirement. For it was a ruggedly designed strategic bomber, a fanged bird-of-prey; built to Warp through Hyperspace, attack targets at extreme range, then return safely to base with its crew of five. The Poltergeists were forty-nine meters long with variable-geometric wings, augmenting two thrust-vectoring engines. This lethal combination allowed the Poltergeist to enter atmospheres of planetary bodies and adjust its flight and handling characteristics accordingly and with alacrity; thus enabling it to destroy the targets it hunted on the ground or in deep-space with equal impunity. To fulfill its mission, the bomber stored all of its firepower within its internal weapons-bay. As no exterior hard-points existed on the Poltergeist, the weapons-bay payload assortment consisted of some of the most deadly weapons ever brought to the battlefield; weapons ranging from medium- to high-yield laser and energy weapons, hybrid explosive-power lasers, kinetic explosive ordnance, and plasma weapons, but a few of the weapons the bomber could employ against Pulsarian targets. In addition to weapons, the Poltergeist possessed an avionics and astronics suite enabling it to track and interrogate up to a thousand targets simultaneously and prioritize weapons to destroy those targets; it could also mask its presence on the battlefield through a fog of scanner and sensor jamming.

Lieutenant Arashi Greysen always felt a surge of pride course through her whenever she flew the Blackghost. It was an incredible machine—an antique, yes—but it was still fast, lethal, and able to withstand tremendous punishment. She'd already been on twenty missions with this Poltergeist and the bomber just didn't show mission fatigue like the newer FB-27 Phantasms she had flown a few years ago. Some would say that the Poltergeist was a step down from the Phantasm. Not Greysen. Just because the FB-27 was newer didn't mean that it was better. Pilots lived or died by the machines they flew and Greysen simply trusted the FB-25. On her last mission, she remembered coming off the bombing run at more than 87,000kpx; with burners lit, she put the Poltergeist into a 10 G reversal to avoid enemy fire and the bomber responded without hesitation. True, one of the engines flamed out seconds later and it took nearly two minutes to re-ignite, but it had gotten them out of the danger area, and the tension the flameout produced in the cockpit was a lot better than getting blown up in the stratosphere of a Pulsarian-held planet. After that mission, Greysen had "Goblin Warrior" stenciled onto the bomber's nose along with a cartoonish image of a greenish beast with huge breasts, and bloody fangs as sort of a tribute to the bomber's tenacity.

"Goblin Warrior" along with eight other FB-25 Poltergeists from the 22nd Omega Strategic Bombing Wing, were patrolling the outer-marker of the Omega asteroid system. The bombers were not flying in any type of formation, they were covering entire zones independently. And none of the nine bombers could 'see' the other, as a result of the thousands of asteroids tumbling about and thus preventing ocular identification. Neither Greysen nor her co-pilot could see any of the other bombers simply because several billion kilometers of cubic space separated all of them—and all nine bombers were patrolling the *same* sector.

The Omega asteroid system was vast, easily bigger than any ten-planet star system; more than thirty billion kilometers across and several hundred million kilometers thick. So vast in fact, that it had to be divided into zones, each zone sub-divided into sectors. Immediately outside the system, interstellar space, was known as the blue zone, where comets crackled in hundred or thousand year orbits; very few asteroids existed in this region, and those that did were dregs of ice, crystallized methane. Core-ward was the yellow zone, located at the fringes of the gravitational wake of the system where dust particles lingered among a few tumbling asteroids covered in ice and quartz. Next was the green zone where asteroids numbered in the tens of thousands; as long as a pilot stayed sharp, it was fairly easy to navigate within this region. Not so with the red zone, a deadly spiral of rock and debris where asteroid numbers climbed into the millions. At the core was a deadly region where the asteroids numbered into the tens-of-millions, the black zone; sometimes called the 'death zone' by pilots. It was a region where flying went from 'simple stick-and-throttle inputs' to a pilot fully acknowledging that a 30-second lifespan was actually 29 seconds of borrowed time. Holding the entire system together in a somewhat coherent gravitational package was a white-dwarf star no more than two-hundred kilometers across, but with a density of a billion metric tons per cubic centimeter.

Second Lieutenant Hamn Yorkers ignored Greysen's stick and throttle inputs and glanced at his chronogram. "Coming up on the patrol sector," he informed her.

"Concur," the navigator, Lieutenant Khardoc said, feeding his data directly into the copilot's flight monitor. "Sector Orion-Alpha-two-four-niner locked in."

"Roger, that." Greysen snapped the fingers of her right hand then returned them to the control yoke. His left hand now rested comfortably on her thigh. She could relax a little now. "Two-four-niner."

"On my mark. Three, two, one, mark. Time hack: twenty-three, zero-five. Not bad." Yorkers glanced at his pilot. "We're twenty minutes ahead of yesterday's patrol schedule. Now let's hope nothing happens in the next eight hours."

"Copy that," Greysen noted. She eased them around several asteroids, examined her instruments briefly—all indicators looked good: engines, fuel flow, cabin pressure . . . routine. She returned her gaze to the viewports in front of her.

"I'll never get used to being this close to the enemy while traveling so damned slow," the navigator/defensive systems officer whispered. Seated behind the copilot, Lieutenant Khardoc tapped figures into a datapad. He slid the datapad into his flightsuit pocket and joined the copilot in staring out the forward windows with his own pair of macro-binoculars. Two Frigate Advancers floated more than 40,000 kilometers downrange. If the Pulsarians detected them, they'd only have seconds to evade before the lasers poured in.

Greysen and her crew's mission, along with eight other Poltergeists snatched from the Ion and Photon squadrons, was to patrol the different zones and sub-zones of the system and gather intelligence on the assembling Pulsarian fleet and report everything they found back to their headquarters without being detected. Hidden within the borders of the black and red zones was the Omega System Command Base. Headquarters of the 22nd Strategic Bombing Wing—among several dozen other combat groups, squadrons, and wings—and home to more than 200,000 base personnel, all wondering when and how the fleet of assembling Pulsarian warships would attack them. Pulsarian weapons could navigate the green zone with diligence and skill, but getting through the red-zone would require—

Despite the feelings of her navigator, Greysen nudged the throttles back another notch, slowing the bomber's speed even more. She had to keep the Poltergeist's heat signature down to a negligible level or they would tip off the Pulsarians to their presence. It also meant she had to fly without deflector screens, because even the cleanest deflector emissions could be detected from thousands of kilometers away. She couldn't utilize the bomber's powerful EVR-V5 space scanner either, or its RWP-97 vulnerability detector, because both could leave a residue even the laziest sensor officer onboard one of those Advancers could detect. Thus, the use of EDM macro-binoculars by the copilot and navigator. Intelligence gathering was useless if you didn't live long enough to report back what you've seen.

She stifled a yawn, rolled the bomber gently around a stadium-sized asteroid and asked, "so, what's the count on them now?"

The copilot, Hamn Yorkers, raised his EDM binoculars and zoomed in on the Advancer. "Well past four hundred. All registered in our on-board data system and catalogued for weapons."

Greysen whistled sharply. "How many of these bastards did we track on our last patrol?" Greysen slipped them past another tumbling boulder. She shook her head. "There's at least fifteen asteroid systems in this area of space alone—the *Puggies* would have to pick our asteroid system to snoop around in." She paused, flipping a switch to her cool-air re-circulation system—it was getting damned hot in the cockpit.

"Four hundred Advancers," Yorkers breathed with dismay.

"By the *Saints* you only need a dozen bloody Advancers to invade a well defended planet," Khardoc added, trying his best to shut down the rage brewing in his chest. The slow speed the bomber was traveling made him feel vulnerable and it was difficult to hide his feelings in front of the others—especially the human female. "What are the Pulsarians doing way out here—dozens of parsecs from a civilized star system?"

"I should think they're waiting for a chance to kill us," Yorkers quipped nervously.

"That's not very damned funny, boy," the navigator, Khardoc retorted.

"Didn't mean for it to be."

"I don't think they have the capability to locate our base." Captain Cornel Atlas, the bombardier/weapons officer said. He tabbed toward Greysen. He may've out-ranked her, but since she was flying the bomber and not him, he answered to her. "Do you think they'll locate the base?"

"With four hundred Advancers," she shrugged, "they'd be incompetent if they didn't."

"Who says that the Pugs are trying to find us," Yorkers ventured hopefully. "Maybe they're just here to test some new weapon system? What if they aren't looking for our base at all, maybe they'll just vaporize the entire asteroid system."

Greysen just glared at him.

Khardoc said, "you need to quit reading comic books, boy."

"Graphic novels," Yorkers said quickly. "But you must admit that the odds of the Pugs just Warping into this particular asteroid system when there are more than fifteen similar asteroid systems within this region, is simply astronomical."

"No pun intended," Greysen said.

"Uh, right," Yorkers said. He didn't know what a pun was. "But our base is hidden *inside* a planet-sized asteroid, one of hundreds in the red-zone. And it's constructed entirely beneath the surface. No way they find us, even if they went to full power on their sensors while in orbit."

"I agree," Greysen said. "Theoretically, the Pulsarians could spend years trying to locate the base. Still, though, four hundred Advancers is a big-ass number by anyone's arithmetic"

"The *Puggies* wouldn't bring that many into play just to waste time looking for a single asteroid base, would they?" Atlas asked.

"Who knows how the Pulsarians think."

"Navigator, plot escape vectors into my computer for the red zone," Greysen breathed, shoving a stick of gum into her mouth. "If we're detected, I wanna be able to get us out of here in a hurry. Look at that." She pointed out the window. "That Frigate Advancer is a little too close." She began working the gum as if possessed.

"Concur."

She had reason for concern. Four hundred Advancers was more than plenty—but it was just a number and didn't take into consideration the firepower, the size, the volume of just a single Pulsarian warship. The Pulsarians called all of their war-making starships Advancers. Advancers, synonymous with conquest, with striving forward, ever forward, never retreating, plowing through planetary defenses, shattering blockades; engaging in the conquest of the galaxy. Advancers came in a concrete number of types and sizes but in many thousands of different classes; yet all were configured in the shape of ocean dwelling manta rays—to Greysen's human eyes anyway. As cephalopods glided along the sandy grit of sea floor, so too did the mammoth Pulsarian space vessels with smooth contours, glide majestically through the vacuum of space. The comparison in appearance of the ocean-dwelling creature and the Pulsarian technical marvel couldn't be disputed. But that's where the comparison ended, for the Pulsarian version was kilometers long, possessed conformal weapons batteries, defensive fields, containment shields, Warp capable engines, fusion reactors, quadra-line matter/anti-matter generators to name but a few differences.

A Frigate Advancer was more than a kilometer in length, yet was one of the smallest warships in the Imperial Armada, and could—given the right conditions on the battlefront—take on planetary defense batteries, ward off hordes of enemy fighters, wipe out cities one by one, or choose to turn the entire surface of a world to molten slag. And that was just simply outlining its basic capabilities. During their last patrol, Greysen and her crew had seen gargantuan Battlecruiser Advancers, the mainstay of the Pulsarian fleet; Dreadnought Destroyer Advancers, fearsome extreme-range planet killers, and a host of others in various types and classes that could exact destruction as easily as the lowly frigate.

"I'm getting a new cluster of signals in sector Orion-green-five-seven," the electronic warfare officer said, making his presence known from further back in the cockpit. The copilot turned to the left and squinted into the binoculars. "I can't—there's something strange here. Standby." William Forge adjusted passive indicators on his ECM equipment.

"I'll edge us closer, then." *Here's where you earned your pay.* Greysen put two percent to the engines, flipped the old bomber over a tumbling asteroid, and danced over and under eighteen more.

"Yeah, looks like I'm getting passive signals from a new un-catalogued task force," Forge stated.

"Damn, that's at least forty more Advancers," Yorkers said. "If they break five hundred, that's a Combined Fleet, isn't it?"

"Think so," Greysen said. "All we can do is catalogue them then report back." She turned to Yorkers. "You see anything, yet?"

The copilot didn't answer.

"Can you see anything?"

The kid brought the binoculars down slowly, his mouth agape.

"What is it?" Greysen demanded. "What do you see?"

Yorkers stared at her, his hands visibly shaking. "One of them is a Capital Mothership Advancer."

"*Good Lord!*" Khardoc's rage boiled over into simmering dread. He began muttering to himself in a language Greysen didn't understand. There were perhaps four or five CMS Advancers in the Pulsarian Admiralty—in the entire galaxy—and one of them was now present in the Omega Asteroid System. What had the boy been saying about odds? When the Pulsarians invaded Minerva, the human capital planet, they hadn't at all bothered with the employment of a CMS Advancer. Now there was one here.

Greysen stared out the windows, her body numbed with fatigue and anticipation.

****

"Gentlemen, I would like to take this time to congratulate you on the most successful campaign since this war started—the *Trhevhea* operation. The Delgradus Star Corridor is ours. The Federation is weakening under our continued, relentless attacks. They are *this* close to surrendering but are too damned stubborn to realize it. This is a very dangerous time for the Federation as well as for ourselves. The path before us will be difficult indeed. But it is a path we have to take—we must take."

Marshal Admiral Rouldran Petti's voice echoed slightly in the cold, mutely lighted conference room of his Capital Mothership Advancer, his flagship *Nryevae.* He paced as he spoke, polished boots clicking loudly on the mirrored finish of the metal floor. With his gaze hitting the officers in the room with glacier-cold concentration, Petti knew he had everyone's full attention. "For at the journey's end, we will have Shiborium." He paused. "And we will have the war."

There was muted approval from the forty flag and battlefield officers in the room. Twenty of whom sat about the massive, blacken marble conference table which had taken weeks to polish to its present gleam. Near the head of the table was Admiral Aldar Dehyhitte, the *Kr'andoc-Threatta V'hriam* carrier task force commander and senior in battlegroup operations. He was in a crisp, forest green uniform, arms folded, not willing to allow his feelings about the matter to be too overtly revealed. Across from him was General Preafect Sergon of the 950th Straaka-Vohm Straterium, in the midnight blue of the Straaka uniform. He was obstinately reclined, his fingers clasped before him; his thoughts hidden beneath an emotion of calm. Next to him was Admiral Sagan Thravagon, unusually quiet for once. Further down the table were Admirals Vanktagetti and Nogon, both attentive and polite. Near the opposite end of the table sat General Hveritte nodded his approval and Admiral Steiner Merwinette who did not. Seatec along the conference chamber's vaulted walls were a select assemblage of legion and cohort commanders, Advancer captains and Spark Racer group commanders. Like their superiors seated at the table, their uniforms were sharply creased, collars were tapered, rank insignia and medallions boldly displayed—they however, seemed more enthusiastic about the Marshal Admiral's preamble than any of the higher ranking officers seated at the table.

Petti finally moved behind his high-backed recliner, as if it were a shield. He'd need it, for sitting before him were vipers who wouldn't hesitate to strike if they sensed his battleplan would melt under the intensity of enemy fire. Petti, his battlestaff, and his SSK in the field, had prepared the plan for months, anticipated every possible counter-move the Federation could make, threw in random elements of chance and how the Federation would react to those. There was no other way. The plan would work, the plan had to work.

Petti made a slight gesture with his left hand and a three-dimensional holographic projection appeared above the conference table. It shimmered lazily, like mist, then quickly solidified into an image that could almost be grasped. It presented a rather simplified schematic of captured areas of Delrel Federated Republic space and its relation to the gargantuan Pulsarian Empire.

"Look here," said the marshal admiral. "We have Delgarada task forces moving here, here, and here." By his verbal indications, fleet icons appeared on the floating map and moved to preprogrammed sectors. "We have the DFR's November Command tied up at the *interior* north. Two operations are currently reasserting themselves with the bombing in the Valiant sector. And within days, our brethren in Combined Fleet East will be in position for an all-out invasion of Scion."

"Finally, the Admiralty is letting us do something," Admiral Steiner Merwinette snorted, "instead of just sitting around and letting the damned Federationers back in this war."

Despite his popularity—or, rather, infamy—many in the conference room shared Merwinette's appraisal of the strategic situation. The war with the Tertiary Alliance had erupted like an exploding star, the enemy losing system after system against the Pulsarian onslaught. When the Alliance finally decided to assert itself, the Delrels were still beaten back, their casualties mounting; even their vaunted Gladatraus Guardians were of little help. Within two years, Minerva had been captured. The cost on both sides had been enormous, but in the end the human capital planet belonged to the Pulsarians. Everything was going to Admiralty plan. Or so it seemed. Conservatism began to numb the Pulsarian momentum. Many thought that the time to attack Shiborium, the Dracterian capital, was ripe; others didn't. Why wait? No one wanted to forward a reason other than the staggering losses suffered during the capture of Minerva. Could they afford another a capital planet so soon after Minerva? Again, no one .d a reason. As far as Merwinette was concerned—and he matter for years—they were resting forces that really didn't /hile the enemy was busily drilling and building up their resolve He felt the conservatism was merely a reflection of severe inco ncy developing within the halls of the Admiralty. Partly due to the fact that their enemy was adopting new tactics on the battlefield. Instead of meeting the Pulsarians full force, they began to husband their forces; if they were at a disadvantage they would not fight. They retreated, then waited for a better opportunity to present itself before attacking. The enemy would employ strategic bombers to destroy re-supply and logistical shipping instead of the traditional targets on the surface of a planet; they'd unleash fighters by the hundreds to kill Carrier Advancers. Then switch tactics, employing hit-and-run attacks on some outpost when logic demanded that a brigade of fighters would've been more beneficial and less costly. No one in the sacred halls of the Admiralty could see that the Delrels were mixing unconventional attacks with large-scale operations and doing it with seamless cohesiveness. In doing so, they were adopting a strategy of attrition. No one in the Admiralty wanted to acknowledge that their clever enemy could win the war by not losing it. It seemed so blatantly obvious, especially when one considered that the Pulsarians outnumbered the Federation in personnel in the hundreds of thousands and material in the millions of tons. How could they possibly hope to win? But it could be done and had been done in the past. When faced with a superior force, the Federation could win by wearing the Pulsarians down, by dragging out engagements, by forcing the Pulsarians to adapt to situations they weren't accustomed to, by making the whole damned war too costly for them to wage. By the time the Admiralty realized this, they were themselves victims of their earlier successes. Having never learned defeat and the humiliation that followed it, the Admiralty became bewildered. Orders were slow in being issued, tactics took too long to develop, counter-attacks never materialized. The past three years of war with the Federation had turned into a bloody stalemate. Yes, there had been a few victories; however, one must remember that the Federation had also claimed its own share of victories. The war was spiraling into a bloody mess and the Admiralty had been too slow to adapt to the changes. The generals and admirals along the frontlines could see it all along. The war could've been over years ago; but because of doctrine, because of unyielding rigidity . . . they had allowed the Federation back into the war.

Petti cleared his throat as he looked down the table toward Merwinette. "I rather doubt the Admiralty had anything to do with our new orders."

All eyes turned back toward Petti.

"My orders come directly from the Emperor himself."

"Madness," Sergon said. He slammed a gloved hand down onto the table. He shook his head. "Does he intend to use us as an instrument in the

Federation's annihilation?"

For years, factions within the Imperium and the Admiralty had waged a bitter war of ideas, of words—sometimes blood—in determining the manner in which the war with the Federation should be conducted. There were those near the Emperor who wanted the Delrels wiped out completely, total sterilization from the galaxy. The Admiralty thought differently. They wanted to conduct a civilized war—yes, they'd kill, slaughter, enslave—but who wanted to settle on a burned out cinder of a world, with no subjects to rule, no wealth to amass? Emperor Arginian Kriltergon V had ordered Xerxes be sterilized two hundred years ago during the bloody Concordian Annexations. An entire race had been systematically hunted down and eradicated because a corrupt Emperor wanted another trophy added to his collection. He'd done it to the utter infamy of his name. And within years of the action, he too was 'sterilized' by the very same admirals and generals he'd given the original orders to. It seemed all too obvious that the current puppet occupying the throne had ignored history . . . or was being told to ignore history by the bootlicking lackeys appointed to his counsel. Just because the Admiralty was currently suffering from senility didn't mean it lacked the resolve to remove an Emperor.

The Admiralty had another ally other than history; they also had the Senate—a Senate which had competed against the Imperium for thousands of years. But they could be just as fickle as the Emperor. As for loyalty—well, treasure took care of that. And if that wasn't enough, then all that was required was for a few of them to start disappearing due to mysterious circumstances—and that in itself could alter the voting to get a controversial measure passed or dropped—whichever was required. The Senate could be just as dangerous as the Imperium. Pulsarian politicians hunted each other with the same relish that Advancer captains hunted Delrels. If anyone was going to save the Pulsarians from themselves and conquer the Federation, it had to be left to the professionalism of the generals and admirals along the forward edge of the battle area.

"With respect, Admiral," Admiral Nogon mused, creasing his fingers. "Do you think we can trust the Imperium?"

"Come now," General Hveritte interrupted in a harsh whisper. "We serve the Empire as we serve the Imperium."

"You're not worried that we're now circumventing the Admiralty and reporting directly to the Imperium?"

"I don't care where our orders come from, as long as they allow us to kill Delrels."

"And what if we return to the dark days of pogroms, are you prepared to have the blood of millions of innocents—"

"So what—they're sub-sentient."

"Gentlemen, please," Petti began again. With another wave of his hand the holograph disappeared. "We are on the threshold of making history. It starts here, it starts right now. As you are all aware, we are on the edges of the Federation's Omega Command Asteroid System." The galactic schematic disappeared, replaced by a representation of the asteroid system. "The Delrels have a base within this swirling mess. We will attack their base, eliminate all opposition. This base is the doorway to Shiborium; we open it, Shiborium is ours. I have orders from the Emperor and the support of the Senate. They want this miserable war to come to a close and have selected me to carry out their wishes. We have a window of two weeks to carry out the plan—"

"Two weeks," Sergon boomed, cutting the admiral off. Sergon glared at him. There was dedication to the plan—they all wanted the war to be over. But there was also professionalism. One couldn't be ignored at the expense of the other. And Sergon wouldn't dedicate his forces to a two-week window. There were two infantry fighting corps within the still assembling fleet. Sergon's forces had been selected by Petti to carry out the assault on the Star Force base while everyone was still in Hyperwarp transit—days before the General knew it was located within an asteroid system. They hadn't even located the damned base yet. The Spark Racers and sensor/reconnaissance platforms scheduled to map the asteroid system wouldn't be launched for another three hours. And Petti wanted him to attack an invisible base, hold it, and ready his Straaka for the Shiborium invasion, all in less than two weeks?

"With respects, Admiral, this isn't Shiborium," Sergon insisted. "This is still an asteroid base we're addressing. To get to Shiborium, you say we must take this base, but we're nowhere near to accomplishing the first objective—"

"Then, Preafect, you make sure you can accomplish the first objective. The Federation scum are on the run and this opportunity must be seized. Once we begin a major operation to take out a key strategic point, they'll never expect us to make an immediate move against the Shiborium star system . . ."

"Admiral, no one in this room wants to defeat the Dracterians more than I. I understand what you want to accomplish, but my Straaka . . ." He suddenly trailed off. "They may be able to take the asteroid base in a matter of hours, perhaps a day. What about Shiborium? That won't be a lightning strike. An invasion there, while taking days to finalize, could take months to execute. And I want to make damned sure that when my Straaka are on the ground, they aren't torn to pieces so you can meet some arbitrary schedule."

"General, your concern is noted. But don't let tactical concerns cloud your strategic thinking—let your colonels worry about tactics. I want an end to this war." Petti paused. He felt his heart racing. "With Minerva and Shiborium under our control, the Aracrayderians will not be able to stand alone. We all know this—by the devil, we've known this for years but refused to act. But I'm telling you now—all of you—this is the course of action I've set. We have more than enough forces to accomplish both tasks.

We will succeed or die in the attempt."

****

Lieutenant Greysen always felt that the last hour of a mission was always the most intense, the most dangerous. For, it seemed, when you were the most fatigued, when your lower back started to ache, when your attention waned, that's when the attack came.

She and her crew had been monitoring the assembling Pulsarian forces for more than seven hours. But total seat time, however, was nearing twelve. Since it had taken them a little under three hours of flight just to reach the sectors to start their patrol. She was looking to returning to base, which would take four, maybe five hours, because she didn't want to lead the Pulsarians to the base—why make it easy for them? Once there, she and her crew would debrief for an hour. They'd then have eight hours to do what they wanted (mostly sleep). Then she'd wake up, grab breakfast, sit through an hour-long mission briefing with her crew and the crews of other bombers; then another hour for the pre-launch briefing, then they'd be at the start of another sixteen-hour-or-so spy mission. Taxing on the fortitude, true, but nothing could completely erode dedication and training. In this arena, Greysen led by example. She didn't yawn, didn't complain about the throbbing in her lower back, didn't whine about the dryness in her eyes.

"Lieutenant Greysen," Lieutenant William Forge called from his electronic warfare station. "I'm getting concentrated search-and-sample scans from the Pulsarians now."

Greysen wasn't alarmed, yet. "Can they see us?"

"Negative," Forge said. "Too much clutter around us." He leaned closer to his instruments. "But the signals are increasing in strength—incrementally. At the current rate of increase, they're bound to stumble on us in an hour or so."

"Hell, we'll be long gone by then," Yorkers quipped.

"Yes, but the bomber crews assigned to replace us won't," Khardoc, the navigator shot back.

"That's their problem—"

"Where are the signals originating from?" Greysen wanted to know.

"From the Destroyer Advancer one thousand megameters downrange; tactical area two-four-zero, nominal."

Greysen was about to tell them to keep an eye on it when Forge suddenly exclaimed: "My God, I've got a Frigate Advancer now sweeping the area with fire-control scans."

"What?"

"Yeah, he just popped up," the EW officer said. Which wasn't exactly true, since the bomber wasn't actively tracking elements of the fleet, just sampling their scans and counting hull-armor. In the vastness of space, the only way the bomber could actually 'feel' if an enemy was there was whether or not that enemy radiated—had its scanners activated. Optics were helpful, but not completely infallible. Anything greater than one thousand megameters range couldn't be detected reliably in this setting and situation. There was only so much space a bomber could passively take notice of without giving away its own position.

"Yeah, I have him too," the bombardier added, tapping furiously at his instrument's passive settings.

Within seconds, every warning system began to light up and whine for attention in front of Greysen and Yorkers.

"Fuck'n hell!" Yorkers breathed.

"Blazer. Blazer. Blazer." Forge began interrogating his computer again. "I think they have us."

"Roger that," Greysen said calmly. "Defense grid on-line."

"Roger." Yorkers began aligning the FB-25's ranged deflector systems, his fingers jerking in spasms. They'd be protected from proximity blasts and near misses, but a direct hit—the Poltergeist's armor would more than likely protect them; but they'd lose teeth or suffer concussions. If the deflectors failed and they took more than one direct hit, they wouldn't have to worry about a few missing teeth . . . or anything else for that matter.

"Alert the other bombers that we've been tagged," Greysen told her copilot. "Give them target information and vectors for attack."

Yorkers did as he was told, feeling his guts twist and tumble as he did so. Things were moving too damned fast. *They were actually going to attack a Frigate Advancer? They wouldn't last ten seconds.*

"Weapons," Greysen barked. "I want an optimum package—I don't care if we fry our systems on the attack. I don't want these bastards to shoot at us on our egress." She nudged the throttles forward with her right hand, her left gripping the control yoke madly. The FB-25 swooped around an asteroid, then yaw-pitched around two more.

"Copy. Orion-Two weapons package selected."

"Navigator, plot a course for our egress. Make sure these bastards can't track us back to base. I don't care if it takes us six hours during the return."

"Copy, that."

"Ions Seven and Nine, and Proton Twelve have received information and are forming up for attack," Yorkers stammered. He still couldn't believe that they were going to attack. Even with three other bombers lining up . . . against a Frigate Advancer they'd need at least eight bombers in all—at least! Making matters worse was that the Pulsarians didn't seem to be aware of the other bombers on station; they were just focusing all of their attention on them. It was sickening—everything was sickening. The way his stomach felt, the way his voice sounded, their attack tactics. *Why the hell weren't they jamming the Advancer?* Because at this range they only thing they'd succeed in doing would be to highlight themselves further. And they'd have more than a single Advancer trying to kill them.

"Good," said Greysen. She leaned forward in her ejection seat, the five-point harness trying to hold her back. "Increase power to deflectors."

"Nova. Nova. Nova. They definitely have us," Forge yelled. "They have us locked up with their fire-control scanners."

At that instant—actually before the lieutenant said anything, an alarm began strumming throughout the cockpit.

"Warning. Incoming fire," the flight computer told Greysen in her left ear. *"Warning. Incoming fire."*

Greysen swung the bomber savagely to the left. She counted to three, then brought it around to the right with equal violence. Space outside became stroboscopic as red and blue Pulsarian energy poured in. The bomber rattled. Greysen grunted, then swung right again, pitched the nose up, then down. "Weapons, do you have a firing solution?"

"Affirmative," said Atlas. She always asked at the exact moment he was ready—uncanny. "Gonna burn up the sky."

"Does anyone see any wildcards out there?" Greysen asked. Wildcards were Advancers or Spark Racers loitering in the area, waiting for the chance to kill them when they least expected an attack.

"Negative," Forge said. "Looks like we're cleared hot."

The Frigate Advancer loomed quickly through the viewports. Arcs of energy and light screamed from its hull, superheating the space around the FB-25. Again, Greysen increased speed. She bit her lip, her eyes narrowed. The bomber jolted.

"Weapons away, weapons away," Atlas shouted over and over as he released a wide-spread of energy and laser munitions.

Greysen flipped the bomber away from the frigate. "Increase power to rear deflectors."

She didn't need to say anything, it was already done.

"Steer heading two-three-zero," the navigator advised.

"Roger two-three-zero," Greysen returned. She yanked on the control yoke, inverted them, went to 'max-burner' for three seconds, then shut the engine down to 'max-cruise'.

"Ha, we did it," Forge shouted. "Cooked 'em good. The other bombers hit 'em hard. One Advancer scratched from Imperial service."

"Nice work, gentlemen." Greysen showed no signs of relaxing.

"Is it hot in here, or is it just me?" Yorkers chimed in.

"Kill the deflectors," Greysen ordered. "Okay, standard procedure people—everyone go through your damage checklists and then go through them again. Alright, let's go home."

****

"I don't like this," Sergon muttered.

"Come now General, you said you were with us." Petti stopped pacing, put his hands on the table and leaned forward.

"I am. But it is madness to take our orders directly from the Imperium and not the Admiralty." Sergon rubbed his chin. "The Federation can be beaten—will be beaten if the Admiralty will give us sound strategy to move on. My legions can go anywhere in the galaxy, anytime, and defeat whatever force is put in front of them. However, I'd feel more comfortable if the Admiralty were involved."

"It's because they can't think in strategic terms that they are not," Admiral Dehyhitte snorted.

"If it'll make you sleep better, General, you can report these proceedings directly to the Admiralty yourself." Petti straightened and folded his arms.

"I intend to."

"But after we have captured Shiborium, not before."

"What difference will it make, Admiral? The message via sub-space will take weeks to reach Admiralty Headquarters."

"By then your Malactites and Battlebarges will have reached the surface of the Dracterian capital planet." Petti moved around the conference table to stand over his most famous General. "This is an opportunity we must seize. You take this asteroid base and the path to Shiborium will be wide open."

"Logical," Dehyhitte said.

Sergon knew that both admirals were right. History clearly showed that when the humans defended their capital five years ago, they did so fanatically, if not somewhat incompetently. The Dracterians weren't fools, they'd make damned sure that they wouldn't make the same mistakes the humans did.

Dehyhitte liked Petti's plan and was his most ardent supporter. Going in to attack the asteroid base would present them with a host of battlefield challenges they hadn't faced before. They'd all have to learn to adapt to an ever changing mosaic of tactics and random circumstances. Honing their skills here would ensure they made fewer mistakes when they set out against the Dracterians.

Admiral Merwinette ran a gloved hand through his hair. "Your plan is sound, Marshal Admiral, and I'm glad you have Admiral Dehyhitte's full endorsement. However, the risk is that the longer we tarry here, will it not give the Dracterians and the Tertiary Alliance more time to prepare their defenses on Shiborium?"

"We're still going in with a Combined Fleet," Dehyhitte snorted.

"So what? Even with our sub-space disruption programs running—we must hit the Dracterians now."

Petti was on the cusp of saying something when Sergon interjected: "I happen to agree with the strategic soundness of our Marshal Admiral's plan. My only objection is that we're doing it without orders from the Admiralty. No matter how well dug in the Dracterians may be, our forces need to be bloodied before we go in there with no substance to cover our swagger."

"Maybe your swagger, General," Merwinette shot back, "not mine."

"Then what the hell's your worry, Admiral? You should be more willing than any of us to cut the guts out of a few Dracterian women."

"Why the sudden change, Preafect? And of course I'm ready to gut a few Dracterians. But there is something going on here that I don't like. And it doesn't involve the non-involvement of the Admiralty. Like General Hveritte, I don't care where our orders come from a long as we get to do what we've been bred to do. But there's something going on here; something I can't see . . ." as if to emphasize his point, Merwinette let his gaze bring in the admirals and generals in the room, finally to focusing on Petti. "I don't like the plan. We shouldn't do this. We should pace our forces, call up the order of battle and move onto Shiborium without delay."

Again Petti had a retort poised on his lips and again it was General Sergon who wiped it away. "The strategic plan is good. We stick with the plan."

Petti smiled as Sergon said this. He didn't trust Sergon; he was a strutting, career climbing viper—but you had to take your allies where you found them, no matter how you planned to eliminate them in the future—

"I agree," Dehyhitte said before Petti could finish his thoughts. "We follow the plan. The sub-space deception will help us. The Dracterians know damned well we want to take Shiborium . . . we've flirted with the idea for years. But the Tertiary Alliance is scattered throughout the galaxy, there's no central concentration of forces . . . except for perhaps November Command."

"They could move that entire command into the Shiborium System and we wouldn't—"

"November Command isn't going anywhere," Dehyhitte said, cutting off Merwinette.

"Narterium is as much a prime strategic point as Omega Command is," Sergon added.

"Narterium is not Shiborium and it definitely isn't this rock we're about to attack."

"Perhaps not," Petti said finally. He clasped his hands behind his back. You could only allow your admirals and generals so much rein before you had to pull them in. All in all it was a good briefing. It let him know whom could be trusted and whom could not. Allies were useful up to a point. When their usefulness was fully taxed, they simply had to be swept aside. But as with all things, timing was everything and the timing here couldn't be more perfect than now. "Our orders, gentlemen, are clear and we will take Shiborium in two weeks. The Admiralty may've led us astray in the past. But today we're on the move . . . When Omega Command falls, it opens and shuts the door on the Dracterians. When Shiborium falls, the Aracrayderians will not be able to go on."

CHAPTER VIII
HYPERSPACE

THE *Mekadore Traveler* blazed through Hyperspace at 3,125 Lightspeed, cutting through webs of cosmic string, disrupting the patterns of racing tachyons and outstripping cryogenic clouds of ultra-dense eobic particles. In its awesome wake, starlight wrinkled and distorted into chaotic patterns of multi-hued fragments, then obliterated into shards of nothingness. Dust and gases sparkled while ions danced along its hull.

Dannen Leers casually strolled onto the observation deck of the *Mekadore Traveler,* ignoring the tremendous display of sheer power and speed cascading before him. He gently settled himself into one of the four padded, fire-retardant recliners, taking more than a minute to find a comfortable position. Finally easing back, he nearly screamed. Spikes of pain seared through his ribs just under his left pectoral muscle. Leers bit down hard, squeezing his right hand, fighting through the sensation. Years ago someone once told him that Omnitraus Officers healed themselves quickly but erratically—the saying didn't make sense then and it sure as hell didn't make sense now. They also said that Omnitraus didn't need to take pain medication—such medication was meant for real injuries: severed limbs, exploded organs, grotesque fourth degree burns and not broken bones or bruised egos. Leers couldn't remember who told him these lies, or if he'd made them up in his own adolescent mind—the way he felt right now, snapping a couple of pain meds sounded reasonable, if not logical. In another day or so he'd be fine—*fine, keep telling yourself that, pal.* And if he wasn't, he was going to take the damned meds. But it wasn't the pain that was keeping him awake during his 'sleep cycle.' It was the thought of all these recent ground-pounding assignments he had to participate in. They were occurring more frequently and they weren't doing his body or his flying any good. Yes, his Omnitraus ranking mandated that he excel in these missions as he would in the cockpit of any fighter, way out in deep space; it didn't mean that he had to like it though—and it didn't mean that he was immune to injury or probable death. But if he had to die—if he had the choice—better to do so while he was flying than on the surface of a planet.

What the hell had happened on Darmen? The heat, the swirling sand, that huge sun dominating the sky, it all just kept battering his mind, relentlessly hammering away at his thoughts; it took keen concentration to think of other matters. Like whether or not he should take pain meds. And when he returned to base, the mission coordinators who had 'volunteered' him to go to Darmen in the first place, would ask him what he thought when *this* happened, what he was thinking when *that* happened—didn't he have an evasion plan to cover this, didn't he have a contingency to cover that—it'd be a seemingly endless round of questioning, euphemistically called a debriefing, that was bound to last hours. Oh, they'd be polite during the inquiry, courteous to a point; then they'd shut down their computers, fold up their charts and ask him to volunteer for another mission, to which he'd say yes to his utter frustration and fury. Once Intelligence Command got their hands on you, they'd forget you were ever a pilot and treat you like another operative. So much for being a pilot, so much for being an Omnitraus Officer.

Leers examined his surroundings. He shouldn't be here. To come so close to dying only to have the Gladatraus pull him out at the last instant was—as much as he hated the thought of dying, the thought of a rescue by the Gladatraus was more than unsettling. Did the presence of the Gladatraus signal something more sinister? He hoped not . . . there could be any number of reasons why they rescued him in the manner that they did—only, they weren't keen on filling him in as to the reason or reasons why. It was more than just discipline and rank, it was their mandate; you just couldn't ask a Gladatraus Guardian anything—you couldn't even *think* of asking them.

He knew he'd been extremely lucky on Darmen—but what about the crew on the KR-91 Infiltrator? What happened to those navy people who had brought him across time and space so that he could carry out his 'failed' mission. They were dead, had to be. . . as much as he'd wished they'd survived—no it was a wasted thought, a futile exercise. If they had been alive, the Gladatraus would've rescued them too. Too bad, just when he was getting used to them—he didn't consider them to be friends or anything—but it would've been nice to have knocked back a few cold ones with them and just complain, just harp on everything that didn't go as planned. Yeah, he could tell them just how frantic and scared he was on Darmen—first, though he'd cuss the skipper out for dropping him more than twenty kilometers off target. Universe, he'd barely gotten to know those navy blokes and now they were gone and here he was safe and sound. He didn't know whether to be grateful or mad.

Then again, he'd always had a knack for being lucky—if that's what you wanted to call it—a knack for cheating death. As a matter of historic fact, Leers had been doing just that from the moment that he was born.

It started with his father Everson Leers; a man he hadn't known because Everson had been killed mere weeks before Dannen was born. Dannen didn't know all the details, but he knew that his father had been an officer in the Minervan defense forces and a test pilot. During a flight-test assignment, Everson Leers' VF-95X Valkyrie began to break apart during high-speed touch-and-go landings, one malfunction quickly following another—his father was faced with the dreaded split-second choices many test pilots all too often encounter. Do you eject, knowing that ejecting in a modern space-superiority fighter meant doing so at speeds that approached mach three, with the added risk of slamming into a concrete abutment that lined most tactical runways, or one of the chase planes monitoring your progress high overhead? Do you retract the landing gear, add power to the engine and try to sort through the problem at higher and safer altitudes? Or do you or just say, 'the hell with it,' cut power to the engines, extend the braking flaps to reduce airspeed and just land the plane? Nearly two decades after the incident, Dannen had read the Safety Board's report of the 'mishap'—that's what they called it, a *mishap*—it revealed that his father had retracted the landing gear and added 10% power to the engines when the Valkyrie suddenly exploded, killing him instantly.

Had it been the right move? The report didn't indicate such—it was simply one of those 'deals' that happens, and there wasn't anything a pilot can do about it—not even Everson Leers. And everyone in his squadron thought of Everson as a prime pilot, the top tenth in his squadron. He was buried with full honors on Minerva's moon, Hylus, in a small plot of land near the testing and evaluation center that he shared with the graves of dozens of other test pilots who had lost their lives while trying to explore the limits of their machines.

After the funeral, the mother Leers had never known, Camilla, boarded a transport to Yanattii to live with Everson's brother Darthorn Leers. The transport never made it. Just off the fringe of the Yanattii system, the transport came under attack by hostiles of unknown origin. During the attack, his mother had been mortally wounded. The transport captain, himself badly wounded, placed Camilla in an escape pod containing a stasis chamber charged and activated—effectively 'freezing' his dying mother and unborn baby. The escape pod raced away from the battle and drifted in deep space for three weeks before a courier ship retrieved the tiny vessel.

When the stasis field was de-activated, Camilla Leers had already perished from her wounds; Dannen, in-turn had to be ripped from her and placed immediately in an incubation/recovery unit to ensure his survival. By a margin no thicker than a micrometer, the child lived and was adopted by his uncle Darthorn. Like his brother, he too had been a test pilot in the space service, but possessed a multitude of other talents, some of which had nothing to do with testing experimental spacecraft or the exploration of Hyperspace. His uncle had been sheriff once, after a short stint as a bounty hunter. He'd been a mayor of one of Yanattii's cities, a lecturer, owned several manufacturing firms on Varmoria, a casino on Ulysses, and before the outbreak of the war, worked as a lawyer and part-time starship driver on Desdemona.

Darthorn had introduced Dannen to flight simulators before most kids—human, that is—could even pronounce their own names. Darthorn didn't know anything about raising kids, so he treated Dannen like a tiny adult. He took him on dangerous hunting trips, taught the youngster how to track and shoot, and how to handle a multitude of laserarms. Before his eighth birthday, Dannen had spent more time in recreational endeavors than he did laboring in static classroom settings; well before his tenth year, Leers could hunt on his own, and knew more about laserarms than most of the homesteaders on his uncle's planet. While most kids were learning how to ride bicycles without hover wheels, young Leers was practically soloing in sub-orbital spacecraft. Every other weekend his uncle would take him up in rickety spaceships just so the kid could get a taste of space travel. One weekend Darthorn suddenly decided that the kid was ready to fly on his own. Dannen found himself strapped inside of a cheap, remanufactured rocket trainer with more than a million pounds of thrust at his fingertips and more than twenty-thousand kilos of liquid hydrogen-three, and nitrogen just waiting to explode if something went wrong. His first solo was an experience that he never forgot. The terror of it, the sheer exhilaration, was something that stayed with him for days after that first flight. He couldn't shake that feeling, didn't want to shake that feeling. Soon he was skipping classes so that he could work odd jobs in order to save up enough money to purchase the fuel he needed for more flights—whoever knew that liquid nitrogen could be so blasted expensive. With his grades slipping, Leers fought for more and more seat time, hoping to one day to make the transition from orbital flights to sorties into deep space. Maybe even land on another planet. However, on his sixth orbital flight, the youngster encountered his first in-flight emergency. One of the engines burned itself out early, before he could reach orbital altitude. Dannen thought about aborting, he thought about ejecting the spent engine, he thought about cutting the fuel flow, he even thought about enriching the mixture of the remaining engines that were still working. All at once it came flooding back to him, a lesson he learned from his deceased father. Sometimes you could do everything right and still die—sometimes you could do everything wrong and just 'luck' yourself into surviving. Leers decided to eject the dying engine and abort the flight. He was so rattled after that, he swore to never cut classes again and when he did fly, he'd do so with a sense that it could rip you apart and burn you alive if you didn't show the proper disciple, the proper respect.

For his part, Leers had always tried to remember the lessons his uncle had taught him. Sometimes, though, it was easy to forget—with thrust-vectoring engines, flight-computers that could actually 'think,' astronics that improved on a monthly basis, it was easy to forget, to allow complacency to dictate your actions. Complacency could kill in the cockpit and being an Omnitraus Officer, complacency could kill on the surface of an enemy-held planet. Like Darmen. Then again, that hadn't been about complacency, it was close to carelessness coupled to incompetence.

One of the things that Leers couldn't ignore was the fact that he was Omnitraus. To fail in a mission was bad enough for any professional during war, but to fail as an Omnitraus was a crime not too easily compensated for. No matter how hard he tried to shake it, the lingering doubt persisted. It went back to his training. For Omnitraus Officers were arguably the most highly trained military professionals in the entire Tertiary Alliance—not mentioning, of course, the Gladatraus Guardians they all hoped to become. They had the expertise and weapons training of commandos, the skill and daring of fighter pilots, the intelligence and guts of test pilots, all within the body of record-breaking decathletes. With all that ability, with all of that skill, they were still primarily fighter pilots.

What set them apart from other pilots was their ability to fly multiple types of spacecraft at the snap of the fingers. The combat pilot who flew the VF-94E Vagrant couldn't readily adjust to the flight characteristics of a VF-87C Vampire. Just to master the VF-84 alone, the pilot had to have gone through a four-month flight school, which included hundreds of hours of both simulator and actual seat time. The pilot would learn emergency procedures, combat configurations, and other flight aspects of the Vagrant from the old A model to the newer H models. More likely than not a pilot would stay with a particular variant of a fighter for at least five years and would be loathed to go from a G model to an E or vice-versa. An Omnitraus Officer though, had to be able to go from a VF-81 Vixen to a VF-97 Vision (and all of their different variants) at a moment's notice and do so with the same skill and ability of a pilot who had ten years of dedicated in-seat experience.

Before they were pilots, Omnitraus were gifted children—in Leers' case, being human meant that he had scored extremely high on intelligence and perception tests and could handle a multitude of divergent tasks simultaneously. As Omnitraus candidates aged, Command groomed them to be among the elite pilots; and because they were so talented, adaptable, high-spirited, Command also trained them in other specialized duties ranging from covert operations to orbital assault, and intelligence collection to infiltration. Omnitraus had to be proficient in all-aspect, all-environment survival training, small-arms employment, demolition, and SAR (search and rescue) missions. The duties of Omnitraus during war were wide reaching and far ranging, made all the more relevant if they survived long enough to earn their Gladatraus ranking.

When assigned to an operational base, a typical day for an Omnitraus Officer would start with two hours of calisthenics followed by small-arms training. After breakfast, he might spend an hour briefing and pre-flighting before spending two hours of flight-training which might include ground attack runs or fighter-to-fighter engagements, followed by another briefing and two more hours of flying. Free time was rare and it wasn't looked at as something to be cherished. Omnitraus were always busy, always training, always honing their skills. If Leers had been slated to fly a mission, his schedule would be different, yes, but no less busy. He might spend two or more days in transit through Hyperspace followed by several hours creeping to the target, an hour attacking the target, followed by two more days in Hyperspace for the return trip back to base. The rigors of such an assignment would be so taxing he'd need an entire day to recover. More times than not, though, he'd be slated to fly another mission, or go through brutal survival training, or re-qualify in zero-g hand-to-hand combat. The task saturation of Omnitraus was relentless and unforgiving. Leers knew that if he couldn't perform to the peak of his ability at all times, he was no good . . . and with other Omnitraus in close proximity, the competition, the struggle for excellence was all the more heated.

Sometimes it was so intense that a crack in the armor would begin to reveal itself. Sometimes the crack could be mended; sometimes the armor blew apart at the seams—which led his train of thought to N'ckshell Slayton.

N'ckshell carried more baggage than most Omnitraus Officers had a right to carry—now with Rook onboard. . . something was bound to happen. Something bad—

From around the corner the smiling Dracterian appeared. She too ignored the celestial display through the viewports and calmly strolled toward one of the other recliners. "May, I?"

She sat before Leers grunted an affirmative.

"Do I detect a bit of hostility?"

"N'ckshell, I really don't feel like talking."

Slayton shrank back, her pointed ears arching out further than usual. "To me, or just talk in general?"

"Pick one."

"Why not? Especially when there's so much to *talk* about." Slayton made a point of gesturing toward their surroundings. "I know how you get at times being cursed with human ancestry, but you must admit, despite your feelings, that there's something wrong here."

Suddenly Leers forgot about the soreness in his body and the bloody mess on Darmen. Despite her fierceness, N'ckshell often had a gift for observing details most missed. "What are you talking about?"

"This," she whispered, pointing to the deck, her eyes narrowing on the walls. "I don't like this. We both should be dead. Not a single one of those intelligence strategists said anything about Gladatraus Command being involved on our missions. Not one word was spent—"

"Should they've said anything?"

Slayton leaned away from the human with a smirk of bemused sarcasm lining her face—"God, you're thick."—an instant later simmering malice replaced it.

Leers wasn't intimidated, he'd seen her eyes glaciate many times. "N'ckshell, you should know by now that when you make your eyes do that it doesn't bother me like it does most humans. Besides, the details of our briefings went into so many contingencies and counter-contingencies that I almost fell asleep during most of it—"

"What are you saying?"

"That I'm not surprised they left something out."

"Left something out? Yeah, kind of funny that you should say that."

"Say, what?"

"You know as well as I that to involve the Gladatraus is no small matter—it's *not* something they would leave out." Slayton shook her head. "Adding to this situational *omission*, the not-so-small matter of our mutual friend, Rook."

Leers felt his stomach tingle. She was right, not a word had been mentioned about a third Omnitraus Officer's participation during the mission. If, indeed, Rook was part of Operation Gorgon. Who the hell knew? Perhaps they'd get their answers when they arrived back at base . . . but until then, who the hell knew? He and Slayton hadn't been told squat by the Gladatraus Guardians flying this Rhoderium Crab. And he wasn't about to demand any answers from them either. That was one thing you didn't do, make demands of the Gladatraus. With their battle-armor, they could incinerate you with a thought.

"I don't like any of this," Slayton said. "Too much is being thrown at us at once. I'm glad the Gladatraus were around to pick us up—we both should be grease stains by now or, at the very least, waiting for the next round of Pulsarian interrogations to begin."

"You mean beatings."

"Whatever." Slayton stood. "A couple of days ago when the Guardians said that we were going to divert to check on another Omnitraus Officer operating on Nijimegan, I had no idea it was going to be Rook." She took a deep breath, shivering. "Maybe you're right, Dannen. Maybe this ship isn't big enough. Almost every thought I have involves killing him."

Leers winced. The tingling in his chest turned into heated dread. "Universe, N'ckshell, you still don't blame him for what happened on Minerva, do you?"

"I don't know," Slayton screamed. Her eyes were wild for a second, then calm, trying to glaciate. "I don't know."

"But it was more than five years ago," Leers reasoned. "He lost his parents that day and you—" Leers could see his friend's chest heaving. The Dracterian was struggling to keep her emotions in check and failing. If something wasn't done soon to calm her . . . she might . . .

"N'ckshell, everything's gonna be okay."

"No, everything's not going to be okay . . ."

"Take it easy, N'ckshell." Leers slowly rose from his seat.

"You fucking take it easy," Slayton screamed, tears welling up in her eyes, fully glaciated now, a crimson shield. "The whole bloody universe can take it easy—"

Leers reached out, trying to console his friend—Slayton slapped away his hand with the speed of a striking viper.

"Don't touch me—"

Leers slipped, stumbling into her. Slayton, sidestepped, pivoted in a blur launched three punches to Leers' mid-section. The human crumpled under the assault, his left hand trying to protect himself, his right reaching out—too slow. Slayton brought her boot around in a spinning kick which caught Leers on the side of the face. Leers hit the deck hard, a jolt of pain crackling from his face to his ribs, then to the back of his skull. Before passing out, the last thing he saw was Slayton leaving the observation deck in a berserking rage.

CHAPTER IX
HISTORY OF BETRAYAL

THE cheetah struggled to pry his eyes open, his muscles refusing to work, feeling as if they'd been surgically lasered shut. His head throbbing, mouth pasty, he tried to open them again and failed. On reflex, he sniffed the air, reassured somewhat that he was in the medical ward of a starship and not the rotting holding cell of a prison barge. He could feel the slight vibration of the engines through the bed. Those engines were running quite smoothly—almost too smoothly—there wasn't a terrible hum, and the bed wasn't shuddering either. He'd never felt an engine so smooth before. *Where am I?* If he could just open his eyes, he could find out. He tried again, summoning enough effort that left him panting and out of breathe. Finally, he began to bring his dark surroundings into focus and again the question returned. *Where am I? On a starship, yes, but whom does it belong to? Am I a guest or a prisoner?* It never occurred to him that he might be both. The last thing he remembered was the image of—*no!* Logan Kiasar. *Take a minute and calm yourself because Logan's dead.* He knew he didn't kill Logan, but who did? Then there was Nijimegan. What was Logan doing on Nijimegan? More important, what was *he* doing on Nijimegan? He needed answers, needed to remember. He tried to sit up but couldn't manage much; the bedding kept him firmly in place. His head pounded remorselessly. He laid back down breathing deeply when another scent hit him—*my God, someone's in the room with me . . .*

"Didn't think that I'd ever see you again," N'ckshell Slayton chortled, finally stepping through the threshold. "Old friend."

Rook's heart raced. He knew that voice. It didn't belong to Logan but something from the deep recesses of his mind told him that a confrontation with this individual could be just as bad. He'd barely had the time to orient himself when the Dracterian from his past stepped forward. "Nor I you," the cheetah rasped. He blinked, working his eyes, trying to gain more clarity. If his head didn't throb so badly he would've— no, the sickening disorientation went beyond the pain between his searing temples to his thumping chest. With fogging vision and dizziness, his muscles didn't seem capable of doing anything with alacrity. He could breathe, he could form words and that was about it. Helplessness, isolation seeped into him, a rising sense of desperation speared his chest. He hadn't seen the Dracterian in years but he knew that tone, he had heard it before.

"Funny, I finally find you in exactly the position that you left me in back on Minerva all those years ago." N'ckshell smiled.

"What would that be, my love?"

"Helpless." She began to pace the room, the smile suddenly vanishing. "Do you know it took a supreme effort on my part not to leave you in a heap on Nijimegan? Do you have any idea?"

"No, but I think you're going to tell me—"

"Shut it, shut your mouth." Slayton suddenly lunged toward the bed, placing her forearm against Rook's throat. Rook gasped, gagged, tried to move, failed. His eyes squeezed shut, his nostrils flared, trying to draw in air.

"For once in your stinking, pampered life, you're going to listen to me," Slayton hissed, her face just centimeters from the cheetah's. "You're going to listen, even if I have to kill you to do it—"

"You're going to kill me anyway—" *you rotten little . . .*

"For five years, I've wondered why you betrayed me." She released the pressure on the cheetah's throat ever so slightly; allowing Rook to breathe, but just barely. . . "And killed the only person I've ever loved."

"*I* didn't kill her, you fool . . ."

Slayton flexed her forearm into the cheetah's throat again. "Sometimes it doesn't matter who kills whom or who gives the order. All that matters is the end result."

Horror filled Rook's mind as he tried to move, tried to breathe. The room, though dark, was rapidly fading into indistinctness blending with the Dracterian's face. Horror turned to rage—if only he hadn't been so weak, he'd rip her face off her skull. Had he been healthy, he could bounce the Dracterian around the room with ease. But now, he was no more threatening than a cub. If only he could—out of the corner of his vision he saw that the

Dracterian was holding a knife.

Without warning, Slayton bolted away from the bed. Tears flooded her eyes, savagely she wiped them away. Rook watched, dazed—what in the name of God was happening here? The Dracterian seemed to be gripped in a flood of conflicting memories, emotions, madness—she didn't know what to do next, what she was feeling. Suddenly the Dracterian began sobbing, then her face flushed with anger, she lifted the knife, stared at its wicked lines and began crying—or was it laughter? The knife fell, clattering on the deck and the Dracterian just stood there staring at him, at the enemy whom had betrayed her all those years ago, the enemy who had murdered her love, and at the friend whom had saved her life countless times.

The Dracterian took a step forward, hesitated, sinking to her knees, head down. If she wanted to kill him, why didn't she do it? It would be so easy now. Rook knew he couldn't fight back.

"What are you staring at?" Slayton screamed suddenly. "What do you want from me?"

"Nothing," Rook gasped. His throat hurt like—"N'ckshell, if you're going to kill me, kill me, quit talking. Or at least give me the privilege of a descent cigarette—"

"Go and shite."

"No, you go on, my love and avenge the death of a traitor."

"She wasn't a traitor, you piece of shite, she was . . ."

"A traitor," Rook snarled. "And remember, dear friend," Rook spat the words out venomously. "Her actions and those of her followers led to the death of my parents and thousands of others. Thousands, N'ckshell. It should be me exacting revenge on you."

"On me?"

"Yes. You were trying to protect her."

"She was innocent."

"My God, N'ckshell. What fantasy universe are you living in?"

"I'm not living, I'm dying," Slayton screamed. "Look at me! I'm a wreck. I don't know what to do. I want to kill you—then I don't. I'm dying inside. I don't know what to do and when I finally do something it always comes out horribly wrong. I don't trust what I'm thinking or saying."

"N'ckshell, what in God's name are you talking about?" Rook felt more adrenalin course through him. He could feel his toes tingling.

"I don't know." Slayton turned away, trying to bury her face in a bank of medical equipment. She wanted to leave the room, but in her utter shame, her legs refused to move. So she sat there weeping.

"N'ckshell, listen to me." Rook's chest was heaving in mighty quakes. "Are you listening?"

Slayton's acknowledgment came in the form of a hated glare.

"Good, because I'm only going to say this once. Your 'girlfriend' betrayed a lot of good people that day. She and her cohorts killed a lot—"

"No she didn't—"

"You're not listening." Rook felt out of his element. He was terrible at counseling troubled souls and the Dracterian's went beyond mere trouble. She was obviously damaged beyond what seemed possible. Rook sat up, ignoring the arcs of pain shooting through his body. With startling swiftness, he leaned over the frame of the bed, seized Slayton's tunic and pulled her. His face contorted as new spasms and shocks rocked him. "She killed my parents . . . my parents . . . and if that's not enough, she killed your sister, N'rsha."

Slayton tried to use martial hand forms to break the cheetah's grip, but to no avail.

"Must you continue to delude yourself; must you continue to consume yourself with these lies?" Rook gave a snarl and shoved the Dracterian away. He settled back in his bed, spent, racks of pain continuing to torment. He closed his eyes, not caring what happened now. If Slayton decided to kill him, so be it. After all these years if she decided that she and only she was the one betrayed . . . if she thought she was the only one to lose someone close to her . . . then the Dracterian was under more psychological stress than he or anyone could imagine. The question was, how deep did it go, how far ranging was her pain? Rook opened his eyes. Just how damaged was N'ckshell? Rook blinked. He saw a friend in need of help, his help and all those who loved her . . . not a rival who needed killing.

"Well, N'ckshell, are you still going to kill me?" Still, Rook couldn't help pushing the envelope.

"You know I can't do that."

Good. "Then what?"

"I don't hate you like—"

"My, my, I can only tell you how thrilled I am to hear that." With the sarcasm still lingering he added, "we both know that Theri Tissuard killed your traitorous thrall."

"Please, don't say that."

"She was—face it and embrace the truth," Rook continued. "Damned near slept with the entire senior class . . . she didn't love you, she used you, used everyone and later tried to have all of us killed, including you."

Despite her rigidity, Slayton felt her guts sag, tears forming at the corners of her eyes. It was all true and she knew it. All of it and then some. All this time she'd harbored an irrational hatred for an individual who had saved her life on a number of occasions. And for what . . . this consuming hatred, it screamed at her, ripped at her; cold one instant, searing hot the next—what did it mean? And here it was Rook. What would she do when she met Theri Tissuard? What would she try to do to her? What would she say?

"I'm finished as an Omnitraus Officer," the Dracterian finally said. She wiped her eyes and nose.

Rook looked around desperately. "Don't say that, love."

"Well, it's true. Who would trust me leading a strike?"

"Quit N'ckshell, you forget yourself."

"I don't care. My capacity to reason, clearly, has left me; has been leaving me ever since that morning."

"My God, N'ckshell, what happened that day affected us all. Please listen. That's what wars and traitors do. They use you up, until you're a wreck of your true self. But, my dear friend, you have to remember that you are an Omnitraus Officer—it's more than a title or rank, combat fatigue or not, billions of people are depending on you, depending on us to protect them."

"The weight of the galaxy being carried on the shoulders of so few—no one else is as mentally ruined as I am."

"You sound sane now."

"Of course," Slayton said, her posture relaxed, shoulders squared, tears now gone, but the redness in her eyes frosted. "I slip in and out of it. I have no control of my emotions."

Rook raised himself to his elbows and whispered, "So you no longer think I killed that . . ." He was about to say 'whore', but thought better of it. ". . . woman of yours."

Slayton smiled briefly, as if she knew what Rook had hidden from her verbally. "No, but the sense of betrayal lingers; my corrupted sense of loss is agonizing. I know the truth of the matter, yes. But an hour from now—perhaps closer to a week, I may find myself in a blind rage again. This conversation completely forgotten."

"Let's hope the Pulsarians are in your presence and not I."

"Yes, let's hope." She sniffed and wiped her eyes. "I'm sorry, Rook."

"No you're not, my love. But you ought to be." Rook smiled. "What was said today should've been said a long time ago. Only what happened back then . . . there was just too much killing. The Pulsarians brought the war to us that day and nothing's been—"

Dannen Leers entered the infirmary. He looked at Rook, said nothing and continued to scan the room. Slayton rose from the deck in the recovery corner. Her eyes bulged, and darkened, obviously she'd been crying. Leers ignored her.

"What's going on here?" the only human in the room demanded.

"Dannen? I didn't know you were here as well." Rook looked around. "What ship are we on? A Rhoderium Crab?"

"Rook, you're a genius," Leers snapped, folding his arms. "But I asked you a question."

"Everything's a-okay, good friend Dannen," Rook mused. He cracked a toothy smile and tugged on a whisker. "Lovey and I were catching up on what brought us all here."

"Like hell." Leers cast a wary eye at Slayton, then again at Rook. "You two hate each other."

"Dannen, we didn't get cast into the fires to dredge up old injustices—"

"Hey, I'm not dredging up anything." Leers pointed at Slayton. "She nearly exploded getting in here."

Again Leers looked to Slayton who had remained silent during his entire exchange with Rook. Slayton glared back at him and mouthed the words, *fuck off.*

"What?" Leers mumbled, flabbergasted, unable to comprehend what was happening. He'd entered the room fully expecting to see blood being spilled to find nothing.

Rook threw the sheets to one side and moved gently from the bed, a medical smock hanging loosely from him as if they were royal robes. Gripped in his clawed left hand was a Hellington Standard Snub-nose laser pistol.

Slayton saw the weapon and felt her insides jump slightly. "You had that with you the entire time?" Hers was a strained whisper.

Rook feigned a shrug and said simply, "Yes."

"You could've killed me."

Lucky for you I didn't know I had this damned thing lying beside me. Rook shrugged again.

"Will one of you please tell me what's going on?" Leers demanded.

"Friend Dannen, I'm shocked." Rook looked at Slayton. "He hasn't changed one erg in five years."

"No, the human hasn't," Slayton said mildly. "Dannen can be so thick at times." She looked at Rook, the inhuman fiend she had mistakenly loathed for so many years. She felt foolish, supremely embarrassed. How had she let her emotions get the better of her after all these years? Was she really so out of control? A maverick, a live-wire (whatever that meant) as her human compatriots had always called her? Or had she been merely an actor in a tragedy that she had created? No, it hadn't been entirely her creation. Those events had transpired on Minerva. Hundreds of thousands had died. She lost more than a girlfriend, lost more than her classmates, lost more than her sister; she'd lost herself, her essence. Over the years, she'd nurtured a hatred that hadn't been justified. Garnered a reputation that wasn't hers to begin with. Yes, she'd had something to do with it, had been instrumental at spreading the blame. There was more than enough of that to go around. It was beyond time to forgive and—but not forget, it'd be the only way she'd learn not to make the same mistakes in the future.

"I'm sorry, Rook," she mumbled. "I've let my emotions get the better of me."

"Now I believe you." Rook paused, considering. "You wouldn't be Dracterian if you hadn't." He threw the weapon on the bed.

Slayton huffed, "Only humans refer to an entire group of people as Dracterians."

Rook held up a claw in a mocking gesture.

Slayton grabbed Rook by the shoulders and hugged him, tears flowing freely from her eyes. "It's good to have you back."

"Don't lie," Rook said, squeezing her tightly. He stepped back and sat on the bed's edge. "Lovey, I wish the circumstances were different."

"Wish the circumstances were different," Leers thundered. "Wait just a damned minute the both of you."

"Would you have preferred that we have killed each other?" Slayton challenged. She began drying her face, her eyes returning to normal.

"Yes, it would've cut down on all my confusion," Leers fired back. "And you, N'ckshell, I still owe you one. My ribs are killing me—you might've set back my recovery for another two freaking days—"

"I can't help it if you're clumsy."

Rook snickered at the two of them. Some things never changed; always fighting, always trying to outperform the other. He took a deep breath; not because he was suddenly reminded of their immaturity, but because now he wasn't feeling so well. For the first time, the trauma inflicted against him by the force beams made themselves known. A low growl escaped his throat as the floor danced briefly in front of him.

"Gentlebeings, you'll have to excuse me," he said softly. "It seems that I'm about to lose control of my bowels."

Forgetting about Slayton, Leers felt more embarrassed than his friend did. "Crap, maybe we should get out of here then."

"Not the words that I would use Dannen, but damned accurate," Rook snorted.

Leers shoved his way past Slayton, who reluctantly followed, and activated the courtesy screen behind them. He turned toward Slayton, and said, "In the future, if you ever come at me again like you did on that observation deck, I'll—"

"Go and *shite*, I already apologized for that," N'ckshell spat. "Do you expect me to do it again?"

"Apologized?" Leers barked, "to who?"

"*Thicky* should be your call sign instead of *Duke*. As I remember, it was you pointing a weapon at me on Nijimegan."

"What? Did I just miss something here?"

There was a whoosh of door mechanisms behind them. Rook ducked into the alcove. "Where am I, by the way?" Human and Dracterian didn't respond at first.

"The *Mekadore Traveler*, flown by . . ." Leers finally mumbled.

"Guardians Draystar and Jasmine, thank-you," Rook finished. He took an easy step forward. "Second question is, where are we going?"

"Who knows, the Gladatraus haven't told us shite," Slayton said.

"To the Omega Command Headquarters base," Leers said in a huff.

"Dannen, you don't know that for sure."

"Do you two ever get along? I thought you would've managed some semblance of maturity during the past five years."

"Rarely," Slayton answered.

"And after all these years, I thought it was just me."

"No, it has nothing to do with—" Leers stopped himself and sighed. "It is good to see an old friend again. Just wish the circumstances were a little different."

"As do I."

"There's so much tension and stress in the air that . . ."

"None of it created by me," Slayton chirped.

"Did I say you?"

"No, Dannen, you never do; it was in your tone. . . it's always in your tone."

"My dear friends, please, we have enough to concern ourselves with without this continued bickering," said Rook. "There have been issues in the past that have been resolved and issues that have not. I think we should look to the future especially since it seems that we're not going to my base but yours. Narterium's a long way from Omega Command; it seems that I'll be working with you two for a while."

"Seems that way, yes," Slayton said. She moved away from Leers and Rook.

"Trouble is," Rook mused, "that I seem to be having problems with my short-term memory."

"Do you think that's wise to say on board a Rhoderium Crab?"

"Why do you think I'm whispering? I have certain images in my mind but nothing connects. I need help before the debriefing. I know what they'd ask at November Command; I know how to read them and how to respond. But your base is different, with different procedures, different—"

"I think it'll be about the same, Rook," Slayton said. "You make it sound so ominous. Besides, I didn't witness any of the action on the ground on Nijimegan."

"I did," Leers stated.

"What were you doing there, anyway?" Slayton asked Rook.

Rook's bushy eyebrows arched. "An operation."

Leers folded his arms. Same old Rook. Secretive, even with friends. Had he forgotten that there were times when you had to share information with those around you, just to avoid feelings of mistrust and betrayal? With Slayton capable of slipping in and out of her own unregistered madness, now was not the time to bring that back up. As much as he cared about his friends, he didn't know what had taken place in the medical ward. The relationship of N'ckshell and Rook went back more than a dozen years and 'complex' didn't begin to describe the bitter rivalry, the closeness, the camaraderie, the life and death struggles the two had endured. Separated for more than five years did nothing to simmer their vulcanized friendship. It was difficult for the human to understand what drove the two to violent confrontation one minute, respect the next. Then again, Leers knew he had to be careful. One of the things they were both good at was setting up a third party. You'd think they were fighting each other when they were really camouflaging an attack against you.

"Rook, N'ckshell and I were talking about this earlier. What were you doing to warrant the attention of Gladatraus Command?"

Rook wasn't budging, "As far as I know, I wasn't doing anything to attract their attention."

"Hopeless," Leers breathed.

"Rook, you were on Nijimegan doing something that went beyond the latitudes of a simple business trip—judging from your attire when we pulled the rescue."

"You mean when *I* rescued him."

"Whatever, Dannen, you barely succeeded in that."

"Because Rook's safe house crew tried to kill me."

"Finished?" came Rook's raised whisper. "You two must understand that I'm not required to tell either of you or the Gladatraus flying this ship the details of my mission. I've obtained information that's vital to the survival . . ." he trailed off, patting down his smock, looking for . . .

"It's in a munitions vault with the data me and N'ckshell stole."

"You were on Nijimegan too?"

"No, not till late in the game. I had a mission on Darmen, a Pulsarian Outland world and N'ckshell had a mission on Elst. So you see, Rook, we're all in the same game. Hell, we might even be on the same team."

"How am I to know that?"

"Because you're here," Slayton said. "God, you're starting to sound as thick as Dannen."

"That proves nothing."

"What? D'ya think me and N'ckshell routinely pull Ops with the Gladatraus in tow?"

"Who knows?"

"The Gladatraus knew," Leers said. "Because I wasn't told lick when I set out for my portion of Operation Gorgon." Leers hoped that by saying the codename of he and Slayton's mission would spark some cooperation from Rook. Nothing emanated from Rook's cool exterior.

"I don't know what Operation Gorgon is and I don't care. I was given strict parameters for my mission, strict rules of operation that I won't violate because I'm with you two."

"Friends who happen to be on a Gladatraus Rhoderium Crab," Slayton hissed. "Gods, you are as thick as Dannen. If ever the Pulsarians captured you, they'd have such a damned time trying to pry anything from you."

"Training dictates that I don't make it easy for them," Rook said. "Or you."

"So that's it?" Leers shrugged. "You ain't gonna say anything?"

"Not until after I've been debriefed by the proper authority. And then, only if it's deemed permissible."

"If you want answers to all of your questions, follow me," came Guardian Jasmine's chilling, metallic voice.

She had seemingly materialized out of nowhere. They hadn't even heard her approaching, her silence unnerving. Leers felt a chill run down his spine. What exactly had she heard and how would she react? She stood in the passage behind them, decked in gleaming gold and turquoise battle armor and battlehelm. A sword, serving both function and form hung on her left hip draped over a leather and silk sash. Wild eyed and awed, Leers forced himself not to gape at the specter before him.

"Omnitraus Officers, your formal and first briefing begins in thirty seconds," she said simply. "And Mr. Rook, you may consider me 'the proper authority.' "

The three Omnitraus remained magnetized to the deck.

"Attendance is of course mandatory." She paused, started to turn. "I might add that the structural integrity of the *Mekadore Traveler* is second to none but the slightest whisper can be heard from across the ship." Her helm swiveled from left to right slowly. "Mister Rook, do you feel well enough to attend?"

"With respects my Guardian, I feel much better." Rook glanced from Leers to Slayton, hoping that Jasmine's armor couldn't detect his lie or fear.

"You don't look better."

Rook shuddered.

"Very well. If you want to change out of that smock into something more professional, we shall wait."

Again Rook shuddered. It would take him a quarter of an hour to change into uniform, his muscles burned with fatigue, and the swelling nausea washing through his torso told him that sudden movements were bound to be painful. "That's quite alright, my Guardian."

"My name is Jasmine. You would do me a great honor by saying it and dropping the 'Guardian,' understood?" She whirled out of the entranceway and disappeared into the darkness of the Rhoderium Crab.

"Very good," Rook said. "You can call me Rook without adding the 'mister.' "

Jasmine paused in mid-stride and turned slightly in Rook's direction. Leers groaned. But the Gladatraus continued on in silence.

"You're an idiot," Slayton hissed in Rook's ear.

Slayton and Leers each took Rook by an arm and practically dragged him after Jasmine. She activated the doors to the conference room, which slid aside with a double hiss. The room was surprisingly spacious and brilliantly lighted, unlike the stark darkness of the rest of the warship's interior. The walls were lined with razor thin monitors and tactical displays; a weapons vault to the right of the entrance and a specialized tactical and spatial vanguard station to the left. At the center of the room stood Guardian

Draystar in black, gold, and grey armor and helm, gauntleted hands clasped behind him. His expression, as always, completely hidden beneath the malevolent stare etched on his helm, perhaps speaking silently for him.

"Welcome onboard the Mekadore Traveler," he said. "There's plenty to cover and frankly I don't know where to start. I promise you that this briefing will not drag on for the forty hours we have left to go for Warp deceleration. As you probably know by now, our destination *is* the Omega Command Asteroid Base. Once we get there, I'm quite sure that we'll have to endure another briefing."

He brought his thick arms from around his back and folded them across his chest. "By the way, I'm Guardian Derek Draystar and this is Guardian Jasmine. She may've already introduced herself. I'm just saying it to be courteous because I'm damned terrible at giving speeches. But the past three weeks have been a confusing blur for both myself and Jasmine. And I'll wager that you three are wondering why the hell Gladatraus are involved with your missions. Make no mistake, Jasmine and I hate this as much as you do. We had no idea that Intelligence Command had three Omnitraus Officers operating deep within enemy held space when we arrived at the Omega Command Base.

"Why were we there? Jasmine and I had been leading counter-invasion strikes against the Pulsarians as they made their push for the Genarra and Yanattii star systems." As if on cue, a schematic of the star systems materialized in front of him. Icons in blue swirled to engage defending icons in red and orange. "You all may've been briefed about Pulsarian activity in those sectors before you set out. . . "

Leers nodded in the appearance of diligence; he didn't know anything about Pulsarian activity in that region. Strategically speaking, he always thought that the Pulsarians would likely move deeper into Aracrayderian space and hope to isolate both Shiborium and Narterium. Hitting Yanattii and Genarra seemed more like further action to solidify their hold on Minerva—which they had taken five years ago. It surprised Leers when Rook suddenly spoke up.

"Yes, I know of Pulsarians releasing bombing squadrons in the area," he supplied. "But anything more than that I don't recall."

Slayton remained silent, not even examining the floating projection, simply mouthing the words: "*Brownnoser.*"

"The counter-strikes were a nightmare to say the obvious," Draystar continued. "Defensive cohesiveness between the two star systems was poorly coordinated—constant bickering between the governments on both Genarra and Yanattii—with one Rhoderium Crab covering more than nine trillion cubic kilometers of space . . ." Draystar let his words linger, his battlehelm shaking slowly. "The situation turned from bad to a total shit show in a hurry." He gestured toward the other Guardian in the room. "Jasmine, you can jump in at any time."

While Jasmine gave details of the battles, Leers felt his shoulders sag. It was always like this, defeat after defeat. Now he had two Gladatraus telling him that they couldn't protect two star systems. Two. Not a large number. How many billions were now languishing under the yoke of Pulsarian tyranny? How many suffering, how many dying in concentration camps? He shifted his feet, even in the micro-gravity, they hurt like hell. But it hardly compared to the pain he now felt seeping into his heart. Two star systems, bombed, invaded, captured; and he hadn't known a damned thing about it. He focused on the Gladatraus standing before him. If they couldn't stave off the attacks in this—his eyes assessed his environment—the most powerful weapons platform ever built . . . what the hell could he, a lowly mistake-prone Omnitraus Officer, ever hope to accomplish? Not even a question he cared to entertain. Forget about inadequacy—what about the power around him? You had to hit the Pulsarians with whatever resources you had and keep hitting them. The only problem with that was once you ran out of resources, once you ran out of time. . . death wasn't too far behind.

As Jasmine finished with the tactics of the battle, Draystar spoke up again, "all this leads me back to the question of how Jasmine and I arrived at the Omega Base. In reference to the loss of the star systems, we were tasked by the Yanattiian planetary governor to ferry more than a quarter million refugees from the battlezone to a safe harbor. The most logical choice was the asteroid base." He pointed at Leers and Slayton. "Many of them were traveling in space vessels so badly damaged and shot-up it would've been an insult to call them starships. I was thankful that we didn't lose any on the way there."

"We would've pushed on to Shiborium," Jasmine interjected. "But too many of them couldn't make the journey without repairs and/or fuel. Not to mention the people onboard who needed medical attention and food—at least two rations a day."

"Universe, Guardian Jasmine, a quarter of a million people in our asteroid base," Leers started muttering. "That's way too many to feed and shelter. . . "

"Yes, they'd better repair their ships quickly," Slayton added.

"It's not your concern, Mr. Leers," Jasmine said. "Nor yours, Snappy. Colonel Granx can handle the logistics of the situation."

"When we get back to the base, it might be difficult to—"

Jasmine folded her arms. "Dannen, your concern is understandable but greatly misplaced. You can't be responsible for hundreds of thousands of people. There are others with rank who can carry that burden better than you. You're primary function is with the flying of fighters and leading others with your training into battle and nothing more."

"I understand Guardian Jasmine; sometimes though, it's difficult to separate myself from those larger issues . . . helps me feel better when I'm leading strikes."

"It's a reasonable response. Just don't let it overwhelm you." She regarded Slayton and Rook, "or either of you."

"I wonder how the General is dealing with the crisis," Slayton wondered, half attentively.

"Just the point I was about to address before we all diverged," Draystar said. "You'd think he'd be enraged to suddenly find himself directly or indirectly responsible for so many citizens. To have so many suddenly show up on his doorstep pleading for protection—since the location of that asteroid base is a highly guarded secret outside certain military circles. But he was more than ecstatic to see us—frantic to put it mildly."

Draystar took a pensive step back, his hands gesturing, but his mouth not finding the words to say next. Finally, he just said, "Admiral Doss, chief of Intelligence Command, and the direct coordinator of your missions, has been killed."

"What, how?" Leers croaked.

"I knew it," Slayton snarled. "I knew something—I knew it." She slammed a fist into an open palm.

Jasmine held up two armored hands to settle them down. Rook especially looked sick. "We don't know too many of the details. We'll get more when we arrive. An investigation has to be completed by now; if not still in progress."

"I can't believe it," Leers said. Doss had handpicked him for his mission. Said that he had great expectations on its success. Just go to Darmen, steal the information, then get the hell out. Simple. Now he was dead and—

"Not only Admiral Doss," Draystar was saying, "but his entire staff as well."

"General Varxbane, who knew of your missions, but wasn't directly involved, asked Draystar and I to do whatever it took to pull all of you out."

"All of them killed . . ." Leers' voice diminished.

"It's worse than that, I'm afraid," Jasmine continued. "There were two relay stations which were meant to monitor your progress—also destroyed in a Pulsarian ambush."

"I always felt something was wrong," Slayton said. "This is just too incredible."

Rook looked at him. "True. But what I don't understand is why my mission was compromised. I didn't take my orders from Omega Command—I've never seen their asteroid base. Heard of it, yes, but that's it. I received my orders from Commander Thallen on Sklavenlium well within the Narterium star system; a million lightyears away."

"The galaxy's not that big, Rook," Slayton snorted.

"Lovey, please, it's just an expression," Rook snapped. "The distance from your Omega Command to November is extreme to say the least." He looked toward the Gladatraus. "How could this have happened?"

"Who's behind all of this?" Slayton wanted to know.

"Again, the details aren't finalized as yet," Jasmine said. "Wish we knew more. I do know that Commander Thallen is Admiral Doss' deputy-director of the DIC branch. You were insurance, Rook, in case something went awry with his primary efforts starting from the Omega Asteroid."

"Primary mission." Rook said, rubbing his forehead.

"Commander Thallen, even though he's in one of the dozens of independent branches that make up Intelligence Command, reported directly to Admiral Doss. He received his orders from Doss."

"So is Commander Thallen dead too?"

"Don't know, Rook. As you said, November Command is a million lightyears from Omega Command. But since your mission was also compromised, we can only speculate."

"Something neither of us is prepared to do at this time," Draystar interjected.

Leers took a deep breath, exhaled slowly. "Let me see if I'm reading this right because I'm not as smart as Rook or as intuitive as N'ckshell. Admiral Doss and his staff were murdered *after* me and N'ckshell set out. A couple of relays stations in charge of 'monitoring' our missions were then destroyed by the Pulsarians. I didn't know anything about any relay station—I wasn't briefed on them." Leers looked at Slayton. "Were you?" Slayton simply nodded.

"Nor were you meant to," Jasmine interrupted. "Anything you don't know can't be used against you in the possible, however . . ."

" . . . Unlikely event we are captured and interrogated," Leers finished.

"Excellent," came Draystar's flat tone. "That's the general gist of it. Whatever you three stole has already directly or indirectly led to the deaths of thousands."

Leers stared at him fighting the violent spasms jumping from his throat to his chest to his groin. Suddenly he didn't feel so damned glib. "It's a miracle we're alive then."

"It's not a miracle," Draystar said. "It's called Gladatraus Command."

Jasmine laid a hand on Draystar's shoulder. "You shouldn't look at it strictly in those terms. The information you've stolen has the potential to save millions."

It was good to hear, but it didn't make Leers feel any better. "Who's behind all of this? Who can take out an admiral and his staff on an asteroid base in the middle of nowhere, then alert the Pulsarians to destroy relay stations, and almost succeed in having us three killed? Who's capable of orchestrating these things?"

"Indeed," noted Rook. "No single individual can be in several locations at once and sub-space transmissions can't . . ."

"Travel infinitely fast," Slayton finished.

"Yes, like you asked before; who has that sort of reach? Not to mention the influence over the Pulsarians."

All three Omnitraus tilted their heads toward Draystar, almost in unison.

"Have any of you heard of the codeword 'Cyclops?' "

Three negative nods gave him his answer. "Rook, you asked who could be in so many places at once; who could pool Pulsarians resources to strike devastating blows against us. It's Cyclops. A traitor, yes, as you may've guessed. But he's more dangerous than any mere traitor and assassin, believe me."

"And as fate or bad luck would have it," Jasmine broke in. "And you three certainly seem to have more than your fair share . . . it all goes back to the Pulsarian invasion of Minerva."

"You don't mean. . ." Leers fumbled for wording.

"The very subject you three were discussing earlier. Yes, the same individual who was responsible for all the betrayals and killings on your campus and dozens of others on the planet. Cyclops was instrumental in assassinations of top government officials, disruptions in communications, the destruction of an entire defensive grid. All of that was Cyclops." She took a step forward. "I've heard your conversations. Shocking to say the least and very un-Omnitraus Officer like in its content. However, you all are so very young and very stupid. Believe me when I say there's plenty of blame to go around."

"Too much," Draystar added.

"So let's end this nonsense, these resentments you've been carrying for five years and move onto more pressing matters." N'ckshell flinched, feeling her knees getting weak. "Rook, your behavior that day was no better than N'ckshell's."

"But I didn't—"

"Excuse me," Jasmine snapped. "I didn't ask for an explanation."

"Pardon me, but N'ckshell—"

Jasmine muzzled him with her gauntlet and squeezed. "When I speak, I'll not be interrupted. Is that understood?" She removed her hand. "The task which lies before us is difficult. We must all set aside the past and its trauma and move on. You three were friends once. Remember what brought you together what keeps trying to tear you apart. You have a common enemy. Focus your energy on that and move on. You all are among the most gifted of the Omnitraus Officers . . . you can't make the journey alone. Whether you like it or not, you need each other."

"This is war, kids," Draystar said. "No more games, no more playing nice. Billions of our people have died at the hands of the Pulsarians. Billions. Now think about that for a while and let it sink in. We're not talking about a few thousand killed in a single attack. We're talking about attack, after attack, after attack . . . from Minerva to Ruby Royale, Scion-Alpha, now finally Yanattii and Genarra. Our enemy is hitting us on many fronts. The task ahead isn't just difficult, it's staggering. Remember this, teamwork is absolutely essential to our survival. It's us versus them on a scale that covers a *galaxy*. Cyclops is one of us, not a Pulsarian—and we have no idea who the hell he is. None"

"And he's operating on our base," Leers mumbled, more to himself than anyone else in the room.

"Exactly," Jasmine said.

"Cyclops has to be stopped," Slayton said. "Even though he's on our base, he's now isolated. Now's the chance to surround, contain, and put an end to him."

"That's the obvious answer to the problem," Jasmine said. "But you're forgetting one thing. There are now more than a 200,000 refugees stranded on your asteroid base as well. When those refugee ships get repaired and the fuel that they need, Cyclops can slip away."

Leers began swearing before she could finish. "I'm sorry, but this whole thing reeks."

"Yes, it does, Mr. Leers. But things are going to get worse—far worse from here on out."

CHAPTER X
WARRIORS OF THE STRATREALM

THE chamber was dark, all sources of illumination cloaked, the air thick with the sickening stench of Vardavian cigars and pipe smoke from burning ginger infused tobacco. Yet, as turbid as the room was, it was not quite as tenebrous as the souls who inhabited it. For the chamber was the conference room in which any one of its inhabitants could order the deaths of thousands, or hundreds of thousands—if they felt the compulsion, the pleasure. The terrible destructive power of each of these predators now held in check could at any time be unleashed, obliterating those who opposed them. They were the masters in the violent mosaic of galactic warfare who honed their craft to a razor's edge and issued orders from within the walls of this chamber to unleash a legion of Straaka, or a phalanx of *landt'phizers* to do their murderous bidding. The atrocities committed on Corradora, the rape of Ruby Royale, the systematic extermination of two million peasants on the planet Rallius—all ordered from within these walls.

This was Star General Preafect Sergon's Command Conference Room located deep within the metallic bowels of Admiral Aldar Dehyhitte's flagship. The nerve center where battle plans, scenarios, contingencies, tactics and doctrine were developed.

The highest-ranking individual in this chamber, of course, was Preafect

Sergon himself, commander of the infamous 950th Straaka-Vohm Straterium. He took a long pull from his cigar, the euphoria coursing through his body as the acrid smoke filled his lungs. The officers standing around the holographic image projector were his field commanders, masters of their deadly trade, all taking puffs and pulls from their cigars, though some of them truly despised this ritual. Despite their feelings, all regarded the three-dimensional projection of a typical planetoid—more commonly referred to as an asteroid by most modern cultures—having the size and mass of a moon or dwarf-planet, according to the data floating next to it. The planetoid rotated on its longitudinal axis slowly, detailed features in the shapes of mountain ranges, pock marked continental plates, and several craters easily the size of a city revealed themselves in crisp clarity.

The predators moved in close, for this unremarkable rock was where the DFR had the Omega Command Star Force Headquarters Base hidden.

"This is it, my brethren," Sergon said, his voice booming in the chamber, reverberating off the cold, thick metallic walls. "This is our enemy's so-called Omega Sector Defense Command Headquarters Base for the Protection of the Sentient Beings and Their Advancement in Civilized. . ." Sergon trailed off as his officers chuckled at his mirth. "Doesn't look like a threat. Not *much* of a threat at any rate—but there are more than a hundred-thousand Delrel personnel stationed there—human, Aracrayderian, and . . . Dracterian," Sergon let that last word hang in the air before continuing, "who love nothing more than killing Pulsarians. We saw proof of this a few days ago when we lost a Frigate Advancer." Sergon studied the data scrolling from top to bottom on the image projection as the muttering grew around him.

"Some aspects of our attack will be fairly straight-forward," Sergon continued. "We shan't deviate too far from doctrine. We'll employ maximum firepower on their weakest point; maintain barrages along these axes here, here, and here . . . academic, in most respects. What isn't and what will pose a slight problem for us is the fact that we must travel, undetected, through the denser regions of an asteroid system and launch an attack against a base that is principally beneath the surface."

A collective wave of groaning and cursing filled the chamber. Sergon held up a gloved hand. "We have to accomplish this feat within thirty hours of our launch, which is exactly five hours from now."

"By your command, it will be done." General Fradviks Pendergon said, then simply nodded, a long-time friend and perhaps Sergon's closest ally in the room. As the deputy commander of the 950th Straaka-Vohm Straterium, his responsibilities to Sergon and to the more than 120,000 Straaka sometimes required more than simple diligence could afford—being deputy commander exacted a bloody toll sometimes too grim to catalogue. Adding to his responsibilities as deputy commander of the 950th was his own command of the famed *Tolk-Mech* Division, a fast-attack Malactite battlegroup. Pendergon was Sergon's shield as well as his sword, a dual duty he hated, but simultaneously relished.

Standing next to Pendergon was General Charlol Resdragon, commander of the *Kraam-Mech* Straaka Legion, which had been all but devastated during the invasion of the DFR's strategic frontier planet Cajetanus seven years ago. Resdragon barely survived, but proved to be a fit leader when his phalanx of untested Straaka replacements destroyed stiff opposition on Bemera three weeks later. While Resdragon may've nodded in unison with Pendergon, he wasn't going to agree with what Sergon was going to say next. He wasn't an ally of Preafect Sergon, and he sure as hell wasn't one of Fradviks Pendergon.

"None of the reconnaissance probes have even located their base yet," Resdragon snapped before Sergon could continue. "All we have before us is a schematic of what we estimate their base looks like. Add to that the high probability of it taking a week, at best, to scan this bloody system. Not to mention the fact that a Frigate Advancer was destroyed earlier in an ambush."

"Well, that's the Imperial Armada for you," Pendergon said drily.

"If they can take-out an Advancer without warning, what chance do you think our Straaka will have in slow moving Malactites?" Resdragon asked.

"A better chance than they will within the bloated walls of these Advancers, I should say . . ."

"Do you actually think that we can keep pace with the Marshal Admiral's attack schedule?"

"Not only do I intend to meet Admiral Petti's two-week timetable, I intend to shatter it," Sergon interrupted, stepping between his bickering generals. "The danger here is great. I'm glad that you sense that, General Resdragon. However, a triumph here will net rewards greater than any danger we're going to face in this asteroid system. With our combined forces here, we outnumber the poor Delrels 50,000 to one."

"Too bad we won't be attacking them with the entire Combined Fleet West," Resdragon said. He folded his arms. "When we go against the Dracterians, those numbers will be reversed."

"Yes, and the swords of our Straaka will already be stained. After this campaign, our Straaka will be more than ready to kill Dracterians." Sergon placed knotted fists on his hips and made a pretense of studying the ever-changing projections in front of him. He knew, as well as all the other generals in the room, that the Dracterians were among the most savage and cunning warriors in all the DFR's Tertiary Alliance. If any single element of his fighting corps wasn't ready, he'd be leading his Straaka into a burning abattoir. No competent commander would in theory allow it—however, battlefield circumstances rarely cared about how competent you were. Sometimes events took place that ripped away all control and the only thing you had left was tenacity. Sergon hoped that by throwing his Straaka into this asteroid engagement, it would sharpen their skills, make them adapt quicker to the unknown. An engagement within an asteroid system had never been attempted, at this scale, and would present its own unique set of problems. The Straaka would have to adapt or die. In the weeks to come, the Dracterians would throw so much death their way that they'd all wish to be fighting inside of an asteroid system again.

"This battle will be a test in regards to Straaka preparedness to fight a well-concealed but determined foe," Sergon continued. "For a number of years our enemy has, more often than not, run at the approach of our Malactites and Battlebarges. They know the end is nearing for them, their major capital planets have fallen—or will fall. We hold many of their industrial/economic centers . . . but across the galactic front, their resistance continues to be stout. Their November Command is still strong, perhaps the strongest it's ever been. And I expect no less of an effort from this Omega Headquarters Base. We must be prepared to have everything thrown at us at once. And when we think that they can't possibly do anything more, expect them to keep coming." He paused briefly, then continued. "They will launch a high-density force of their fighters and attack-bombers with little or no warning."

"Yes, it is a Star Force base we're attacking," Pendergon muttered aloud. He didn't think they had much to concern themselves about. Fighters were dangerous and incredibly useful on the battlefield—but they couldn't be utilized to win a battle by themselves. What concerned him was, "Electronic Warfare. What is this base's operational rating?"

"At least a four, maybe a five," Sergon answered.

Pendergon huffed disdainfully. So, not only were they going to have to evade asteroids, they also had to worry about tracking ghosts. When it came to scanner jamming and deception, the Delrels were the unsurpassed masters. A level five was the highest, but a level four could be just as nightmarish. Like most Pulsarians, Pendergon saw little use in deceiving a victim before you destroyed them. He thought of jamming as trickery, something used to mask weakness. To the Delrels it was serious art— infused into every aspect of their battlefield doctrine. For it went beyond jamming scanners and sensors, there was communications jamming, deception, flanking attacks, feints, reversals, cloaking fields—all of it sometimes combined and layered making electronic warfare the deadliest of arts. When employed with competence, jamming could make a commander think that an attack was coming from one direction when in fact it was coming from another. Pendergon was loath to conclude that not only could jamming hide weakness, but it could hide superiority as well.

While Pendergon and others like him were loath to utilize jamming, preferring a straight toe-to-toe fight with their enemies instead of trickery, many had to admit that their own foray into electronic warfare had played an integral part in the capture of Minerva.

"Who's their base commander?" Resdragon asked.

"Star Force General Varxbane," Sergon said. As if on cue, the holographic projection changed instantly to reveal the image of a massive Aracrayderian Gorilla, smartly uniformed with rows of campaign and service ribbons displayed on a barrel chest. In spite of themselves, several of Sergon's generals took a step or two back in the face of the awesome two-meter tall image.

"His intelligence is supposed to be near genius," Sergon snorted. *If a beast can be truly intelligent.* "All but a legend in their experimental testing and evaluation flight centers. Whatever fighters we may face, this Varxbane may've tested and flown years, if not decades ago. Aside from testing, he was a fighter squadron commander on Ruby Royale; became a wing commander on Grenididan; a division commander on Narterium . . . now the Delrels have given this ape his own major command."

"Impressive," someone mused.

"Indeed, yes," Sergon conceded. As much as he hated matching wits against this abomination of natural law, he was quick not to let his prejudice underestimate Varxbane. Many Pulsarian commanders had, and many weren't alive to learn from their mistake.

"His pilots are highly trained and well-motivated, as we've witnessed through the destruction of a Frigate Advancer days ago. I don't intend to be the object of sport for the Delrels, my friends. The danger here is not like any we've faced before." His faced creased sympathetically. "An entire operation conducted within an asteroid system? You ought to kill the poor bastard who so blindly allowed himself to be led into Marshal Admiral Petti's trap."

The tight laughter which followed was rueful, if not at all volumed in uncompromising loyalty.

"And make no mistake," he continued, "the danger to us and the fleet is very real indeed. They know this region, we don't. They're well versed in tactics we haven't even considered. And when they come at us, *my brethren*, they will hit us with fighters, attack-bombers, strategic bombers, and high-speed interceptors. I expect nothing but chaos to reign on the battlefield. However, in the end, we will prevail and it will be all the more glorious because we will have beaten them on their home field."

He looked to Resdragon and said, "As far as the actual location of their base is concerned—that information still eludes us. Our dear marshal admiral has ensured me that data will be provided after we launch . . . which is about all we can expect from him."

"Quite true."

Sergon creased a brow and folded his arms. "However, here's what they can expect from us: the *Tolk-Mech* Division will be at the speardhead of our attack, employing maximum firepower and disruptive jamming to annihilate their scanning attempts. We will have two Malactite jamming platforms operating just outside the battle area," Sergon said. "They'll maintain formation from 10,000 to 50,000 kilometers out and will wipe out the entire spectrum, if necessary. The *Volkr-Ghelk* Straaka Legion will be in the second wave—landing after the *Tolk-Mech* has reached the surface. Two *Straaka Rhom* Assault Phalanxes will also deploy with Malactite and fast-attack Battlebarges for support. Providing cover will be three, maybe four squadrons of Spark Racers and *Shall'Avacher*s under Admiral Dehyhitte's personal command." Sergon paused to nod toward the Imperial Armada liaison officer. "More than twenty-five thousand Straaka on the move and killing as many Delrels as we can; we will take their base in under twelve hours."

"Impressive," Pendergon mused.

Sergon looked up briefly and caught Resdragon's steely glance. "I'm sorry, Charlol, but your *Kraam-Mech* will have to sit this one out."

"As the General wishes." The steel vanished. There wasn't anything he could do about it except launch a formal protest and he didn't want to do that. Besides, he didn't like the idea of attacking a Federation base within an asteroid system in the first place. If his Straaka were going to be used, let them be used in assaulting the Dracterian capital.

"We shouldn't have too much to worry about—chaos notwithstanding."

"To the devil with that," General Ommarr Threshergon barked. The legion commander of the *Volkr-Ghelk* Straaka Legion knew full well that when the Delrels started shooting, they'd do everything in their power to kill him. Delrel tacticians called it 'severing the head of the serpent'. By throwing everything at the commanding elements of the invasion force, they hoped to throw an entire invasion into disarray. The Pulsarian response to this was to exact an even heavier toll on any force trying to execute such a plan—generally it worked.

Threshergon stepped forward. He was known throughout his legion as an intellectually fit commander; clever, proficient—if not somewhat hotheaded. "Begging the general's pardon,"—impetuous or not, he always employed respect and adhered to strict military protocol no matter how informal the setting—"but you make it sound as if it will be easy to cut through their fighter screen and take their base."

"Oh no, general, I said nothing of the sort," Pendergon said. "However, we're not attacking a heavily fortified planet. They don't have a planetary defense fleet hanging above this . . . this rock, ready to take shots at us while we make planetfall. Our attack should be a straight-forward operation." *Easy enough for you to handle, my friend.* His gaze narrowed on Threshergon.

"Take a look at this," Sergon said, indicating all to follow his gesture to the projection. "According to intelligence, their entire base is constructed beneath the surface of the planetoid."

There were rumblings of astonishment in the dark chamber.

"It only makes sense," another general ventured above the din. "Their base is within an asteroid system. To protect themselves from the constant meteor shower, they would be forced to construct their base beneath the surface."

"A wise observation indeed," said another, "it negates the necessity of a massed shielding array."

"Yes, but an asteroid striking the surface is still an asteroid strike and the effects can still be devastating no matter how far beneath the surface their base is."

"They have interceptors."

"True enough."

"There base is sensor shielded as well," Sergon added. "Detection won't be easy."

"Incredible," Threshergon said. "Such misplaced effort."

"Straaka landings will be difficult," Sergon continued. "They won't have the luxury of operating in the familiar battlefield environment. Our Straaka will have to operate within caverns and mammoth underground complexes both natural and artificial without fire-support from the Malactites or Battlebarges. The APCs might be able to navigate some of their corridors, but I'm not going to guarantee it. Make sure your Straaka units go over their starship boarding procedures—it'll be useful in this environment. Also a review of inner-city combat tactics may prove valuable as well."

Threshergon shook his head. It was a lot to digest in so short a period of time.

"Once your Straaka are inside, they will have to rely on their superior training, speed, and numbers." Sergon walked around to make sure all of his subordinates keyed on his every word.

"They can't afford to get pinned down, and neither can either of you. Crush all resistance, utterly. The infantry we will face will be no match for the Straaka. The base is protected by a Retainer force numbering well under a thousand. As you know, they are not frontline combatants—they mostly put on parades and guard the base's fighters."

Some of the generals let out tight snorts of mirth.

"They won't pose a threat. The real danger lies in approaching the base, getting through their fighter wall. That's where the challenge lies. Because of this, we are going to adopt a new tactic. In the past, we've approached the target en masse. Our Malactites and Battlebarges would go in under the protective cover of Battlecruiser Advancers under optimum circumstances—Destroyer Advancers at worse. Upon reaching the surface, the *Shallh'Avachers* transporting the tanks would act as a low-orbital protection. Not in this case. Here, we'll have no such protection, no such cover. All elements of the invasion will approach the planetoid on its own track to avoid detection. As I've said, General Varxbane's pilots are among the best the Delrels have to field against us—add to that their knowledge of this region—a large force approaching them will be easily detected, sorted, then destroyed. Our Malactites are good machines, but against swarms of enemy fighters, they make even better coffins."

"Excuse me sirs, but while we're on this subject—exactly what type of Delrel fighter are we expected to run into out there?" a colonel asked.

Pendergon activated several controls on the image enhancer. The image of the spiraling asteroid system rippled and faded, replaced by a two-dimensional schematic of four different types of Delrel fighter. Immediately the officers began to breathe a collective sigh of relief. All of the fighter types displayed were old. The outlines of the deadly VF-95 Valkyrie or the supremely lethal VF-98 Vigilante were not on the schematic—thank the *Lords of Stralolem*. For the VF-95 and the VF-98 were highly capable, lethal, and for all intents and purposes equal matches for the Spark Racer THV or the newer Spark Racer XXR. What was projected, however, were the mean, heavy-looking outlines of the VF-94 Vagrant; the serpentine and smooth lines of the high-speed interceptor, the VF-97 Vision; the clumsy, but reliable VF-87 Vampire; and lastly, the sleek, powerful interdiction-bomber, the VF-81 Vixen.

Indeed, the Delrels were quite capable of defending themselves from a surface attack or Malactite suppression. But the Spark Racers escorting the Malactites would even the odds on the battlefield, somewhat. The VF-97 Vision was fast—much faster than the XXR—but, in being so, it sacrificed firepower, maneuverability, and armor. As for the Vampire and the Vixen, all they could do was bomb planetary or orbital targets, useless in fighter-to-fighter engagements. The pilots on these fighter-bombers were not trained in the deadly art of knife-fighting—all they could do was bomb planetary or orbital targets from extreme or close range. On the other side of that spectrum was the menacing shape of the Vagrant, a different beast altogether, for it embodied the toughness of a bomber while being as agile as a knife-fighter. The Vagrant was heavily armored, powerful and had an excellent sustained turning rate within close proximity to planetary influences as well as a wide array of weapons it could employ against any potential adversary. Strangely, it looked more like a brick with wings and guns than a fighter. It was a deadly opponent not to be taken lightly—but realistically speaking, in a one-on-one fight with a Spark Racer XXR, with all things being equal, the XXR would beat the ungainly VF-94 Vagrant every time.

"As you can see, the Spark Racer XXR has numerous advantages over its closest rival, which, I feel, is the VF-94 Vagrant—their 'F' model to be more specific," Pendergon said. Against his loyalty to the Emperor, the Great Houses of the Stratrealm, and the Empire, Pendergon had to admit that he rather liked the massive look of the Vagrant, an opinion he'd never admit openly. "Their fighters are a threat, but I don't think we should be overly concerned. As mentioned earlier, if we are detected before we are anywhere near their base, we'd have to contend with asteroids as well as their fighters. But they too will face the same challenge—but they'll have to contend with the combined firepower of the invasion force and they will never know when our Spark Racers will pop up. Not to mention the *Shall'Avachers*. They can't come after us and down our escorts at the same time."

Resdragon smiled and gazed around the conference chamber. "Throughout the battle, the Delrel scanner systems will be reduced to static, garbage. We're not going to waste time with games—false inputs, deceptive measures. Those take time. We're going for total denial. Without their radar and scanners, they will be blind."

"Now this is how the battle will proceed," Sergon said. The projection flickered, once again showing the asteroid. "I will lead the first wave of the assault on their base in my own fighting vehicle. Threshergon, you will lead the second wave and Mitragon, you take the third and final wave. Each wave will contain twenty-five Malactites. We'll each be escorting thirty-three Battlebarges into the invasion zone. It is our task to bomb the Delrels into submission and protect those Battlebarges. The Delrels will no doubt target the barges because they are lightly armored and will carry the bulk of our Straaka. Each component of the invasion force will go in alone unescorted. This is incredibly risky, but we can't afford detection. Our success depends on stealth more than anything else. It's a tremendous body of asteroids out there. That can be an aid as well as a hindrance."

"We will have to pick the finest Malactite pilots in the command and our best fire- and weapons- comptrollers. Our crews will have to direct an all-out effort toward success. An all-out effort. Nothing will take precedence over our final objective: the destruction of their base. Nothing."

CHAPTER XI
TRANSIT

DANNEN Leers turned down another dark corridor, which led directly to the flight deck of the *Mekadore Traveler*. There wasn't anything overtly unusual about the passageway, save the fact that the minute change in gravity made his stomach protest somewhat. Then again, it was always like this on Gladatraus Rhoderium Crabs; they weren't built with luxurious comfort in mind. The medical center was a steady one-G environment because recovery from injury took place quicker than in a zero-G environment. But that wasn't true for the rest of the ship where the rates of gravity could be changed to suit certain functions. Behind the cushioned walls were conformal, articulating interior armor plating that hid laser rifles, auxiliary power units, medical supplies, and parts and accessories for environment suits. In that regard, all Gladatraus Rhoderium Crabs were alike. Form always followed function. However, some Gladatraus flew warships that were bigger, some smaller, some faster, some with defensive capabilities that staggered the mind. The last Rhoderium Crab Leers had been on was the *Magika*, sixty meters in diameter and bigger than the Rhoderium Crab he was presently on—that was almost a year ago. *A year. Had it been that long?* He remembered that the *Magika* was not quite as dark as the *Mekadore Traveler*, it was a bit cooler too.

He entered the flight deck to see Guardian Jasmine at her pilot's station checking and interrogating Hyperspace passage numbers. Leers said nothing to announce his presence, standing as best he could at attention with a battered body.

"Relax, Mr. Leers," Jasmine said, her attention refusing to leave the cascading data before her. "I'll be with you in a few ticks."

"Engine output is nominal," the flight computer stated dryly. "There may be a few bumps ahead, but I'll warn you before the rattling starts."

"Thank you, Nancy." Jasmine turned. The hard stare etched on her battlehelm froze Leers in place even as she said, "Come in, have a seat." She gestured toward Draystar's command chair.

Leers took a step forward then hesitated. No, to sit in that chair would be a display of wanton arrogance. He heard what sounded like laughter hissing from underneath Jasmine's helm.

"What is it, Mr. Leers?" She folded her arms. "Are you intimidated? Worried perhaps? Draystar's in his rest cycle. I don't think he'll kill a lowly Omnitraus Officer for sitting in his seat."

Still Leers refused to move. It—the whole thing seemed presumptuous.

A hot trail of vapor shot up from Jasmine's helm. She reached up with two gloved hands and pulled the helm from her head. Leers stopped breathing. *Universe.* Once armored, Gladatraus never revealed themselves to those they outranked, and never ever to Omnitraus. Leers felt his face burning. Not because she was revealing herself to him but because she was laughing at his discomfort.

"Calm yourself, youngster, you're not going to turn into stone if you look at me." She smiled pleasantly. "Were you expecting an old hag with reptilian hair?"

Leers nodded absently. She had to have been more than thirty years his senior, but she looked no more than two—five would be pushing it. And her features were clearly that of a Dracterian; black and red strands of hair falling well below her sharply pointed ears told him that she was an elder member of N'ckshell Slayton's clan. The way she moved, her hands on the instrument board, the way she looked at him. Some Dracterians looked at humans as if they were vermin. Not Jasmine; she looked at him with respect.

"I, ah, beg your pardon, ma'am," Leers stuttered.

"Don't call me that. I'm not your wet nurse. And don't call me Guardian Jasmine either, because I know you're about to. Just Jasmine—you can extend the same courtesy to Draystar as well. In fact, he'll probably let you call him Derek from time to time, if you get on his good side."

Leers swallowed; they were slightly more relaxed than the Guardians onboard the *Magika.* There, they never let you forget that they were the Gladatraus and you were Omnitraus—as if an Omnitraus ranking was lower than insect shit. What Jasmine was doing was so unusual, against every protocol he'd ever learned—Guardians always requested a prefix before their names—always.

"And stop staring at me like some loathsome first year cadet."

Leers nodded, not knowing what to say.

"As you are quite aware, Draystar and I do things differently than most of our colleagues. We work well together. Don't let our lax nature dull you into thinking that we disregard professionalism. We adhere to it more strictly than any two-pack, by-the-book, jar-heads you're apt to find."

"Understood." Leers sat in Draystar's command chair reluctantly.

"No you don't. Otherwise you wouldn't have said anything."

Coded messages chimed through the console next to her. Jasmine flipped a few switches nonchalantly and silently regarded the human sitting next to her. There was something odd about Dannen—no, not odd, different. Unlike most humans in the galaxy, his skin was dark, and his hair, although closely cropped, was wooly, but neat and textured. He wasn't Caucasoid—he was—she couldn't remember the word right now—not that it mattered. Somehow, though it seemed terribly important . . . perhaps she'd remember later.

"According to Nancy, your sleep cycles have been irregular," Jasmine stated frankly. "What's the cause of this?"

Leers shrugged. "I don't know."

"Is it your injuries?"

"No, I'm recovering fine." As if to remind him of his plight, the entire left side of his body tingled. The sensation wasn't pleasant. He looked down, not wanting to talk about what they were going to talk about. When the Gladatraus asked a question, you'd damned well better sort out an answer.

"I've made too many mistakes." He looked up, slowly.

"Mistakes? Dannen, how many people were killed because of your mistakes on Darmen?"

"I'm afraid I don't understand what . . ."

"The hell you don't—you know exactly what I'm asking. You just refuse to answer, damn stubborn human. I repeat . . . How many people died because of the complacent mistakes you made on that planet?"

Complacent? What the hell? I did everything I thought I needed to do—"I don't know . . . the crew on the Infiltrator—"

"You had nothing to do with their deaths. Nothing at all."

"But Draystar said—"

"Nothing! They were all dead from the start and it had nothing to do with you." She paused. For some reason, she could see Leers wasn't listening to her. He was attentive, true—but the words weren't penetrating. *Damn, these humans and their guilt.*

"Imagine if the captain of that patrolship had delivered you to that planet well within mission parameters instead of just outside of them. You would've completed your mission in under three hours instead of ten and you'd be dead by now."

"I thought that—"

"Your problem, Dannen, is that you think too much. You overanalyze when you should leap right in. Sometimes you can't avoid making mistakes. We all can't be perfect. Nor are we expected to be. All that's expected of us is that we maximize our abilities so that others can do the same and hopefully, with skill, and faith, we can find our way out of this nightmare."

Universe, I hope so . . . I still think I could've done more to—"It's difficult to deal with all of the killing and seeing your friends die. About four or five months ago, we lost nearly an entire fighter squadron in an ambush. My squadron was across the system and you could hear them screaming for help on the radios—but we were too far out of position to do anything."

"Remember, you're not the only one to deal with these feelings."

"Yeah, I suppose you're right."

"I never 'suppose' anything, Mr. Leers. I'm always right."

Leers looked away as his stomach rankled. Laughter struggled vainly to escape through his lips, but the pain in his chest was too great. He croaked instead.

Jasmine smiled.

"I shouldn't say such things when you're in the condition you're in."

This made Leers croak louder, his face contorting in misery.

"It's good to see you laugh," Jasmine noted mildly. "Or trying to execute a close approximation of laughter. You've been brooding about the ship like a depressed midshipman who faces the grim prospects of being keel-hauled without the luxury of a vacuum-suit."

A tear streamed from Leers' left eye. He couldn't hold back the laughter, his ribs protesting in a gnashing agony that went down his spine to his tail-bone. Trouble was, he didn't know what was so damned funny. Nothing Jasmine had said—rather it was how she had said it.

Finally, the pain had become too great and the young human straightened in the command chair, his face tight. He wiped away the tears. "I apologize for losing my bearing. It won't happen again."

"No need for apology." Jasmine folded her arms. "A little introspection is good . . . a little laughter, good too. But, as with all things in life, they must be carefully balanced. Sometimes we forget these simple lessons."

"And during a war is when they're most important," Leers mused.

Jasmine smiled. "My dear, boy, I think you're learning." She quickly tapped several codes in her console. "Now tell me, how's your flying?"

"Good." Finally something he didn't feel too terrible talking about. "I'm assigned to the Ranger Squadron back at base; we fly the VF-94 Vagrant, the E model."

Jasmine grimaced. "The Vagrant's spaceframe is older than you are."

"Don't tell the Pugs—I mean, the Pulsarians that. They may have better machines, but their pilots are too aggressive. They fly right at us like we can't shoot back." He looked at Jasmine keenly. "You know, if we had the machines to match theirs, there would be no stopping us."

"I know. You're no different than any other pilot, any other theatre commander in the Tertiary Alliance. The Pulsarians have the numbers and they have the machines. But there is something that they lack, that we have a lot of . . . desire."

"Right now, I'd be willing to trade desire for the ability to fight back. Have you seen their Spark Racer XXR in action?"

"Of course I have."

"I tangled with three of them last year. Three! I killed two; but I could barely keep pace with the fight in my Vagrant. My flight—" he suddenly shook his head "—we killed six of them before we had to bug out."

"You managed only two kills?"

"Well I suppose I could've—you know, might've—"

"Relax, Dannen. Consider this: you and your Omnitraus have to be strong, you have to be steadfast and bold. Things look dark, yes; maybe even desperate. Even with losses—we can make it back into the light. We're still strong. Right now all of the major commands are training pilots by the thousands. Manufacturers are designing and building more and more fighters. Infantry units will be equipped with weapons that can duel Pulsarian weapons on an even basis. Someday, we will turn the tide."

"I know, but I keep thinking about the constant killing. Sometimes none of it makes sense."

"Believe me, you are no more confused and frustrated than I am. Imagine, if you will, how the Pulsarians will feel a year from now—five years! They won't know what the hell happened to their Empire."

"I wish I could believe . . ."

Jasmine clasped armor-clad fingers together and simply said, "Start believing it, Dannen, start." Jasmine studied his reaction. He was so young, even for a human. But how long could they hold out, these youngsters who called themselves Omnitraus Officers? Would they dedicate their lives to the cause? So many of them had died. So many of them had been driven . . . "Tell me, young Leers, what is the history behind this delusion *kirsa* Slayton seems to be suffering from?"

Leers felt a sudden jolt, he thought their meeting was all but over. It had sounded like a conclusion to him and he was more than ready to leave the flight deck. He looked at the forward viewer absently. He didn't know where to start. He'd known Slayton for more than a decade and had witnessed her fiery temper masked by paranoid calm, surrounded by a cool exterior. As strange as it sounded, you never knew which N'ckshell Slayton you'd be greeted by on a day-to-day basis. Dannen and a select few others of whom Slayton called friends were used to the tantrums, the icy reactions, because like it or not, N'ckshell was a damned good fighter pilot and an utterly ruthless Omnitraus Officer. She stayed calm under fire when others seemed on the edge of going berserk. She would go wild with rage and charge while others wanted to stay put and hold their position. Strangely, as Leers contemplated what he was going to say to Jasmine, he found himself wondering what actions N'ckshell would've taken on Darmen had she been placed in a similar situation.

Leers noticed that Jasmine was still staring at him waiting for an answer.

"Please excuse my silence, Guardian Jasmine." Leers shrugged. "I just don't know where to begin. I mean— N'ckshell is a good girl—I mean Dracterian. She's a prime pilot. She'll lead you in a fight. She'll shut-up when it's her turn to follow. When you're in a knife-fight and you start to feel that creeping dread—she's got your back." Leers snapped his fingers. "Just like that, she's there, no questions asked."

"I can see that she's loyal to you and loyal to the cause. You haven't answered my question, have you?"

"No, I guess I haven't."

"Is the subject that difficult to talk about?"

"In a way it is. So many people died that day. People who you thought were friends turned out to be enemies. Just utter calamity, the killing, and then having to retreat."

"I was there."

Yeah but you didn't see the same insanity that I saw, Leers declined to say out loud. "Rook was due to walk during his graduation ceremony later that morning and . . ." Leers stopped. "Rook's parents were killed that day. N'ckshell lost her—one of her older sisters, N'arsha, was killed." Leers shut his eyes, his chest burning with the acute sense of loss. "I was in love with N'arsha . . . Universe, I still miss her."

Jasmine reached out and squeezed the youngster's hand into her own. "I'm sorry for your loss. Those were terrible times for us all." She saw him bat his eyes quickly, trying to hold back moisture. Human males were like that, Draystar was like that.

Leers abruptly cleared his throat and said, "I remember those days on the campus. Everyone seemed to have this invasion fever." He looked at Jasmine as if to confirm his memory with actual historic events. "No one was certain that the Pulsarians were actually gonna attack Minerva. We listened to what the newsies had to say; we had our own in-class intelligence briefings. Many of us thought that the Pulsarians didn't have the resources, let alone the nerve to attack Minerva. Everyone thought that they would invade the Valiant star system instead, right? Everything pointed to Valiant: sub-space communiqués, intelligence intercepts . . . it had to be Valiant. And whenever the Pulsarians probed the Minerva star system with their Spark Racers, they met overwhelming force, right?"

Jasmine silently agreed. Knowing all too well what Leers was saying with the extra benefit of being one who had lead intercepts against probing

Pulsarian attackers. The Pulsarians would Warp in at the outer edge of the star system, as if doing so would hinder detection, make a run along the outer ring of planets where they would be then destroyed before a single item of intelligence could be collected about Minerva. The intercepts, the killed Pulsarians, had become so routine that many commanders felt confident that they could repel any invasion.

"I remember thinking," Leers was saying. "That the week of graduation would be a perfect time for an invasion. The Prime Minister was vacationing on Ruby-Royale, three lightyears away. A lot of the Minerva defense forces—I don't know how many or the exact units—had been sent to Valiant, because we *knew* the Pulsarians were gonna attack there. The army was scheduled to parade through Minerva's capital. It was like we were setting ourselves up for an invasion. And that's exactly what the Pulsarians did. Had us thinking Valiant, Valiant, Valiant when they attacked Minerva."

Leers paused, considering the immensity of Pulsarian timing. "That morning we were all in the Hall of Heroes when the craziness started."

Jasmine folded her arms. "Hall of Heroes?"

"Yeah, it was a corridor, prep-chamber, leading to the open-air auditorium," Leers said plainly. "Where they had statues and busts of the student-warriors of high academic standing. Funny how I always wanted to have a bronzed bust of myself in there someday with that golden light shining down on it." He paused for a moment, thinking he sounded silly. "That's when Rook said that Wionna Weather was a traitor—called her out in front of everybody. It happened so fast. There were about a hundred of us in the hall—when he and Theri Tissuard just let go with a flurry of accusations, stating evidence, pointing fingers, cursing. It was crazy. I thought they were *all* crazy. Wionna was the class valedictorian and holder of the *Shield of the Hermitage*. She was just forty-five minutes away from giving her speech for the opening ceremonies and a eulogy for her roommate Bianca Bond . . ."

"Excuse me," Jasmine said.

"I'm sorry," Leers said. "I'm flying all over the place. Bianca Bond was Weather's roommate who had committed suicide just two weeks before graduation. Just like that, no explanation. Right when the daily rigors of academic life on campus start to ratchet down a bit she kills herself. The rumor mongering went out of control as I remember. She was an Omnitraus candidate and close to Rook. They weren't lovers or anything, they were just close."

"I understand," Jasmine mused. "What did you think about her?"

"I didn't like her, truth be told," Leers blurted out suddenly. He looked down for a moment. "I always thought she was a little on the uppity side—you know, old-world money." Leers looked down again, summing things up. "Bianca kills herself, but a few of us didn't believe it for a second. I mean, Bianca had all the money in the galaxy. . . And the Bastian Academy has its first non-Omnitraus valedictorian in over fifty years, in Wionna—not mentioning the fact that she's also holder of the *Shield of the Hermitage*."

"I don't understand."

"Like I was saying about the school's history, no Omnitraus candidate has ever been both. It's just too damned hard. Impossible. And here comes Wionna, a non-Omnitraus student, and she wins both."

"My next question is, what does any of this have to do with Rook and N'ckshell Slayton wanting to kill each other?"

"Rook was at the top of his Omnitraus class, a full point above Theri Tissuard, when Wionna is selected as valedictorian because of the unfortunate 'accident' with her roommate, Bianca."

"I see . . ."

"It gets worse. Wionna and N'ckshell had a thing for each other."

"What do you mean by a 'thing?' "

"A relationship," said Leers. "If you wanna call it that. I mean, N'ckshell had plenty of boyfriends . . . but there was something about those two. Wionna wasn't exactly as sweet and innocent as she pretended to be. If I could be perfectly honest, she was on the loose side and damned near slept with the entire class."

Jasmine gave him an icy stare.

"Sorry, I forget myself." Leers lowered his voice. "But she had sexual relations with a lot of the jocks on the Bombardier team—maybe it was just hyped. Then she and N'ckshell started hooking up—"

"And you saw this?"

"No—I didn't see it." Leers paused for a moment then added, "Not to be crude, but everybody knew that Wionna got around, but her favorite, it seemed, was N'ckshell."

"Go on," Jasmine said.

"To earn the *Shield of the Hermitage*," Leers continued. "I don't know if you know this or not—you have to compete in the 'Riddle of Dromnegra'; it's a twelve-hour endurance event where you compete individually against dozens of others, solving puzzles, advancing over ravines, scaling up cliffs, running through wilderness, setting up ambushes and 'eliminating' foes. I won't get into the rules and everything but Rook was in the event as was N'ckshell and Wionna. It was nearing the end and the few who remained were exhausted, just dripping or lathered in sweat. N'ckshell has a clean 'kill' on Wionna but misses. Two hundred meters away, no wind, no obstructions, no distractions and she misses; eliminates herself from the competition. This then gives Wionna a two point advantage over Rook and puts her in prime position to score a 'kill' on him. She does and gets the trophy. Rook should've won that thing hands down."

"I see . . . so when did this competition take place?"

"Three days *before* Bianca commits suicide. Once that happened, Wionna was named class valedictorian. It didn't end there. Rook and N'ckshell didn't have much to say to each other. In fact, they avoided each other and if they just happened to be in the same lecture hall, they fought. I mean they went after each other, I mean—drawing blood, gouging eyes, type of fight. I had a devil of a time keeping them apart.

"Right before graduation more rumors began to spread about Wionna. More than the sex, a few of the students began to question her possible involvement in her roommate's death. The timing of it seemed a little too perfect . . . if you get my meaning. I didn't see it. Rook and some of the others did. Turns out that Wionna and several others were plotting to blow up the graduation ceremony. Sounds like paranoid fantasy. But it was to coincide with the Pulsarian invasion. They had totally seeded the campus with high-explosive charges. Rook and some others found raw explosives in the history lecture hall just an hour before the ceremony was to begin. And you wouldn't believe where she had hidden the detonators . . . under N'ckshell's bed."

"What was N'ckshell's reaction?"

"Total shock. She may've been madly in love with her, but she's no traitor. We set out to disarm the bombs but we didn't know all of the hiding places. N'ckshell kept asking her why, why, why? She was crying, pleading with her to end it . . . and Wionna just looked at her like she wasn't there. I tried to be more direct, because we were running out of time . . . finally Theri just shot her and Rook hit N'ckshell with a stun beam because she went berserk. At the moment that I had caught N'ckshell to keep her from hitting the ground, the Pulsarians started bombing the capital. We never found all of the bombs Wionna and her traitors had planted . . . we barely made it off the campus alive. Rook lost his parents." Leers stopped, breathing deeply. "There were more than a hundred thousand people on that campus that morning . . . all of them blown up. There wasn't anything we could've done to save them. We tried, but it was just no good. . . there were just so many bodies strewn around. I never want to see anything like that ever again."

"I'm sorry, Dannen," Jasmine said. "We did everything we could to hold the planet but—"

"I know you did the best you could. Everyone did their best, including Cyclops. I didn't make the connection then or a few hours ago. It had to have been Cyclops who masterminded Wionna's plot to blow up the school. Wionna was smart but not that sophisticated. Bianca musta' found out about it and was killed."

"That's the way the official report reads."

Leers looked confused.

"I'm sorry, Dannen. I knew the ending, not the beginning; not the facts behind Rook and N'ckshell's hatred. I was aware of pieces of their story but not the whole sorry episode. I often wondered what Cyclops would gain by destroying your school, the Bastian Academy you called it?"

"Aside from taking out Omnitraus candidates—"

"There were other academies on Minerva."

"We had the largest contingent of Omnitraus candidates as well as future engineers, physicians, pilots and other service officers."

"I always thought Cyclops was a sick and twisted maniac; but the magnitude of this scheme. . ."

"And now he's running around the asteroid base compromising missions and killing people."

Jasmine retrieved her battlehelm. She slid it on with a metallic hiss. "His days are numbered."

"I hope you're right," Leers said finally. "Not only about Cyclops, but also about some of the other stuff you said as well."

"The war, you mean?"

"Yeah."

Jasmine's simple, yet unsettling answer was to leave the flight deck.

CHAPTER XII
GALACTIC CARTOGRAPHY

MANY simply called it Hyperspace; Draystar was among them. The spectacular multi-dimensional realm of time and space, where quantum dynamics flirted with Warp theory, thus, allowing starships to breach the so-called light barrier after thousands of years of human deep space exploration. It was by no means a secret that the many scientists within the Delrel Federated Republic didn't have a firm grasp of what faster-than-light travel *truly* entailed—Pulsarian scientists weren't available for comment. Was a starship actually moving beyond lightspeed (370,000 kilometers per second, or 1,000,000kpx) or was the space around the starship moving beyond lightspeed? Was there any movement at all? Was the space around the starship being folded, or as some had argued, Warped; thus, bringing objects many lightyears away closer to the subject ship. No one could design a computer model to accurately determine exactly what was happening. Traveling from one star system to another involved risk and wasn't as clean as those outside the scientific community thought it to be.

Scientists and engineers built computers that could approximate, but that was really the extent of it. Many Warp theorists were divided into two opposing camps. Those who believed that space was being Warped and those who believed that the starship was actually achieving FTL speeds; the debate raged as pilots took machines into deep space to both settle the debate and to push technology to the limit. Wrestling with FTL, Hyperspace, and Warp dynamics was just as furiously competitive in establishing scientific milestones as breaking the sound barrier had been thousands of years ago when humans began to take flight in the mechanized birds that they created. Many pilots had lost their lives in the pursuit of breaching the sonic barrier. Now engineering interns could scratch-build machines that could dance around the speed of sound as if it didn't exist; their machines could fold it, bend it, stretch it, shatter it, re-assemble it and manipulate it with elemental ease. FTL and Warping were beasts of an entirely different, sometimes violent nature, only allowing manipulation to a certain degree before fighting back. Within a certain set of parameters, a starship could be 'observed' as traveling 200 times beyond the speed of light as it ventured from one star to another. With the rules properly applied and obeyed, such a flight would be routine. But disobey the most seemingly rudimentary flight characteristics and that routine flight would become an instrument of death for the pilot and crew aboard that ship.

This was where the test pilots came into the picture. They were the rugged, brave souls of myth who suited up, climbed into experimental starships, and put the machines through the rigors of stripping, folding, and shredding space. If the current rule of Warp travel mandated that a ship fifty meters long, weighing more than a hundred tons needed to maintain a Warp Run for at least forty seconds before it could safely Warp space, then the engineers and the test pilots wanted to know why. Even though the rule may have been established by another experimental team more than twenty years ago, the rule had to be challenged. Maybe the original test pilot pushed a similar machine to the limits, got 'freaked' and decided to 'pull it back' in before killing himself and destroying the machine. Perhaps the data from twenty years ago was somehow flawed, or skewed as a result of an older engine design and perhaps even an older computer. The possibilities and testing options could reach into the billions; precisely the reason why engineering teams and their test pilots routinely pushed themselves and their hardware to the edge, sometimes beyond it, either to shatter old rules or to establish new ones.

There were literally millions and millions of different spaceframes to put through the paces to establish new rules for Warp or FTL space travel. The real benefit of all the testing, or as some would say 'risk-taking', was that it was giving scientists a better picture of how the Universe worked. However, it seemed that the Universe was bent on not allowing piss-ant scientists full mastery of its design—as if it were all being orchestrated by some unknown force—at least that's what Gladatraus Guardian Derek Draystar always thought, especially when some unfortunate soul blew himself or herself apart trying to push it.

But there was more to being a test pilot than just breaking speed records across the infinite void. If a manufacturer wanted to test a prototype navigation computer, the test pilot went up in his experimental ship—usually designated the x-platform—and put the new computer through the foundations of Warp flight, knowing full well that if the damned thing malfunctioned, he likely find himself on a trajectory to the nearest galaxy without any means of return. Not that it would matter; the pilot would've long succumbed to hypoxia centuries before attaining a tenth of the distance.

Draystar chuckled at that thought as he entered the empty flight deck of the *Mekadore Traveler* and paused before taking the command chair. They had been decelerating from 6,729 times the speed of light to 275 FTL just an hour ago. Nancy, the flight computer, had handled the deceleration with ease in his and Jasmine's absence. But the 'rules' mandated that he run his own set of tests before relativistic speeds dropped below 16 times the speed of light. Funny how a Rhoderium Crab, one of the most advanced starships in the galaxy, could drop from 6,729 FTL to just 275 FTL in a quarter-hour, but needed a full hour to drop from 275 FTL to 27 FTL. Draystar didn't agree with the computation, because it was one of the 'rules' that locked you into a certain set of parameters without much in the way of deviation—it seemed so asinine. At the back of his mind, he knew that some poor sap flying a Rhoderium type starship fifty years ago had probably 'rushed' the deceleration and had probably died in the process. Which was why he was here now, on the flight deck, to run his tests, and ensure everything was in readiness for proper decel into normal space. Still, it'd be nice to push it, to see if the hour rule of deceleration from 275 FTL to 27 FTL could be broken. But if the *Mekadore Traveler* decided that it didn't like the breach of protocol and exploded, he'd never hear the end of it from Jasmine.

"Ah, the rules," he breathed to himself. He took his seat and began running the *decel* program. "It'd be nice, when all of this war business is over, to really ring this baby out a little."

"I'm not a testing platform, Draystar," Nancy said politely, "I'm a warship. Warships are built for fighting, not speed."

"Oh, I didn't know you were awake," Draystar said drily. "But you are extremely fast—when you want to be. I'd like to know *how* fast."

"My Warp threshold has been long established by the most senior—"

"You're in a mood. Has Jasmine been messing around with your personality chip? Don't answer that. Now that I have your attention, I'm gonna need the fuel computations for a round trip sortie to the Shiborium star system and back to the Omega Asteroid system. I expect that we're gonna be burning up a lot of space in the next couple of weeks. . ."

"What makes you think that?"

"If the last couple of weeks are any indication . . . also, please include computations for possible combat as well."

"I'll have your program ready for you in thirty seconds . . . or less."

Draystar cut off a light-hearted chuckle and began his regimen, *Jasmine has been re-programming Nancy's personality template.* As he worked on the computations from his end, his thoughts drifted back to when he was a boy and had gotten into an argument with another child about the difference between a starship and a spaceship. The other kid said that there was no difference, but Draystar knew that there was, but couldn't quite verbalize the disagreement and let his fists do the arguing instead.

The primary difference between a spaceship, per se, and a starship was in their respective drive systems—a 'spaceship' flew from planet to planet within a set star system while a 'starship' flew from star system to star system via Hyperspace. A spaceship's top-speed neared, but did *not* exceed sub-light. It could lift itself from the surface of one planet and land on the surface of another planet. Starships, in general terms, didn't have this capability since their design allowed for interstellar travel only, employing shuttles to fulfill the orbit to surface role. Starships, as tradition and engineering demanded, were many times more massive than spaceships; they ranged from several hundred meters long with a spatial displacement of over four thousand metric tons, to carriers and dreadnoughts of over a kilometer long with over four hundred thousand metric tons of spatial displacement. It wasn't difficult to imagine the enormous strain, power consumption, and torquing these mammoth beasts had to endure just to get them from the surface of a planet into orbit—or, conversely, the extreme heat and hull-scattering vibrations they had to endure to get from an orbital position to the surface of a planet. Was it any wonder why starships remained in space and never ventured to within a few thousand kilometers of a planet? Or try imaging a kilometer long starship trying to make planetfall and the vertical climbers and main engines quitting? The resulting catastrophe would be—forget about rogue comets or asteroids, a malfunctioning starship slamming into a planet could end all life on that planet in a matter of hours. Thus, starships didn't have the necessary drive systems available to make planetfall and possessed an incredible array of planetary buffers to keep them away from any planetary body, or well outside the 10,000-kilometer safety zone. It would take a starship captain and the engineering chief days to weeks to override all of the safety systems to get a starship of more than 4,000 metric tons to actually land on a planet. But with shuttles, cutters and an array of escape pods, why would anyone want to risk destroying themselves and their starship to land on the surface of a planet?

Space travel was about specialization. Even after thousands of years of galactic exploration, nothing was taken for granted and the complexity of the Integrated-Hyperspace Drive systems, Warp-navigation systems, Warp-particle deflectors and a multitude of hundreds of other sub-systems and integrated components was testimony to that. Specialization was the rule augmented with the keen desire to keep crews in space alive in the least and averting a planet-wide catastrophe in the highly remote worst case. Specialization was a laser beam focusing on allowing space vehicle very little latitude outside of their performance envelopes. Specialization was a rule. In ancient times, it was unlikely that a helicopter could fly inverted at speed surpassing mach two, or a thirty-six gun frigate with all of its top-sails dismasted traveling at better than a hundred knots—such scenarios were impossible to realize. Specialization existed from the times of galleons roaming the oceans being powered with wind and the sweat lathered backs of slaves at the oars, to the dawn of the computer age when armored aircraft supported advancing infantry troops on the ground, to the modern era of intergalactic space travel.

However, there were a few space vehicles not locked into the spaceship versus starship specialization rule. These vehicles were chiefly military in design. Yes, there were a few corporate designs and even fewer civilian designs—but the space vehicles that routinely broke the specialization rule were indeed military and the warship that epitomized this was the Gladatraus Rhoderium Crab.

It was the spaceframe of a potential vehicle that determined how it would perform in the many environments of space. All it took was guts, skill, and uncompromising engineering to expand a space vehicle's role. Back during his flight-testing years, Draystar was positively pleased to get the opportunity to put the elegant AL-80L Starliner through its paces, for it was designed with wings that allowed it to enter planetary atmospheres and could thus, take-off and land on a planet's surface with relative ease; its elongated body could hold more than four-hundred travelers in luxurious comfort. But of primary importance to Draystar was the machine's dual engine rating that stressed brief Warp Runs, pushing it into Hyperspace with speeds topping Warp Eleven—well within the realm of many high-performance military vehicles—totally unheard of within civilian space travel circles.

The AL-80L was fast, but lacked the ability to attack targets, carry ordnance, or protect itself with weapons grade shields and screens. All it could do was ferry passengers from star system to star system and it performed this task admirably—with considerable financial reward to the companies within the travel industry that purchased the AL-80L in record numbers. But if you were a combat pilot and were tasked with attacking targets without having to worry about passengers, you might try a FB-25 Poltergeist (of course you sacrificed speed and edible in-flight meals) but you could attack and *kill* targets which is what combat pilots wanted. Any flight engineer, given the time, would be all too happy to explain why the AL-80L was good in its particular field and the FB-25 in its. What if a combat pilot wanted it all . . . the blending of speed and comfort, ruggedness and survivability, the ability to kill and defend—wanted all of that compacted within the most capable spaceframe that strained engineering capabilities to the limit? Draystar would be the first to say that you need look no further than the Gladatraus Rhoderium Crab.

Many engineers knew of the incredible capability of Gladatraus Rhoderium Crabs by reputation and eyewitness accounts only—of course many had worked with Omnitraus Officers all the time—but once those Omnitraus became Gladatraus, they were never heard from again. As distant observers, they knew that within a spaceframe of fifty to eighty meters in diameter, the Gladatraus warships could boast the firepower of most frontline battlecruisers which ranged from 800 to a thousand meters long! It had the maneuverability of many space superiority fighters, those venomous metallic gnats that only range from twelve to twenty meters long. The Gladatraus flight deck was similar in layout to the cockpit of the FB-25 Poltergeist. The mystery was how all of the diverging, wide-ranging abilities could have been compressed into a functioning, versatile, multi-role weapons platform. Not many knew that the Gladatraus themselves didn't know how it was all accomplished, just that it was. Which was all well and good for Draystar because he didn't give a damn one way or the other.

"Well, Nancy, I think that just about does it," he said, clasping his armored fingers behind his head.

"I agree with you, sir. All lights are green. I'm ready to burn up the sky."

"Well, burn it up all you want," Draystar cleared his throat. "Just make sure I'm not around when you do."

Guardian Jasmine entered the flight deck carrying Draystar's battlehelm. "You left this in your private berthing area, sir." She let the helm float to the commander. "Remember, we have guests on board."

"Thank you." He guided the helm toward a nearby panel and let it hover in the weightlessness. "I don't think our Omnitraus guests would be too horrified by my appearance."

Jasmine leaned toward him and cupped his chin in her hand. "You're not bad for a human." She gently massaged his chin. She always liked that divot in his chin. She also liked the thin lips that seemed ready to form a snarl as quickly as they could a smile. Her fingers caressed his lips then glided up the tanned, oyster-sheen skin. With her free hand, she deactivated the sealing mechanisms of her helm and pulled it from her head. She stared into his metallic blue eyes and stroked his parched white hair. With ease, she stepped over the edge of his commander's chair, straddled his lap, leaned forward and began kissing him fully on the lips.

After a few moments, she pulled away.

"Long time since we've done that," Draystar said.

"Too long."

They began kissing again, with renewed vigor and intensity.

"Maybe you two should focus on the deceleration," Nancy's voice echoed in their ears.

Jasmine pulled away, licking her lips. Looking at him slyly she said, "Um, humans taste so good."

Draystar felt his cheeks heating. "You've been so frisky lately, what's going on?"

"Well, do you want me to stop?"

"Not particularly, no," Draystar mused. "But, we have work to do and the ever dutiful Nancy is right. We should focus on the Warp deceleration."

Jasmine kissed him deeply again, running her fingers through his hair. She tilted her head away and smiled, "routine and boring." She gave him quick pecks on his cheek and forehead and lifted herself off his lap. She resealed her helm and sat in her pilot's chair. "Any word?"

"None," Draystar answered. "I've sent out three requests for clearance into the Omega Asteroid System and not a word back from them."

"Do you think there's a reason for this?"

"Oh, all of a sudden this isn't so routine and boring after all."

"You know what I mean."

"Well, I hope not. I've known General Varxbane for a long time. But this is downright . . ."

"I thought you said that he hated you."

"Well, that was true, at one time; when I was a lieutenant, we didn't get along well." He retrieved his helm and sealed it into place. "Time changes many things."

"If you say so." Jasmine began examining her Warp deceleration indicators. Everything appeared to be within norm. "With all those refugees probably still stranded at his base, the food situation must be reaching critical levels by now."

"Right. My main concern is where do we take them next. We'll have to take them somewhere out of harm's way. Desdemona, or even Valiant would work . . ."

"No, they're too far away," Jasmine finished.

"Maybe. Once we land at the asteroid base we'll debrief with Varxbane and his staff and come up with a plan."

"Sounds good to me," Jasmine agreed, then adding, "anyplace would be good as long as it's not Shiborium . . . Oh, I see you've already set Nancy up with a flight plan that lists Shiborium as our primary destination."

"It's a logical choice," Draystar countered mildly. "You don't need star vectors to see that."

"And your little wifey is there."

"Don't call her that."

"So all of this, um—let's take the refugees to the Desdemona star system, or Valiant, was just talk then?"

Draystar took a deep breath and let it out slowly; his adrenals were starting to run wild. "Look, Jasmine, we can't keep doing this thing that we're doing."

She held up an armor hand to silence him. "Were you thinking about her while we were kissing?"

Another sigh whistled from beneath Draystar's helm. "No, I wasn't. And that's what scares me."

"Pardon the interruption but we're coming up on the optimal re-entry point," Nancy said.

"Your timing's impeccable, my dear," Draystar said, his eyes sweeping over the flight systems and the deceleration indicators flashing urgently before his eyes.

"Your timing's shitty, Nancy," Jasmine said. She leaned toward Draystar, placing her hand on his thigh. "Don't think that this is over. We're still going to finish our discussion before we're within a lightyear of Shiborium."

Draystar felt the burning in his stomach suddenly turn to ice. He mumbled a reply which Jasmine took to mean the affirmative. There was no way out of this now and Draystar knew it. He was going to have to break off their affair. Trouble was, he didn't know if he'd survive it. "Ah, Nancy, where are the Omnitraus kids?" Draystar asked absently—anything to take his mind off the beautiful form of his pilot and their future.

"They're on the observation deck arguing about everything under the sun," Jasmine answered for the flight computer. "Again."

"Could be worse, they could be trying to kill each other," Draystar said. "Nancy, tell them to strap themselves in. We'll be re-entering real space soon near an asteroid system—might get a little bumpy."

"I already have, Draystar," Nancy said. "They say they're ready for anything."

"Switch to re-entry mode," Draystar said.

"Roger, switching to re-entry mode," Jasmine acknowledged. She inhaled deeply then let it out slowly. "Braking thrusters energized and ready. Emergency Braking Thruster's on stand-by."

"The clock is operating," Draystar declared.

"All systems nominal," Nancy declared. "Starting the count-down."

On the observation deck, Leers, N'ckshell, and Rook were strapped into their recliners and discussing the more technical aspects of deep space fighter-to-fighter combat. They had been at it for the better part of an hour and being confined to their seats hadn't hampered their enthusiasm in the slightest. All three knew the Warp deceleration was taking place, and all three ignored its implications for the time being. Trading stories about fighter combat was more important.

It was Slayton's turn now and she began 'hand-waving' as she described a recent deep space fighter-to-fighter engagement with the enemy.

"My point of reference for the VF-94 Vagrant," she was saying, suddenly folding her arms, "was that I had *no* point of reference."

"Beg your pardon?" Rook said. "Everyone on this deck knows that the thrust to weight variable—"

"Look, it's not quite as fast as the VF-97 Vision," she explained. "And it's not nearly as maneuverable as the VF-95 Valkyrie."

"From what we hear," Leers added with a huff. He wagged a couple of fingers Rook's way and tapped him on the shoulder. "But you're the expert on that machine."

"Everything that I've told you about the Valkyrie is true—you can read the reports yourself if you don't—"

"*Anyway*, it's actually heavier than a VF-87 Vampire, if you can believe that," Slayton continued forcibly. "So when you go on a bombing run in the Vagrant—say your target is a refinery on some oxygen rich planet—you can actually stay in your dive a few seconds longer than you could in a Vampire . . . I mean, the Vagrant is crazy that way. So I ended up ass over teakettle, diving right smack into the enveloping explosion—shrapnel's clanging off the canopy. Ah, shite, I thought I was going to—"

"Must've been terrible. . ."

"That's not all," Slayton continued. "There are times when you're flying tight with your wingmates when you hear, *'break, break, break!'* So you break hard—you don't even think about it. You pull the stick back, but fucking hell, you're still going straight."

"Yeah, it's some machine," Leers added drily.

"Can't be as bad as that," Rook countered.

"But it is," Slayton insisted. "And making matters worse, in between missions, we get to maintain our proficiency and training by flying in a fucking asteroid system."

"So?"

"When was the last time you trained in an asteroid system, my friend?" Leers inquired.

"Well, eh, we try to avoid them," the cheetah answered. "Seems to reflect a higher degree of intelligence to do so."

"Must be nice."

"We can't avoid them," Leers said.

"Look you two, it's not as if I've never flown or engaged an enemy from within an asteroid belt—I just try to lead the fight *away* from such navigational hazards. Besides, asteroid belts are about as common as—"

"Who said anything about an asteroid belt?" Slayton asked sarcastically. "Dannen and I fly and train within an asteroid *system*—an entire system of asteroids, mate. Do you understand? That's where Omega Command is, that's what it is. One asteroid patrol after another—no avoiding it."

Rook only succeeded in hiding his horror for a moment. "Are you saying that your entire command has to fly in that mess?"

"Yeah," Leers answered for Slayton. "Fighters, bombers, shuttles, everybody. . ."

"All except the cargo jocks and jockettes," Slayton added. "They get to use our base's shield corridor."

"I beg your pardon?"

"We have a huge deflector array," she answered, looking at Rook as if he'd suddenly grown a third eye. "It can project a magnitude seven deflector corridor from our asteroid base to just about any area within the blue zone of the asteroid system."

"Actually, it can produce a magnitude nine particle shield well into the green zone," Leers interjected, "a distance covering more than 200 million kilometers, at least."

"At least?" Rook snorted. "Am I supposed to be impressed?"

"Does November Command have one?" Slayton asked.

"No. But we don't need one either, Love."

"Which brings us back to my original point," Slayton said. "Your November Command is three to four times bigger than Omega Command; you have more than four times the machines and you have *newer* machines, while we get *hand-me-down* pieces of shite. Shite that we have to fly through a bloody asteroid system just to maintain proficiency. Shite that we have to take into combat lightyears away from any allied star system just so we bomb some 'suspected' ammo dump or detonate yet another Pulsarian refinery."

"Sounds like both you *lot* are blaming me for your assignment to this back-water Omega Command," Rook said defensively. "I had nothing to do with that."

"We're not blaming you," Leers said, "but it'd be nice to—"

"Omega Command sounds rather ominous," Rook pressed on, "but it's too small and too remote to be an actual command base by any stretch of the imagination, to be painfully honest. Besides, you all aren't on call to protect a populated star system—"

"Oh, but we do get called out to protect 'populated' systems all the time—star systems dozens of lightyears away," Slayton countered. "And we do it in a shite-box machine that's designed to carry out a vast array of missions, but it just can't do any of them well enough to qualify for shite."

"What are you talking about?"

"The VF-94 isn't specialized in any one area," Leers said. "Unlike the VF-95 that you fly—now that's a space superiority fighter first and foremost."

"But we can use it to bomb targets too," Rook said, "in a pinch. Or we can hit orbital weapons platforms from stand-off, target lock-down distances."

"But the Valkyrie is a knife-fighter first and foremost, correct?" Leers pressed.

"The Valkyrie *is* what the Vagrant is *not*." Rook whistled sharply through his teeth. "Even the name, Vagrant, sounds rather, shall we say . . . ghetto?"

"Oh, Rook, for fuck's sake, just admit that you guys get treated like royalty in November Command while we get to eat shite and have to love it."

"She's right."

"I'm not the minister of defense or the comptroller for weapons acquisitions—you two need to learn to fly and fight in the machines that you're given and enough with whining."

"Universe, you sound like a colonel that I know," Leers huffed.

"Are you referring to 'Buckethead' or 'Muffintop'?" Slayton asked.

"'Buckethead Dargoinne."

"Nice."

"What are you two going on about?" Rook asked.

"You'll find out," Leers answered. "Much to your disgust."

"I can hardly wait."

"You know, we've been going back and forth about this, but we're forgetting one thing," Leers said. "N'ckshell has a point and a valid one. It's not about the machines that we have the luxury—or curse—to fly. It's about us, this is about pilots. There is no comparison between our training and tactics and the typical Pug. Pug pilots ain't the best trained. They're too aggressive and what's worse, they don't know their machines."

"For sure," noted Slayton.

"A few months ago," Leers continued, "before we set out for these missions; N'ckshell and I were assigned to escort a couple bombers to smash a Pulsarian high-yield, multi-phased, sub-space communications beacon, when we get jumped by a flight of Pug fighters—I mean the newer Spark Racers, the XXR models. And it was just the two of us—and the two bombers against four XXRs. Not a second after N'ckshell calls 'tally-ho', we break. And I'm chasing down an XXR—he's maybe fifty kilometers in front of me when the threat warning receiver picked up another Spark Racer slicing down on my six o'clock position . . . And my weapons officer in the backseat is just screaming about this new threat—then she decides to get sick."

"Ralphing Rita?" Slayton queried.

"Yeah," Leers answered. "Not my favorite WSO."

"Are you two serious," Rook asked. "This sounds like part of your last story."

"It ain't," Leers said. "So don't worry. So I cook off two port side Shards and kill the Spark Racer in front of me. But I still have one on my tail and I'm reversing like a psycho to lose this rat Pug—but I can't. He's fifty kilometers behind me, I reverse, and we're literally canopy to canopy with only two kilometers of separation. And I'm thinking, *crap, this ain't good*, so I break into his path, but he reverses and he's behind me again. Meanwhile, the bombers are blowing the hell out of that communications array, so they were fine. But I can't get rid of this Pug bastard because I'm in a Vagrant and the damn machine won't let me. Then before I know it, a *second* XXR is on my tail trying to kill me."

"Two," Rook interrupted. "No way you could've survived that."

"I mean, I'm chaffing, flaring—shutting down my deflectors, doing everything I can to keep me and my WSO alive."

"Well?" asked Rook, "were you killed?"

"I killed both of them, it wasn't even close," Slayton said with a flourish.

"They were so focused on killing Dannen, that they didn't even see me."

"Great pick-up, Stinger," Leers admitted. "I thought I was gonna start ralphing like Rita."

"Saved your ass," Slayton sang. "And that has to be a record. I bagged three Pugs literally within seconds of each other."

"Let's not get carried away," Leers said. "I was thankful, Rita was thankful. But my cockpit smelled like a horrifying nightmare. Needless to say, the next mission I fly, I won't have ole Rita in the backseat." The three of them shared in a bit of laughter when Leers added. "But it proves what I've been saying for the better part of a year now to anyone who'll listen to me. Training and teamwork will beat better equipment and naked aggression every time."

"Every time," Slayton said. "Still be nice though, if *everyone* had machines that could match the enemy's. Not just November Command."

"Back to that, are we?" Rook hissed.

"You know what I mean."

"Get a transfer to November Command," Rook said. "We'd welcome your services."

"Thanks for your confidence," Slayton said. "But all indications point to our timely arrival to Omega Command. We have a more urgent need. Besides which, Dannen's girlfriend won't let him—"

"N'ckshell, please!"

"You have a girlfriend, friend Dannen," Rook chirped, then chittered, "this sounds like a topic I'd like to discuss. Tell me about her."

"No, let's not."

"She a bomber pilot," Slayton said.

Leers just glared at her.

"The Phantasm?"

"No, the Poltergeist," Slayton said. "You should see her ass, Rook. Even through her uniform—"

"Enough," Leers warned.

"You must be really smitten by her to protect her so fiercely," Rook said. "Let's hear more."

Slayton opened her mouth, looked at Leers then remained silent.

"Go ahead," Leers said. "You seem to like her as much as I do."

"She's from Desdemona," Slayton said. "She's a lieutenant and her name is Bags—"

"Mags," Leers corrected. "I call her Mags. It's short for—"

"Maggie," Rook guessed.

"No, Maiko," Leers said. "Her name is Maiko Arashi Greysen. I just call her Mags."

The *Mekadore Traveler* suddenly lurched as it began to slow. The colorful mosaic through the elongated viewers altered somewhat.

"Thank God," Leers muttered.

"Ah, we're making normal space reentry," Rook said, rubbing his hands together.

The Rhoderium Crab lurched again. This time the strain continued unabated. The three of them were pressed gently against their acceleration straps. None of them fought the sensation. There was no need to. In a matter of seconds, it would all be over. Leers listened to the inter-ship speakers as Jasmine's voice ordered full power on the braking thrusters; Nancy started her own count-down at T-minus ten seconds. At seven seconds, Draystar ordered reversing thrusters. He then ordered cut power to the Hyperdrives—the speed brakes were extended, causing the warship to buck violently under the strain. At three seconds, the reversing brakes went to fifty-percent military power . . . the Rhoderium Crab lurched even more, the colorful mosaic was obscured briefly then dazzled into more coherent points of light . . . Leers caught a brief glimpse of a large brownish, gray mass set against the back drop of stars speeding toward them at a frightening rate. It was the Asteroid System as big as any star system and it seemed to be racing right for them! Soon it filled the heavens . . . the sub-light engines came on line, shields were energized. Proximity alarms bellowed urgently, followed by the ear-splitting howl of the hostile fire warning alarms.

"What the hell—" Leers shouted, barely heard over the alarms. "Not again, I don't believe this."

"Don't believe what," Rook shouted back.

"It feels like we're coming apart," Slayton yelled.

Through the forward viewer, a vast leviathan filled the monitor. A damp chill raced down Leers' spine as he immediately recognized the outlines of the Pulsarian Advancer. Energy bolts rained down to greet them.

CHAPTER XIII
FIRE WAVE

THE *Mekadore Traveler* burned out of Hyperspace into tidal waves of annihilation—destructive energy searing the fabric of normal space. Explosive carnage raged along the deflector shields of the Rhoderium Crab as it slowed to sub-light. Staccato energy bolts, arcs of multi-hued fury, sought desperately to end the Rhoderium Crab's flight. On the flight deck, Jasmine cursed, eyes tracking the cascading deluge of data to her left and right, and cursed again. In a flash she was certain that the universe was going to explode around her and there wasn't a thing in hell that could prevent it. Alarms wailed within her battlehelm's audio systems, alarms sounded on her instrument panel, warnings flashed their urgent message on the monitors in front of her. Nancy, the flight computer, was also vying for attention while Draystar—his armored helm rotated toward her—she couldn't hear a damned word he was saying. . . . The deck shuddered, main lighting winked on and off.

Reflexively Jasmine's left thumb tabbed the alarms off. Crimson light washed over the flight deck. An invisible fist sledgehammered into the *Mekadore Traveler* throwing both her and Draystar against their harnesses.

"What?"

Draystar said, "I said 'now I know why the asteroid base wasn't responding to our calls while we were in Hyperspace'."

Another shutter followed by more rattling.

"We're taking heavy fire," Jasmine wailed.

"No shit—do you think?" Draystar shot back.

"Must be an entire Pulsarian taskforce out there—if not two," Jasmine opined. "Nancy, what are we up against? What's out there?"

The forward monitor was awash in jamming noise. An image would solidify for an instant, revealing the billions of stars in the galaxy, then would again disappear under a wave of noise.

"Standby, one," the computer said coolly. "I will have coherent, structured scanner returns in fifteen seconds."

"Shields are holding," Draystar declared.

"Good," Jasmine noted. She knew that it wouldn't make a difference once the Pulsarians quit flinging cheap lasers at them and decided to hit them with heavier warheads. And it had to be the Pulsarians—Federation doctrine forbade firing upon a starship during re-entry without identifying it first. Then again, there have been rare instances of Delrel commanders behaving exactly like the enemy was behaving now. For enemy forces waiting in normal space held a significant advantage over forces making the normal space re-entry transition. When starships decelerated and made re-entry, the effects on normal space were about as subtle as a stun grenade exploding next to your ear. The release of energy was enormous—instruments millions of kilometers away would spike suddenly—then just like that, the readings would disappear. By that time you were certainly guaranteed a hot reception.

There were ways, of course, to thwart re-entry detection, or at the very least disguise the magnitude of the boom. But that would entail knowing that the enemy was present in the exact same sector of space where you were executing your deceleration from Hyperspace—neither Draystar nor Jasmine had any notion that there were Pulsarians within the Omega Asteroid System.

Jasmine knew that the explosions rocking the ship would soon become more devastating than astonishing. Being onboard a Rhoderium Crab eased her concerns, somewhat. Having shielding in-place eased them more. To have someone actually open on you the moment you crossed over the verge was unsettling no matter how prepared you were for the possibility.

"Nancy, how about that threat assessment?" Draystar barked.

"Still working."

"Nancy, you're gonna have to work faster." Draystar studied his Warp re-entry authenticators, verifying the warship's course and speed. One of the most rudimentary tasks all pilots had to perform was checking their position and comparing that information against the starchart and the stellar chronometer. A monumental waste of time on a Rhoderium Crab, but it kept Draystar from harping on Nancy every two seconds.

Another burst rattled the *Mekadore Traveler.*

"Shields holding," Jasmine read the indications from Draystar's auxiliary, all in an effort to keep her commander calm. "No problem, no problem." Not that Draystar ever lost it, but he had a knack for barking and making unnecessary demands when he felt things were deteriorating, or weren't moving fast enough. Jasmine didn't relish having to pilot the ship while keeping her partner's emotions on an even keel. For it all hinged on Draystar. He could get them through daunting, seemingly hopeless situations when training demanded retreat. Likewise, he could make a simple missile run a labor too great to tolerate if things didn't 'appear' to be going just the way he thought they should.

Draystar slammed a metallic fist against the console. "Goddamnit, Nancy, what's taking so long?"

Jasmine bit her tongue. Fifteen seconds hadn't even passed yet and Draystar was already starting to—All he had to do was wait. The Pulsarians were strong, dangerous adversaries, but the *Mekadore Traveler* could deal with them on more or less equal terms. They had the firepower, the speed, and maneuverability, and the protection system of shields and screens.

Deflector shields could be 'erected' ten meters away, a hundred meters, or even several kilometers away and acted as an invisible wall in which to protect the subject vessel from outside attack. Setting up shields ten to fifty meters was the standard operating procedure during a battle. Highly versatile, shields could be 'rigged' at a variety of settings, and thus afford protection from a variety of weapons. They could be specified to hold off high-explosive weapons, set to ward off penetration weapons, re-configured again to hold of fragmentation or heavy concussive weapon effects. There was no single best shield setting that could protect against them all because laser and energy warheads simply behaved differently on contact with different deflector barriers. The list of shields and they're various functions was almost as long as the list of weapons which could be employed against them; this Jasmine was acutely aware of—as well as the knowledge that defensive systems always seemed to lag behind weapons.

A close partner of the deflector shield was the deflector screen. Often confused as being the same by noncombatants—the role of the screen, however, was to act as a secondary piece of armor. Screens were highly effective in protecting the target vessel against near-explosive damage, but did little against direct hits. Screens acted as insurance should a weapon breach the outer shield; it would try to bleed more energy from the weapon before it impacted the armor of a vessel. Like shields, screens could be angled to protect different areas of the ship at varying power levels and settings; screens burned considerably less power than shields. True, they didn't offer the same level of protection, but any pilot would rather fly into combat with them than without them.

Draystar provided more power to the deflector screens; he didn't know why, reflex found his fingers hitting switches. While he may not have known who was firing at them, or specifically, what type of weapons were being fired, he knew that they were impacting the starboard, lower quadrant shields—none of the energy had made contact with the inner screens as of yet. The shields weren't taking direct hits; these were more like glancing blows—but they sure as hell felt like direct hits. The weapons were low- to medium-yield munitions. If one of them got through it wouldn't destroy the *Mekadore Traveler*, but it could go a long way towards crippling the ship.

Meanwhile Jasmine too, was acting on reflex, and had begun bringing the warship's weapons on-line. A quick glance at Draystar's boards told her where the majority of the fire was coming from. She activated the weapons on that section of the ship. At her disposal were the two omni-directional Pinser guns on the right claw, three starboard low-yield omni-directional Legion guns, and two forward medium-yield multi-lateral guns; she took a second to put two of the four main forward batteries on stand-by. That left more than sixty percent of the *Mekadore Traveler*'s weapon ports deactivated . . . for now. If the threat outside proved to be a serious one, she could go to immediate stand-by on any of the remaining weapons, then go to full power in a matter of seconds thereafter. That is, if Draystar traded deflector power for weapons power. Which he'd probably do once he got the threat assessment from Nancy.

With the weapon ports ready, Jasmine called up a list of weapon packages she could hurl at the Pulsarians. At the top of the list was a laser called the Shard, a powerful weapon that could tackle a wide variety of targets that weighed anywhere from 5,000 to 60,000 metric tons, from ranges of a hundred meters to distances of up to 25,000 kilometers and beyond. Versatile, yes, but up against a target the size of an Advancer, utterly useless. Unless the Shard was being solely utilized to punch holes through Advancer shielding and screens, a duty it was more than apt to perform, allowing her to use heavier weapons to do the serious damage; weapons like the Harpoon or the Skean. The Harpoon was an energy warhead capable of producing one stardamm of explosive force, equal to about ten-thousand kilograms of high explosive—it didn't tackle targets, it destroyed them. A truly destructive weapon against armor, but it tended to bounce off the flimsiest of shielding; which was why it needed help from the Shard. Precisely the reason why these weapons were used in tandem. The Skean, on the other hand, could burn its way through most shielding (depending on range and aspect angle) and could shred armor. Instead of exploding, the Skean would instead bore through to rupture fuel cells, control systems, or kill personnel. Employing eight Shards and three Harpoons netted the same results as one Skean, but only required 20% of the power. This was the choice—or dilemma—of modern warfare; which weapons to use, in which order to employ them and how best to use them. Like the deflector issue, some worked better than others, some robbed more power than others, some seemed totally useless while others seemed capable of cracking open planets. Again, it depended on the targets, range, and how much power you were willing to spend to destroy it.

The weapons at Jasmine's disposal didn't limit her to the just the Shard, the Harpoon, or the Skean. They were just at the top of her list and the most commonly used. She could also employ the Mace, a heavy bombardment weapon with enough power to flatten cities; the Diamond that produced a heavy ion discharge to convert enemy starship control systems into useless piles of junk; the Halberd, a long-range, medium- to heavy-yield, multi-purpose bludgeoning weapon. The list was as long as were the recommended targets. Then there were the different classes, or phases within the weapons themselves, such as the Shard phase one, phase two, and so on—another list of potential targets until it oftentimes led to 'paralysis by over-analysis.' Something starship captains couldn't allow themselves to slip into when all it took was for an enemy to fire a single ray of light to utterly destroy you. Jasmine, however didn't consider herself to be an ordinary starship captain. She could do more things, execute more maneuvers than most captains ever dreamed possible.

Suddenly the harsh noise on the forward monitor disappeared to reveal the brilliant starfield. The image died, awash in noise again, re-solidified for an instant to be replaced by a tactical plot of their current position and sector.

"Preliminary indications put us at the outer perimeter of a Pulsarian taskforce," Nancy stated even as Draystar and Jasmine could read the data on the monitor before them. "They have us on their space-track scanners only. No weapons control scanners as yet. Their sensor probes are just now coming on-line."

"They're firing blindly at our Warp re-entry signal and nothing more," Jasmine said. "Once their panic subsides at our unauthorized arrival, once they have us identified as Gladatraus, they'll go to their heavier weapons."

"Not going to let that happen, not today," Draystar muttered. "Nancy, plot a course through the asteroid system and relay all data to Jasmine so that we can get there while not leading them to the—"

A violent burst of energy knocked Draystar forward savagely. *What the hell was that? Were the Pulsarian devils already throwing heavy munitions their way?*

"Disregard last, Nancy," Draystar barked. That last blast had caused him to bite his tongue. Felt like he had bitten right through the damn thing. Tasting blood he said, "Let's tell these bastards who we are and show them what we're capable of."

"I don't know Draystar; are you sure we shouldn't just get to the base and—"

"I'm getting goddamned sick of turning our backs to the enemy," Draystar said, cutting Jasmine off. "Every time we get a chance to engage them we run. That's all we ever do. Run."

"I know but—" She never got a chance to finish before an explosion cut her off.

"No, damn you, we fight." Draystar shook his fist at her. "Today we fight."

Meanwhile Nancy was busily reading the target list of the task force they were racing toward.

"Are you with me?" Draystar asked his pilot.

"You know I am." *I have my reservations, but I'm not going to launch a formal protest now*, Jasmine thought.

"That's your cue Nancy, bring all primary battle systems to full power," Draystar ordered. There was no other way to announce his intentions to the Pulsarians than to light up all of the *Mekadore Traveler's* systems. In seconds the enemy would get good readings; once that happened, once the inevitable panic started to run through their ranks, Jasmine would light them up.

Jasmine activated her weapons and control monitor. She swallowed, feeling the pit of her stomach rage with fire then freeze into a blizzard almost simultaneously. *Universe, we're actually going to tackle a task force, actually gonna dive in and take those Pugs out. When was the last time we'd ever done anything like this? Three years ago? Seven. How about never.* Facing three or four Battlecruiser Advancers was one thing. A task force had enough firepower to destroy an entire star system. *Universe. More than forty Advancers against one Gladatraus Rhoderium Crab.* She glanced at the monitor again. Okay, forty-one Advancers to be painfully precise. From the look of them, this had to be an invasion type task force or a smallish assault force. She knew this because there was a lack of Carrier Advancers in the formation and that was disappointing. You take out a Carrier Advancer or two and you also take some of the most highly trained professionals in the Pulsarian fleet, their pilots.

****

Admiral Steiner Merwinette kicked the human thrall from his bed as the general alarm sounded throughout his Dreadnought Destroyer Advancer *P'kaflam*. She would have protested, but remembered he had the power to vent her into vacuum if she displeased him, like he'd done with so many others. Merwinette rushed naked to the primary communit. The monitor remained blank, he communicated via voice-link only.

"Report," he barked.

"We've identified a Gladatraus Warcruiser entering our sector in zone twelve," the officer of the bridge reported excitedly.

So?

As if sensing Merwinette's growing inclemency, the bridge officer quickly added, "it has already attacked and put out of action two Destroyer Advancers on the outer marker of the perimeter. Captain Kra Votogon reported contact—"

"What the hell did you just say?"

"Captain Votogon reported contact with the Gladatraus nearly two minutes ago and has—"

"Before that," Merwinette shrieked.

"Two Destroyer Advancers have been put out of action . . ."

"Maintain current operational status until I reach the Combat Control Deck," Merwinette said plainly, feeling his pulse rate slow. "Do not take any action whatsoever unless I give the order."

"Understood, Admiral."

Merwinette began dressing himself, his thoughts hinging on the upcoming fight with the Alliance's most deadly of warriors. So, they've come to fight—time to show my true mettle after so long a holiday. He glanced behind him. The human female of whom he had treated so roughly seconds ago rejoined her sisters on the mammoth bed. Merwinette paused, his gaze icy . . . no longer aware of the slaves or of the pleasure they had given him . . . he saw through them, to the raging energies of battle, to his fate. "Time to kill the enemies of the empire," he simply said.

****

Jasmine put the Rhoderium Crab in a tight spiral away from the two burning Destroyer Advancers. The surface of the warship registered gravitational forces pushing slightly beyond 20G's, however, within the steeled frame of the *Mekadore Traveler* those forces felt no greater than 2G's. Jasmine felt no comfort in the relative lack of sensation, didn't pay attention to it. It meant to her was that she was putting the *Mekadore Traveler* through maneuvers the lumbering Advancers couldn't follow, that their weapons would have a difficult time, at best, to track. So much the better since they weren't about to get smoked just seconds into the engagement. Several minutes from now who knew what the outcome would be.

"Switching shield configuration, now," Draystar announced in the seat left of her. "The Pulsarians aren't shooting anywhere near us." The Rhoderium Crab rattled as if to disagree. *You see, when you attack these cowards they don't know how to react. Show a bold front and they forget how to use their weapons.* "Looks like their point-defense is still active. Come around on a flak suppression run then finish them, Jasmine."

"Copy that," Jasmine replied. She released her grip on the steering yoke long enough to flex her fingers and give her knuckles and wrists a good cracking. *Finish them?* She thought. *They're already burning . . . half their crews are probably dead. There's really no need to go back and destroy them utterly. If you want to punish them so badly Draystar, just let the bastards burn.* "Coming around."

She pushed the throttle forward slightly. The burning hulks were a mere five thousand kilometers in front of them now. She could see them clearly on the forward monitor, crackling, spewing flame, escape pods launching—

not many of them though. If those destroyers went now, the Pulsarians in those pods would be dry-roasted. Probably what Draystar wanted all along.

"More sporadic fire," Draystar said. "Nothing to worry about."

Jasmine didn't comment. She focused on the tactical plot, her weapons list and her current configuration for attack. The Advancers were just sitting there, vainly trying to defend themselves. She'd put weapons into these monsters before, but somehow these two just seemed pitiful.

She squeezed the firing stud on her control yoke. Outside, twelve Shards raced away from each of the four main forward batteries of the *Mekadore Traveler.* Without shielding or defensive screens to protect them, the supercharged hybrid lasers destroyed gun-mounts, sensor domes, and punched holes in the superstructures, thus weakening the Pulsarian warships further.

Without hesitating she followed up by putting ten Harpoons into both targets each and finished them with a pair of Maces each. Jasmine winced as the heavy energy weapons raced away from the Rhoderium Crab. A single Mace each should've done the job, two seemed like overkill. She didn't like wasting munitions. You destroyed your enemy with the least amount of effort and energy as possible. But she watched the plot as the four warheads raced away. It was over in less than a second. There was a blinding flash, two blinding flashes really, but they were timed so closely together that her Dracterian's mind couldn't track the subtlety of it. She could clearly see the magnitude as both Advancers blew apart in a wash of angry yellow light.

"Confirm the destruction of two Destroyer Advancers," the flight computer, Nancy stated.

"Copy that," Jasmine noted, busily cutting at the controls and bringing the Rhoderium Crab around toward their next targets which were . . .

"Tracking two more Destroyer Advancers on an intercept course, bearing two-three-niner-point-one," Nancy said.

"Concur," said Draystar. "Matching shield angle to target bearing. Jasmine, they're yours."

"Roger."

"Wildcard, wildcard, wildcard—" Nancy warned.

"Where are they," Draystar barked, "how many do you see?"

"Battlecruiser Advancers entering the area," Nancy warned. "On a direct intercept course, flanking the destroyers."

"Confirmed," Draystar said. It was no easy feat to snuff out two Destroyer Advancers—although with a Gladatraus Rhoderium Crab, they made it appear so. Battlecruiser Advancers were a beast of a different sort. Draystar couldn't remember the last time he'd tangled with the mainstay of the Imperial Armada. But he knew, as any damned fool would tell him, that an encounter with these killers was an encounter best to be avoided. Within these Advancers came the engines for both speed and maneuverability, city-wrecking firepower from its guns, and a defensive capability that made it a tactician's worst nightmare. Once you spotted the dreaded Battlecruiser Advancer, you lit your burners and ran. Structurally speaking these Advancers had no weaknesses. However, Draystar knew of one: the Pulsarians within the hull. They'd be just as over-confident and over-zealous as the now dead crews on the first two Destroyer Advancers.

Draystar regarded the tacplot for a second. It'd be tempting to go after the battlecruisers first and ignore the smaller, weaker destroyers. But he wasn't dumb enough to allow Jasmine to fly them within the firing envelopes of four Advancers at once. No, he had to play it safe, but aggressive. Hit the destroyers, smoke 'em, then go after the battlecruisers. Once that was done look for more targets to burn.

Again the tacplot told him that target designation one was destroyed. Target designation two (the two Narta class Destroyer Advancers) was thirty-thousand kilometers downrange and moving in; target designation three (the two Drocokal class Battlecruiser Advancers) was also closing fast, running a parallel course, fifteen-hundred kilometers off the port beam of target designation two and thirty-three thousand kilometers downrange.

"Jasmine, take target designation two," Draystar ordered. "Stay away from the battlecruisers for now."

She merely nodded and steered the Rhoderium Crab to the right of the Destroyer Advancers. She wasn't about to fly between them and it seemed that Draystar was thinking the same thing.

"Why the hell aren't they firing at us?" Draystar wondered out loud. "They have us within range."

"They sense a trap," Jasmine said briskly. "Two destroyers have already been killed in a matter of seconds . . . what would you do?"

Get a firm picture of what I'm up against, then go all out to destroy it, Draystar was thinking.

"Exactly," said Jasmine, as if reading his mind. After flying together for so many years, sometimes she knew what he was thinking before he did.

"Registering phased-two target track scans from the lead Advancer in target designation two," Nancy informed them. "Signal's clear, standing-by for incoming fire."

I see it, Draystar didn't say. Of course he could throw out jamming emissions from the Rhoderium Crab; temporally blind them in an effort to delay their firing cues and thus save his shields and screens a little while longer. *But why do that—besides it making perfect sense. Let the Pulsarian bastards see exactly what they were up against before they died.*

"Shields are going up on both Destroyer Advancers," Nancy noted further. "Onthon type. No readings on the Battlecruiser Advancers in target designation three at this time."

Onthon class shields only meant that they would have to fly closer to their targets before weapons release. A package of Skeans and Harpoons could be released now, but that'd do nothing more than provide them with an extravagant light-show and not much in the direction of two dead targets. If it hadn't been for the presence of the nearby Battlecruiser Advancers (or the proximity of the rest of the taskforce for that matter) they could hold their position and trade blows with the destroyers for hours before the Onthon shields failed and the Crab's weapons made killing blows against their hulls. And the reverse effect could be made true if the destroyers decided to trade blows with a relatively stationary Gladatraus warship. Scenarios only fools would entertain. Jasmine and Draystar were just as determined to destroy their enemy as their enemy was as determined to destroy them. The captains on the destroyers knew that the Rhoderium Crab would have to move in close to get good hits against them and in doing so would fly within their point-defense systems. The barrage that would follow would be of such lethal intensity that the Gladatraus would have to break-off or risk serious damage to themselves, by that time the battlecruisers would have them in range.

Jasmine had barely a second to analyze this before she took action. The Pulsarians, everywhere, no matter what sector of the galaxy you were in, no matter what taskforce you were against, or even the Pulsarian captain on the bridge—were predictable.

She increased speed, cut power by fifteen percent, sheared to the left, fluttered the throttle, reversed and dove for the destroyers again, bringing her speed up and readied her weapons.

Ten Shards burned into the Onthon shielding of the closest Advancer followed by a pair of Harpoons. The resulting explosions against the Advancer's hull must've sent its captain into a state of paralyzed shock. No point-defense weaponry greeted the agile Rhoderium Crab.

Six more Shards lacerated the shielding to allow more Harpoons to pound the hull and into the decks below. Six tenths of a second later four Skeans plunged deeper into the hemorrhaging Advancer. It wouldn't be long now. But Jasmine didn't wait. She drove the ship a mere hundred meters above the Advancer's inferno engulfed hull, through evaporating shields and targeted the second Advancer. The results were just as spectacular as with the first destroyer. Both Advancers were now drifting aimlessly through the void, their hulls breached, eruptions of flame spewing from the stricken vessels. Neither Advancer had fired a shot in its defense; Jasmine's attack had been so lethal, so swift.

The Battlecruiser Advancers moved into position.

Jasmine caught her breath. She could see them plainly on the main viewer. *They're expecting me to attack*, she thought, *to fly right in there, bold and stupid.* She reversed course and headed back for the burning Destroyer Advancers. The battlecruisers followed, slowly, rays of superheated energy lacing from them. The Rhoderium Crab lurched from the near misses. Jasmine groaned, picked a weapons package with the fingers of her right hand and turned the warship around with her left to face the battlecruisers once again. Her jaw tightened, cold shivers spread from her sternum to her fingertips. Every impulse told her not to face these steely leviathans, to alter her ship's angle of attack and make a run for it. That was the sensible thing to do. However, because she was in a Rhoderium Crab, the Gladatraus thing to do would be to press the fight, right now, cold and without hesitation. Launch a blow-through attack and put enough distance between them and her ship before they could prime themselves for a counter-offensive. Yes, that's what the Gladatraus had been trained to do, and probably what those Pulsarian captains were waiting for. Not today. No blow-through attacks, no raking, no running.

Explosive energy rattled the Rhoderium Crab; the Pulsarians were throwing enough energy at them to flatten a city every three point five seconds—Jasmine had the readings right in front of her. In seventeen-point-two seconds the shields, at their current setting would buckle, the screens would follow . . .

Jasmine jinked the *Mekadore Traveler* left and right, pitched up and down, increased throttle, decreased throttle. Taking action now—not waiting for the damned defensive systems to fail, then trying to figure out a way to stay alive—*Universe, don't make it easy for the Pulsarians.* Within seconds the subtle inputs put her in directly in line with the damaged and burning destroyers and the fast moving battlecruisers. She smiled grimly at the results.

Several of the incoming laser and energy beams missed them completely and slammed into the hulls of the destroyers. One of the destroyers pitched forward violently—nearly a hundred-thousand metric tons of titanium, rharerium, steel, glastisoid, carbon composites, several million kilometers of conduit, high-density networking cells, and laser optics; all of that and a substantially bit more, was consumed in a cloud of vapor several kilometers long. More than three thousand Pulsarians obliterated by the batteries of the Battlecruiser Advancers.

The incoming fire from the Battlecruiser Advancers diminished, but it still came. Seventeen point two seconds to shield failure turned to forty-five seconds, then ninety seconds, then—it didn't matter anymore. Jasmine brought the crab forward to press the attack against the stunned Pulsarians onboard the Battlecruiser Advancers. She primed the four aft batteries. She had only seconds now. Timing was crucial. She had planned to salvo the aft batteries and finish the remaining destroyer behind her before tackling the battlecruisers but stopped short when she heard Nancy say:

"Registering new targets now, entering our threat-sphere. Target designation-four is composed of two Frigate Advancers and one Lightcarrier Advancer."

"A carrier?" Draystar looked at his readings. Sure enough, there it was, flanked by the two frigates.

"Heavy jamming emanating from target designation four."

"Is the carrier launching Spark Racers?"

"Cannot confirm at this time."

"What the hell can you confirm?"

"Two Frigate Advancers bearing—"

"Damnit, Nancy, I need—"

"Draystar!" Jasmine snarled, "I'm trying to concentrate." Ignoring any reaction she might've gotten from Draystar, Jasmine quickly released a Mace warhead at the Destroyer Advancer behind her. Readings indicated that it had just thrown up an auxiliary shield to protect itself, to buy time while the damage control teams worked to put the fires out and the engineers worked to bring the engines back on-line. At least, that's what Jasmine had reasoned they were doing. Wasted effort. Valiant but wasted. The single Mace smashed through the hastily erected shield and exploded against the hull. Its conflagration was just as spectacular as its partner's. Both Advancers in target designation two were now destroyed. Now Jasmine refocused on the battlecruisers and the new threat looming on the horizon—and do it without distractions.

She quickly re-routed power to the forward batteries—it only took half a second to release four Maces at battlecruiser 'alpha' and six toward battlecruiser 'beta'. The resulting explosions were stupendous, each many times the size of the Advancers Jasmine had targeted. The battlecruiser were well protected and emerged on the other side of the hell-storm rattled but un-bruised.

Meanwhile, Draystar, unfazed by Jasmine's rebuke and Nancy's continued lagging, sent jamming energy toward the Battlecruiser Advancers. Both were now ten thousand kilometers downrange, their space-track scanners useless. Their weapons-control radars were far from ineffectual. Even with the jamming in play, the Pulsarians could approximate the location of the Rhoderium Crab, but they still couldn't get a firm lock-on. The jamming wasn't absolute protection from weapons fire. They worked for a time, but then you'd better have a backup plan. Again, as far as target-lock went, the Pulsarians would have them for about a millisecond—no more than a thousandth of a second, Draystar was certain—before they'd lose acquisition. He had the readings vividly displayed in front of him. What the Pulsarians needed was a full second and they'd have the Gladatraus absorbing direct-hits. Draystar's function was to keep that from happening though. A task made incredibly easy since the Advancers were many times the size of the Rhoderium Crab. There was the rub for the Pulsarians. They had the unenviable task of trying to track something that equaled their deflector technology, did well with firepower and weapons employment, but was so damned small, fast, and incredibly agile—more than any fighter they would likely face. Draystar sent more jamming waves towards the Pulsarians and kept an eye on the threat board.

"Nancy, I need a dedicated two second burst toward target designation four," Draystar ordered. "Let them know where we are."

"Do you want me to engage them after I'm finished with the battlecruisers?" Jasmine asked.

"High-aspect blow-through only—this is taking too long. I want to locate the flagship of this taskforce with our heavy weapons package hot."

"Roger that," Jasmine said. They'd be facing a Dreadnought Destroyer Advancer, a killer that was the equal of five Battlecruiser Advancers—she hadn't forgotten about the two giving her fits right now. Well, she'd toyed with them long enough . . .

****

Dannen Leers couldn't help but grip the armrests on the recliner as the battle unfolded before him and his friends on the observation deck. What he saw went beyond anything in warfare he'd ever witnessed before. He'd been in one versus one 'knife-fights' with Slave Racers at speeds in excess of 87,000kpx, in two versus two fights against the newer generation of Spark Racers in the low to mid-orbits of enemy-held planets, escorted bombers on high-speed raids, strafed Straaka on the ground—he'd seen a lot, had been through his fair share of blistering space-combat, but nothing prepared him for what the *Mekadore Traveler* was doing to this Pulsarian taskforce. He could tell from the awed astonishment marking the faces of his friends, that they too were sharing his feelings.

On the three displays were target information, interception data, weapons being employed by the Pulsarians, the deflectors in-place to thwart those weapons, variable angles-of-attack, weapons aspect ratios, jamming frequencies, G-loads, structural integrity—Universe, every bit of information you needed for a fight was right there in a seamless, coherent package. The heads-up display on his trusty VF-94 Vagrant was nowhere near as explicit. It gave him target data, threat warnings, what weapons he had armed, how many G's he was pulling, firing cues—but certainly not what the Pulsarians were using against him. Not what deflectors they had in place, not how fast they were going, and certainly nothing on the status of the battle. These Gladatraus Guardians had everything, everything displayed for them . . . how could they lose a fight?

Leers flinched at the sight of a Battlecruiser Advancer icon winking from green to blue, to red, then winking off completely. The words 'target designation three-alpha destroyed' flashed before him. Just like that . . . Mere seconds to destroy one of the widely deployed warships of the Imperial Armada. If he were lucky—extremely lucky—it would take him leading two squadrons of VF-94 Vagrants and perhaps a half dozen tactical bombers; all of them brimming with munitions and several minutes of supreme, concentrated effort, to accomplish what these Gladatraus had achieved in several seconds. Half his forces would be killed in the process and the survivors would be so badly shot-up that they'd barely make it back to base.

But the Gladatraus weren't doing that . . . No, they were lining up the second battlecruiser, the so-called 'target designation three-beta.' Leers blinked, nearly missing the devastating results of the *Mekadore Traveler's* first salvo. The battlecruiser's forward deflectors had been shredded to 65%, specifically the high-azimuth teinagon section. Not a split second later, down to 32%—the other nineteen areas of the deflector shield were running at 100%—then again, the *Mekadore Traveler* hadn't hit those areas with anything. All it had to do was breach a small section, pour weapons into it before it could heal itself; Leers just watched the results with horrific fascination.

He barely had to wait three seconds before the words 'Target designation three-beta destroyed' told him all he needed to know about the fate of the Battlecruiser Advancer. He felt a sudden chill come over him followed by a surge of exhilaration. One simply didn't snuff out a warship called a battlecruiser, no matter if it belonged in the Imperial Armada of the Admiralty or the Star Fleet of the Tertiary Alliance. Guardians Draystar and Jasmine had killed two in under a quarter of a minute. He took his eyes off the elongated monitors for a moment and glanced at his friends. He didn't know about them, but he was determined now, more than ever to command a Gladatraus Rhoderium Crab on his own. This was the answer to all of those questions he'd asked himself years and years ago. You could do a lot of good in these machines. The justice he'd exact against the Pulsarians would be just the beginning.

"Looks like we have a couple of wild cards entering the fight," came Rook's terse analysis.

"Why are you so worried?" Slayton challenged. "Let them come."

"There was nothing in my tone to convey concern, dearest one."

"You were the one who argued that the VF-95 Valkyrie was the best fighter in the galaxy. Well, what do you think now? The Valkyrie's flight and weapons envelope is nowhere close to this." Slayton shook her head slowly, tsking to herself.

"An idiotic comparison to say the least," Rook countered. "Where in the Alliance are you going to find Omnitraus Officers flying Rhoderium Crabs?"

"They're called Gladatraus Guardians." Leers shrugged as he said this.

****

Merwinette entered the combat command deck of the *P'kaflam* amid a torrent of frantic, yet determined activity. Officers raced to and fro barking orders, received loud responses from the enlisted ranks, then barked more. Indicator beacons on small monitors mirrored the urgent flashes displayed on the primary tactical plot, which measured more than ten meters by ten meters. To the untrained eye the immense room with its multi-layers of independently articulated raising and lowering platforms, floating holographic imagery; Armada com-officers in gleaming battledress, non-commissioned officers in dull blues and grays—the scene would look chaotic, a malfunctioning conduit of Pulsarians, hardware and information. However, amidst the mounting intensity of mechanical and organic noise, there was purposeful, well-directed order.

A smartly uniformed Commander Arkon Isterette bounded up to the admiral before he could fully take his second step into the cauldron.

"Earlier reports confirmed, Admiral," Isterette said. "There is definitive contact with a Gladatraus Rhoderium Crab operating in our sector. It Warped into normal space approximately—"

"It didn't come from that system of asteroids?" Merwinette asked, already knowing the answer. If it had come from the asteroid system, why wait until now to attack?

"Negative, Admiral. All sensor readings report Warp re-entry burst in zone twelve and . . ."

Merwinette looked at the officer as he spoke, barely listening as he covered the devastating assault the Gladatraus was exacting on his taskforce. After a pause in thought, he turned to a nearby communications bank.

"Bridge, status," he barked.

The officer on duty snapped to attention on a nearly monitor. "All systems are operational, Admiral. Engines, nominal. Primary and secondary batteries, nominal. Defensive screening and shields, standing by for your orders."

Without commending the officer of the bridge for his crew's efficiency, Merwinette said, "Activate defensive screens, shields on stand-by only. Maintain heading and course. Do *not* maneuver to intercept the Gladatraus."

The bridge officer blinked, but didn't dare question Merwinette's order. "As you command, Admiral."

Merwinette turned to Commander Iserette. "Let the Gladatraus come to us. Maintain course and cruising speed no matter what they do."

Merwinette studied the floating tactical plot above him. At its center was the icon of his flagship, the Dreadnought Destroyer Advancer *P'kaflam*. Flanking it were four Heavy Cruiser Advancers; the *Atherdral* commanded by Commodore Phatheon Taszergon, the *Akkerfak* commanded by Captain Phaton Kingergon, the *Adhirhom* commanded by Captain Final Krilergon and the *Aggervhom* commanded by Commander Ater Routergon. Yes, they were professional and would keep formation and tactical attitude with him, no matter how much firepower the Gladatraus rained unto them.

"Gladatraus is moving into zone four," a nearby officer reported, even though Merwinette could clearly see his enemy's position on the display above him.

"The *Orgevort* and the *Hydervort* are moving in to engage the Gladatraus directly," Commander Arkon Iserette said, *the fools*, he didn't add. "The Lightcarrier Advancer *Hrerhom* is moving into a parallel course configuration to search for survivors of previous engagements."

****

Draystar felt a tinge of concern as the *Mekadore Traveler* continued to rattle and shudder under the intense barrage coming from the two Frigate Advancers ahead. He shifted shielding alignment, decreased power to the screens and directed jamming emissions toward the antagonists; he still couldn't break their target acquisition scans for more than a few seconds. He could drop the deflectors completely, but with all the energy the Pulsarians were directing at them a near-miss would be about all the Rhoderium Crab's hull armor could take. As he had always known, but feared, the Pulsarians were getting smarter with their attacks. What the skippers on those Advancers wanted was to hold them at range, keep them at a distance while constantly changing up munitions and demand assistance from the other Advancers in their taskforce.

The obvious tactic for the Gladatraus would be to push in close—while taking as few hits as possible—to point-blank range and let them have it. What angered Draystar about this option was that it was keeping him away from that Dreadnought Destroyer Advancer at the heart of this taskforce. Pulsarian attacks up to this point had been random and careless; now they were engaging him with concentration and patience. Soon, more Advancers would come into play and he and Jasmine would be forced to retreat.

"They're reacting quicker to the weapons I'm throwing at them, damnit," Jasmine reported.

"Target-lock is getting more difficult to achieve," Nancy added.

The Rhoderium Crab heaved violently to port, righted itself, then pitched to starboard.

"Draystar, do you think we should bug—"

"No," Draystar barked. "I want their flagship. I want the Pulsarian commanding this taskforce. I told you before, we're not running."

"We've bagged more Pulsarians in the last several minutes than we have in the last several months," Jasmine said calmly. "If we continue to push this attack the danger to ourselves will be greater than any danger we've faced in the past."

"Then Jasmine, I suggest that you fly this thing to minimize the danger."

"What the hell do you think I'm doing?"

"Playing with them," Draystar fired back. "You fly this ship like a Gladatraus Guardian and quit—just quit toying with them, please."

Jasmine grunted and brought the Rhoderium Crab around violently. Much in an effort to shake her commander as to spoil Pulsarian aiming solutions. Regaining her situational awareness she cut speed, jinked, rolled to port, then increased power, narrowly avoiding several Pulsarian Javelins and a barrage of Daggers. She returned her concentration on the Frigate Advancers on the main viewer. These Advancers didn't have half the firepower or reputation of the Battlecruiser Advancers, yet the manner in which their captains chose weapons and rates of fire, made them an even more formidable foe.

She increased speed and dove the warship toward the nearest Frigate Advancer. Six Pulsarian Javelins tore through space after her. Jasmine jinked hard left, then returned violently to the right. The warheads screamed by to explode ten kilometers away. It felt much closer and the jarring heaves that resulted nearly bounced her and her commander from their seats. Jasmine quickly concluded that the Advancers were data-linked, sharing scanner and weapons information in an combined defensive effort. *Here they come again.* Six Javelins, three from each Advancer, followed by a pair of Falchions, screaming from each Advancer. *Okay, they're starting to get serious,* Jasmine thought. And it confirmed once again that her antagonists were data-linked. Up to this point the Pulsarians had been trying to dispatch them independently—as if a single Advancer were a match for a single Rhoderium Crab. Now they were coordinating their efforts and utilizing better weapons employment, and from the difficulty she was having getting a solid target-lock; the Pulsarians were also layering their deflectors better using selective jamming for maximum effect. Perhaps Draystar was right, maybe she should be more determined in her attacks, stop trying to kill them with finesse and start landing more devastating blows of her own. Then again, human males had to be right about everything.

The fingers of her left hand tapped quickly at her weapons board. She quickly reached forward and cued for a better scanner lock, cycling through a hundred settings in under five seconds.

"Target acquisition re-solidified," Nancy informed her.

"Good," Jasmine said. "Stay on that track and keep improving. Improvise and stay ahead of the Pulsarians. "

"Copy that."

Another fusillade of Falchions raced by the Rhoderium Crab. Jasmine released a torrent of Harpoons in response. She didn't like the answer. The Harpoons simply exploded against the Pulsarian deflectors. Instead of targeting both Advancers she focused on the closer of the two frigates and released another salvo of Harpoons. Again, the resulting explosions confirmed that the Pulsarian deflectors were behaving exactly as they intended them to. She could sneak in a few Shards, but stinging them wasn't what she was after. She banked away from the Frigate Advancer for two seconds, then dove toward it again releasing ten Harpoons. She had to dodge two Javelins and a rain of Dirks too numerous to count. Several hit the shields, which Draystar was able to swat aside with his own well-practiced deflector inputs. Jasmine continued her attack run. The fire from the second Advancer no longer a factor since her new pattern put the first Advancer between her and it. Eight more Harpoons struck the first Advancer's shielding; explosive geysers plumed into space, shredded shielding residue vaporizing under the intense heat in a shower of blue and red sparks. Jasmine released a single Mace and powered the Rhoderium Crab away.

In less than two seconds the Mace struck the Frigate Advancer's port shield. The contact created a huge disruptive bulge that caused the shield to bow in on itself. Three-point-two nanoseconds later the shield came in contact with the hull, the pressure so great the hull itself splintered into the elemental molecules that had once formed the armored composites. The energy from the exploding Mace raced through at a third the speed of light—its effects however lasted less than two sevenths of a nanosecond. All it needed. For Jasmine had chosen her target well. The point of contact was less than fifty meters from the Frigate Advancer's primary engineering and drive decks. The Frigate Advancer ripped itself in half as its fusion reactors detonated. The anti-matter coils leading to the Warp engines exploded in a horrifying flower of raw plasma several nanoseconds later.

The explosion knocked the Rhoderium Crab around. Jasmine lost control momentarily, regained it in time to hear Draystar's dry comment: "Cutting it a little close aren't we?"

Jasmine didn't reply as another thermal wave shuck the warship.

"Target designation four alpha destroyed," Nancy reported.

Jasmine increased throttle by two percent and flipped the warship over to engage the second Advancer, now ringed in a plasma storm from its exploding partner. Jasmine released two Maces toward it. On the monitor she could see the second Advancer completely wreathed in flame and the scarlet of rapidly evaporating deflector residue. The Maces hit causing the Advancer to literally bend on its spinal axis. The engines vented yellow and crimson flame moments before shutting down completely. Jasmine turned the Rhoderium Crab away from the frigate and headed for the retreating Lightcarrier Advancer.

"Target intercept effectiveness, regained," Nancy stated evenly.

"Negative jamming from target designation four," Draystar noted.

"Roger, that," Jasmine answered. "That second frigate in target designation four should be on the way out in a few minutes."

"Yeah, I can see escape pods on my scanner," Draystar noted.

"Wildcard, wildcard, wildcard."

"Talk to me, Nancy."

"New players entering the fight," Nancy answered. "Confirming new targets in zone twelve. One Dreadnought Destroyer Advancer, two Battlewagon Advancers, one Heavycarrier Advancer, and—"

The flight computer was cut off as a violent explosion jarred the warship. Jasmine regained control as smaller explosions began to rattle it. "There she goes," Jasmine said as the Frigate Advancer exploded.

"I'm making this new group target designation five," Nancy continued.

"Copy that," Draystar said, leaning forward in his seat. "Make that Dreadnought Destroyer Advancer the alpha in this group. The Pulsarian taskforce commander is on that Advancer."

As Jasmine waited for Draystar's instructions she sent laser and heavy-energy munitions toward the retreating Lightcarrier Advancer. She could easily manage destroying it while setting up for Draystar's next attack command, which she knew would be the alpha in target designation five. Tackling a Dreadnought Destroyer Advancer would take some doing—more than that, it would require more guile and nerve than she presently had. Dreadnought Destroyer Advancers were just so colossal—it'd be best to set-up an attack with another Gladatraus Rhoderium Crab. Early in this fight they might've had a better than even chance at tackling it. Now, this late in the fight . . . with the Pulsarians changing their tactics, coordinating their attacks, and actually thinking, the task they now faced would be a daunting one. The Pulsarians would examine the munitions she'd been employing to destroy their brethren and would erect wall after wall of different deflectors to thwart the effectiveness of her favorite attacks. This meant that Draystar would also have his hands full with the continuous re-alignment of their own deflectors, thus ensuring that they stayed alive long enough to kill the Pulsarians. Already Jasmine didn't like what they were flying into . . . she hadn't liked the idea of attacking the taskforce to begin with. Although the effort had allowed her to kill more Pulsarians than she thought was immediately possible, now with the Pulsarians reacting quicker and smarter to their attacks—the surprise that had worked before was gone. Worse, they were about to attack a Dreadnought Destroyer Advancer, with powerful Battlewagon Advancers flanking it. The jarring near misses they had been experiencing were about to become ax handle blows to the face.

As if to confirm what she was feeling the Rhoderium Crab began to rattle and shudder.

"Incoming fire from the Battlewagon Advancers," Nancy informed them.

"Switching shield configuration," Draystar acknowledged. The warship snapped up violently. "Damnit, they can't be staying up with me this quickly. Jasmine, if you haven't figured it out already, ignore the battlewagons, go after that dreadnought destroyer."

"I've already concluded that one," she said flatly, while thinking, *I hope this works. Because if it doesn't we are going to look awfully silly during a Pulsarian interrogation.*

"Good," Draystar said quickly. "Make sure we have an immediate egress for the asteroid base. I think we've hurt them enough for one day. Pick a weapons package that will get the job done in one pass."

Jasmine released more destructive energy toward the Lightcarrier Advancer, then paused. It exploded in a wash of blue light and frenzied sparks. "Are you authorizing the use of the Gladius?"

"Yes, confirmed," Draystar said, trying to keep pace with his deflector inputs against the incoming weapons fire. "You are authorized to use the Gladius."

"Roger, that. Energizing weapons package Rhoderia." She called up the list on her weapons board. The Gladius, while not necessarily the most powerful weapon on the warship, was perhaps one of the most devastating. It was a dual-functioned weapon packing a massive heavy Proton explosive coupled with a disruptive Ion warhead. The problem with employing the Gladius was that it robbed so much power from the other systems of the Rhoderium Crab. Every other weapon from the Mace, to the Shard, the Harpoon, the Skean, and on down the list, could be fired independently or in tandem from any of the *Mekadore Traveler's* numerous weapon ports. But firing a single Gladius warhead required the use of all four of the forward main batteries, whilst completely shutting down the four medium-yield omni-directional Pinser guns and the two thorax mounted medium-yield guns. There were other guns on the *Mekadore Traveler*: the six aft Basilisk Barrage Batteries, the four Quartzmark missile launchers—but those and other weapons were primarily used against smaller targets of which the Battlewagon and Dreadnought Destroyer Advancers clearly were not. Their fighting effectiveness was greatly diminished until they fired the Gladius. They had to endure thirty seconds of vulnerability as the Gladius powered up before they could—

"Hey, Jasmine, try to stay away from those damned Battlewagon Advancers," Draystar ordered, knowing full well that he was stating the obvious. "Getting a heavy barrage of jamming from them now. Making it difficult for me to select the proper deflector to defeat their weapons packages. Let's make this attack quick and decisive."

"I'll do my best," Jasmine said. Hell they were already within the medium- to long-range weapons envelops of three Advancers. What else did he expect her to do besides her best? She didn't want to ask.

Draystar examined his threat indicators again. All of the current jamming that the Pulsarians were trying to blind and disable them with was indeed coming from the Battlewagon Advancers. Not a whisper was coming from the taskforce command ship, the Dreadnought Destroyer Advancer. Draystar interrogated his systems further. Nothing from the Dreadnought Destroyer; no long-range scanners, no immediate range finders were searching for them, no fire-control radars, nothing.

"Nancy, are you getting any signals at all from the alpha in this target group?"

"Nothing. No emanations. All signals are originating from the Battlewagon Advancers."

"Why the hell aren't they trying to get a reading on us? They have to know we're coming after them by now?" *Why don't they acknowledge us?* "Nancy, are you sure we're not getting any readings from them?"

"Affirmative, Draystar. There are no signals originating from the alpha."

"Can you believe this?" Draystar asked Jasmine. "What the hell are they up to?"

Jasmine wasn't about to offer a reply. The Rhoderium Crab rattled, then quaked. She held the control yoke in firm hands, looping the warship around in a tight spiral, before returning to her attack pattern. She had twenty seconds before she could fire the Gladius. She'd fly in close and would place the Gladius right through their command decks and would then—

—the sub-space communications panel began chirping frantically.

"What the . . ." Draystar mumbled. "Who the hell is trying to contact us now?"

"Is it the asteroid base?" Jasmine asked. The annoying beeping in her ear was distracting her from the target run. "We'll know in a few seconds."

Then another tone filled the flight deck, this one more virulent and imposing; a tone unmistakable to any Gladatraus Guardian.

"Universe," Draystar breathed, "it's the Gladatraus Recall."

"No," said Jasmine. "It can't be, can it?" She released the control yoke and began punching at the communications panel authentication suite. She already knew the incoming communiqué was as authentic as the Rhoderium Crab she was flying. The last time she had heard that familiar tone and the message to follow was during the Minerva invasion.

Draystar was equally as confused and as out of sorts as Jasmine. The Recall was no small matter. To be so involved in a battle, to be keenly set on killing your enemy to be blind-sided by that chime that went beyond urgent was something neither he nor Jasmine was used to. It could've been a desperate Pulsarian trick; a ploy to distract them from the attack. But to emulate a Gladatraus Recall meant that you actually had to be onboard Gladatraus Supreme's Rhoderium Crab, the *Sterling Star*, to transmit the code. Then the Pulsarians had to know the *Mekadore Traveler*'s command code, another impossibility. No, this signal was real, it's meaning concrete.

"Read it, Nancy," Draystar ordered.

"General alert status: triumvirate. To all Gladatraus Guardians of Gladatraus Command, attention. To all Omnitraus Officers of Gladatraus Command, attention. All Guardians and Officers are to report to star system 775 immediately . . ."

Jasmine raced down her astro-navigation list on her auxiliary monitor. She already knew what the code meant. Star system 775 was the Shiborium star system. Seeing it on the monitor confirmed her dread, her heart freezing.

"What about the refugees?" Draystar asked. "I can't leave them here. I promised them I'd take them to a safe port before I dumped them into General Varxbane's lap at that asteroid base. We can't leave them there."

"I know," Jasmine whisper. The refugees had to be putting an incredible strain on the base's limited resources. Now there was a Pulsarian taskforce present and who knew what else waited for them.

Meanwhile Nancy was still reading the communiqué, "All other orders below any command level authority are hereby rescinded. Repeat: all other orders are rescinded, effective immediately." Nancy stopped then added.

"There's an additional attachment which reads, the *Mekadore Traveler*, Guardians Draystar and Jasmine are hereby ordered to retrieve all data and materials concerning Operation Forge and report directly to Gladatraus Supreme immediately. All Omnitraus Officers within the Omega Asteroid System are also ordered to—

"Incoming fire in zone twelve," Nancy suddenly shouted, "Javelins, Javelins, Javelins!"

Jasmine slammed the throttles forward and yanked on the control yoke savagely. She almost evaded the incoming warheads. The first Javelin tore away the port high-aspect shield as if it didn't exist. The second detonated against the secondary layer in a wash of light. Wasted shield slag belched into the vacuum creating an amber cauldron of heat and flame. The third Javelin, its reactive skin bleached of most it energy ran through the fragments of the secondary layer and glanced off the underlying darta-class deflector screen. Traveling so fast it detonated behind the Rhoderium Crab, adding more heat and flame to the expanding cauldron. The fourth Javelin breached the over-taxed screen and ripped the rear-most portside leg away from the warship. Frenzied sparks erupted from the vacant socket.

The Rhoderium Crab didn't shudder this time—this time it quaked, it jarred, it rocked all at once in a violent motion that nearly split the warship in half. The lighting in the entire warship winked and died. Everything just stopped. Silence. Then just as suddenly, systems came back on-line and the lighting relit as the harsh thunder outside rose to a devastating crescendo.

Another explosion rocked the warship as three undetected Scimitars scored hits. The blast was so powerful that it momentarily peeled the forward deflector shield back like the skin on an orange and allowed flame to swallow the entire warship in a cloud of spent gases for several seconds.

"Well that wasn't exactly the smartest thing we've done, my dear," Draystar said over the alarms.

Jasmine never liked being called 'dear.' She let it go, there were more urgent matters to deal with. "We've lost a leg, but other than that, damage appears minimal," she said.

"I have a problem," Nancy said.

"What is it," Jasmine asked.

"I can't shut down the power to my severed leg. There's an enormous power drain there. If we fly to the base, the Pulsarians will be able to track us all the way."

"I'm on it," Jasmine said getting out of her seat.

"Okay, as soon as you lock down that power drain we're on our way to the asteroid base," Draystar said. "In the meantime I'm getting us out of the battle area. I'll slice into the red zone of the asteroid system, where I'll fly around until you get the job done." Jasmine nodded. "They won't follow us there." Anything bigger than a Frigate Advancer was just too damn big to risk venturing into the red zone of the asteroid system. "If they do we'll lose them."

Jasmine leaned toward him. "It'll only take a few minutes to locate the problem. A few more to analyze it. A couple more before I can shut it down."

"Sounds good. Get going."

"Draystar, don't ever call me dear again. You know I hate being called that." She saluted and sprinted from the flight deck.

Draystar watched the star field wheel around wildly on the forward monitor as he pointed the Rhoderium Crab towards the denser part of the asteroids. He released the Gladius targeting the Heavycarrier Advancer, not really caring if it scored a hit or not—if anything it would give the Pulsarians something to think about and the resulting explosion would shield their retreat somewhat. *Damn, we're retreating again,* well at least we hurt them this time. He took bitter comfort in that and throttled the warship into the asteroids.

CHAPTER XIV
THE AFTERBURNER PIT

THE *Mekadore Traveler* thundered over the craggy landscape of planet-sized asteroid that held the Omega Command Headquarters base. The Omega Command Asteroid Base was a Star Force base, and home to the 91st Omega Command Attack/Interdiction Division, the 101st Strategic Bombing Division and the 19th Strategic Starlift Division. Most Star Force Commands had their fighting assets spread throughout a particular star system or several star systems with defensive responsibilities covering three-square parsecs or more. Omega Command was truly unique in that all of its assets, from the headquarters command structure down to the mechanics repairing fighters, were on the same site, beneath the surface of an asteroid the size of a planet. It wasn't headquartered in a densely populated star system and thus had no protective responsibilities whatsoever. Its mission was to provide strategic support of the larger neighboring commands. Whenever they needed bombers to augment a raid; or tactical fighters to help with a sweep, or more cargo-haulers to help move infantry from one star system to another, Omega Command readily provided said support.

The limb-severed warship streaked twenty meters above the life-less, pockmarked surface at 11,800kpx. Muddled hues of burnt umber, burnt sierra, beige, gray, and desert gold blurred by in the *Mekadore Traveler's* wake. Ahead of the warship was the sprawling Kinteesen Mountain range—the base was there. Hidden beneath the awesome fortress of rock, iron ore, nickel, cobalt, and poleirium; beneath more than a million tons of rock.

The original discoverers of asteroid MT-476 had been Dracterian pirates and mercenaries of the *Mosvar-Shev* who used the base from which to stage raids against Aracrayderian shipping and rival clans more than three hundred years earlier. The pirates had the dual benefit of having their base within a dense asteroid system and having it completely beneath the surface; safe from prying eyes and the most sophisticated sensing devices. After a ten-year struggle to put an end to the activities of the *Mosvar-Shev*, an Aracrayderian assault force finally located asteroid MT-476. Rooting the pirates out of their clever nest was a venture that took nearly a year of bloody fighting. Asteroid MT-476, the *Mosvar-Shev*, and the violent uprooting remained forgotten for nearly a hundred years. Until an Aracrayderian engineer, Kangnoch of the Family *Varnion dov Shire* decided that strategic advances of such an asteroid base had to be utilized. Kangnoch and his team of a hundred engineers and thousands of laborers set about drastically improving on the original pirate lair. The new base was constructed underneath the Kintessen Mountain Range with a great deal encroaching beneath the neighboring Kryderain Range and the Blackerton Flats.

It had taken more than two decades to construct the vast underground complex that easily covered the area of several connected cities. The Aracrayderians used the base to keep a wary eye on their long-time foes the Dracterians. And the base was pivotal in the signing of the Non-aggression pact of 4867 that kept the rival governments from engaging in anything tenser than a simmering Cold War (of course, the Pact did nothing to quell Dracterian violence among themselves). Then again, the Pact hadn't been designed for that purpose.

However, with the formation of the Tertiary Alliance came the legal unification of the Paranhoor Republic, which represented the Royal Family and the peoples of the Aracrayderians, the Nasercrayderians, and the Aracrayderian Commonwealth Territories; the United Worlds of Shiborium representing the Dracterians from Shiborium, Nikatus, and Narterium; the Republic of Minerva representing the human faction. The cold war between the Dracterians and the Aracrayderians ceased. Dracterian internal violence continued to flare from time to time, never completely extinguishing itself outright no matter how many missionaries the humans sent to Dracterian worlds. The industrial and military matrixes of these divergent houses of galactic power were merged to form the defensive forces of the Delrel Federation. The fully integrated army became known as the Strike Force, a massive organizational body that included heavy-weapons infantry, a fast-assault specialized force of marines, orbital gliders, space defense, amphibious assault, as well as a force of close-battle support spacecraft to include tactical bombers and tactical fighters. Next was the formation of a fully integrated navy, or Star Fleet, sometimes called the Derellian Fleet. As the second largest armed forces branch of the Tertiary Alliance, it included Warp-capable capital ships: battlecruisers, destroyers, minesweepers, and the colossal half-kilometer long tactical fighter carriers. The starships and warships of the Star Fleet numbered into the tens of thousands, and while they were drastically smaller than the Advancers of the Imperial Armada; they made up for it with skill, tenacity, cunning, and simply refusing to engage when set against a superior force. The final branch on the armed forces tree belonged to the Star Force, an organization of highly skilled pilots flying tactical fighters and bombers, strategic bombers, space-borne warning platforms and cargo-haulers. Although it was the smallest branch, the daring exploits of its pilots made it as well known and perhaps even more popular than the other two branches combined.

The *Mekadore Traveler* slowed to a crawl, 980kpx, as it entered the base's point defense grid. Seeded through this alert zone and shielded beneath the surface were dozens of scanner control and infrared guided pulse-laser cannons, 'big-weapon' emplacements (90 and 120mmx Thorium blasters, and 220mmx Triaxial-phased blasters) that could knock out Battlecruiser Advancers with ion or proton loaded warheads. Two of these big guns appeared out of the ground and aimed their nasty muzzles at the warship as it roared by. They weren't going to shoot it down; it was standard procedure to lock onto every starship that arrived here to keep the weapon's controllers in practice and proficient. When the *Mekadore Traveler* passed out over the rocky horizon the guns were lowered back beneath more than one hundred tons of rock. Boulders slid smoothly into place to hide all traces that the cannons ever existed. There weren't any sharp angles or straight lines to mark where weapons had been, mute testimony to the genius of engineer Kangnoch.

Suddenly, out of the midnight sky, two sleek, elongated VF-97A Visions appeared to take up escort positions about the Gladatraus warship. Looking like two venom-dripping wasps, the Visions were Omega Command's red carpet committee. The VF-97A was the Star Force's new fast-attack, high-speed interceptor. With a crew of one, the Vision was thinly armored, but heavily armed with offensive weapons and external Hyper Warp Velocity boosters that could be attached beneath the wings and spaceframe. It was just over twenty meters in length, with a wingspan of ten meters. It could go where needed, crossing parsecs to blast an enemy to hell and then return to base without the need of CFX-2 or CFX-7 transports to ferry them back and forth. Any fighter could have a booster pack strapped onto it, but as far as the VF-97 Vision was concerned the mating seemed to be permanent.

The *Mekadore Traveler* banked on final and reduced speed further as it approached the awesome Mount Gruirron. It was a dormant volcano that had existed in that state for more than seventy-five million years. In fact, the entire Kinteesen continental plate had no seismic or volcanic activity whatsoever. The ship, along with its escort, maneuvered up the face of the volcano for thirty-seven kilometers and then into its yawning throat, which was more than six kilometers in diameter. There were other crepuscular access areas to the base constructed strategically throughout the Kinteesen Range, but these were for fighter type spacecraft only—even a Rhoderium Crab would have a difficult time trying to wedge its bulk through one of those. The warship and the Visions dropped into the dark abyssal, the volcano swallowing them.

Down they went. Two kilometers, seven . . . Diving down in a ramrod 90-degree angle, the three ships continued down the dark esophagus. The Visions extended their speedbrakes and turned on their landing-approach and anti-collision running lights. The Rhoderium Crab followed suit as they approached a thick metallic shield door made of sensor-absorbing composites splitting in eighths, each octave moving aside just enough to let the vehicles through. There was no straining metal or laboring drive systems. Like the base, these doors were meticulously engineered to perform perfectly and efficiently. No rumbling machinery squealing, no thunder coming from stressed-out steel.

The doors closed behind the vehicles as they continued on down the esophagus . . . nineteen kilometers, twenty-seven. Another set of thick shield doors moved aside to permit passage. Between the first and second doors, atmospheric pressure had been equalized since the area beneath these second shield doors contained a breathable atmosphere.

The three spacecraft emerged into a cavern that was stupendous, massive, and fantastically lighted. Clearly dozens of kilometers across in every direction, mammoth lighting dishes dozens of meters across seemed to be placed everywhere along the stalactite studded ceiling. Then there was the flora and fauna along the floor; millions of mosses, lichens, and ferns, serving to supply the base with breathable atmosphere. The moss didn't augment the life support systems, the life-support systems supported the moss's incredible oxygen producing abilities. There was water present too. Aside from providing rare and common ores, thousands of asteroids within this Omega asteroid system were a chief source of water, albeit frozen. But the water within the cavern was in its liquid state. At the east end of the cavern was the Kinteesen waterfalls, booming and thundering with spray and steam. An incredible sight made all the more spectacular with the addition of underwater lighting.

This massive batholith called the Afterburner Pit by the base's pilots. Because this is where it all happened. Sixteen tunnels snaked away from the Afterburner Pit, some running for hundreds of kilometers, to connect to other smaller caverns, which housed entire fighter squadrons. The Astra Squadron, for instance, had a twenty-two kilometer tunnel that ran from here to its hangar of thirty-two VF-97A Visions to the northeast corner of the Afterburner Pit.

Being unable to match the crab's slow speed performance and maneuverability, the two VF-97A Visions peeled off the escort and streamed to the gaping tunnel that led to the Asteroid Interceptor Squadron's hangar. Both pilots saluted as they powered away. The Gladatraus warship saluted with a smooth fluid-like motion of its right pincer; it swerved and glided toward the general-purpose hangar, its legs hanging limply away from its body.

The Omega Command Headquarters Base, although designed as a Star Force base, from which to stage fighters, fighter-bombers, and strategic bombers, did have the facilities necessary to service the mammoth starships of the Star Fleet and the tenders and tinkers and troop transports of the Strike Force. So it wasn't unusual to see an occasional battlecruiser docked in one of the auxiliary hangars being loaded with munitions, or fuel or taking on supplies, or dropping off an entertainment troupe. As the *Mekadore Traveler* threaded its way through the massive cavern, Slayton and Leers were surprised to see what looked like an entire task force parked among the stalagmites. The first starship they saw was a two-hundred meter long Hornet class destroyer. It was an old, dilapidated, wreck and obviously a long way from home—the starship belonged in a museum. But there was nothing ancient about the eight, 99mmx deck-guns which—well-worn from recent use—looked fresh from the factory.

Leers gaped in horror at the civilian starships position haphazardly throughout the cavern, dispersed amongst the Star Fleet vessels. They were everywhere, dozens, perhaps even a hundred of them: starliners form Xendra Cruise Lines, battered merchant vessels, cargo haulers, tugs, cruisers, cutters, dilapidated Derek & Hans transports, skiffs and galleons. They were parked—no, heaped up—all about the cavern. Leers always thought of the Afterburner Pit as a pristine setting, a place to take your girl for a walk on one of those rare occasions when he wasn't preparing for a mission. This was a place of sublime beauty and calm, it made you forget that you were inside a remote rock in the middle of a hostile asteroid system. The peace only interrupted by fighters racing away through the Afterburner Pit for a mission; the interruption only lasting several seconds. And with the raging Kinteesen Water Falls, the green, red, and yellow hued mosses and lichens like carpet along the cavern floor, the stalactites and stalagmites, and the incredible lighting; who couldn't fall in love with the place. The Afterburner Pit was never as filthy and as polluted as the name implied—it was the opposite; starships raced in and starships raced out—they didn't disturb its beauty. Leers was appalled by the sight of the wrecks lying around. Their beautiful base looked like a nasty, reeking junkyard, a compost pile of components and metal. Many of the battle damaged starships were leaking fluids, black greasy slicks that spilled onto the cavern floor and formed pools, those smoking grease lakes steamed and bubbled like a disaster on the old kitchen stove. Fuel lines and power cables were everywhere, as were maintenance tugs and uniformed technicians who scrambled all over the many hulls like ants at a picnic.

Earlier, Leers had wanted to impress his friend Rook with the beauty of the cavern, the Afterburner Pit; he thought the name would throw off the cheetah, make him think that it was a burned out desecration. Sadly, it was exactly what it looked like now. But there was more at stake here than beauty being abused.

"Now we have primary ident on how bad the evacuation of Yanattii was," said Rook, folding his arms.

One of the monitors split-screened to reveal a cluster of refugees waiting in what appeared to be a food line near the hulk of a starship. The image looked so out of sync that Leers found it difficult to identify how he was feeling. There was a machine representing the highest degree of technical fortitude and a ragged collection of humans stood beside it in a state of misery and despair, at the very edge of survival.

He turned toward the cheetah. "You know Rook, when you're in your fighter, blazing along at 98,000kpx, you never get a chance to be this close to the misery, the heartbreaking desperation of it all," the human mumbled.

"There's that," Slayton said, "and the fact that our base is dozens of lightyears from any population center. For years we've been insulated from all of this."

"Well friends, you're in it now," Rook said. "Looks like the war has arrived at your doorstep."

"Those Pulsarians are gonna wish that they had never pursued those people here. We have a chance against their taskforce." Leers pounded his armrest. "And with Guardians Jasmine and Draystar with us, we can't lose that fight."

"You're forgetting one thing," Slayton said. "That Gladatraus Recall. We may not have a Rhoderium Crab to lead the attack."

"So?" Leers barked. "We have two divisions here—we can take them."

"What if there's more than one Pulsarian task force out there, then what?" Rook asked.

"So?"

"And if that recall also involves Omnitraus Officers? What then?"

"We don't know that," Leers said, scratching his head. "I'm not leaving without a fight, Rook."

"Speak for yourself," N'ckshell cut in. "Dying on this rock—just doesn't do it for me."

"Friend Dannen, you're bravery is without question. N'ckshell is right, though; Jasmine was awfully vague about what the recall was about. If that recall involves us and if it has something to do with the information we *nicked* on our missions, we may not be around to help with the fight."

"May not be around? Rook, those are our people down there; forced from their homes and starving. How can you disconnect yourself from that?"

"Because I never forget that I'm an officer and sometimes there are more important things we have to consider—"

Leers dismissed his observation with a wave of his hand. "Shut-up, I don't wanna hear anymore."

Slayton thought about adding her own commentary but fell silent.

The Rhoderium Crab banked down and threaded its way through a well-lit tunnel/corridor at the north end of the Afterburner Pit that led to the base's main starship hangar that rivaled the Afterburner Pit in size and volume. Along the way they passed over what was once a Star Fleet destroyer. It was a so heavily damaged that it didn't look like a starship anymore. It was about a hundred meters long, with eight—Leers and Slayton counted them—99mmx deck guns; all of which were blackened, carbonized, dented and or missing several hullplates, mute testimony to the ferocity of its retreat from Yanattii.

They emerged into the main hangar and were immediately greeted by the sight of an eight-hundred meter long heavy carrier.

"Is that," Leers started stammering, "is that the *Stern-Strike*?"

"Looks like it," Rook answered.

"How do you know that?" Came Slayton's sneering query.

"It says so on the monitor," Rook said pointing to the obvious.

They flew fifteen meters above the *Stern-Strike's* flight deck. Deck personnel looked up from their work as the Gladatraus warship flew by. Along the deck were the treating shapes of VF-98 Vigilantes, the newest frontline fighter for the navy (newer and more capable than the slightly older VF-97 Vision); there were the old, navy version VF-94 Vagrant multi-role fighters (its greatest time in service ended decades ago); the VF-86 Vanquish; the old and sturdy surface, and large-scale, attack fighter-bomber; finally there were several EI-95 Probes, surveillance and warning space craft. Also on deck were several flight-deck re-fuelers, cargo carriers, weapon haulers, mobile carts filled with tools, components and spare parts.

Next to the *Stern-Strike* were three battle cruisers, the all-purpose work horses of the Star Fleet. Among them was the famed *Toronaga*, which took on and defeated a Dreadnought Destroyer Advancer. A supreme achievement when one considered the latter vessel outgunned the *Toronaga* twenty to one. Here, the *Toronaga* achieved victory through sheer tenacity and the unbridled stubbornness of her crew in the face of such staggering odds. The Federation needed more starships like the *Toronaga* and the tough-minded crews to serve on them.

But the *Toronaga* didn't look so fearsome now. It was just as battered, just as broken as the other starships in the hangar.

****

Star General Preafect Sergon, commander of the 950th Straaka-Vohm Straterium, moved uneasily in his ejection chair. He was strapped down tightly within the dark, cramped confines of his KM-750 Command Malactite's cockpit module—not exactly the place he wanted to be with a Gladatraus Rhoderium Crab flying around. Sergon examined his surroundings, eyes sweeping pass the tactical information display, the weapons board, the main-threat board, the flickering lights here and there. It might as well be his coffin; he could already smell the baited anticipation emanating from the bodies of his cockpit crew, as if it steamed from the soul of a living entity. Or was the smell akin to something worse? Was it fear? Best not be. As rotten as the presence of a Rhoderium Crab was, fear had to be dealt with and shut aside. The Asteroid System was big and death could claim them in a variety of ways and in a variety of forms . . . to just focus on one aspect was counter-productive and dangerous.

The presence of the Gladatraus didn't signify a cancellation of the planetoid invasion. They were already within the asteroid rain, too late to turn back. Certain aspects of the attack would have to be revised, but on the whole the attack was still on course. He only wished that he and his forces were better armed to meet any Gladatraus contingency. His Malactite bristled with space-to-ground munitions, anti-fighter weapons like the Gaff and Dirk, even heavy bombardment weapons. But nothing that could take on a Rhoderium Crab with any success. It would've been nice to have planned for that eventuality in advance and packed Javelins or even a Pike . . . but that was always hindsight's luxury.

The six diligent Malactite pilots didn't turn from their work on the instrument panels or the large monitor in front of them to regard their leader. They couldn't, busy as they were guiding the Malactite through the asteroids. Each pilot was attired in full armored battle dress, which contained leggings, chest armor and a battlehelm equipped with communications and an emergency oxygen container that provided oxygen for up to a hundred hours. Useless, because if they had to eject in this asteroid system under battle conditions, it would be weeks before their bodies were discovered.

Sergon's Malactite was already in the swirling chaos and his second squad was just starting to disembark from Dehyhitte's Advancers when the report of the Rhoderium Crab's arrival sent shockwaves through the entire fleet. Despite his professional cool and decades of service, he nearly went into a frenzy. That's what the sudden presence of the Gladatraus did—even though they were attacking Merwinette's forces millions of kilometers away and in another sector. Never in his life had Sergon felt so utterly useless than that moment the Gladatraus were identified and the general alarm spread through the entire fleet. To go one-on-one with the Federation's ultimate weapon meant death in no uncertain terms. Not that he was one to back away from a fight with the Gladatraus. Even if he engaged them with hypothetical Javelins and Pikes, he was sure that he'd find his death in this coffin of titanium, fiber-optics and steel. But, he reminded himself, there'd be no better way to die than in a struggle with your enemy. Bring them on, these Gladatraus. Let's see their mettle matched against his.

Far from being a fool, Sergon requested that his forces be augmented by ten more Malactites armed with Gladatraus killing weapons to strengthen the rear echelon, and at least five more squadrons of Spark Racer XXR models. Admiral Aldar Dehyhitte immediately approved the launching of the ten Malactites—especially since he was also joining the planetoid attack onboard one of his *Shallh'Avachers*. But the request for additional Spark Racers had been overwritten by Admiral Rouldran Petti. Even though he didn't give a reason, Sergon knew the Admiral feared the Gladatraus and wanted as many Spark Racers as possible on patrol to protect him. After all, Petti wasn't Straaka and placed a high premium on his hide. But the good Admiral would provide them with two additional squadrons of Spark Racer THVs, of which each would be equipped with heavy weapons suited to dealing with starship and Rhoderium threats. Rhoderium Crabs were incredible machines, yes, but they were not invincible—there were ways to deal with them; given room, accuracy, speed of the assault, they could be dealt with—and without the tremendous loss of Pulsarian and machines that was usually associated with the taking of a Gladatraus Rhoderium Crab.

Sergon would press with the invasion and it would be successful. He still had Admiral Dehyhitte's force of six *Shallh'Avachers* to provide high cover for his Malactites, Battlebarges to augment cover fire, and *landt'phizers* for the main surface assault.

Sergon jumped slightly as a proximity alarm shrilled for attention. An asteroid some twenty meters in diameter split the void between them and the number two Malactite. It was traveling at 72,000kpx as it sped by. Another asteroid, this one more than two-hundred meters across rolled on a collision course toward them. The boulder dwarfed the Malactite, which opened up on it with its main deck guns. Four shots and the boulder split into a billion glittering fragments.

The number two Malactite moved up closer to Sergon's command Malactite. It was smaller than his KM-7500 Command Malactite, but the VM-7100 was still a tempest of weapons and explosive firepower. In general, all Malactites were composed of two main structural components: a fighting module and a command module. The fighting module was roughly shaped like a tortoise shell, but was an incredible fifty to eighty meters in diameter, depending on the class. Armored plating was massed upon armored plating, and energy weapon domes covered the surface like boils and warts. There were smaller anti-fighter pulse-laser guns strategically placed about the mammoth fighting vehicle, along with heavy weapons launch tubes with sensor pods and reflective scanning grids. At the exact center of the big tortoise shell was the command module, which was similarly shaped, but only ten meters in diameter. The Malactite pilots controlled their bloodthirsty fighting vehicle from here. The command module rotated on its own axis and could augment the fighting module's firepower with its own weapons' suite.

The Malactite's role on the battlefield was high-orbital bombardment. With its heavy armor and massive shielding array, the machine could go toe-to-toe with planetary defense batteries and fend off fighters simultaneously. Its armor could take tremendous punishment, which became a weakness because the armor and shield generators took up so much room, robbing space necessary for fast, powerful engines—a Malactite's engines were small; thus, the machine was slow and usually popped up on enemy radar like an apple ready for plucking. So it had no choice but to holdout during heavy bombardment and had been constructed with that thought in mind. The Malactite's secondary role was to support the infantry. The standard tactic was to lay off a city, surround it with three to five Malactites and bomb it to the point that the advancing Straaka battalion columns would encounter a demoralized, battle-shocked enemy unable to defend themselves.

Sergon tried to relax as he studied the multicolored symbology dance on the tactical display. Nothing but millions and millions of asteroids, a seemingly endless shower of flying rock. Relax.

Sitting here, strapped in wasn't serving any purpose. The General decided to disconnect himself from his ejection chair and take a walk through the cramped command module and fighting module, which was forbidden—once a Malactite entered hostile space every officer and crewmember was required to stay at their stations battle-ready and alert. However it was his prerogative to make sure that everyone on board the Malactite was ready to kill Delrels with unequaled ferocity. Fear was a disease that had to be snuffed out before its paralyzing infection spread.

****

The MI-347 Pulsarian Command Shuttle folded its long wings up, locking them into final/landing position as it descended to the landing pad in an explosion of snow, ice and vertical climber steam. Outside, Four Straaka, their surcoats flapping in the frozen air, moved underneath the vulture shaped shuttle as it touched down and clapped its landing gear into place with three heavy, inter-locking, anti-gravity, anti-environment holding collars in an attempt to keep the frigid winds of Elst from blowing the shuttle over. The shuttle's drive engines and vertical climbers powered down and the Straaka choked and gagged on the sudden expulsion of ozone and gas. The Straaka hurriedly finished their work and fled the scene as the main ramp lowered and locked into place.

The Straaka Keptein Meitgon watched all of the bustling activity from the relative warmth of his command center viewing room. He sipped absently at the steaming cup of tea then set it down on a dusty, seldom used desk.

Hmmmph, so the bloodthirsty SSK have sent one of their lap dogs to question me about the run-in with that Omnitraus Officer, eh? So be it. Meitgon was too arrogant to feel any apprehension about the meeting. He'd done everything in his power to kill the Federation spy—against orders—and he had succeeded. Besides, what were last minute orders when one was dealing with the Omnitraus? No, the Dracterian had to be killed and she was dead. The fool, despite her so-called superior training, had skied right off the side of the mountain and perished. Her body hadn't been recovered due to the severity of one of Elst's unpredictable winter blasts that had lasted for more than four days now. And bio-scans, while not being too reliable, hadn't detected any life-signs—Meitgon knew that no one could survive a 2,000 meter plunge and the severe cold weather temperatures, Omnitraus or not.

"Here they come," the Straaka sergeant behind him said, peering over the Keptein's shoulder to take a good look at the SSK.

"Yes. Go down and escort our guests up here." Meitgon folded his arms and huffed. "This shouldn't take long. He'll conduct his investigation; ask why the Dracterian's body hadn't been discovered—that's because it's been covered by more than ten meter of snow and ice." Meitgon smiled. "And we'll send the SSK on their way."

The Sergeant saluted and hurried out into the crowded corridor.

Meitgon loathed the SSK. Damned counter-intelligence police force didn't know a damned thing about the true meaning of warfare or how to handle the real enemies of the Empire. They were nothing more than a collection of paranoid fanatics who saw—no, imagined—treasonous activity around every corner. Meitgon wasn't blind to their power, however. The SSK was an organization with a little more than 200,000 fanatics who could go anywhere, do anything they damned well pleased, all in the name of security.

The SSK bootlickers weren't to be trifled with—200,000 fanatics in the galaxy was an absurdly small number especially when compared to the Straaka whose numbers swelled to more than two-hundred million—but the SSK seemed to be everywhere.

Meitgon remembered a long time ago during his tenure at the Straaka Ghelk-Mech College. He and his comrades were enjoying a little time off at a cafe, sipping spiced tea, complaining about the curriculum, minding their own business, when a woman sitting two tables away complained too loudly that gruesome ambassador to the Federation embassy had more political sense in one of his toe-nails than the Emperor did in his entire head. Meitgon and his comrades balked when they heard this but thought nothing of it. Besides, many citizens had misgivings about the growing tensions between the Empire and the DFR, and they thought nothing of it. But not more than five minutes after the woman had made that comment was she arrested by the SSK and hauled off to jail. Someone in the cafe' had overheard her comment—an innocent comment, because Meitgon felt the same way at times—reported her and the SSK had responded with their legendary zeal.

Meitgon learned later that the woman was released a month later, beaten and broken, but alive. She was lucky. The SSK executed most others on the spot. Those were the dark times before the war, when citizens were rounded up and slaughtered just for voicing political opinions too loudly. There were even rumors of SSK killing generals for refusing to carry out the Emperor's battle plans to the letter. *Madness.*

And now several of the SSK's prime bootlickers were on their way up to question him. He knew one would be Major Bblaes Netergon of Nijimegan Security. What a blasted joke. He was going to be put to the task by some position holder all the way from the Frontier. Meitgon felt insulted. If they really wanted something from him wouldn't they have sent someone from their Headquarters? Even worse, this Netergon outranked him. Meitgon didn't like this one bit.

Meitgon retrieved his shoulder holster and laser pistol from the horizontal filing cabinet and strapped it around his back and chest. He slid the weapon into the holster and stood in front of his desk. Caution. That's all it was. He'd be damned if they were going to haul him off to prison without a trial, without a fight. And—just as an afterthought—he clicked the weapon's safety to the 'ready' position.

Meitgon felt his stomach heave as the Straaka Sergeant entered with three SSK. Immediately Meitgon knew which one was Netergon. He was difficult to miss. With those hard eyes, that thin predator's nose, full lips and whitening hair, this was Netergon. And strangely, he appeared to be the most intelligent looking SSK scum Meitgon had ever seen. Right away he hated Netergon.

"I am—" Netergon started.

"Major Bblaes Netergon, SSK Nijimegan operations," Meitgon finished. All three of the new arrivals were wearing armor and weapons. But Meitgon didn't let that observation faze him. "Elst Outland Base and Strategic Operations welcomes you. There's spiced Vrag root tea if you wish it."

Netergon wasn't amused by any of this—these Straaka were too infantile, inept and arrogant to realize that true power in the universe could be better administered with ideas than the point of a weapon. And this Meitgon was no different than his brethren.

Netergon strolled casually into the room, scanned it and handed his parka to one of his aides. There was a chair for him to sit in but he didn't take it. "Received your report," the Major said without preamble. Formality wasn't necessary here—then Netergon's scan caught a glimpse of the other's shoulder holster—*perhaps he does know why I'm here.*

"Yes, and . . ."

"Keptein, do you have a problem with adhering to strict military protocol?"

"No, Major, I do not."

"Not that it really matters." Netergon paused to examine the intricate cravings on the display shelf. "My interview will only take a minute—with or without your cooperation."

"So, major, why is the SSK here," Meitgon sneered. "Checking to make sure we're all registered party members and that our loyalty to the Emperor—"

"Nothing as absurd as that," Netergon answered evenly.

"What, may I inquire, is it?"

"The Federation agent."

Meitgon didn't say anything.

"Look Keptein, I've traveled from one end of this galaxy to another. Five blasted days in Hyperspace to arrive on your beautifully frozen wastewater world. I'm not in the mood for pissing around. I'm conducting an investigation here, and from this moment forward you *will* answer all of my questions and you *will* answer them clearly, concisely and to the point. Is that understood, Keptein."

"Yes, Major," Meitgon sneered. "Please proceed."

"The Federation agent," Netergon started again. "You had orders to let her escape. Why didn't you follow—"

"Major, that Delrel spy killed more than twenty of my Straaka. Now add to that, the fact that she ripped restricted data from our storage files—"

"What were your orders, Keptein?"

"—and then wantonly destroyed Imperial property. It was my duty, Major—it's my duty to do everything in my power to destroy an identified enemy of the Empire. With special emphasis to those identified as one of their elite Omnitraus."

"Your duty is to obey your orders!" Netergon boomed dangerously. "Why didn't you obey your orders?"

"I know my duty. I did it and nothing more."

"So, without considering the broader implications of your actions you killed her."

"Yes."

"Where's the body?"

"There is no body. The Dracterian spy plunged to her death on the north face of this mountain as witnessed by four of my Straaka." He thought, *you read my report—you should know that.* "The weather retarded our efforts at recovery. A storm blew in and I would have lost more men conducting a search just to identify a corpse. Besides, our sensor probes did not pick up any life-signs."

"You received orders from the SSK that there may be an Omnitraus agent loose on your base. Later, you received an amendment to those orders from Combined Advancer Fleet West not to touch this agent, and you went ahead and killed her. Is that correct?"

"How could I have received orders from a fleet that doesn't exist?"

"It exists now."

"Let me tell you something, Major," Meitgon sneered. "When a report comes in that we have a Federation spy running wild on my base—not just any spy, but one of their Omnitraus—I do everything in my power to destroy them utterly. Utterly—do you understand? Your late orders said to hold back and observe; but I will not do that and let her kill my men and steal restricted data. Letting an Omnitraus go is insane and irresponsible—just so you SSK can play your games—"

"Keptein, you are formally charged with treason and willfully disobeying your orders."

The words were like a bolt of lightning. "What? What are you talking about? Didn't you hear anything that I have said?" He reached for his weapon. Instantly the two SSK were on him, but not before he could pull the weapon free and aim it at Netergon's head. He pulled the trigger—nothing happened. What? The weapon hissed and nothing else. Then the two SSK were wrestling for the weapon and Meitgon fired again. Nothing.

"No," Meitgon shrieked. "You can't do this." He looked at his Straaka sergeant, who only stood there, smiling it seemed.

"Take him outside and shoot him," Netergon said coolly.

"What—you knew!" Meitgon was screaming at the Straaka sergeant now. "You tampered with my weapon, you traitor! You filthy traitor!"

Struggling against the two SSK, Meitgon was dragged from the room.

"Excellent work," Netergon said.

The sergeant saluted. "Major, several merchant ships in orbit at the time of the Omnitraus' escape reported seeing an Gladatraus Rhoderium Crab dropping into atmosphere. It is possible that after all this the Delrel did manage to escape."

"Of course the Delrel escaped," Netergon folded his arms. "Meitgon is a fool. Just because he scanned for life-signs and didn't find any doesn't mean that the Dracterian was killed. He should have re-aligned his scanner to scan for something uniquely Dracterian. Cells, DNA, anything—but Meitgon didn't do that. He probably turned on the scanner, didn't find any life and turned it off—he didn't investigate."

"I see your point, Major."

"You're in charge of operations here until a replacement is assigned here." Netergon moved to the window and looked down. Meitgon was dragged to the landing pad, his arms locked behind him. One of the SSK pulled out a pistol, aimed it at the base of the Straaka's skull and fired. "Remember this lesson, Sergeant. When you receive orders from a higher command, you do your damnedest to carry them out, no matter what your feelings concerning those orders may be. Or, your career will meet the same end as Meitgon's."

CHAPTER XV
THE BWRC

THE *Mekadore Traveler* rested at the northwest corner of the main hangar, directly in front of the NW-11A entrance. The Gladatraus warship had to circle the hangar for fifteen minutes before a dented and hull-fractured transport could be relocated to a connecting hangar.

On the stalagmite-studded deck, technicians rushed between injured starships in small speedy drone carts. The carts could pull up to five trailers behind them and carried tools, spare parts, replacement maintenance teams, and food and drink for the haggard labor teams.

Because this was principally a Star Force base, the tech crews were more acute to the repairs and logistics of fighters and fighter-bombers, than to these bigger starships. There were different schematics to consider, different parts, an entirely different layout—they had tech orders on the fighters and the fighter-bombers, but not the starships, which were all unique in their design. Repairing them would cause relentless headaches for most, but some looked to it as a challenge.

Leers watched all of the activity through a set of binoculars he had borrowed from the armory of the *Mekadore Traveler*. He studied the activity on the deck of the carrier, *Stern-Strike*. He could not hide his fascination and awe; the carrier was stupendous and looked strangely odd 'sitting' on the ground within the cavern, instead of majestically floating in the black void of space. He wondered how something so enormous could fit inside the cavern. *Very carefully*, came a quick reply. The helmsman had to be a real cool hand.

Leers leaned against the massive starboard pinser-claw of the Rhoderium Crab, then scanned the civilian craft next to the mammoth carrier. The food line was gone. The meal servers were cleaning up. He felt a sense of helplessness he hadn't felt since he went on a mission to liberate hundreds of detainees at a Pulsarian concentration camp last year. The rescue, according to the mission planners, had been more than successful. But there were thousands they had to leave behind. That sense of not being able to do more was a feeling he didn't like. As he watched the lines disperse next to the starship, he couldn't help the feelings of pity, of sadness for these people. But with these people, there was hope. There had to be. Someone noticed that he was staring at them as they broke down their cooking equipment, and waved. Leers smiled and waved back.

Rook stood next to him, arms crossed, whiskers twitching anxiously. Both human and cheetah were attired in the standard grey Star Force all-purpose duty uniform. It consisted of grey slacks tucked into a pair of boots and a black turtle-neck shirt beneath a grey double-breasted service coat, which was tapered at the waist and gave the two an exaggerated 'V' shaped frame. Rook yawned and loudly cracked his fingers, giving the impression that he might stretch out on the sandy floor and grab a quick nap at any second.

Ignoring both human and Aracrayderian, Slayton began pacing back and forth, occasionally passing a stalagmite that wouldn't move, no matter how many times she kicked it. She was attired in a crimson and black starrior uniform; a uniform worn only by Star Force fighter aces. It consisted of a stiff collared shirt tucked into jodhpurs, which were, in turn, tucked into a pair of glossy black boots. It was a uniform that demanded attention be paid to its wearer, for he or she was a professional who had accomplished something fewer than eight percent of all Star Force pilots had achieved. To be an ace meant gaining ten kills; Slayton had triple that number. She looked more like an arrogant clergy than an Omnitraus Officer.

Standing with the kids, while at the same time making sure that he didn't stand too close to them, was Colonel Marks Dargoinne. He was General Varxbane's chief of staff and aide. He was also chief of base operations and the administrative commander of the Battle Warning Readiness Center. Dargoinne had his hands in everything. There was nothing that didn't go on in the base that he didn't know about. He wore a neat, crisp, three-piece duty uniform with service cap. He didn't need to wear the damned cap—everyone in the Star Force hated wearing them—but Dargoinne, because he was Dargoinne, followed every regulation with unwavering diligence. Many of the base's personnel called him 'Buckethead' because of it. And in doing so giving a vivid description of Dargoinne's rigidity. Of course, Slayton and Leers were among his most ardent detractors. The reasons Slayton and Leers held the Colonel in such ill regard were numerous. When asked, Slayton would be quick to point out that Dargoinne often conjured up all manner of unrealistic contingencies and tactics for the base's flight crews to execute under the most severe combat conditions. Leers would just as quickly add that if pilots didn't like it, too bad; if the wing commanders protested, so what; Dargoinne didn't care. Pilots were pilots. Either they flew the missions he requested or he'd ground them and get someone else to fly. They were at war. He had no time for pilots who questioned orders, let alone pompous Omnitraus who thought regulations or orders they didn't like never applied to them. It was never a simple matter of reminding them of what they were fighting for. Threatening to ground them seemed to work though.

The colonel and two armed guards were there to escort the Guardians and the Officers to the BWRC. There, they'd all attend a mission debriefing and another general briefing that would fill them in on the base's current operational status. They would have a lot of questions and—

Draystar and Jasmine strolled down the ramp, their boots clicking rhythmically, Leers chuckled as Dargoinne performed a clumsy double-take at the awesome presence of the two Gladatraus. With their imposing stature, their gleaming armor and helms, Dargoinne swallowed hard on reflex alone—he'd seen these two before—weeks ago, but their aura, their magnificence, was staggering to those not accustomed to being within their vicinity on a regular basis. Embarrassed, he snapped a quick salute, which the Gladatraus returned with undue respect.

"This way, please," Dargoinne directed, starting for the thick exit doors.

Leers set the binoculars down next to the boarding ramp of the *Mekadore Traveler*—they'd be safe there, no one was dumb enough to steal something in such close proximately to a Gladatraus warship. He joined everyone as they fell in behind the colonel, including the two guards, who activated their weapons. Leers didn't think that an armed escort to the BWRC was necessary, especially with two Gladatraus Guardians present in full battle armor. But if the General wanted it that way, so be it, no one argued with General Varxbane.

The thick blast doors moved silently aside and the group entered a corridor that was cut directly into the rock. Leers explained to Rook that this particular corridor was the longest in the entire base, branching off to tributaries that led to hundreds of main corridors, secondary passages, light-vehicle thoroughfares, and emergency access ways, which in turn led to dozens of the command and operations sections of the base. There were perhaps twenty thousand kilometers of these passages carved throughout the labyrinth of the asteroid base.

The group paused before a set of turbo elevators; Dargoinne pressed the service request button and was greeted by a friendly availability beeping.

All followed the Colonel into the elevator, which was large enough to hold a sports arena, and rode down two kilometers. When the mammoth doors opened, they entered a wide and brightly lighted corridor. Unlike the first corridor that was attached to the hangar, this one was crowded and noisy; base personnel were everywhere. Twenty meters up the corridor was a cluster of pilots doing a bit of 'hand waving' (the way pilots reenacted engagements). They only stopped because the presence of the two Gladatraus Guardians was enough to send shudders down the most resolute and arrogant. The pilots saluted the Guardians as they strolled by, not because duty dictated for them to do so, but out of respect, then went back to their hand-waving as if nothing had happened. Next to the pilots were comptrollers in blue uniforms and crescents on their shoulders; across the corridor were administrative personnel in khaki, and further up were mission-techs, programmers, officers and enlisted personnel. There were humans of multiple ethnic backgrounds and nationalities: Minervan, Yanatiian, natives of Ruby-Royale with pale skin, natives of Desdemona with ebon hues, humans with the flat faces and wide palms of Carthorn. There were Dracterians, from Shiborium, Narterium, and Nikatus. And Aracrayderians of multiple species: black panthers here in gando-tech uniforms replacing launch-control conduit; a squat, meter-high armadillo shackled down with a massive tool belt barking orders at them; two smartly uniformed lions with golden manes—pilots from the Prancer Squadron; an elephant of massive proportions in an uniform of an AWF-19 scanner officer. The variety of species, the staggering combinations of sentient beings reminded Rook of November Command and could've gone into the hundreds of billions, but the asteroid base could only hold a fraction of the rich diversity of the Tertiary Alliance. Individuals from the nearest to the farthest reaches of the known galaxy, assembled here—as they were on other Federation bases—all with the sworn duty to defend those who couldn't defend themselves from the ravages of the Pulsarian Empire. All sworn to uphold peace, order, and good government. In a galaxy of staggering political and technological complexity . . . the components of freedom and the will to defend oneself could be exquisitely simple.

They continued on. Before them the corridor opened up into a canyon more than three hundred meters across and five-hundred deep. Dozens of razor thin catwalks connected to corridors and tunnels, gleaming escalators lead to thoroughfares at different levels above the vast chasm. Five hundred meters below the group were the raging waters of the Kinteesen; the same river that raced away from the Kinteesen Falls within the Afterburner Pit.

"*Now* what do you think of our humble little base?" Slayton beamed. She stopped and nudged Rook in the ribs.

"Very impressive, Lovey. I'm liking what I see."

"That's what I like about you, *Pussy*. You never seem to find enough words in that limited lexicon of yours to fully express yourself."

"Yes, but I do believe that the chief designer of this base was an Aracrayderian, no?"

"He's got you there, N'ckshell," Leers said.

"Maybe, but the original discoverers were Dracterians, no?" Slayton said, mimicking Rook's diction.

"A collection of bloodthirsty cut-throats who had nothing to do with the present condition of this base."

"For someone who has never been to our base before, you sure do know a lot about it."

They crossed the canyon and entered the command section of the base and followed a granite gray security hall leading to the BWRC. The lighting here wasn't as severe as that in the other halls. Armed guards with side-arms displayed stopped the group before a set of twenty-meter high shield doors for a security check. Dargoinne handed one of the guards a set of orders, which one of the guards took his time scrutinizing. Satisfied, he punched in the entry code and let them through the doors that slowly moved aside with a deep purr and sharp hiss.

Immediately, Rook noted that the BWRC was dimly lighted and packed with hundreds of personnel. With the only sources of light coming from glowing monitors and massive wall mounted displays, it took a few moments for his eyes to adjust. He surveyed the room, noting that here and there were long glass plotting maps, which looked just as out of place as the metallic filing cabinets at the opposite end of the room; there were multi-dimensional tactical tables, conduit ran along the ceiling, secure comm gear were on desks, equipment containers piled several meters high. But most of all, there were rows and rows of computers, rows of scanner monitors, rows of sensor scopes. At each station was an operator, sometimes two, and behind the operator was an analyst. Each analyst reported to a controller, who was in charge of a certain row of operators and analyst. The controller reported to the section chief, or the shift commander, who was usually a lieutenant or a captain. This officer reported to the deputy duty officer, who then, for all intents and purposes, reported to Colonel Dargoinne. And, of course, Dargoinne reported to General Varxbane.

Forty meters into the BWRC, they approached the imposing form of General Varxbane, a huge, one-hundred-year-old Aracrayderian Gorilla with a coat of brilliant silver fur; most of which was hidden behind a custom tailored uniform of crisp lines, gold insignia, and highly polished metal. He was fierce in appearance and in his loyalty to the Federation—also, he was quite famous. During the glory years of flight-testing, Varxbane—then a lieutenant—was a member of a short list of totally fearless test pilots who dared to break performance and speed records in experimental spacecraft that rattled, shuddered, and exploded without warning. There were many test pilots who probed the frontiers of the galaxy, many never returning. And those who did came back, had harrowing tales of phantom zones, quasi-stellar disruptions, omnipotent beings, unresponsive controls that did the opposite of what you wanted them to, negative voids, time shears. The list went on and on. And Varxbane had probably seen them all.

When Varxbane was a major in the Star Force, he ran into—literally—a brash young lieutenant Derek Draystar fresh out of the Omnitraus Officers auxiliary. Varxbane hated the kid, not because he was human and constantly smelled of overbearing confidence, but because he was never wrong, flew recklessly, and often came within a hair's width of morting himself and destroying good machinery. With Aracrayderians, no matter the specie or gender, to be a test pilot simply meant that you had elected a technical profession—albeit a dangerous one—and were seeking to improve piloting skills first and your career second. But Varxbane felt that for humans, and to the highly imitative Dracterians, being a pilot meant that you had joined a righteous fraternity, a secret society were competition, boasting, and carousing were the order of the day. It went beyond flying and involved beer-call after hours, followed by pursuing the opposite sex until the early dawn, getting two, perhaps six hours of sleep and doing it all over again. And Draystar epitomized that arrogant, swaggering individual and had honed the human version of a test pilot to an art form. Despite rank, or rather because of it, they'd butted heads constantly. Varxbane wasn't impressed with Draystar's Omnitraus ranking—to him he was just another pilot—he had to admit, though, the kid flew like a demon.

Seeing him now, Varxbane felt a familiar pride warming his soul. Approaching was a Gladatraus Guardian of the highest order, one of the best. Approaching was a man and not that 'tail-chasing' kid; a responsible family leader with a keen sense of duty. Besides which, Varxbane didn't know what humans meant by 'tail-chasing', since they had no tails to begin with. But if it meant that by not doing it made them more mature, so be it, it must be true.

It was good to see his old student again, Varxbane mused. Rotten timing and circumstances wouldn't allow them to catch up on the last decade or so—on the old times. There was so much that he'd love to tell Draystar and he was sure there were stories Draystar would share with him.

"Good to see you again, Guardian Draystar," Varxbane boomed. He held out a massively clawed hand. Draystar grabbed it and Varxbane shook the hauberked hand vigorously. Varxbane ignored Guardian Jasmine and the three Omnitraus Officers.

"Got here as quickly as we could, General," Draystar said.

"Your timing is most impeccable, as always," Varxbane stated evenly. "I'm glad you brought back my Omnitraus Officers. Alive and intact I see." With a massive hand Varxbane shoved, rather than guided Draystar toward the central briefing room. "We haven't much time. Things are quite busy here."

"Noticed that on the way in, General. Have more refugees arrived?"

"None since your departure. You're no doubt aware of our Pulsarian friends."

"We took quite a pounding when we made normal space re-entry," Draystar said. "But we gave as much as we got."

"That couldn't have been helped. If we had sent out a transmission to warn you about them, we would've given that Combined Fleet the exact location of this base."

Draystar stopped. He and Jasmine exchanged glances. "Did you just say a Combined Pulsarian Fleet?" Varxbane grunted a reply. "I thought it was just a Task Force we ran into."

"My friend, there are more than five-hundred Advancers out there searching for this base." Varxbane sounded as if he were apologizing.

"I wasn't assigning any blame," Draystar said. "If I were in your boots, I would not even have considered sending a transmission in warning."

"However, you do feel that you flew into a trap," Varxbane quickly added. He was about to go on when he noticed Rook. He only had four Omnitraus stationed on his base. This one was new. "Who the hell are you?"

Rook stopped, surprised. "Omnitraus Officer and Star Force Captain Rook, General, at your disposal."

"Yes, I can see you're Omnitraus." Varxbane thundered over him. "What's your command?"

"November Command, General, stationed out of Narterium."

Varxbane's mind began to race. "You're the . . ." he didn't finish. He looked at the Gladatraus. "He's the . . . "

"That's right," Jasmine said.

"What?" asked N'ckshell. "I don't understand."

"Remember, during our briefing onboard the *Mekadore Traveler*, I said that Rook was Admiral Doss' insurance policy," Draystar said.

Slayton simply shrugged and followed the others into the conference room.

The conference chamber was divided into three sections; two preparation rooms and one primary briefing room. The briefing room was centered with a massive table of marble and oak, with twenty high-backed recliners ranged about it. All seats were occupied and there was an assortment of coffee mugs on the table, some half-filled, some steaming hot, others hours cold. There were ashtrays near some occupants filled with smoldering butts, personal datapads scattered here and there, half-eaten sandwiches, charts, and miniature image-projectors. The conversation in the room was just as scattered and disheveled as the briefing room itself. Of all the people seated at the table or milling around it, Leers could only recognize a half-dozen or so. The others were base personnel he'd never meet before or officers from the Delrellien Fleet.

"Attention on deck," an unidentified admiral demanded at the far side of the room.

"As you were," Varxbane said, waving them down.

Leers balked slightly at the 'attention on deck' command—though he didn't necessarily have to come to attention since he was with the General and two Gladatraus Guardians. 'Attention on deck' was a command that belonged in the navy and had no business on a Star Force base. Leave it to the Fleeters to come in here and impose their protocol onto everyone else.

"Find seats," Varxbane said.

As Jasmine and Draystar entered, several colonels retreated from their assigned seats and the table altogether. Varxbane remained standing and made quick introductions. The Fleeter who brought the deck to attention was Admiral William Walthersen of the 12th Yanattiian Defense Fleet—the other eleven had been destroyed. And from the weathered look affixed to Walthersen's face, the narrowness of his fleet's survival was apparent.

He was a stout individual in his fleet cloak; roughly squared features that made him appear more intense than handsome. Perhaps in his mid-fifties, Leers decided, with more than half his life spent in the service.

Across the table and further down was General Foster Starguard, the third highest officer on the base. No introduction needed here. She was the leader of the 91st Omega Attack/Interdiction Division, which Leers and Slayton were nearly at the bottom of a long chain-of-command, and were her direct subordinates. As with Jasmine and Draystar, if she wanted something done, the Omnitraus Officers would have to do it because they were pilots assigned to her division—although said orders would pass down through wing and squadron commanders, respectively. But the presence of Jasmine and Draystar complicated matters somewhat. Regulations demanded that the officer with tactical command of a situation, regardless of rank, could control the actions of the Omnitraus Officers by assigning them specific tasks, if necessary. A determination had to be established just who had tactical command of the current situation. And with the introductions not yet over, the current situation had yet to be established.

Leers shifted uneasily in his chair. After serving in General Starguard's command for more than two years, he had nothing but deep respect for her. But after spending several weeks in Hyperspace with the Gladatraus and witnessing how they took apart elements of a Pug taskforce, the question that tore at him was whom should he follow? If given a choice, would he fly into combat in the cockpit of a VF-94 Vagrant, or would he stay with the Gladatraus—yeah, find a nice comfortable place on the *Mekadore Traveler* to sit and maybe open up a few cans of beer, and watch them rip through more Pug battlecruisers and destroyers. Rook was lucky in the fact that he wasn't assigned to this base, he could take orders from the Gladatraus. Leers sighed and thought, *sometimes I guess it's better to be lucky than to be good.*

Further down the table were more Star Fleet officers; Leers missed their introductions. Didn't care. Next to them, however, were Colonels Piercenan of base security and Granx, an Aracrayderian walrus and chief of base administration. Leers didn't envy either one of them their jobs. If a Pug fighting force made it to the surface of the asteroid and attacked their base, it would be Piercenan's job to fight Malactites and tanks with laser rifles and grenades. And he'd have to do it with a security personnel and 'augmentees' barely numbering five hundred.

Colonel Granx, on a separate matter, had to make sure that all classified and sensitive items of probable intelligence value weren't captured by the Pulsarians in the event they did blow-through Piercenan's forces. A tremendously daunting task when one considered that on a Star Force command base, the term 'anything of probable intelligence value' ranged from simple classified documents to spare parts for tactical fighters. The BWRC would have to be gutted of all its systems, a process that could take weeks under normal circumstances. But Granx also had to consider the fighter and bomber squadrons spread throughout the region and their equipment . . . the logistical nightmare he faced was nothing short of migraine-stabbing insomnia.

By the time the introductions were finished, Leers didn't care who was seated at the table or who was standing around it. For they all had the same thing in common; their action or lack of action could lead to the deaths of many. Admittedly, it didn't take a genius to figure their situation was dire in the fairest of terms . . . suddenly Leers felt sick.

"Just before your arrival, my staff and I, the base commanders and administrators, and the personnel from the Star Fleet were attempting to come up with a plan to deal with that Combined Fleet."

"So who's the Pulsarian admiral commanding this Combined Fleet?" Jasmine whispered to herself.

"We haven't anything firm," Colonel Dargoinne said. "An educated assessment would place Marshal Admiral Rouldran Petti as the commanding Pulsarian."

"Indeed," answered Varxbane. "Welcome to this corner of hell. We're up against more than five hundred Advancers; more than was unleashed against Minerva during the first wave. But we are well-hidden within this asteroid system and well-protected underneath the surface of our asteroid. The only question is how long we can remain hidden."

"No problem," Draystar said. "Jasmine and I will stay here until the refugees are ready to leave, and then we'll—"

"What are you saying?" Varxbane demanded. "Did you not receive the Gladatraus Recall?"

"We did, but—"

"But nothing." Varxbane lowered his voice. "You and Jasmine must obey the Recall. You must leave at once. I don't know what was ordered, or the magnitude of the order. But a Gladatraus Recall is not something that can be so easily ignored or mistaken for anything other than what it is."

Draystar wasn't backing down. "Pardon me, General—"

"I will not. You must leave here. There may be greater things at issue here. Matters that we may not be aware of. When was the last time that a Recall was issued?"

"Minerva—but that—doesn't—"

"Leave us to our fate here."

Draystar turned toward the stunned officers and non-comms sitting or standing around the table. "You'll please excuse the General and I, we have matters to discuss in private."

Without a further word, Draystar grabbed his old instructor fiercely by the arm. Two of Varxbane's guards started to follow. Draystar held up an armored hand to halt them. Varxbane glanced to those in the briefing room as if to apologize for the sudden solecism.

Leers watched as Varxbane was forced-marched into the adjoining briefing room. The gasps in the room confirmed what he was feeling. It had happened so fast. Jasmine stood.

"Who can tell me what the current alert status is for this base?" she asked.

Meanwhile, in the adjoining room, the door didn't fully hiss shut before Draystar tore into Varxbane as if he were a second year cadet. "General Varxbane, I've known you for quite a long time, have nothing but the deepest respect for you. But I'm going to tell you something and I'll only say it once. I will not surrender those refugees to the Pulsarians. Damn the Recall. I will not surrender them!"

"They are not your concern."

"Every citizen of the Federation is my concern. Damnit, I took an oath. Jasmine took an oath—even those Omnitraus kids—they took an oath."

"And part of that oath is to obey the orders of Gladatraus Supreme, Draystar. She doesn't issue them lightly."

"I can't do it."

"You've heard the Gladatraus Recall?" Varxbane asked pointedly. He already knew the answer.

"Yes, so . . ."

"You *have* to report to Shiborium, as you were ordered. A Gladatraus Recall rescinds all other orders."

"I'm not going." Draystar thundered, folding his arms. "Not yet."

"What do you mean?" Varxbane roared. "Clarify your position, for the record."

"I'm not gonna abandon those citizens, for the record. We've lost Yanattii. I don't know how many millions the Pulsarians slaughtered. But those 250,000, I'm not gonna leave 'em here."

"Draystar, think! I asked you before: when was the last time a General Gladatraus Recall was issued?"

"As I said, during the campaign for Minerva."

"A Gladatraus Recall is never issued without merit."

"What makes the humans on Yanattii any different than the humans on

Minerva? There's no difference. People are people. And I will *not* leave these people!"

"My friend, this is far greater than you or I—than any of us. What the Omnitraus stole could be the one thing that turns this bloody mess around and saves all our worlds."

"I won't start by sacrificing these people. These lives are important. As a Guardian, I've sworn a duty to protect them, from the lowest to the highest. I'm no good unless I can do that . . . is it any wonder why we're losing this war?"

"Because individuals like you don't follow orders."

"No, it's because all I've done is follow orders—to the letter. And what's the result? More shattered lives. More wasted opportunities. It's always the same 'fall-back' strategy that amounts to nothing. Why? General, if we're not in this war to protect the citizens, what are we in it for?"

"To kill Pulsarians. We do that, we win the war."

"Not this Gladatraus."

"You are not making this easy, my friend."

"General, this is your Command Sector. By the articles of war, you are in command of Jasmine and I since we've evacuated the Yanattii sector. You could order me to leave."

"You know damned well that I'll do nothing of the sort." Varxbane began pacing. "So, Draystar, what would you propose we do?"

Draystar considered his friend's current stance. Varxbane was backing down, offering to work as a team instead of as rivals. "Speaking to you from a purely tactical point of view, there is only one course of action we dare take. And once again, I'm afraid it's the painfully obvious one."

"Retreat."

"Well, yes and no." Draystar waved his arms about hopelessly. "I hate retreat more than anyone on this base, including you, my friend. I don't like the taint of it." His armored helm rotated slowly. "But I grant you that something big is on the horizon. The Recall orders Jasmine and I to move with all available speed to the Shiborium star system. It even includes taking Dannen, Rook, N'ckshell and any other Omnitraus Officers on this base with us. Aside from that, I can only guess. Factor in Cyclops, losing two star systems in Genarra and Yanattii, the presence of a Combined Fleet poised to destroy this base—a base on the edge of nowhere. Something's brewing."

Varxbane stroked his chin. "Do you suppose that the Pulsarians are here to take back what those Omnitraus were sent out to steal?"

"Who knows what the Pulsarians are thinking."

"Retreat, eh?"

"A total evacuation of this entire Command. Against a Combined Fleet, you cannot hold out. I could barely hold out against a task force—and that's a hell of a thing for a Gladatraus Guardian to say. We may be able to surprise them with a couple of strikes; but in the end they will destroy us and those refugees. I promised to take them to a place of safety. A few weeks ago, what I said was true. Not anymore."

"Could you so casually refuse your orders from Gladatraus Supreme? I've met her once. Believe me, she's not a woman to be trifled with."

"Nevertheless, I will not leave without those refugees and I will not abandon this base so you all can be slaughtered by the Pulsarians. If I'm to understand my duty to the Federation, one of its central tenants is the protection of her people."

"The Recall has Gladatraus Command reporting to Shiborium," Varxbane mused.

"Imagine Gladatraus Supreme's astonishment when I report to Shiborium with not only myself and Jasmine, but the Omnitraus, and your entire Command. Who knows, she might resign and vote me Gladatraus Supreme."

Varxbane allowed himself a small grunt in amusement. "And the refugees?"

"And the refugees," Draystar repeated. "It seems that I'll be taking them to a place not much safer than this asteroid, in a strategic sense. But there they can breathe un-recycled air, eat fresh vegetables. For a time they will be safe. The Shiborium star system has billions of Dracterians who will welcome them. Who will fight for and with them?"

"Draystar, you're quite noble."

"Don't waste such a word on my actions, General. I'm only doing what I think is necessary for survival, nothing more."

"Survival, indeed," Varxbane boomed. "Then fight when a better opportunity presents itself."

"Staying here is—"

"You're right. I've already begun preparations for Command to evacuate this base."

"What?"

"I'm sorry, Draystar. But there's still a tremendous amount of work yet to be done. The movement of an entire Command is not as easy—"

"This was your position from the beginning?" Varxbane's idiotic shrug did little to quell his rage. "Why didn't you tell me this before? You let me believe—"

"I'm sorry, old friend."

"Why didn't you tell me?"

Varxbane turned away from the armored form. "Because, after all these years, I didn't want you to think that I was a coward." The gorilla leveled his large amber eyes at his friend. "There it is." Varxbane shrugged in spite of his honesty.

"I would never think that," Draystar said. "I think you're a manipulative prig, but certainly not a coward."

Varxbane reached for a nearby pitcher of water and a couple of glasses.

"A drink then, to our strategic evacuation. May it leave the Pulsarians positively thunderstruck. I don't know what I despise the most, being called a coward or a prig."

"You choose one, General. And while you make up your mind, you might have someone fetch us something stronger to drink."

CHAPTER XVI
RANGER SQUADRON . . . POLITICS

THE three Omnitraus Officers exited the diastolic disorder of the BWRC and entered the brightly lit corridors that constituted the core of the asteroid base. It was more of a retreat than anything else. The colonels and generals were going to be busy in the extreme and it was best to stay out of the way and let preparations run their natural course. After Guardian Draystar's disagreement with General Varxbane, the meeting had reconvened, and had lasted more than three hours. Leers had never been present during an evacuation planning session, the complexities of the details were more than he had ever imagined. During the battle of Minerva, everything was chaotic, every-being for itself. The hysteria, the panic was something that he didn't want to experience again. The generals and colonels of the base were determined to slip past the Pulsarian blockade and Warp to Shiborium. But slipping past a Combined Fleet would take some doing. So they laid plans, changed them, argued and re-worked the details. Draystar asked the Omnitraus to leave, the youngsters really couldn't offer any solutions; and their constant fidgeting was a distraction. If they needed assistance, he'd call on the Omnitraus; but until that time, Leers, Slayton and Rook were free to do whatever they felt necessary to prepare them for the rigors of the next few days.

"Now that's the kind of debriefing that I like," N'ckshell said as they started down another busy corridor, "short and oh so sweet."

"Short my ass," snorted Leers. "I thought we were never gonna get out of there."

"You know, I've been wondering," Rook said rubbing at his whiskers.

"Wondering what?" Leers asked. The human scratched his head.

"Wondering where it is that we're going." Rook ignored his last comment.

"Better question is where's Draystar going," Slayton said. "He slipped out of there rather slyly."

"My guess would be to find out more about 'you know who'."

"Whom, are you referring to?"

"Whom do ya'll think?" Leers huffed.

"Cyclops."

"N'ckshell this ain't a secured area—"

"So what, who cares—we're still inside of the BWRC," Slayton countered with an irritated shrug. "Besides, the whole bloody base probably knows about Cyclops by now; it shouldn't be such a secret."

"But still."

N'ckshell shook her head vigorously. "Dannen, you're such a dildo. It should be your call-sign instead of Duke." She took a deep breath heaving her abdominals in and proceeded to mock her friend. "This is Dildo Leader, *I'mah* painting four bandits on *mah* radar. . ."

Rook shot her an amused stare then eyed Dannen. "How do you put up with this?"

"Believe me it ain't easy."

"Dildo Leader has *ah'* tally . . ."

"Are you through?"

"Where did you say we were going?" Rook uttered with a stifled giggle.

"To our Squadron," Leers answered. "I'll introduce you to several friends—"

"Nice of you, friend Dannen, but I would like to eat first."

"Didn't you eat on the *Mekadore Traveler*?" N'ckshell asked him.

"The squadron has a nice little bistro," Leers supplied.

"It does?" Rook arched his eyebrow. "Lovey, to answer your question I ate regretfully very little food on that Rhoderium ship. I can't eat the food on those ships, I just can't. It tastes too manufactured, too antiseptic."

"Besides food; if we tangle with the Pulsarians, Rook, it'd be nice to have you up there with us," Leers said.

"Dannen please . . ." N'ckshell let the scorn lather her words.

"What? We can use all the help we can get."

"Our Squadron is so rank heavy right now, that—"

"Is it?" Rook asked, "How many pilots do you have?"

"Too many, would be a conservative answer for you."

"I'll just ask the squadron commander," Leers said ignoring her. "I'm sure he'll—"

"Dannen, are you willing to give up your seat for Rook?" N'ckshell wanted to know.

"No."

"Neither am I, because that's what it's going to come down to."

"I'm sure we can talk to some of the guys and make room for Rook."

"We? You mean you."

"Yeah."

"Wait a second, Dannen my good friend, this is happening a bit too fast for me."

"Don't worry about it, Rook. I can get you a seat."

"No, thank you."

"What do you mean?"

"What type of machine do you people fly again?"

"The Vagrant E, why?"

"Not the Valkyrie."

"No, Rook—and we already discussed this, remember?"

"There isn't a Valkyrie within ten lightyears of this base," Slayton said.

"Yes, the Vagrant," Rook said, thick with sarcasm. "Now I remember, how quaint."

"Hold it right there, Rook. The Vagrant's a good machine. It's a reliable machine and can gun your brains out while you're looking for a button to push in your precious Valkyrie."

"Come now, my friend, you should hear yourself. We both know the Vagrant's a trashcan."

"No it ain't."

"Yes, it is," Slayton said.

"Nobody asked you."

"He's right, Dannen."

Rook held up his hands. "Alright, all hassling aside and faced with no other choice, I'd fly the Vagrant. I won't like it, but I'd do it. However, I will not take some pilot's seat just so I can fly. I'd need a few hours in the simulator, then a couple more hours to familiarize myself with the spaceframe, then there's the astronics, weapons . . ."

"You can do it easily, you're an Omnitraus Officer."

"Stop saying that. It's not that easy; never that easy. It's more than just flying the fighter, it's putting that machine through aggressive combat maneuvers and learning what I can and can't do in that machine and unlearning all of the tricks that I've learned while flying the Valkyrie. Then I'd have to get acquainted with your squadron mates who won't like the fact that, 'here comes another Omnitraus Officer we're being forced to accommodate.' And a pyramid of other complications too damned numerous to list."

"So, your point is. . ."

"That's your response to everything non-Omnitraus?" Rook looked incredulously. "It's no wonder they don't like us—but my answer is still a respectable no."

"Damn, I guess. Sure would've been nice to have you flying with us."

"Speak for yourself," Slayton parried.

"If we were going to be here for more than a month, then I'd take you up on your offer," Rook said. "Tell me about your squadron—what do you people call yourselves again?"

"The Ranger Squadron." Leers went on to explain that the Ranger Fighter Squadron was directly subordinate to the 1st Omega Tactical Fighter Wing, which, of course, was directly subordinate to the 91st Omega Attack/Interdiction Division. Under the 91st there were three fighter wings with three squadrons each for a total of nine squadrons on the asteroid base in all. Sister squadrons of the Rangers consisted of the Boulder and Echo Fighter Squadrons. Typically speaking, however, most Star Force Fighter Wings consisted of four subordinate squadrons, not three—the Rampage Squadron had been unceremoniously re-assigned to Shiborium a couple of years ago to make room for more FB-25 Poltergeists from one of the bomber wings. To make room for all of the new equipment and personnel, the entire headquarters staff of the 1st OTFW had been moved within the cavern that housed Ranger Squadron. No squadron commander liked the idea of having the wing commander literally down the hall from you, asking questions about day-to-day operations, looking over one's shoulder—but the wing commander left squadron matters to squadron commanders—usually. In an operational sense, all fighter squadrons maintained between twenty-four and thirty-two identical fighters, with more than enough crews and technical staff to maintain them; the three squadrons under the 1st OTFW were no exception. Regulations demanded that at least eighteen fighters had to be combat ready at all times, no more than five could be used in training student pilots, while two would be utilized for emergency maintenance stand-by.

Many command generals (General Varxbane not among them) didn't view Omega Command as a *real* command. It wasn't located within a planetary system, it didn't regulate interstellar commerce, it was remote—more than a dozen lightyears from any habitable star system. Theatre commanders, while viewing Varxbane's asteroid base as a viable and important strategic center, thought of it as nothing more than an outpost . . . an outpost constructed with the sole purpose of supporting them. When population centers came under attack, Omega Command provided help—Omega Command didn't get help. That was the rule.

It was a rule Leers didn't like; however, it was a rule he and the other pilots had to live with. For the most part, fighter wings were designed to be malleable. Fighter squadrons could be moved and reassigned to different wings within the command division, or they could be moved and re-assigned to a different division under a different command—but it always depended on the strategic situation: where were the Pulsarians attacking, which systems were feeling threatened and so on. . . . Regulations concerning wing and squadron cohesion, just as important as malleability, were ignored at the expense of the pilots. And it affected morale—Leers and Slayton had literally flown missions all over the galaxy. There'd be little rest, no recuperation, before they'd have to fly more sorties across time and space. Aside from all that, at least the food in the cantina was good.

"These are difficult times we all have to face," Rook said picking up the conversation again. "Things aren't any easier in November Command."

"Yes, but there's a million pilots there," Leers countered. "There's probably just under a thousand pilots here at Omega."

"True enough, but you didn't have any civilians to protect," Rook mused. "Until now."

"That's right, until now—ain't nobody's coming to help us either."

They moved toward the huge station platform where it seemed that half the base was waiting to board travel tubes. There were seven levels with three tubes each. Cargo platforms, elevators, escalators, anti-grav lifter pads with black and yellow caution placards were everywhere. The travel tubes looked like thick, elongated, gleaming torpedoes with windows and conformal sliding doors. Each floated centimeters above hydra-dynamic magneto rails that snaked away from the station into tunnels leading to the other areas of the base. Areas that included auxiliary command, computer central, fighter operations, Kinteesen Park, Varett Botanical Gardens, as well as the hangars to the various fighter wings and squadrons. There were more than 10,000 kilometers of rail laid throughout the Kinteesen Range, all beneath the surface.

When Leers relayed this information to Rook, he was thoroughly amazed. The asteroid base was truly larger than it seemed—in fact the usage of 'base' was a cruel under characterization of the labyrinthine cities constructed below the surface of the planetoid.

There were large monitors everywhere relaying schedule information and travel tube availability. Rook examined one of the monitors and was confused. None of it made sense. It was a gaggle of multi-colored shapes and symbols with time symbols that read vertically instead of horizontally—some of it seemed backwards. But he hurriedly boarded a 'green' tube, chasing after his friends. He strapped himself into a rather comfortable seat. The train was very crowded and Rook wondered how Varxbane and his staff were going to evacuate this base before the Pulsarians attacked. Until now, Rook had never fully realized the enormity of it all. This wouldn't be a simple evacuation by any means. It had to be accomplished with Star Force cargo haulers—naval merchant shipping didn't exist on this base. With the merchant vessels, the task would be enormous . . . without it, well . . . it was a paragon without equal.

The travel tube snaked its way through the dark tunnels at 300kpx. It was a wild, light reflective ride that lasted barely ten minutes. The train came to a gradual halt and the three exited with a dozen other personnel. They emerged into a vast cavern, a kilometer in diameter, the stalactite ceiling more than two hundred meters above them. They were standing on the transport's station platform, which, itself was some fifty meters above the dusty cavern floor—this was a good day, Leers noted; usually the ground was muddy. But the cavern was brilliantly lighted; dozens of Geenenht Manufacturing lamps, each more than ten meters long and three across, were arranged along the ceiling. This was the home of Ranger Squadron where pilots could laser lasso an asteroid, so claimed the squadron emblem on the wall.

Rook smiled a toothy grin and found his heart pounding as he split away from the others and walked up to the guard railing; the sight beneath him warming his blood. He saw twenty VF-94E Vagrants assembled like waiting birds of prey on the cavern floor at their marked hardstands and then another five parked further down the tarmac at a range of two-hundred meters.

Rook knew that the basic VF-94 fighter called the Vagrant was just over twenty meters in length, with a wingspan of eleven meters. Two immense Rand & Drake VF-180HBVA (Hyperballistic/Vector Augmenting) engines powered the fighter. Each was capable of generating 2.5 million tons of thrust on planetary surfaces with atmosphere and a gravitational force of 1G. Outside atmosphere and in near- to high-orbital positions, the Vagrant could cruise at speeds ranging from 20,000kpx to 120,000kpx. At still greater distances from planetary bodies, its speed could exceed 287,000kpx. And while the Vagrant didn't have Warp capability, it could easily be fitted with Hyper Warp Booster Rockets, or 'fast-packs' as the pilots called them, enabling the Vagrant to support long-range missions anywhere in the galaxy.

The Vagrant was a multi-role fighter that could fly surface attack missions in support of infantry or conduct fighter interdiction missions; thus it came in eight different variants arranged alphabetically from A (the oldest) to H (the newest and rarest model). The variant designation didn't indicate that B models were better than As, or that Ds were better than Cs, it just indicated that some models were faster than others, that some were stronger than others, that some had better ground tracking radar while others had better long-range space scanners.

The Vagrant held a flight crew of two—a pilot and a weapon system and scanner officer. They sat in tandem. The Vagrant wasn't large enough for the side-by-side seating arrangement that was found on the mammoth VF-81 Vixen. Its primary weapon was the RG-4 railgun, which could shoot armor-piercing projectiles at targets such as Spark Racers or Malactites at nearly 150,000kpx; the pilots called them 'disks' or 'wafers'. Along six weapon pylons mounted beneath the wings and fuselage, the Vagrant could carry the

LPT laser guns that fired the Shard weapon, or the VPM energy rifle that fired the ultra-lethal Harpoon, or gun mounts that fired highly-charged Maces—the list of weapon types was as long as the list of missions the beastly VF-94E could fly.

Rook continued to scan the hangar/cavern. There was a control tower at one end, a ground control building below it, maintenance shops, and hot-refueling pits. There were also four black and yellow emergency crash vehicles parked against the east wall. There wasn't a lot of activity in the hangar at the moment; in fact, only four of the Vagrants had mechanics and technicians swarming around them. But this was only a small part of Ranger squadron, Leers informed the cheetah. The rest of the squadron—offices, dining facilities, the armory, and personnel quarters—was located beneath the cavern floor and behind the cavern walls.

Dannen and N'ckshell flipped their identity badges to the two stern-looking Retainers standing before the access way leading to the rest of the squadron. To the left was a solid wall of rock kilometers thick, behind was the entrance to the travel tubes, to the right was the hangar floor, fifty meters beneath their feet. The only way down was through the Retainers and down a long flight of stairs. And from the look of the guards, they weren't going to let anyone pass without proper authorization. The Retainers immediately recognized Leers and Slayton.

"Welcome back, ya'll," the battle-armored sergeant said slinging a blast pike over his shoulder. He saluted. "Been kinda quiet around here without you two causing one ruckus after another. Your badges, please. Thank-you. And you would be?"

Rook felt for his badge in his coat pocket.

"This is Omnitraus Officer Captain Rook," Leers spoke up as Rook finally located his badge and handed it to the sergeant. The sergeant studied the badge, perhaps a bit too closely, handed it back to Rook, saluted, then waved them through.

"Security's tighter than usual," Slayton said as they moved passed the guards and the energy fence and started down the stairs.

"Keen observation," Rook answered.

"T'harum, agfe weium 'thaim, ecs ecs Sihium!"

Surprised, Rook turned to the source of the salutation. He immediately recognized the language and he knew the female voice that it belonged to. The voice belonged to Slayton's sister, L'ennell Slayton. She wore a mid-night blue flight-suit with the shoulder patches of the Echo Squadron and the rank insignia of a full colonel. On her right wrist was a solid gold anti-shock high-resolution chronogram. A *Sheaghe* original, of course. Years before being assigned to the Echo Squadron she flew VF-94F Vagrants from Desdemona and the 43rd Tactical Fighter Division, 202nd Princess-Vermillia Tactical Fighter Wing, Storm Squadron commander, and had helped the humans in that sector repel repeated Pulsarian attacks. She was a cunning and utterly merciless fighter pilot who gave enemy pilots no quarter. She acted like a fairy-play romantic outside the cockpit; posed as a knight who gallantly went up to meet the enemy to engage in the ultimate test of skill and bravery. But once the Shards flew, she was anything but chivalrous. Every dirty trick, flanking maneuver, deceptive sleight of hand, stick-and-rudder, booster input she could employ she did. And with a ferocity that belied her beauty. Her job was to fly and kill Pulsarians and leave romance to poets.

She had the same pale, milky white skin that her sister had and sharply pointed ears that were partially hidden behind her beautiful long velvety black hair with streaks of crimson. She was, however, taller than her sibling.

"Where were you? I haven't seen you for weeks," she repeated, speaking Delrel Primary now. She rushed up to her sister and embraced her tightly, kissing her cheek. She pulled back to tug on her sharply pointed nose. "How are you?"

"I'm fine," N'ckshell said, exasperated. She pulled away from her smiling.

L'ennell smiled back, satisfied that she had succeeded in embarrassing her younger sister yet again.

"Where have you been?"

"On a—we'll talk about it later."

"Last time you said that you disappeared for a month," L'ennell said sarcastically. "Does it have anything to do with this Cyclops business? Don't look so damned shocked, the whole base is talking."

"So it would seem." The younger Slayton glared at Rook and Leers.

"Hello, Mr. Leers," L'ennell said, hugging the man. "Wherever you go, my sister is not so far away."

"Well, someone has to keep her out of trouble." For the first time Leers noticed that she was wearing a shoulder holster with Fleeter laser pistol. "Nice weapon."

"We have to be cautious with all the Cyclops hysteria and—" she noticed Rook and smiled. "What's your name? No, don't say anything, let me guess."

Rook stood shocked. He'd been a family friend for years and hadn't expected to see another Slayton stationed on this asteroid base and hadn't expected to receive such a greeting from one—then again the Slayton's seemed to be everywhere. "Very funny, Colonel Slayton."

"Ah, Rook," she said, nearly bursting into laughter. She grabbed his arm and squeezed it. "You're always so serious; even after all these years. What brings you here? Gods, all we need now is for my brother C'riss to be here and we could have a family and friends reunion like the old times. As I recall, you were stationed at November Command. If things weren't so bad around here, I'd be thoroughly pleased to see all of you."

"What, you know my Command, but you can't remember my name?" He hugged her. She spoke so quickly, Rook had a difficult time tracking her words.

"Are you here for reassignment? That is, before the retreat."

"Unfortunately, no. And it's not a retreat, it's an evacuation."

"Call it what you will." A serious glint sparkled in her eyes. "Things are going ugly here, fast. We have a Pulsarian Fleet lurking about. There's this business with Cyclops. And our food is running short with a million refugees here."

"Not quite a million," Leers said.

"Does it really matter?"

"It's good to see you and my sister finally getting along," Colonel Slayton said. "Friends?"

"Sis."

"Uh, yeah," Rook said, shrugging. "I guess."

"Rook, try to sound more enthusiastic than that," the younger Slayton hissed. "For years I've wanted to kill you—don't look so shocked, sister—but when the moment came I didn't—okay? All because of something Cyclops did on Minerva. But it's over . . . history as they say. I want to 'move on' and not have my sister or other people continually remind me of it."

"That's good," L'ennell Slayton said evenly. "You both make better allies than enemies."

"If you say so."

"Rook!" The younger Slayton made a motion of punching the cheetah in the ribs, who dodged and launched his own humored shot to the Dracterian's face.

That was good to see. Their behavior seemed normal, L'ennell thought. One never knew. Her sister could go into a berserking rage with little or no provocation. "But neither of you answered my original question. What brings you out here?" Again, she glanced toward Leers as if he would furnish her with an answer.

"I wish I could tell you." Rook raised his shoulders.

"Damnit, you all." She shook her head disdainfully. "N'ckshell, I haven't seen you in weeks—you didn't say a single word when you left, you just vanished. I know your missions for the Omnitraus are 'need to know' and all that other nonsense, but what happened with our simple code? Remember, we have a code."

"I didn't know you two had a code," Leers whispered to N'ckshell.

The elder Slayton ignored him and continued. "Did I mention that we had Pulsarians everywhere, spies, murder—and you bring Rook here as if nothing's happened? I beg your pardon if I sound a bit tense. But you're the only sister I have left. And I know that what we do is dangerous, you have to warn me before you leave. Please."

"I wish I could tell you," Rook said politely. "Right now we can't say anything."

She smiled. "I wasn't talking to you, Rook. My sister can speak for herself—"

"Sorry Lensy, this time I can't say a word," the younger Slayton shrugged.

"You Omnitraus are so full of yourselves sometimes. You're privy to all of this 'secret-code-breaker' nonsense and you never say a word to your fellow pilots."

"N'ckshell's right, there ain't much to say, really," Leers swore.

"Some things will never change. None of you will ever change."

One thing that hadn't changed was L'ennell—she was as beautiful and as fiery as ever, Leers found himself thinking absently. Or perhaps it hadn't been that far back in his mind. Looking at L'ennell—well it was impossible not to look at her. The four of them had known each other for nearly two decades. And Rook's sparring with the Slayton sisters was nothing new, it could be traced back to when he was a cub just getting used to the tremendous power in his legs and sprinting into walls or furniture.

L'ennell was older than N'ckshell and her twin brother, C'riss, by six years and the twin sister of N'arsha who had died during the Minerva invasion. Every time Dannen looked at L'ennell he thought of N'arsha—every single time. *N'arsha.* My God. She was beautiful! Dannen had loved her. It was more than a simple boyhood crush. He loved her. The pain of her loss had been difficult to erase—N'ckshell could never understand this and perhaps she never would—he had been able to 'move on'—to borrow a term from her; L'ennell had been able to move on as well. This generation of the Slayton family had lost two brothers and one sister. One brother had been killed before N'ckshell was born, the other when the Pulsarians invaded the Commander Star system seven years ago, N'arsha had been killed during the Minerva invasion; C'riss, L'ennell and N'ckshell remained.

"How do you feel, Dannen?" She noticed that Leers appeared to be in a trance and he was absently rubbing his neck.

"Hmm? Oh, I'm fine—really—nothing to worry about." He saw the unmistakable concern in her eye and patted her reassuringly on the shoulder. "Everything's all right."

"Of course you are." She managed a thin smile.

"What were you doing here in the first place?" The younger Slayton asked. "Certainly not to check up on our return and definitely not to embarrass Rook."

"I just got out of a meeting with the wing commander," the elder Slayton feigned disgust. "Gods, I hate talking to her. It must drive you guys crazy to have the wing commander so close—always getting into your business. Anyway, folks are getting nervous with all of the Pulsarians lurking around the asteroid system and I get the feeling that we're going to be asked to fly soon—I'm making sure that we're in a position to kill more of them than they of us."

"Thanks a lot, colonel," N'ckshell snorted. "I was hoping to take it easy for a while. Kill that idea."

"You were taking it easy while you were away," L'ennell said as she turned toward the transport tubes. "And no one's saying anything about how many of them are out there."

"Oh, how many of what?" Leers said stupidly.

"Puggies, you idiot," L'ennell said, tilting her head forward. "Is it just a brace of Advancers or an entire task force we're facing? Nobody's saying a damned thing—nothing. Or is it two task forces?"

"Sure, why not?"

"Good, more of them to kill," L'ennell said. "I'm off to grab a quick nap. Stop by my quarters at 011:00 hours. Or better yet, why don't you meet me near the northern falls. We can eat there. Rook, you can join us too."

Rook was about to say something but waved instead.

"One more thing, Mr. Leers," L'ennell's tone suddenly changed. "You may want to speak with the wing commander before you do anything else."

"Why?"

"Why not." She turned and moved briskly for the transport tube, with a smirk and a slight wave—more of a flick of her wrist than anything else.

"Well, wasn't that a bit . . . odd," Leers whispered.

"I didn't know that your sister was stationed here?" Rook said.

"Sometimes I wish she weren't," Slayton said dryly. "She checks up on me as if she were human."

"What other surprises do you have in store for me?" Rook asked

The question went unanswered as they turned down the stairway and onto the tarmac. They moved behind a VF-94E Vagrant, fuel lines and power cables hanging from it like tentacles. Mechanics swarmed around the machine like drones servicing the queen bee. Leers stopped, noticing a tall figure standing just outside of the frantic activity.

It was Omnitraus Officer Captain Stan McHellington. The man was roughly Leers' size, with hair so blond that it was nearly white. He was deeply tanned, had a lean muscular body and piercing blue-grey eyes set in a handsomely chiseled face. His one-piece, gray, Ranger Squadron flight suit was folded down at his waist; only his checkered black and white hunting shirt—not squadron issue, of course—covered his chest and arms.

"Stan!" Leers shouted.

McHellington whirled. "Dannen, N'ckshell and—me God in Heaven, Rook." He blinked. "What in the name of—" He raced toward the three, trying to embrace all three simultaneously.

"It's good ye're back," McHellington said. "Rook, what tha' hell are ye' doin here? Ah thought ye're stationed at November Command, with ah, Starjax and Theri."

"Why is everyone I run into so concerned about me and November Command? It may be tough going but they can survive quite well without me for a while."

"Hey, ye here to help us fight—ye didn't bring Theri with ye?"

"No, I didn't bring Theri—you know, during beer call she still talks about you—but the Gladatraus brought me here to answer your query."

"Gladatraus?" McHellington glanced toward Leers and Slayton. "What the hell? They're back?"

"Guardians Jasmine and Draystar," Slayton provided.

McHellington frowned. He wanted to ask about his old girlfriend and the Gladatraus at the same time and also tell them about the—"these're the same Gladatraus who had pulled in here a few weeks ago with the refugees and now they bring ye here?" He was pointing at Rook.

"I know," Leers said. "I'm still confused by it all."

"Ah bet."

Rook started away from the others, examining the engines of a nearby Vagrant. "I hear there's another one of our classmates stationed here."

"Yes, Kaltorr's around here somewhere, me laddy." McHellington looked around. "A couple of hours ago he and his crew were at the other side of the hangar pacing their hot-refueling skills—trying not to blow themselves up and the hangar."

Rook grinned, Kaltorr was one of the finest Omnitraus to graduate the same time as he. Kaltorr hadn't attended the Bastian Academy. He'd attended school on Hera, Minerva's sister planet, and had his graduation ceremony violently interrupted when the Pulsarians invaded the star system. No matter what the next few days threw at them, they'd all be able to handle it better with Kaltorr here.

Kaltorr was a fierce, incredibly strong warrior, an Aracrayderian Rhinoceros. He relied on immense physical strength as well as his wits to get him through tough spots. He was a shrewd, calculating warrior. During grueling centrifuge tests, he could withstand twelve times the force of gravity for five minutes without blacking out or causing undue damage to his body. Incredible feats of strength were not uncommon among Aracrayderian Rhinos.

"Tell me, Stan, is he still torturing himself with unnecessary centrifuge time?"

"Oh, no. He's much wiser in his old age, Rook. He just spins an hour in the centrifuge instead of two."

"I can't wait to talk to him," Rook said.

"He'll make his presence known soon enough I'm sure." McHellington turned toward Leers and Slayton. "I've got some somber news, friend."

"What is it?" Leers asked.

"The ah, squadron leader was killed a couple of days ago and the exec is recovering in the base hospital."

"What happened?"

"They were flying a sweep when they got jumped by the Pulsarians. Outnumbered four-to-one—the usual odds. Colonel Starjohns got killed on the first pass. The others barely made it back. But they bagged three of the bastards before they RTB'ed."

"The Colonel's dead." Leers stared at him, his gut aching. "N'ckshell, I think we'd better report in."

"Yes, ye'd better." McHellington's tone was on the sour side. He gripped Leers' shoulder. "I've been assigned to command the squadron the next time we move out against the Pulsarians."

Leers blinked. "What?" he simply stammered.

McHellington simply unrolled the upper-half of his flight suit up from around his waist and pulled it over his hunting shirt—Leers could now see the wing and squadron patches . . . and also the brass insignia of—

"Major," Leers shouted, "you've made major, how? And you have the squadron?"

Slayton felt her face burning. "Uh, oh."

"Yes, me have made major, and ah will command the squadron."

Leers didn't like the tone or the hint of radiance forming on McHellington's face. "By all rights, I'm the next in line for major and squadron commander by a freaking lightyear—not you."

"Dannen, maybe we should . . ." N'ckshell pulled gently on his arm.

"Hey, that's not what the wing commander thinks," McHellington answered, radiating more.

"Is that so?" Leers stepped forward, glancing from N'ckshell to McHellington. "Well, we'll see about that."

McHellington shrugged, "go ahead with ye. Because she's here and—"

Leers turned away from him. "It's wrong and you know it." He paused. "But congratulations on your rank, Major Stan McHellington—but this squadron is mine."

"Ye'll find that difficult to—"

Leers wasn't listening anymore as he stormed down the flight-line with N'ckshell trailing after him.

"While you two report in," Rook called after them. "I'm going have Stan here lead me to some food; don't worry about me." Rook smiled at McHellington.

"That black bastard," McHellington snarled.

"My dear Stanley, there's simply no need for all that."

"What do ye mean? There's plenty of need."

"Simply this," Rook began clipping his next words, "if you are indeed the new Ranger Squadron commander, don't concern yourself with such trivialities. Let Dannen fall on his face. Let him argue his case and let him fail. You'll only appear weak if you rush in there on his heels raising counter claims to his challenge."

"What—there's nothing," McHellington stumbled over his words trying to express five ideas all at once. "Ah, Rook, the devil take ye and yer blasted advice. Blast ye."

"Don't do it Stan—I know about these things."

"But . . ."

Rook merely nodded slowly as McHellington rubbed at his throat. "Ah don't know about this mate. Ah, just don't know."

"I'm famished, remember."

"Alright. The squadron bistro is open—or should be. The choices have been rather limited over the last few weeks."

"It'll do."

CHAPTER XVII
FORENSICS

DANNEN and N'ckshell walked briskly through the corridors of the Ranger Squadron's operations center, then straight on to the hall of the 1st Omega Tactical Fighter Wing. On either side of the corridor were briefing rooms, ready rooms, communications sections, offices, small logistical workshops and a few wing personnel, eyeing the Omnitraus as they strolled by. In a matter of seconds, they entered the command section and moved swiftly through a maze of half-crewed cubicles and workstations, never noticing a lean figure stepping out to intercept them both.

Suddenly N'ckshell slowed. "I don't think this is a good idea, Dannen," she was saying. "There's just too much going on right now—with the Pulsarians and everything else. Maybe we should—"

"No, N'ckshell, something stinks here and you know it. Stan is never that smug."

"I guess it's going to be your funeral because I'm not the wing commander's favorite pilot, remember?"

"So?"

"Look, when a captain gets into a shouting match with a major—what was his name again—never mind. It's not a smart tactical move."

"Whoa, where do ya'll think you're going?" The man, taller than either

Leers or Slayton, demanded. There was nothing polite or respectful in his manner.

Leers almost pushed his way past him—almost, that is until he noticed the rank epaulets, and the sneering upturned lips set against a face that wore more arrogance than professionalism. Colonel M. Jacob Galensen was the operations officer of the wing but often times threw his weight around as if the heavens themselves answer to him only. Leers halted about a meter from Galensen and Slayton nearly ran into the back of her friend.

"Dannen, I'm going to head back to the squadron—"

Leers quickly seized her arm, cutting off her escape.

"We need to speak with the wing commander, sir," Leers answered respectfully.

"Is that so?" Galensen said folding his arms. "The WC can't see anyone at this time."

"She'll see me."

"About what?" Galensen placed the palm of his hand against Leers' chest—Leers didn't know what the hell the colonel was doing or why any of this was his business.

"We can make an appointment for another time . . ." Slayton said twisting her arm out of Leers' grip.

"It's no concern of yours, Colonel, sorry," Leers said, ignoring her.

"Right now, I'm making it my concern, son."

Don't really recall seeing you on my family tree. Leers almost smiled in spite himself, then sighed. There was nothing like silly frat-house intimidation. Leers had endured this kind of treatment before and it didn't have anything to do with rank, or tradition, or who was more intelligent. No matter how hard you worked there was always those stationed way above your pay-grade who seemed threatened by your mere presence. "Respectfully speaking, sir, I don't have to tell you anything—you're not in my direct line of command—"

"Yes, but I outrank you Captain or whatever the hell rank you hold." Galensen folded his arms, his complexion darkening. "I don't know, since you're not in any Star Force uniform that I can recognize."

"I just got back from an assignment."

"That's no excuse. You are Star Force first, Omnitraus second, got it? Or should I make it an operational order for all of the squadrons in this wing?"

"You don't have to do that, sir," Slayton chirped nervously.

"Where were you off to playing commando this time?"

"Sorry, sir, but I'm not obligated to reveal that." *That's it, kill him with kindness and respect.*

"You arrogant little Omnitraus Officers think you can do whatever you please and go wherever you please." He stood just a few centimeters taller than either Leers or Slayton and glared at them. "But know this, you don't see the wing commander until I okay the meeting—got it!"

"Yes, colonel." *Universe, he's serious. Why do I have to deal with this moron?* He caught a brief glance of Slayton standing at his side—the incredulous look on her face confirmed what he was already feeling. *Maybe Stan was right—maybe I should get along and go along—*

"Well? What are you still standing around here for? Move out of operations and I'll contact you when the WC can speak to you."

"Colonel Galensen, respectfully sir, I can't do that because I need to know who will be commanding the Ranger Squadron when we make a move against the Pulsarians."

"Who says we're going to make a move against the Pulsarians? The wing hasn't gotten any orders from the BWRC."

"But, sir, something is bound to happen—"

"The Ranger Squadron has a replacement for Colonel Nate Starjohns. But you probably don't know about that since you were away."

"That's it, sir; Colonel Starjohns' replacement should be me."

Galensen nearly burst out in full-throated laughter. "It should be anyone but you." Instead, he studied Leers and ran a hand through the blonde fibers of his crew cut.

"I beg your pardon, sir, but I've been informed on the current situation and—"

"And you want to cry to the WC?"

"Excuse me, Colonel, but you're way out of line."

"Watch your bearing, mister."

"You watch your bearing," Leers blurted. "I've got more seat time in the VF-94E than Major Stan McHellington—who's also an Omnitraus Officer I might add."

"He knows he's a pilot first and doesn't run off to play commando like you or her."

"Even still, I know I've got more kills, I've flown more missions and I've busted my ass time and time again to prove to you people that I can lead and you continually promote others ahead of me, why?"

"Look, kid—and you too, little gal—no matter how good ya'll think ya'll are, you always make the mistake of thinking you can do or say anything you damned well please. You come and go as you want. I don't care if you are an Omnitraus Officer or not. Maybe if you got busted down to the rank of sergeant you'd show a little more respect."

Suddenly Leers wasn't listening to Galensen anymore. He had to lock down the urge to level the man right then and there—if he had less mental capacity he probably would have. Not that it would've changed the situation, but it would've made him feel a lot better. A second later, it didn't matter how he felt. Two meters away a door whooshed aside and the lithe Colonel Anastasia Zimmer materialized into the work area flanked by her executive officer Colonel Krandersen. She and the rough-looking Krandersen wore crisp black flight suits, but she had a red scarf tied around her neck. She had long blonde locks that hung past her shoulders. She was easily twice the age of Leers but only looked two or three years older. She had been an instructor pilot on Minerva. Picked up her first combat assignment on Valiant, then moved onto Desdemona. She was reassigned to the asteroid base just six months ago. By reputation alone, Leers knew her to be a fierce competitor and solid leader and had only spoken to her once before. She demanded and expected that the more than two-hundred pilots in her command put their intelligence and aggression into every mission they flew. Those who didn't meet her expectations—well, it was better not to tread in the waters of mediocrity around Zimmer.

"What the hell is going on out here?" She demanded in a voice that would've transformed a rainforest into a glacier.

Galensen's right eye twitched nervously as he bent around to regard his commanding officer and the executive officer of the wing. Like an idiot, he saluted, then quickly stated, "Wing Commander Zimmer, we were just about to take our conversation to the wing briefing room when—"

Leers quickly stepped forward and cut Galensen off, "Colonel Zimmer, I'm Dannen Leers with the Ranger Squadron and I request an immediate. . . "

Leers never finished as Zimmer pushed past Galensen and looked up at Leers. "I know who you are, young man. What is it that you want?"

"I beg your pardon, Wing Commander, but I can bring clarity to this situation—" Galensen began.

"I didn't ask you Colonel Galensen, I asked him." Galensen nearly smoldered into a pool of vapor under Zimmer's glare. "Please proceed, Mr. Leers."

"It has to do with the new leader of the Ranger Squadron, Colonel Zimmer; that's the problem."

"And you saw fit to by-pass the normal line of command to address your wing commander directly? It must be some problem."

Having been given clearance to speak, Leers suddenly couldn't find the words to continue. In an instant, his mouth felt pasty and he thought that he was going to slide right out of his skin. "Being blunt, but the line of command is the problem."

"This is preposterous!" Galensen thundered.

"I beg your pardon, sir," Leers said.

"Let him speak, Colonel Galensen, please." Zimmer looked away from Galensen back to Leers. "Where's your uniform?"

"I—"

"Never mind, I almost forgot that you're one of those damned Omnitraus Officers, aren't you?" She folded her arms across her breasts and brought N'ckshell under her steely gaze. "You are as well. You here for the same reason; concerns about the LOC?"

"No, colonel, I'm here to keep Dannen from killing someone," Slayton said and immediately wished that she'd kept her mouth shut. "Bad joke."

"And you're out of uniform as well." Zimmer noted. "How the hell am I supposed to know what rank the both of you are and what squadron you belong to? With those damned Omnitraus utility uniforms you're wearing, I can't even tell if you are pilots or engine maintenance trainees. You look like a couple of goddamned mercenaries."

Colonel Galensen didn't hide the fact that he was taking pleasure in the wing commander's comments. His face began illustrating a wry, but somewhat vicious smile.

"I strongly apologize for our appearance, Colonel Zimmer. We only arrived here a couple of hours ago and . . ."

"I didn't ask for an explanation, Leers. And Jacob, if you can't maintain bearing, you know where your office is."

"Well, ma'am—"

"Don't call me 'ma'am'. Do I look like your grandma to you?"

"The problem is really two fold, Colonel Zimmer—I feel that I've been passed up for promotion and command of Ranger Squadron."

"You were away on one of those secret Omnitraus missions," Galensen interjected shoving a finger into Leers' chest.

"Enough of this." Zimmer looked as if someone had insulted her ancestry. "You two, in my office, now. Colonel Galensen—get out of my sight and stay out of it for the next ten hours. In fact, why don't you just stay in your office the entire time."

She didn't wait for a protest and simply followed Krandersen, Leers and Slayton into her office. As the doors closed with hissing authority, Colonel M. Jacob Galensen just stood there, gawking stupidly in the dimly lit hall.

The first thing that Leers noticed was that Wing Commander's office was spacious, comfortable, and professional. Perhaps a tad bit too comfortable. The office didn't *look* like a fighter pilot's domain it looked like it belonged to a mid-level corporate manager. There were oil paintings on the walls, brass lighting fixtures, three leather easy chairs, a robust bar lined with goblets and steins. There was also an original Regalia sofa with wooden armrests inlaid with brass and sterling carvings. Two end tables with models of a VF-94 Vagrant and the newer VF-95 Valkyrie floating above them finished off the room. Colonel Zimmer glided smoothly toward the rear of the room and made her way behind her mammoth desk. She tapped at a flat panel and several schematics and charts floated before her. Images that only she could see.

As Colonel Krandersen made his way to the bar, Zimmer said, "Alright Dannen Leers, the floor is yours, make your case."

It took Leers five minutes to conduct himself thusly. As he spoke, Krandersen handed both he and Slayton short glasses of non-alcoholic apple cider. In due course, Zimmer moved from behind her desk and leaned against the arm of one of the easy-chairs. N'ckshell hadn't touched her drink, this matter didn't concern her in the least. She politely thanked the wing commander and tried to take her leave, hoping to hell that she didn't run into Galensen on the way out.

"Stay, young lady, stay," Zimmer insisted. "This does concern you."

"At ease, both of you," Krandersen said.

"I just confirmed everything that you told me. But I'm not really a stats sort of woman; I like to hear what a pilot has to say and I liked what you had to say. It reveals your character in ways that numbers on a spreadsheet can't," Zimmer said, moving lightly on the antique rug. She clasped her hands behind her. "According to these charts, you have more than fifty pilots and weapon system officers within the Ranger Squadron. After examining all of this data, I can extrapolate that you have nineteen missions flown and Stan McHellington, who was recently promoted to major, has fourteen. Is that sufficient reason why you should get the appointment and not he? You've flown four missions as a weapon system officer . . ." Zimmer couldn't disguise the slight twitching of her lower lip. She'd almost forgotten that these damned Omnitraus could fly as both pilots *and* weapons officers without loss of proficiency—in fact they could do either duty better than the crews who trained and flew as strictly pilots or strictly as weapons officers. "And your friend McHellington has flown seven as a weapons officer. Interesting, he has the edge on you there. However, after looking deeper into these charts, I see that you have more kills than he does and—even you young lady. You have flown only twelve missions as a pilot and you have more kills than McHellington. Do no mistake where I'm going with this. Kills are not the single most determining factor when figuring out who gets to lead a fighter squadron and who doesn't. It's not that simple."

She took a sip of her drink. "Since the untimely death of Nate Starjohns, I issued an order to the exec that Major Helen Lange be elected commander of Ranger Squadron. Is that correct?"

"Yes, Colonel," Krandersen said. "I signed the order right below your signature."

"But somehow the order was superseded and McHellington got the order." She paused to crack her knuckles. "Mr. Leers, I'm appointing you because you made the bold move to see me during our current crisis without an announcement. You are indeed qualified to be a squadron commander—hell, the whole base probably knows you're qualified. Your timing is piss-poor though. If you had landed here four or five days ago, we wouldn't be having this discussion; you'd be the new squadron commander with the rank of major."

"I don't understand," Leers muttered.

"Lange turned us down," Krandersen said. "Flat refused to accept squadron commander. She stated repeatedly that you'd be a better choice than she would be. She was quite adamant about it, too."

"Even though you weren't around, she could see no one else in that role," Zimmer supplied. "She respects you that much."

Leers looked down, his emotions a brew of survivor's guilt and exultation. He'd thought he'd have to climb a mountain—this almost seemed too—"I don't know what to say." The words stumbled out of his mouth.

"Start with thank you."

****

Being excused from the wing commander's office was more than the most righteous of blessings as far as N'ckshell Slayton was concerned. In her soul, she was through and through a pilot—all of this political wrangling was for other beings. As a pilot, you flew your mission, and if the mission required that you bomb a factory, you did it; if the mission required that you killed enemy fighter pilots, you did it. To spend energy worrying about something else was counterproductive. The only thing that mattered was the mission. Why Dannen Leers felt the need to correct some perceived wrong was quite beyond N'ckshell's understanding. No matter who led the squadron, Dannen would still get to fly, wouldn't he? He would, he knew he would, but Dannen always had an asteroid-headed sense of justice.

Slayton moved along the rock-hewn passageways back to the Ranger Squadron. This section of the base was called the *Hinternoon Caverns*; mostly three connecting caverns, the largest of which belonged to the Boulder Squadron. The Wing Command Headquarters was to the west and Ranger Squadron was to the northwest of Wing HQ. Slayton always marveled at the ingenuity that it took to build all of this beneath the surface of an asteroid the size of a planet. Omega Command itself was still small in comparison, only about the size of a metropolitan. Still, to have all of it beneath the surface never failed to send shivers down her spine whenever she thought about it.

She had to find Stan McHellington and ask him what the hell he was thinking. He and Leers had butted heads a couple of times before; did Stan really think that Dannen would just let this one go? Once Dannen got it in his head that he had been wronged, or just marginally slighted, he would do everything in his power to right that wrong—no matter if there were larger issues, more important issues to wrestle with around the corner.

What if it had been her? What would she do if a friend and fellow pilot decided to put the glide on her promotion? Would she be upset? Something told her that she would be upset. Something else told her that her rival would most likely be dead.

Being a squadron commander was serious duty. It meant pushing sixteen fighters into combat. It meant being responsible for sixteen pilots—including yourself—and sixteen weapon system officers. After several months you would slowly start to pass more responsibility to the senior pilots of your squadron; you'd find yourself flying less and less. As a squadron commander, you'd also be in charge of the training and currency of your combat crews, so much so that all of the flying missions you did fly would be training missions and not combat missions where you actually got to go out and kill Pulsarians. Then before you knew it, some division commander would try to groom you for wing commander, where you'd fly even less than a squadron commander—you'd be lucky to fly two combat missions a year. Was that what Dannen really wanted? It couldn't be. He loved the flying, loved the action of being on the front, tangling with the Pulsarians—not training pilots, even though he was pretty good at doing that too—not writing training manuals and supplements, not debating with other squadron commanders about marrying doctrine with in-close fighter tactics. You'd have to be crazy to give up all of this to become a glorified arm-chair tactician. Perhaps Dannen *was* crazy.

Perhaps she was too, for letting him do it. Well, if either of them was going to go insane in this war, it'd be best to let Leers lead off. That way she could see how he handled it and avoid the mistakes he was bound to make.

She continued down the brightly lighted corridors until she reached the outer edge of the Ranger Squadron. So lost in her thoughts, she was surprised by how quickly she arrived here. She could see the tailpipes of several of the Vagrants lined up. She could see several of the squadron techs working on a couple of the warbirds now. She wondered if she would soon be flying one of them. Before she left for Elst, she led an eight-ship mission to support bombers hitting a Pulsarian supply depot on Ridan-Prime. She got involved in three separate knife-fights with Pulsarian pilots and her Vagrant had been literally shot to pieces. So badly damaged was her warbird that when making her final approach to the asteroid base, her flight systems just quit. She was approaching the asteroid at speeds in excess of 30,000kpx when everything went dark in the cockpit. She attempted several cold re-starts to bring everything back on-line, nothing. With the ground rushing up at her, and the approach controller and her fellow pilots yelling instructions at her—none of which really helped—she somehow managed to chop her speed to a mere 300kpx before landing 'wheels up' on the surface of the asteroid. Some said that she plowed into the ground instead of landing, others said she crunched it *real* good, still there were those who thought the she and her weapons officer were lucky to be alive.

Naturally, Slayton didn't consider it luck. Making a belly landing at 300kpx with a dead stick and no instruments was skill—simple as that. She had been lucky that the Vagrant did not disintegrate while on the return trip home via Hyperspace. That was the lucky part—the part she had no control over. Skill was required to crash land her Vagrant on the surface the way that she did and then have the cool to walk away from it and sign up for another mission. The next mission she got had nothing to do with fighters; before she knew what was happening, she was being rushed to the Frontier in an FB-25, then onto Elst on board Captain's freighter.

This caused Slayton to pause as she stepped out onto the flight-line. It would be nice to know what happened to her fighter. Did they fix it or did they condemn the machine for 'parts only'. *Please, let that not be the fate of my fighter.* She had to find out. But it was quiet; strangely so on the flight-line. Each fighter squadron had a team of mechanics who were always fixing this or taking apart that. When they weren't getting birds ready for missions, they were always training the enlisted mechanics and techs—having them take apart an engine, or strip the astronics out of the cockpit, assembling the components on the floor and having the tech reassemble the whole instrument panel. Sometimes they would organize races and have the entire squadron watch.

She noticed a small knot of techs loading chaff and flares in the counter-measures bay of a nearby Vagrant. She could just recognize . . .

"Sergeant Breton, how's it going?" she said. She stepped up to the four techs, fists on her hips.

Breton looked up from his work and eyed her suspiciously. "What's up, Captain? What are you doing here; I didn't know you were back." He grabbed a towel from the tool rack and began wiping the grim from his hands.

"It's major now, Sarge."

"Congrats are in order then, Major," Breton said with curtness. "You're not wearing a Star Force uniform that I can see, or rank, so how am I—"

"Supposed to know," Slayton finished for him. "A lot of people have been saying that a lot lately."

"Maybe you should do something about it then." He turned back to his mates. "You guys are good to work on this by yourselves for a few minutes? Good."

"Sergeant, whenever you start giving orders to officers, you're supposed to be more subtle about it." Slayton gave him a wink.

"Why Major, I have no idea what you're talking about," Breton said coyly.

"Besides which, I'll change when I'm good and ready and not a second before."

"*Hmmph*, you officers. If someone handed me some new brass, I'd move hell and the Universe to put it on."

"Maybe you would," Slayton fumed. "The more brass you put on, the less you get to fly. But that's the irony though, isn't it? The more brass, the more money you earn, the less fun you have."

"So you want the rank *and* the control to fly as many combat missions as you want." Breton paused. "Isn't that like baking your cake and eating it too."

"I don't know. I've never heard that saying before. But that's it exactly, Sergeant. Unfortunately, the military doesn't work that way."

"Maybe it should. Then again, they have it that way for a reason, doncha' think."

"Oh?"

"Yeah, they can't have their best pilots getting knocked off flying every combat mission the bigwigs dream up. That's what lieutenants are for."

"That's awfully crass of you."

"Maybe, but it's the truth." Breton shrugged. "Lieutenants are a dime a dozen in the Star Force . . . use them up, I say. Or train them up so they live long enough to be captains and majors."

"You don't like lieutenants do you?"

"Busted."

"Did you like me when I was a lieutenant?"

"I didn't know you when you were a lieutenant."

"Do you like me now?"

"Sometimes, when you're not being a pain in the ass, or busting up all of our fighters." Breton took a step closer to her. He had never really had this lengthy of a conversation with her. She only greeted him when she was on her way to shag his suitemate. This was a rather historic moment for them. "I always felt that you—maybe a couple of others—were someone I can talk to like a regular person—not some type of royalty. I can't stand it when you officers snap your fingers at me like I'm supposed to drop everything and show you to the lavatory so's you can blow your noses and wipe your asses."

"Sometimes you violate rank, customs and courtesies too easily."

"Yeah, I know I do," Breton said. "But I'm not the one not wearing a proper uniform on the flight-line now, am I?"

N'ckshell ignored him. "Speaking of lieutenants that you hate so much, where's—"

"Your boyfriend—the only lieutenant I don't hate." Breton gestured around the cavern. "Who the hell knows; they got a lot of our tech-crews working on those reeking refugee ships, trying to make sure they're Hyperspace worthy. We got our own ships to worry about."

"Do you know when he'll be back?" she asked. "Do you know which refugee ships he's working on? Why would he volunteer for that assignment?"

"He didn't have a choice, Major."

****

"So this is where it happened?" Guardian Draystar asked as he followed Colonel Piercenan through the verge of the control room.

"Yes, it is," Piercenan answered, surveying the room himself. "Nothing's been touched since you were in transit. The bodies were removed, of course, they are in freezers at the base hospital."

"They haven't been given autopsies yet?"

"None of the medical staff has that type of training, Guardian Draystar," Piercenan said. "We have fully staffed combat medical teams keen at pulling shrapnel out of you or treating serious burns; but examining corpses for an investigation? No, sir. Besides, General Varxbane ordered them not to touch those bodies."

"He's correct, then," Draystar said. "They'll just have to be examined later."

I have no problem with that, Piercenan thought, *thank the Universe it's not my beat.* Piercenan stepped over the threshold of the control room and let his eyes scan the circumference. There was nothing spectacular about the room. It provided enough lighting that he could see a layer of fine dust was now covering the five metallic desks and the half a dozen office chairs on rollers. Piercenan ignored the unsettling rumblings in his stomach as his mind raced back to the day he and his security team answered the alarm. When they got here, it'd been too late for Admiral Doss. He and his staff had all been gunned down in cold blood. The admiral had a security chief, she was the first to be killed. She got it behind the head as she stood at her post near the entrance. Of the nine people in the room, she was the only one who was armed. In a sickening sense of remorseless professionalism, the killer picked up the guard's weapon and used it to kill the others.

"So, Admiral Doss was killed where?"

"Toward the back of the room near a row of star-charts," Piercenan answered.

"I don't see any star-charts."

"Yes, all of the star-charts and CPU's his team were using are in the security vault in my HQ."

Piercenan's answer seemed to satisfy Draystar. He couldn't read any emotion through the armored battlehelm the Guardian wore.

"So Doss was killed back there," Draystar said, "probably witnessing his colleagues being murdered one by one." Draystar moved toward the nearest desk but didn't touch it. "One by one and there wasn't a thing that he could do about it. And that doorway is the only way in and out of this control room."

"The only entrance."

"Trapped without escape, watching his people being murdered. Not a way anyone should go." Draystar stepped deeper into the room, Piercenan watched as his battlehelm shifted from the left and the right, surveying the scene where the carnage took place. Everyone cut down with no escape, knowing they were going to die. What goes on in a person's head when they're faced with something like that? What were they feeling, what were they thinking? Piercenan knew what the killer thought—it'd be nothing more than stone, vacant logic. Kill these people because those were the orders issued. Nothing more complex or ruthless than that. Do the job, leave no clues, get out . . . get paid.

"We estimate that it took six seconds to execute everyone in the room."

"Yes, I read your report on the way down here," Draystar confirmed.

"How did you mange that?" Piercenan inquired.

"I accessed your report through the mainframe and then had the data streamed across the inner visor of my battlehelm."

I need to get one of those helmets someday. Piercenan thought. *I wonder what else it can do.*

Draystar edged back toward the entrance. "So the killer shot the guard here." He knelt down, "grabbed the guard's weapon." Draystar rose and quickly sidestepped left down the main aisle, "then moved over here where he shot the others."

"Yes, that follows what I wrote in my report."

"Nine people dead in less than six seconds," Draystar mused. "Each victim, except the guard, received a double tap to the chest and one to the head."

"Yes."

"That's almost impossible," Draystar said.

"But . . ."

"I'm not saying that it didn't happen," Draystar said. "I'm saying that the speed and accuracy is simply incredible. With the integrated weapon systems in my armor, I could do it. Guardian Jasmine and any of the Omnitraus stationed at this base could . . ."

"That was my thought," Piercenan said. He already knew the mental path that Draystar was about to walk down. "I checked. Besides Leers and Slayton, there's Kaltorr and Stan McHellington who are the only other Omnitraus Officers stationed on this base. All of their alibis are vacuum sealed shut—iron clad in fact. Kaltorr was a lightyear away flying a mission with the Ranger and Astra Squadrons. And McHellington was with me and a few dozen others at the main firing range for handgun training."

"That's *supervenient* for him to have you for an alibi."

"Very convenient, yes," Piercenan said nonplused. "But that's also in my supplemental report on witnesses and verifying their—"

"I'm downloading that supplement right down and having it streamed onto my optics."

"While you read it, I'll just tell you that we have more than a dozen witnesses reporting that McHellington kid there—some of whom really don't like him, for that matter. But we have his targeting score and encrypted time-hack."

"I see it now."

"Additionally, during that weapons training—don't you think it'd be a bit ironic that McHellington would be down at the firing range proving that he had the skill to carry out these murders in the manner that they were carried out?"

"I already see what you mean," Draystar said, nodding. "Cyclops may be more dangerous than I originally feared."

"I share your fear whenever I start to contemplate what we're up against." Piercenan's stomach began doing flip-flops again. "We have a determined Pulsarian agent working this base with the skill of an Omnitraus Officer. An agent who can kill at random then melt away without leaving a single clue. I don't have the personnel to deal with something like this."

"Even if you did, they'd only be killed."

****

Lieutenant A'llen Krenner was bone-tired and he knew it, hell he felt it. Even though the entomology was human, he felt it immediately described the rotten condition he was in as he stumbled for the elevator. Krenner was what the humans called a Dracterian, and right now being a member of the *Mese'Crait* clan didn't seem all that important. His feet hurt in the mechanic's boots that he wore, from the tips of his toes, his blistered arches, to his heels. His knees creaked whenever he bent them; some of it was his age, as he was rapidly approaching thirty—but his doctor had always told him that they should last well into his seventies before needing replacements. It'd be nice to have those metallic replacements now. His back started to spasm whenever he twisted his torso. His head felt like it'd been in a hydraulic pressing machine. It bitterly reminded him what it felt like to have only six hours of sleep during the past four days. It didn't matter if you were human, Aracrayderian or Dracterian; to go this long with little sleep and even less food—but they had plenty of water and vitamin supplements to add to it—that is, until the water ran out. Krenner felt his soul slowly eroding. As one of Ranger Squadron's tech-mechanics, sleep was the only damned thing that mattered right now. In fact, he'd been ordered to do that and only that for the next ten hours, then report back to Colonel Granx for more duty repairing those refugee ships.

The elevator door opened and Krenner lumbered out totally forgetting that he had ridden the elevator with three other technicians.

"Oh, hey, see you fellas tomorrow," was all his vocal chords allowed him to say. He waved, sort of as everyone started to head for their suites. "We'll start early on the barge-boards on number—er, I forgot the number—you know the one I'm talking about, though. And the weapons pylon needs to be looked at too."

"Take 'er easy, LT," one of the mechanics said through a yawn. Staff Sergeant Donrin Ringer snapped Krenner a raggedy salute. "We'll even save a seat for you. Hopefully, they'll still have some eggs left."

"We'd *better* have eggs—I'm not working unless I get something to eat."

Everyone stopped at once; this was always a sore subject.

"Those damn DP's are going through our stocks faster and faster—like we have an infinite supply or something," Sergeant Ringer continued, suddenly not so tired. He always had energy when talking about the displaced persons from Yanattii and all of the torment they caused. "Every time they have me drive the supply truck with food, they go after it like a bunch of savages."

"We're the ones doing the most work on their ships," Senior Starman Hendersen grumbled, "and they get to eat like royalty."

"They're civilians, what do you expect."

Krenner wasn't listening to their ranting anymore; he'd heard the same statements in one form or another at least a dozen times already today, to say nothing of the past four days. Someone slapped him on the shoulder.

"Someday, LT, you'll make cap'n and you can leave all of this heavy duty crap behind."

"I don't think so," Krenner huffed. "You'll be a Tech-sergeant well before they'll pin captains' bars to my shoulders. Like you humans like to say, *'that'll be the day.'* "

"That's a load of crap, sir," Ringer said. "All of this hard work ain't gonna be for nothing, sir. You mark my words, sir. Something good'll come out of this."

"What if I don't want to wear the rank of captain," Krenner said flatly. "I love being a tech, I love fixing ships. I love breaking things down then building them back up. Once I make captain, they'll move me away from the flight-line to a desk. I'll be staring at a monitor for eighteen or twenty-four hours a day, typing reports and making charts—no thank you, sergeant very much. I'd much rather turn a wrench—do something that'll get my hands dirty."

"Amen to that."

"What has me worried," Krenner continued, "a few weeks ago we were sitting fat and pretty with enough parts for our fighters and then some. Now we don't have any spares for combat. Our pilots might be able to fly one combat sortie, maybe two and we are going to have to start sending them up with cracked seals, ruptured casings and Universe knows what else."

"We can, er, liberate the parts we need from the Boulder Squadron, sir," Ringer suggested.

"They won't have anything. Besides, their mechanics will probably be busy trying to steal parts from us."

"See you tomorrow, LT," Hendersen said, turning away.

"Anyway, we've got good pilots, they can handle it," Ringer noted.

"They're not that good," Krenner said drily.

As they split up, the weariness returned to Krenner. He reached his suite and slid his keycard past the small security sensor and—the damned thing didn't go beep, the door didn't slide aside. Krenner released an all-too-human sigh mixed with exasperation. He moved the keycard past the sensor again—he didn't have time for this shit, not now—he was too tired. He just wanted to shower and sleep, was that asking too much? Right now he was so miserable with fatigue that he might skip the damn shower. But he had to gain access to his suite first. He shared it with four others, two officers and two NCOs—each with his or her own bedroom and bath; they all shared the kitchen and living room/common area and the foyer leading to the main entrance to the suite which wasn't granting him access.

He tried his keycard again. *Shit.* One of the officers must have some underage enlisted female over for a few brews and loud sex. He probably promised her—

The door swooshed aside and Krenner stumbled back in spite of himself. He could smell her before his eyes focused on the almost nude shape of N'ckshell Slayton. She was barely wearing one of his undershirts, one of the clean ones—she was on top of him in an instant, her lips clamping onto his, her arms anchored around like the deadly embrace from a Medusa plant. If he hadn't had such good balance, he would've hit the floor with his back with her on top of him still sucking his face dry with her kisses—not caring that her butt was exposed for all to see.

"Niki," he blurted tiredly. "Niki, baby, I can't breathe—you're killing me."

"Oh, not yet, baby, not yet," she said between kisses. "I haven't seen you in weeks."

"But let's get inside before the enlisted ranks see you and start think—"

"Aren't you glad to see me?"

"Well, part of me is glad to see you," Krenner said with a wry smile. He began guiding her out of the foyer and into the common area. Good, none of his suitemates were around. He could barely see anything beyond her pale face, those gorgeous eyes, her sharp ears—she smelled good. Which was more than Krenner could say for himself. "Baby, I need a shower, badly—before the water's rationed."

"No, you don't," N'ckshell said. She began ripping at the opening of his mechanic's trousers.

"Niki, I'm knackered."

She grabbed a hold of him. "As long as this works, you'll be fine."

CHAPTER XVIII
THE EYE OF CYCLOPS

"GET those charges in place now! Hurry man, move. We haven't got much time," the silhouetted humanoid form yelled at the three space-suited men.

One of them looked up from his work, undoing his helmet. "We are working as fast as we can. These are real sensitive charges. If we rush it too much, we'll all end up stuck to the walls of this cave."

The figure shrugged and clenched his fists. Damnit. This was taking too long. Those charges needed to be set now. The space-suited technician was right. He looked around the dark utility bunker—cave—there were fifteen canisters of TBI-80 seismic explosive charges lying about. They *were* sensitive. However, the technician was wrong about one thing; if one blew, they all would blow. They wouldn't be stuck to the walls of the cave because the cave would cease to exist.

"Alright then, exercise extreme caution. But hurry, time is of the essence. I can't wait around here all day."

"Don't worry, boss. Everything is under control. Remember Admiral Doss. Took care of him, right?"

The dark silhouetted figure moved out of the light flowing in from the deserted access corridor and stepped deeper into the dark bunker. He wore an olive-drab overcoat, the collars up, effectively obscuring his face—not that it mattered, the techs *knew* who he was.

The other two techs unfastened the helmets to their suits. One began to check the UT-4 electron detonators while the other held up a probe-light so that the former could complete his work.

"Okay, I'm rigging the detonator now. It'll take about five minutes."

The other technician picked up the detonator and handed it to the shadowy figure in the overcoat. "When everything is hooked up to that UT-4 you've got in your hand, you can transmit the detonation code through at least a kilometer of solid rock. But, you don't have to be that far away to be within minimum safe distance—a fourth of that will be enough."

With one gloved hand, the man took the detonator from the scruffy technician.

"The amber switch there, arms the explosives—all of them simultaneously. The red one blows the whole cake."

"There's no timed delay?" the man, codenamed Cyclops, asked.

"None. Only Pulsarians use timed delays. Just make sure you're outside of the blast radius when you decide to blow it."

The overcoat-attired man put the detonator inside his left coat pocket and turned . . .

"Hey, where the hell are you going? Wait a minute. We're not finished yet. Don'cha go get'n any funny ideas. You're nothing without us, you hear? Nothing."

"I have some unfinished business to attend to," the man stated calmly, stepping into the day-bright corridor. "You can come along if you like. But it won't be as gratifying as killing Doss."

The scruffy technician threw his helmet aside and rushed out of the small cave. "Where are we going?"

"Upstairs. Up into the deflector shield control room."

"Why? We're going to blow it. The deflector shield projection dish, the back-up generator, the whole thing—and just about everything else within a hundred meter radius."

"There's something that I need to take care of before everything pops. A signal must be sent to the Pulsarians if they are to find us in the middle of this freaking asteroid system."

"I thought the explosion would be enough. The Pulsarians should have their sensor probes on."

"They should, but what if they don't? And even if they did, a small explosion such as the one we're rigging could be easily mistaken as an asteroid collision or a volcanic explosion. And remember, we're dealing with Malactites here. Their sensors are primitive at best. They could fly right by a titan burst and still not pick it up. What the Pulsarians need is a signal that won't be mistaken for some sort of random spatial disruption."

The man moved toward a yellow and black access ladder and quickly scaled it to the service corridor two stories above. He looked around cautiously. This corridor, too, was deserted. He stepped into the corridor and rapidly moved toward the doors that led to the deflector shield control room. Behind these doors were the personnel that controlled the deflector shield corridor which enabled starships the luxury of traversing the asteroid system without having to worry about colliding into one of them.

It had to be blown. The success of the Pulsarian invasion depended on it. There were dozens of contingency plans centered around the operation of that shield—it could do more than provide starships with a safe corridor through the asteroid system—it was powerful enough to protect from Malactite as well as Advancer bombardment. For it could change frequencies and deflection modes as fast as—if not faster—than Pulsarian gunners could alternate weapons and firing commands.

The door slid aside and the man burst into the room with a wicked looking pistol drawn. One of the controllers, a young human female, turned from her monitoring to have the side of her head sheared off by a bright beam of light. Sizzling blood and splinters of bone, flesh and brains exploded in a sickening cloud of flame. She was dead before she hit the floor. A guard met the same fate as he readied his own weapon, determination, surprise and fear registering on his face synchronously. The others in the room heard the violent shrieks of laser fire and swiveled around in their chairs, the terror a solid mask on their faces, their eyes wide with fear.

Mercilessly, the man in the overcoat fired again and again. Sizzling vitals sprayed the walls as the lasers ripped through their bodies.

The overweight, red-headed, scruffy tech staggered into the room. His face contorted in anguish as he looked at the grisly corpses. All but one of them were unarmed—they were all kids! And the girl—she couldn't be out of her teens yet and now she was dead; the shot that had finished her was so grotesque—*My, God*—her eyes were bubbling in a sickening red froth. The tech wheeled over and vomited violently, gasping for air as the bile geysered from his nose and mouth.

The man in the overcoat was furious. "Shut that damn door, you imbecile!" What was wrong with him? He's killed before.

Shaking, the tech hit the activator button, continuing to convulse. The man, unaffected by the gore, stepped up to the deflector shield control system. It wasn't too complex to understand. Power supply system here, which fed energy to the deflector shield control unit, which in turn led to the deflector modulator. Easy. But first he had to raise the entire deflector control housing above the surface of the asteroid so that the deflector could be projected. And those controllers were over there, next to the power supply generator. Convenient. He wiped gory redness from the buttons, switches and computerized gauges with his gloved hand. He needed to see the readings clearly.

Twenty-five meters above the control room, two great slabs of rock slid aside. The DSP rose above the surface of the asteroid. The projection dish itself was fifteen meters in diameter and coated in fine silt. Unseen servos whined and swiveled the dish on its axis until it pointed skyward. All around the base of the DSP were canisters of explosives, all set to detonate at the same time as those in the underground bunker. It was overkill, but the man wanted to be thorough.

From the main control room, he got the green light. The dish was locked firmly in place. He activated the shields and got another confirming green light. In moments, some controller in the BWRC kilometers away would get the energy readings on his control panel and would state politely that they didn't have authorization to activate the beam without orders to do so. If they didn't shut it down then he would have to do it from his location. And that's what the man wanted, for it would take them time to do it.

And by that time, he would have accomplished his mission. He threw the switch to the modulator, throwing out a tremendous eruption of energy.

****

The senior sensor control officer onboard General Sergon's Command Malactite blinked in disbelief as his panels lit up from the emissions screaming across the asteroid system. He lifted the face plate to his armored battlehelm. His computerized optics hadn't been malfunctioning again—he was reading the information correctly. His own tired eyes confirmed that much. He was getting major power readings, almost across the spectrum—indicators were pinging like crazy. He sent out his sensor feelers and tasters to analyze the power source and localize it. It only took a moment. But he had to cross-reference it before he reported his findings to the general. He was astounded by the power. The Pulsarians had nothing like it.

Without further delay, he activated the internal communications system. "Command section, this is the sensor section commander."

Ten levels above him a battle-ready leftenant answered the call in Sergon's command section. "Go sensor section."

"I've got a deflector beam emission of incredible power. Force eight deflective yield."

"Force eight?" an operator next to him echoed in disbelief.

"Very good, pipe it through," the leftenant directed. He studied the readings of the beam on the main tactical monitor. Incredible—the Delrels were sending them an invitation.

Behind him Sergon opened his eyes slowly and studied the readings. *So this Cyclops has come through again for Admiral Petti. Interesting.*

"General?"

"Lock-on to that power source, leftenant," Sergon said calmly.

The officer was far from being calm. He anxiously stabbed at the screen to get an accurate pick on the signal that was still pouring out like a nova.

"General, I have it. It's in sector four. At current speed it'll take 72 hours to get there."

"Increase speed to flank." The general did some mental figuring. "That should get us there in just under eighteen hours, maybe twenty," he added quickly, thinking of the asteroids they had to travel through. "Get underway now."

"It's going to be close, general."

"I'm well aware of the fuel situation, leftenant. All possibilities have been weighed. We'll have more than enough to maneuver and annihilate the Federation base." He leaned back in his seat and closed his eyes. "Now I want you to use the laser induction link to notify the rest of the invasion force and inform our dear Marshal Admiral, Rouldran Petti, of our current situation, on the scrambler, of course. Secondly, send the coordinates to Admiral Dehyhitte. Make sure he gets it along with our ETA so that we can coordinate our attack."

"Yes, General."

****

"When they asked me to take over as squadron commander, no one said a damned thing about all the crapping admin work I was gonna have to do." Leers pushed his breakfast aside and examined another spreadsheet on his datapad. "The Ranger Squadron has twenty-two operational VF-94E Vagrants and thirty pilots, forty weapon system officers—but my dear friend Rook, you wouldn't know what a WSO is because November Command flies nothing older than C-model Valkyries—"

"The best talent gets the best equipment—" Rook countered quickly.

"Here we go again," N'ckshell Slayton chimed in mock disgust.

"At ease, at ease," Leers said. "I've got more than a hundred flight-line personnel I'm responsible for now. You know, mechanics, engine techs, computer jocks, astronics techs, engines, weapons and so on and so forth, etcetera, etcetera."

"You also have your own administrative staff," Slayton said spitting out a few bits of egg. "Let them do it."

"It would be nice," Leers said. "But they are busy with the evacuation plan, which leaves me with all of the battleplan stuff and spreadsheets."

"What exactly were you expecting?" Rook asked. "Congratulations on your rank, by the way. Both of you hit major."

"It's funny how Colonel Zimmer left out the small details about the spreadsheets. Who the hell invented spreadsheets anyway?"

"Dannen, you need to quit with the whining," Slayton said plowing through more of her eggs. "We both make major and you get to command the squadron, you should be happy."

Leers glanced briefly at his shoulder epaulets, then at hers. "Yeah, being a major should be nice."

"Should be, but it really isn't," Slayton said. "I don't like this situation any more than you do."

Rook shrugged. "What situation is that, Lovey?"

Slayton threw down her fork and quit chewing for once as she spoke. "I don't get to command my own flight; no, I have to fly with Dannen, as his WSO."

"Surely, you're joking," Rook said trying to swallow coffee and speak at the same time.

"She's not joking." Leers leaned away from the breakfast table. "Under the Evacplan, Omnitraus Officers have to pair up with other Omnitraus to insure that other squadron personnel can assume their assigned seats—"

"That doesn't make any sense," Rook mumbled.

"You can't have two element leaders fighting over the same seat," Leers said, "or two flight leaders fighting over the same seat, for that matter. Under the battleplan, yeah, I'd have N'ckshell leading a flight—"

"—that's a scary thought—"

"Find a muzzle, Rook."

"—Kaltorr would lead a flight as well as Stan," Leers finished up ignoring his squabbling friends. "But we're operating under the Evacplan—like I was saying—so we have no choice but to maximize the personnel we've got in the fight. And that means doubling up the Omnitraus because I guess we can take it."

"But that's crazy," Rook said.

"It's obscene is what it is," Slayton said, attacking her toast this time.

Rook folded his arms as he spoke, "You know, friend Dannen, this sounds suspiciously like a plan some anti-Gladatraus league would come up with."

"Anti-what?"

"Haven't you heard?" Rook looked incredulous, even for a feline. "You people really are *cutoff* from the rest of the galaxy in this asteroid base."

"Yeah, but what is this anti-league stuff you're talking about?"

Rook cleared his throat and leaned forward. His eyes quickly flashed to the left and right scanning the crowded room. "November Command has a few of them, maybe even Desdemona as well; but there are rumblings that the war is taking too long and—"

"Taking too long," Leers boomed. "Don't they know how big the Pulsarian Empire is for Universe sake? They attacked us! They're murdering our people—"

"Dannen, I know that," Rook hissed. "And keep your voice down, please. But there are people—mostly human if you can believe it—who feel that we're not doing everything possible to end the war."

"What a bunch of shite," Slayton said.

"Easy, N'ckshell," Leers waved her down. "Keep going, Rook."

"That's it," Rook said. "Depending on whom you talk to . . . but I suppose every organization has its more radical elements. I've heard that they actually think that we, both Gladatraus and Omnitraus are working with the Pulsarians to bleed the Federation dry of its resources."

"Are you shitting me?" Slayton whispered harshly.

"And then rule this part of the galaxy with the Pulsarians when—"

"That's ridiculous."

"Is it?" Rook countered.

"You sound like you agree with them," Leers parried. "Remember Rook, you're an Omnitraus Officer too. Ain't you also part of the 'plan' to take over the galaxy with the Pugs." Leers snorted as he chuckled. "This whole thing sounds ridiculous—if these league idiots knew what we do. Knew what we sacrifice to protect them . . ."

"Too bad everything we do is classified," Slayton added. "Well, most of it is anyway. But it's still a bunch of shite."

"My friends, I'm only telling you what I've heard."

"Next time, Rook, keep it to yourself. At least until I'm done eating." The Dracterian gripped her stomach and pushed herself away from the table. "As human women like to say, 'I have to break off a deuce'—"

"That's what men say."

"Whatever, I just hope it lands on some league twerp. My God, of all the things . . ." Her voice trailed off as she pushed her way toward the exit.

Leers watched her leave. "You know, Rook, as much as I laugh at the idea, there were a few valid points you made." Leers paused for a few moments. "When we Warped out of Hyperspace into the middle of that Pug taskforce, man, we were kicking their asses. I mean, if we had more Gladatraus Guardians assembled together at the right place at the right time, the Pugs would get a bloody nose for sure. But we both know it ain't as easy as that, now is it?"

"I agree, this deal makes me laugh as well. You're right, Dannen, whoever these leaguers are—if they even exist—who knows? They obviously don't know how formidable our enemy is, or how dedicated we are. I'm not going to mention how many star systems we have within the Federation, planetary governors, all of them screaming for help—you can't be every place at once. Now with Shiborium being threatened, it's only a matter of—"

"Hey, can I join you gents?"

Leers looked up to see a sergeant holding her tray of fruits and eggs eyeing Slayton's vacated seat.

"Sure," said Leers.

"Thank you," she said, beaming. "It's so crowded in here, ah thought I was gonna haf'ta eat on the floor."

"You can join our league."

****

The human in the overcoat whirled as the communication panel winked repeatedly for attention. The controllers in the BWRC were on to the unwarranted use of the DSP. He ignored the inquiry and added more power to the shield corridor. He wanted to make absolutely certain that the Pulsarians were picking up the signal.

"Come on, red. We're getting out of here." He grabbed the ill-stricken man and raced back to the cave bunker. The other two technicians were finished with their work.

"Yea, we're all done with the work at this end. Everything's ready to pop. Cyclops strikes again. How will they stop—"

"Don't call me by that name, you idiot!"

"I didn't mean to ah—"

"Hey, how's the investigation going?"

"It's going nowhere."

That brought about a great deal of laughter from the three techs. Because of their actions, and the actions of Cyclops, the base was wide open to attack. Nothing could stop the Pulsarians now. The techs continued to laugh. Cyclops could only imagine their shock when their bodies were torn apart by lasers coming from his pistol. They were dead before they hit stone. Cyclops quickly exited the room as alarms began to wail in the distance. In minutes, troops would rush over to investigate. He ran down the service corridor and stepped into one of the two travel tubes. He keyed his destination and waited, waited until he was out of the potential blast radius before he activated the detonator.

CHAPTER XIX
DAMAGE ASSESSMENT

"MY God! What's going on here?" Colonel Dargoinne yelled as he sprinted into the tension-filled BWRC. Alarms blared loudly, personnel scrambled around in panic and confusion—what is this—controllers moved urgently from station to station looking over the shoulders of numbed operators who tried to sort through a deluge of information on the dozens of monitors.

"We lost the entire deflector shield projector site," one of the controllers, a massive, fierce-looking grizzly growled back above the din. His mouth glistened with saliva. "The whole damn DSP exploded!"

"Are we under attack?" Dargoinne asked, trying to keep the panic out of his voice, eyes bulging at computer readings he didn't understand. *Goddamnit, the Pulsarians can't be attacking now.*

"We don't know yet. We can't use the base's scanners for confirmation. But we do have a flight of Visions from the Hornet Squadron launching right now. They'll report soon."

At that moment, General Varxbane, Guardian Jasmine and Colonel Piercenan ran up the transparent stairs to join Dargoinne and a knot of frayed-looking controllers. Piercenan's expression, more than anyone else around him, was grim; after all, he was in charge of base security. And it was his plan to wait for Cyclops' next move. He never expected this.

****

Hornet Leader adjusted his oxygen mask once again as he steered the sleek VF-97 Vision over the craggy smoldering crater that once marked the location of the Deflector Shield Projector. He flew about three hundred meters above the craggy surface of the asteroid and could readily see small space-suited figures and small maintenance vehicles converging on the site. Incredible. Like everyone else on the base, he knew there was a saboteur loose. He knew of some of the things that the traitor had done: the destruction of the EWF-19, the death of the Attack Wing commander . . . He heard rumors of other outrages . . . . *But this! This was utter craziness.* Destroying the DSP would allow the Pulsarians to bomb them with impunity—the saboteur would be destroyed as surely as everyone else. It didn't make sense.

He keyed his mike.

"Ah, this is Hornet Leader. Am flying over the site now," he said into the mike, breathing heavily against the steady flow of oxygen. "Personnel are moving into the area now. Ah, there is no sign of enemy activity. Repeat: there is no sign of enemy activity."

Which was true—because if this was a Pulsarian attack, he and his wingman would be dodging flak about now. No, this was a target selected by the saboteur rampaging through the base—it didn't take a genius to figure that one out. Rumors were flying that it was Cyclops, but it was unsubstantiated because those with the security clearances who knew for certain weren't saying anything.

****

"Hornet Leader reports no signs of any Pulsarian activity," Piercenan reported to the other concerned souls standing around. "If it was an attack, they wouldn't stop with a single bombing and then leave. They'd continue. And why the DSP and not some other target? This is an attack from within. This *is* the work of Cyclops."

"With the DSP down, we are vulnerable to attack," Dargoinne told them all. "Not only does the DSP allow spacecraft to travel through the asteroid system, with protection, but it can also protect the base from a Malactite bombardment. Without it, we're dead."

"How are we going to evacuate without the shield to protect us," Granx asked joining the group. "Most of those civilian starships barely have the ability to fly in a straight line, let alone pulling violent maneuvers to avoid all those asteroids. Cyclops has us on this." Suddenly Granx turned to face

Piercenan. "He's got us good, Piercenan. What are you going to do about this? Do you have a plan? All I've heard is talk. Nothing but talk. And your talk has gotten us nowhere near to capturing this menace!"

"I advise you to throttle-back, colonel," Piercenan said. "You are stepping over the line."

"Is that your answer, colonel?"

"What would you do?" Piercenan challenged. "Somehow I don't think you have the imagination or the fortitude to—"

"Gentlemen, please, I think that's enough for now," Jasmine interjected. "We can't afford to fight like this. We have to sort through this as a team. I thought we agreed on that? No one's at fault. If we let ourselves get caught up in these petty recriminations, the Pulsarians will surely kill us all. And they won't need a super agent either."

Piercenan exhaled heavily and stepped away from Granx. He glanced at the powerful form of the Gladatraus, then returned his gaze briefly to Granx. "You're right. Yes, I'll admit that I've been under a lot of stress. Probably even eaten more aspirin than solid food these last few weeks."

Granx apologized to the slim humanoid then added, "I've been feeling the stress too." Walruses, like Granx, didn't like to admit their weaknesses. But since Granx was in the company of aliens and had, in fact, insulted one, an admission was warranted and wouldn't be a sign of weakness. Besides, Piercenan couldn't help it if he was born a *Gap'poc*.

A controller ran up to the group. "We have a definite confirmation now. Before the DSP was destroyed, it was activated at full power, full deflective output . . ."

"If the Pulsarians didn't know the exact location of our base before, they do now," Piercenan said. "With that thing operating at maximum yield, it could lead a blind dwarf here."

"This is not good," Dargoinne said. He didn't have the slightest idea what a dwarf had to do with any of this.

Varxbane glared at him. Of course it's not good. He needed contingencies to get through this and not his colonels fighting and certainly not adolescent comments that moved them nowhere.

"What do we do now?" Dargoinne asked, immediately regretting uttering a sound.

Varxbane put his fingers to his temples, thinking, concentrating. He was getting one of Piercenan's headaches. "Okay, here's what we do. Until now, I've always entertained the thought of apprehending this Cyclops for questioning. But I no longer think we can be so particular. He may have to be destroyed once and for all before he destroys us."

"But sir, if we can capture him alive; the information we'd find out: networks, future Pulsarian contingencies, contacts," Piercenan was saying.

"*No*, we can't afford the risk," Varxbane countered. "He's too dangerous! And he must be stopped now. At all costs. *Before* the Pulsarians attack, and definitely before we *evacuate*!"

Piercenan shrank back, his shoulders involuntarily pulling themselves together. All of a sudden, the reality of their current situation punched straight through him like a blast from a force beam.

"First things first. We must get things in order. The Pulsarians aren't even here and already things are falling apart. The original DSP was designed to—we must get another DSP constructed and operational immediately—"

"That could take *weeks*," Granx exploded. "We haven't the time or the personnel."

"No it will *not* take weeks, Colonel Granx, because I'm giving you only until all the civilian starships are operational. Once the last one is cleared for space travel, that shield *will* be operational. Do you understand what I'm saying Colonel Granx?"

"With respects, General, I beg you to listen for a moment," the walrus pleaded, looking around for support.

"Alright, you have ten seconds."

"*All* of the logistics teams are working on getting the civilian and Star Fleet ships ready for the evacuation. *All of them.* And they're working around the clock as it is—"

"Then you work them smarter, Colonel Granx. Those refugees aren't going anywhere if that DSP isn't operational. The Pulsarians will trap them here with us. They will be destroyed here with us."

"I understand, General."

"Get the best engineers you can to work on constructing a new shield generator; go amongst the refugees and recruit anyone with a basic grasp of shield tech—there are more than two-hundred thousand of them out there—somebody has to know something. Get out there and get their help. Do what you can, Colonel Granx, anyway that you can."

Granx saluted and sprinted from the BWRC. Varxbane watched him go then addressed Piercenan. "Make sure he has an escort with him at all times. It'd be just like Cyclops to kill the individual in charge of the construction project."

Piercenan turned toward one of his lieutenants and issued the orders.

"Are those two Visions still on station?"

"Yes, General," answered a nearby controller.

"Alright then, have them break orbit and head into the Asteroid System," Varxbane said. "I want them to fly a quick recon mission of the system. No more than a million kilometers out though. I want them to spot the location of the enemy. If they see anything, I want speed, heading, numbers—all of the pertinent information—and report that information to me personally once they've landed. No cross-system transmissions will be allowed. They are to maintain absolute radio silence. And they are not to engage the enemy. I don't care if they are fired upon first—they are *not* to engage, just carry out the recon mission and report back here, clear? Okay, put it all in motion now."

"General, why not send the *Mekadore Traveler* up there for the recon mission," Jasmine suggested. "We're better equipped to scan the area and we can take a bunch of them out before they even know what's happening."

"Excellent idea," Varxbane said. "But I would like for you to remain here."

"Why, for Heaven's sake?"

"Because, once you launch, everyone will see you do it. They won't know what to expect. They might think you're deserting us—making a run for it. Yes, I know it sounds ludicrous. But I need you here as a symbol of our resolve to meet the Pulsarians on a united front. Once they see you take off, once they see you leave—and since many of them know the Pulsarians are on the way—they might lose their will to finish repairs on those wrecks out there . . . Hornet Leader can handle it."

"I see your point, General," Jasmine replied flatly. "I don't like it, but I understand." How many times in the past had she and her colleagues been used as symbols instead of active fighting units? They were the mightiest warriors in the galaxy and for the most part they were held back while *regular* fighting units, although well trained and skilled, died in horrendous numbers. Only when the situation was beyond hopeless were the Gladatraus Guardians called into action. Commanders knew the power of the Gladatraus but refused to use it. She wondered why theatre commanders were like this? *We can fight, why not let us? But instead, they choose to throw regulars into the battle and not Gladatraus; watching them die in droves against the Pulsarian onslaught. Why did they do this? And here's Varxbane, who appeared to be a practical being, doing the same thing.*

As far as rank was concerned, Varxbane and Jasmine were equals. But this was his base and the people here were his responsibility. *He* had the final word.

Varxbane turned toward Piercenan and pulled the colonel aside. "I don't have to tell you that this monster must be captured or killed before we leave. If we take him to Shiborium, he'll be right where he needs to be . . . again."

"I know, General," Piercenan said exhaustedly.

"I know that you're doing your best. This base is too big. Too many places for him to hide. And there aren't enough of your Retainers to search everywhere at once and protect our vulnerable areas at the same time. This Cyclops has got us spread out too thinly. That's his plan. To create confusion and disillusionment in our ranks. By the time the Pulsarians attack, we'll be too exhausted to fight them. But we will not let that happen. We will not show our weakness; the Cyclops must not win."

****

Admiral Rouldran Petti walked down the vast metallic canyon, known as corridor A2-7, within the hulk of his Capital Mothership Advancer *Nryevae*. The corridor was one of many that ran fifteen kilometers along the entire length of the gargantuan CMS Advancer. Petti looked about the brightly lighted canyon; his personnel were everywhere walking this direction and that, carrying out their duties, reporting to stations, keeping pace with battle plans and scenarios, and a multitude of other duties necessary to keep a twenty kilometer long Advancer flying. There were thousands of them. He could see communications officers in the standard gray fleet uniform lined with black battle networks, helmets thick and gleaming, shielded communications cords that could transmit millions of individual nodes of data simultaneously, dangling down to the polished floor or fastened securely to belts or shoulder harnesses. To his left was a standard of Straaka of the *Obver Cvosok* unit marching in cadence down the center traffic line.

Petti suppressed a smile and clenched his fists, quietly struggling to keep the feelings of power radiating within him like a reactor from exploding. The power that he held. All of the personnel in this corridor—the Straaka, the controllers, the comptrollers, mission officers, thousands and thousands of others spread throughout this Advancer and the Advancers of the entire Combined Fleet where the numbers passed a million—were his! They *all* belonged to him. To do with whatever he damned well pleased. They answered to him. True, his admirals and generals had the right to bicker, to alter orders . . . but in the end, they too belonged to him. An entire galaxy lay waiting to be purged, to be exploited; and the Pulsarians around him had dedicated their lives, their ambitions, their very souls so that he could use them in any manner he thought necessary.

War surpassed all other forms of sentient achievement; it was a combination of the ultimate test, the ultimate adventure. War was a constant in the universe and existed without the involvement of sentient beings. Right now there were energies that destroyed stars as well as created them, there were forces within the galaxy tearing apart planets, exploding comets, and it had nothing to do with tactical targeting and the application of firepower. Races like the Pulsarians were simply an extension of the war the galaxy waged on itself. War was necessary and not evil, a natural occurrence. It sustained life and it advanced careers. One did not enjoy life to the fullest without risking something that mattered more than poetry, architecture, drama—life. Without that edge, life was wasted. To fully know it, to extend it, you had to challenge it. No other endeavor challenged an individual more than war.

Over the years, he'd made many an analysis of war and power and had arrived at many conclusions. The one that stayed with him more than any other was that no other race in the galaxy understood war or its application to wealth and power more than the Pulsarians. There were races that could field vast armies, plant impressive navies into space . . . but to what end? Security, protection, exploration and nothing more. The Delrel Federated

Republicans were keen at this, but that's where it ended. They lacked the vision to take military might to the next level—either they lacked the vision or the courage. It could be both. If it was, then the Delrels were truly naïve in the way of intergalactic power. It was sad. Like little children, they would have to be led to the arena and tutored.

Petti paused in the corridor for a second. Looking around him at the brilliant lighting, the ceiling that held its place sixty meters above him; and just to his right the mammoth bronze statue of the ancient God of Conquest, Atvertuk. He was hoisting a gleaming goblet in one hand and a bloodied sword in the another, raised high, always ready to strike. What Federationer would have a forty-meter high statue in the heart of a command ship? Not one. What Federationer starship equaled the technical superiority of the Capital Mothership Advancer? Yes, he had to quickly remind himself that the Aracrayderians had battlestations that easily dwarfed any CMS Advancer . . . but that was the slight, for those stations mostly remained in orbit. The Aracrayderians were clever, yet lacked the vision to go beyond convention. A further indication of their weakness was that they constituted nearly sixty percent of the Tertiary Alliance and yet commanded less than twelve percent of the field assets. The Alliance was commanded primarily by human and Dracterian generals and admirals. If the Federation was a collection of children, then the Aracrayderians were their most infantile.

Keeping pace with the marshal admiral was his smartly uniformed aides, his personal battlestaff advisors. They were on the way to the bridge—at least Petti was—via the longest most indirect route possible, corridor A2-7.

" . . . He also stated that after the sensors picked up the deflector shield disturbance a low-yield explosion followed. Nearly impossible to detect with sensors on passive mode. Malactite sensors at . . ." a blue skinned, gray haired officer reported over the din of thousands of conversations taking place both up and down A2-7. Sound and echo absorbers were in-place and activated along the far walls and ceiling but did little to sponge up all the noise.

"Yes," Petti answered simply as the commander finished his report. Petti was only half paying attention. His thoughts were elsewhere . . . . Then he suddenly added, "Malactite sensors aren't the best in the Empire no matter what mode they're on. The new KM-V950 models are being tested on Phazerlon now. They'll prove more effective than current front line models. But I fear that the war will be over before they can be employed. Besides which, I doubt the Straaka are smart enough to operate them."

This released a hard knot of laughter from Petti's staff because they knew Petti didn't know a damned thing about Malactites to begin with.

"While I'm on the subject of Straaka, what's General Sergon's ETA to the Federation base?" Petti asked.

"Under seventeen hours, Admiral," the gray haired commander said, glancing briefly at a small computerized tablet he held in his left hand. "He's moving at flank speed right now. The Battlebarges are barely keeping pace."

"They'll manage, Commander Thvetti, don't worry."

"Did I forget to tell you something?" Thvetti looked concerned.

"Only that it's an unprecedented operation. Something such as this has *never* been attempted before in history and it's one of the biggest gambles that I've ever undertaken." Petti paused. "Admiral Dehyhitte's report."

"He also picked up the deflection shield disturbance and is on his way to the area. He and his *Shallh'Avachers* can get there in less than two hours. But the battle plan calls for a simultaneous attack. Dehyhitte's forces will provide high orbital cover while the Malactites and Battlebarges sweep the surface. He plans to reduce the closing speed of his forces so that they arrive on target just minutes after General Sergon's move into position."

"Excellent." Petti pounded a fist into an open palm. "And the Spark Racers?"

Another officer moved up to report, "Five squadrons of Spark Racers—from both the THV and XXR classes—will engage Federation fighters that try to intercept the invasion force. Commander Terger Aragon reports that his pilots are shadowing Admiral Dehyhitte's *Shallh'Avachers* and will haddock with them during regular intervals to keep fatigue at bay. Three to four hours away from contact, they will race ahead to engage Federation pilots."

"Excellent. And how are Admiral Merwinette's Advancers faring after that brief encounter with that stray Gladatraus Rhoderium Crab?"

Yet another aide, a captain, moved forward, his expression not matching the dread he felt in his gut. "Admiral Merwinette hasn't released an after-action assessment yet, Admiral."

"What?"

"He refuses my repeated inquiries."

"Damnit, Captain," Petti stopped, turned and leaned close to his subordinate—"you get on a shuttle and you take my request to him personally. You stay on him and stay after him until he files that damned report, understood."

"Yes, Admiral."

"What about the Gladatraus ship? Did it sustain damage?"

"It took several hits from a Javelin salvo and disappeared in the red zone of the asteroid system before we could track it or fully ascertain its damage," Thvetti said.

Petti acknowledged the report with a barely perceptible nod. Petti and his entourage approached a set of turbo elevators, stepped inside and rode to the command level. There they de-boarded and entered the gargantuan, coliseum-like command bridge. Controllers, scanner operators, navigators, weapon system comptrollers and deck gun operators, comm techs, helmsmen and thousands of others filled the vast multi-layered bridge. Before them was a breathtaking vista of the red and black zones of the asteroid system seen through view ports more than four-hundred meters long. Petti stopped to gaze upon the magnificent spectacle, that familiar furnace starting to warm him again. He turned to his advisors.

"That'll be all gentlemen, thank-you. I have other matters to attend to."

The advisors saluted smartly and watched as their leader descended into the technological maze beneath them. Petti moved to an aisle about fifteen meters long. He paused to glance at the dozens of negative readings, feeds coming in by the billions every second. They were probing the red zone of the asteroid system looking for Federation transgressors. It was a waste of time, a scanning operator's nightmare. Their equipment couldn't penetrate the dense shower of rock and raw ores. Their scanner returns looked like garbage. The Federation could hit them at any second and they wouldn't know until they were right on top of them. They could use the asteroids to mask their attack and—

Petti heard the rhythmic clicking of boots on metal approaching from behind. Colonel Kahn Trentergon stepped slowly up to the admiral. The admiral directed his line of sight toward the uniformed zombie standing two meter away from him. Trentergon was a gruesome sight; twisted facial features that resembled the lines on a rotting vulture. His mouth affixed in a downward and disrespectful scowl. His thin frame looked more imposing beneath the greened-gray uniform of the SSK, and the massive Armada overcoat draped over his shoulders. He removed his service cap and offered his superior a salute. Petti returned it and extended his hand, which Trentergon took. Not surprisingly, it was almost too cold to grip.

"I just arrived here a quarter of an hour ago, Admiral. I'm sorry I missed your phase one briefing." Trentergon's voice sounded like it had been filtered through a meteor storm. "Not that any of your fleet admirals or Straaka generals would've allowed me to attend."

"Quite true."

"But the news on the Frontier is in . . ."

"And?"

"Admiral, might we discuss this in a more secure location?" Trentergon made it sound like an order.

The SSK agent looked a little agitated.

"Certainly. This way." Petti moved into a small sealed off room at the back of the scanner aisle that was walled with thick reflective transmetal. Trentergon followed and shut the door behind him.

"Admiral, the reports along the Frontier indicate that the Delrels have taken action to retrieve information about the *Bleqck Shulker* project."

"Good," Petti stated mildly. "That's what we wanted."

"Indeed, Admiral. However, our agent, whom the Delrels call Cyclops, is also aware of the *Bleqck Shulker* project. But he isn't aware of the full extent of—"

"What the hell are you saying?"

"Cyclops, without my orders, or any orders from my section of the SSK, has released priority communiqués to field assets on Nijimegan, Elst, and Darmen, and along Delgrada sectors and had everyone alerted."

Petti stopped breathing, an apoplectic seizure threatened to envelope him if he didn't— He forced his hands on his hips instead of seizing his collar and pulling it away from his throat. "What else do you have? I assume you have more. Did the Delrels manage to steal information on the *Bleqck Shulker*?"

"Yes, Admiral, barely."

Petti let the air slowly out through his nose, relaxing. He'd forgotten how Trentergon's sense of drama sometimes clouded Strategic considerations.

"I shouldn't worry about it then. The operation will proceed."

"Admiral, do you think it wise to go forward—"

"The operation *will* proceed."

"Very well, Admiral, as you command."

"Think about it, Colonel," Petti mused. "This can only work to our advantage. The Delrels are clever, not clairvoyant. Contact Phazerlon."

Trentergon liked this, but it wasn't enough. "And the Delrels, what of them?"

"What of them! They're nothing. They're dying. The project will do nothing more than end their agony and put a swift end to this wasteful war." Petti's expression was sharp, a rapier. "Weeks from now, we'll toast our victory over the Delrel Federated Republic. We will accomplish in a short period of time what the Great Houses of the Stratrealm, what the Senate, what the Admiralty have *all* failed to accomplish in seven years! Seven goddamn years. The DFR as a fighting force will be finished and we *will* win."

****

Dannen Leers held on tightly and braced himself as the RRT-5 Medium-Terrain vehicle rumbled around another set of lichen-covered stalagmites on the floor of cavern Alpha-Beta three. Staff-sergeant Donrin Ringer seemed to be enjoying himself as he gunned the engine of the small three-axled, open cockpit vehicle. Leers had given up chiding the non-commissioned officer; the more he complained, the faster the sergeant pushed the vehicle. Perhaps it was time for a different sense of aesthetic perception.

"Hey, Sergeant," Leers called over the whine of the Vortex-5 engine, "my meeting with the other squadron leaders isn't for another seven-point-five hours."

"Major, with all due respect, sir; those Pug bastards are ah'liable to launch ah sneak attack on us in any moment. Besides which, there's that Cyclops traitor killing officers—like you—and blowing shit up."

"Thanks for your concern, Sergeant."

"You're welcome, sir."

"But I won't be able to fight'em while recovering in a hospital—as a result from the injuries I'm gonna sustain while driving with you—"

"Shit, Major, that Vagrant you fly makes what I'm doing in this here vehicle look like a snail's crawl by comparison."

"What the hell's a snail?"

"You fool'n me, right sir?"

Leers nodded and continued to brace himself.

"Damn, ain't this ah big galaxy or what—hang on, sir." Ringer gripped the wheel tighter and careened around another set of stalagmites then set himself up to attack an intrusive formation of rock and crumbling debris. "Whew-we, that'll take the kinks out if I do say so myself." He glanced at Leers. "Okay, sir, I'm slowing down."

Leers shook his head and scanned the cavern around them. Fifty and one hundred meter-long starships hovered above them on improvised docking mechanisms. Mechanics and technicians barked at each other as they made repairs on the refugee liners. A cart of spare parts lumbered by them. Sparks flew as battle-damaged hull-plates were re-seared to spaceframes. The activity was as well coordinated as it was intense. Leers knew that similar scenes were taking place all over the base.

Leers' line of sight caught hold of clusters of be-draggled refugees. Universe, there were hundreds of them—those with no expertise in starship repair lent a hand whenever and wherever they could. They carried supplies, traded tools, swapped parts or simply sponged sweat from weary foreheads; some drove axle-less hover trucks, or served food to the techs . . . and then there were those who milled around aimlessly, either too battle-stressed to help, or just too damned fatigued to do anything. In contrast to them were the children, who never seemed fatigued. They were running around, playing, laughing and teasing each other, as if this were some great adventure, the danger so far away.

Leers grabbed Ringer by the shoulder. "Stop over there. We'll drop the supplies off next to those kids."

You're not much more than a kid yourself, Ringer thought, cutting in the decel and guiding the vehicle over.

"Yeah, this'll be good. We'll unload the food canisters here."

"Thanks for helping me out on this, Major."

"No problem," Leers said easily. "Besides, the deal was that after I help you unload the supplies, you'd take me anywhere I want to go on this base."

"Yes, sir. That was part of the bargain. But you never said whereto?"

"To the 101st Strategic Bombing Division," Leers said with a sly grin. He climbed out of the cab. "Ion Squadron to be precise."

****

"How much did it cost to build this fortress?" Jasmine asked, her metallic voice finally breaking the silence of the central computer center.

"Oh, I really don't know," Varxbane admitted. "Maybe a billion credits conservatively speaking. It constructed itself mostly."

"Constructed itself? Nanotech construction?"

"Yes, before the ban. But all of the caverns were here billions of years before the Federation arrived. This base is huge but it only occupies about twenty percent of the Kinteesen Range and the nearby flats, and also about ten percent of the Kryderrian Pass."

Jasmine had been assigned—no, she had assigned herself to escort the general wherever he went. Cyclops was still loose and the general's guards had been relieved and reassigned to other posts. Usually, Jasmine didn't like being a 'tag-along', but in this instance she'd looked to it as a challenge. Varxbane was still a target because he knew nearly as much as Doss had—Varxbane just wasn't the mission commander.

The computer center was occupied by a skeleton force of operators and controllers. The controllers were dislodging terminals, CPUs, retrieval systems and monitors from several of the stations and placing them in large anti-grav containers, which would be loaded aboard the massive cargo haulers: CF-2s, CFX-2s, CF-3s, and the grotesquely incredible CFX-7s. The computer systems were high priority systems and must be taken with the evacuation forces. Other systems on the base wouldn't make the journey. There wasn't enough room to take everything—people were more valuable than boxes full of quantum components, nano-micro chips, and shielded diamond coded diodes—no matter how expensive they were.

Everything was under way. Colonel Granx was in charge of it all. But then again, Granx was in charge of everything.

Taking a base like this and packing it all away on cargo-haulers was a difficult task. There were a number of lists that they went by. There was the *must-go* list: the civilians, as well as the base civilians and base personnel; the highest priority list: computers, CPUs, sensor equipment, fighters; the lists went on to total ten altogether. Varxbane was glad that he wasn't in charge of the operation. All he could do was get in the way. That was why he and Jasmine were in the computer center—to get away from the frantic, but well rehearsed activity.

But the activity had just caught up to them.

"What a shame," the ape finally said. "To leave all of this behind. I loved serving here. This was my best command. My favorite command. Flying experimental spacecraft and starships was fun in its time. But it's not something one could've done indefinitely." He sighed, shoulders sagging momentarily. "I doubt that I'll ever get another command again after all this."

"Don't start, General," Jasmine said. "You're an able leader. And as long as there are Pulsarians to kill, you'll get another command. The war is long from being over."

"Do you think so?" Varxbane winced—he should not have asked.

"You marshal your forces with a leadership rarely—"

"No, I meant the part about the war being a long way from being over. We sent those cubs out there to steal information that confirms that the Pulsarians are up to something so twisted and stupendous that it alone will insure *them* victory within months." By cubs, Jasmine knew Varxbane meant Slayton, Leers, and Rook . . . and smiled inwardly. It was difficult to think of them as anything more than children. "And it has nothing to do with Cyclops. Compared to what they stole, he's nothing."

"From the attention that he's been getting lately, I'd be inclined to think differently. I'll admit that I'm slightly curious to find out what is so important that Admiral Doss was killed for it. What is it? What did those boys steal?"

"I don't know for sure. But it's—"

"Tremendous," Jasmine finished. "I beg your pardon, sir. I've heard that before and I feel that I'm getting jaded. Quite a disgusting feeling." She leaned closer to Varxbane. "We can access the information ourselves and find out what's going on."

"No, we can't, Guardian Jasmine," Varxbane whispered back, harshly. "We are not cleared to view that information."

"We *must*," Jasmine insisted. "After all that's happened here and lightyears away on those planets. We have Pulsarians breathing down our necks waiting to attack us. All other options are closed to us. We must, I tell you, we must!"

"No, out of the question."

Jasmine stood up suddenly, her mask glaring down at the ape. Despite his size, power, and rank, Varxbane felt like an infant about to be scolded.

"Where are you going?" He dared to ask.

"To my ship."

"No. This is highly unwarranted."

"I know." She grabbed him tightly by the arm with an armored hand. The general winced in spite himself. "Let's go."

"Alright, I'm going," Varxbane whispered tightly as he stood. "But I'll say you forced me to . . ."

"The hell I am. I'm *you're* escort, not vice-versa."

Jasmine started for the exit, leaving the general standing there dumbfounded. What to do? He knew the answer to that already.

"In case anyone needs me, I'll be on board the Rhoderium Crab until further notice."

****

Leers woke with a start. He looked at his timepiece. Blast, he'd only been asleep for a couple of hours. He sank back onto the pillows. He could hear his beautiful Arashi purring softly next to him. He could smell the fragrance of tulips in her hair, the perfume between her breasts. He lifted his head off the pillow, sighing. Through the darkness, he could see some of the details of her suite, the nearby end table, the vase he had given her last month on her birthday, and the flowers he had given her a few hours ago. Even though ninety percent of her belongings had been packed onto a container pallet and shipped onto a CFX-7 Fathom cargo-hauler, her room looked homier and more lived in than his spartan quarters.

She murmured to wakefulness.

"Didn't mean to wake you." Leers kissed her on the cheek. She smiled briefly.

"Were you trying to slip out without so much as a good-bye?"

"Wouldn't think of it."

"That's what you said last time. Then you were gone for the better part of the month. I don't like it when you sneak away like that. You're supposed to tell me when you're leaving so I don't worry so much."

"You sound like someone else I know."

"Oh—another jealous lover?"

"Not quite. Colonel L'ennell Slayton, N'ckshell's sister, was just saying that this evening."

"I know who she is." *How could I forget—you used to talk about her twin so much . . . difficult to compete with a ghost. God I hate these Slayton women. How many are there anyway*—"With the Pulsarians in the neighborhood, I'd just like to be with you as much as possible. I just worry sometimes."

"Arashi, there are times when I worry about you. That FB-25 you fly isn't exactly the fastest spacecraft around."

"But I have four engines, Dannen. Four. Your Vagrant VF—whatever—only has two; it's not even Warp capable like my Poltergeist. What good is speed if you can't use those same engines to Warp? Doesn't make sense."

"To me it does."

"Then that genius wing commander of yours decides it's a good idea to strap booster packs onto those Vagrants and sends you guys across the galaxy—something else that doesn't make sense."

"I'm good at what I do."

"So am I."

"So I've heard. Tackling a Frigate Advancer. Damn impressive."

In the gloom, Leers could see her smile diminishing. "I was so scared," she whispered. "I know I'm not supposed to admit it; but the attack happened so fast—I just went for it. And my co-pilot—you should've seen his face—he was like, petrified. He just stared at his instruments like a zombie."

Leers sank back a little. "You know, you worry me sometimes."

"Why? Because I'm aggressive? Because I chose to attack?"

"Well, yeah."

"I'm a bomber pilot, remember? I do what I'm trained to do."

"But your mission was simply reconnaissance."

"Why did they load us up with so many damned weapons then?" She folded her arms. "If it had been you, I know you would've attacked."

"That's different—I'm an Omnitraus Officer."

"Don't take that superior attitude with me, Dannen." She sat up in bed suddenly and swung a pillow at him. It caught him square in the face. "What we both do is dangerous and it's not very easy."

"Well, maybe you could do something easier and less dangerous."

"No way in hell, mister." For a moment it almost sounded like a plea. It quickly vanished in the venom to follow. "What do you want me to fly? One of those cargo haulers? Not a chance. They get shot at too you know. In my Poltergeist, I get to shoot back." A tear suddenly appeared out of the corner of her left eye. "Why would you say something like that?"

"I know—I'm sorry," Leers mumbled. "I know you're a good pilot. I'm just—"

Scared, Greysen thought. She leaned into him. "So am I. But I don't think you'd like me any other way, Dannen."

"Then, I reckons we're both doomed."

"Would you like me if I were a brainless beauty?"

"No."

"So, I'm not beautiful?"

Leers stared at her blankly. Where *the hell did that come from?* Emotions tied in a knot, Leers scratched his head and stammered, "of course you're beautiful. What I meant was—what I'm trying to say is . . ."

Greysen smiled, pulling the covers over her breast. She reached over and placed her fingers over his lips. "Quit struggling, sir, I love you too . . ."

"I'm trying to be serious," he started heatedly, then calmed slightly, "why do you tease me so?"

"Because you're an easy target."

"You sound like a fighter pilot."

"But I'm not—don't want to be either. Would you be with me if I were? Or maybe if I were an Omnitraus Officer, would you be with me?"

"I don't care who you are."

"So now you don't care."

"Of course I do. I care about you greatly." Leers folded his arms. "Why are you putting me to the furnace?"

"I'm not trying to burn you. I was just asking politely."

"Sometimes I think you enjoy making me feel uncomfortable. Do you treat all the men in your life this badly?"

"Yes," Greysen smirked, "all of them."

"Ha—now I know you're playing with me."

"Took you long enough to figure it out." She kissed him.

Leers took a quick glance at his chronogram. His heart sank.

Greysen folded her arms. "I hate it when you do that."

"Can't help it," he huffed. "There's so little time and always too damned much to do. I shouldn't even be here. Not that it matters, I had to see you."

Greysen looked away. Leers threw the covers away and climbed out of bed. He began the ceremony of picking his uniforms off the dusty floor. He stopped. This might well be the last time he'd ever see this room again. He looked at Arashi, who was staring at him in the muted light. *What was she thinking, right now? What was going on in the mischievous head of hers?* One of the reasons why he felt so attracted to her was because he couldn't figure out what she was going to do or say next. She was as much a mystery as she claimed he was—perhaps more so. Definitely more so. *What was she feeling right now? Was she scared? Was she . . .* She glided out of bed and stood in front of him.

"Be careful out there," she whispered.

"You too—but I know you won't."

She smiled, then suddenly began sobbing.

"Hey, everything's gonna be alright." He embraced her tightly.

She pulled away, wiping at the tears. "No, everything's not going to be alright. The Pulsarians are going to kill us. And there's nothing you or your Gladatraus can do to stop them from doing it."

Maybe, I don't know, Leers thought bleakly. Taking a deep breath, he said slowly, "then you and I had better make sure we give them our best effort before we go. If it comes to that. I don't believe that it will—"

"Yes, you do, otherwise you wouldn't have said anything."

Leers allowed himself a smile. "That's my line."

Greysen began sobbing again. Leers felt that all too familiar ice envelop his stomach, followed by the burning under his temples. He put his arms around her and pulled her close to his chest. Against a Pulsarian Combined Fleet, they were dead before the fight. It would take more than clever phrases, more than hopeful reassurances. With his shoulder wet with Arashi's tears, Leers felt like crying too.

****

Harsh red light highlighted Jasmine's battlehelm as she leaned close to the monitor. Varxbane stood behind her, his gaze intent, his heart thudding in his barreled chest. He felt like a cub trying to steal treats from the watchful eyes of the *Anjarhator*. This was wrong. But he wanted to see the information as much as Jasmine did. No, he wanted to see it much worse; inside he burned with anticipation—Doss was an old friend—he had to find out what it was that got him killed. What was Cyclops protecting? What was it?

Accessing the data now, Jasmine," Nancy informed them. "Stand-by one."

"Nancy, make copies of this data on disk," Jasmine ordered. "Now you've checked for plagues and—"

"Of course, Jasmine. Do you think that I'd let some filthy Pulsarian virus invade my systems? No way. In fact—"

"Why are you making duplicates?" Varxbane asked, ignoring the computer's tirade.

"In case the *Mekadore Traveler* doesn't make it to Shiborium," Jasmine said.

"But you will."

"What if we don't?"

"Here's the information now," Nancy said.

Jasmine and Varxbane stared at the monitor as the data flowed before them. Several minutes passed and the images shifted and changed to the utter and absolute horror of the two viewers. Varxbane had viewed preliminary data but he hadn't expected this!

"My God."

CHAPTER XX
DARKNESS DESCENDING

COLONEL Granx hurried down the granite carved corridor at almost a run, as base personnel scrambled about him trying to carry out his last minute orders. There weren't nearly enough of them, the Pulsarians were closing in—there was just simply too much to do and not enough time. Moreover, every time he thought he had something covered, two more items would crop up demanding his attention. Every few seconds, he'd snag one of his enlisted people and ask them to perform this task or that, check up on this piece of equipment or that, look for this person or—as if they had nothing better to do than to have him pile on even more tasks, when they could barely handle those they already had.

Breaking down a base and moving it out from under the noses of the Pulsarians was no simple endeavor in any terms. Nevertheless, this was a command base with more than 200,000 base personnel and enough equipment and hardware to construct an entire city. And they had to do it on near empty stomachs.

One of the sergeants politely reminded Granx of that, to which the colonel replied, "I don't care how you feel about it, Sergeant," Granx thundered, "this is Omega Command—the finest in the Star Force—not a pissing party. Now get it done and report back to me when you're finished."

The man stormed off mumbling something, but having the good sense not to do it too loudly.

Colonel Mranz was still breathing heavily when he caught up to Colonel Granx. From the call, it sounded urgent and probably was.

Before he could even speak, Colonel Granx said, "Here's the thing that has me thoroughly worried about this evacuation . . ."

"The readiness of the refugee ships—because I've seen—"

"No, no, no," Granx said irritably, "I'm not concerned about that at all."

"Is it the fuel situation?" Mranz said quickly. "Because, Colonel, we have more than enough. So much that we're going to be giving the Pulsarians a lot of it when we depart, unless someone comes up with a plan to dispose of it all—safely without blowing us all up."

Granx suddenly paused in the middle of the corridor, his expression troubled. "I hadn't thought about that—but that isn't it either."

"What is it then?" Mranz slipped two thick fingers to his throat and pulled his collar away from his neck. His collar felt like a constricting vice every time he spoke. Mranz felt his irritation building because Granx would not spit out what he was thinking. To enlisted personnel, he was full of bluster, to officers, regardless of rank, less so. Obviously, it had to be important or he would not have called him here at this hour.

"If you'd stop interrupting, I'll tell you." Granx began massaging the stubble on his forehead; an audible sigh escaped his flaring nostrils. "It's not the refugees, it's not the fuel—or the food—which we're running out of. It's *our* evacuation that has me concerned."

"I beg your pardon."

"It's *us*, my friend; we don't have enough cargo-haulers to get all of *our* personnel and equipment out of here."

"What are you saying?" Mranz insisted impatiently—the solution was obvious to him. "We'll have to leave some of our equipment here."

"We can't do that," Granx countered. "We can't do that—some of this equipment—if the Pulsarians get their hands on it . . . if they can analyze the core matrix of our computers, or get a hold of some of our sensors. We can't let them at our equipment. Everyone knows that Pulsarian shield technology is years, if not decades behind our own technology."

"Can't we just destroy this equipment?"

"Yes and no—we're wrecking as much of it as we can—some of it, though, is crapping expensive."

"Colonel, I can't believe I'm hearing this."

"I'm not the only one thinking this."

"Does it go higher than you?"

"Can't say. We all have our duties to perform."

"We can't leave our people behind."

"Of course we can't." Granx's shoulders sagged slightly. "Even if we got rid of all of the so-called non-essential equipment from General Varxbane's list and *all* of the important equipment—and I do mean all of it—everything. We'd still be asking more than nine-thousand base personnel to stay behind."

"*My Universe.*"

"Bad situation it is indeed, because we can't ask them to stay here—who would volunteer for that?"

"I wouldn't."

"I was merely being rhetorical."

"What are we going to tell General Varxbane?"

"This was something that I've been thinking about for the past three hours and the reason why I called you down here in the middle of your sleep cycle." Granx found himself staring absently at the cragged walls of the passage and almost couldn't bear the weight of what he was about to say. "There's enough room for our people on several of those refugee ships."

"By the *Pit of Kragindra*!" Mranz thundered. "We can't ask our people to board those leaky, festering, broken-down, infested garbage carrying . . ."

"It's either that or they'll have to stay here." Granx began patting his tunic pockets for his cigars and didn't find any. "I've given it a lot of thought and there's no other way. And, when we do this, we can also load the essential and non-essential equipment too—"

"So that's what this is really about, eh, Colonel?"

"Not exactly," Granx almost hated bringing this up, but, "there's one more thing and then I'm through putting in last minute requests. Somebody, or a group of somebody's, will have to stay behind and scuttle the DSP as soon as the refugee fleet is safely away from the asteroids."

"Colonel Granx, I'll let General Varxbane know that you volunteer."

"The hell you will."

"The general already has a plan for that contingency."

"That's one item I can scratch off my list. Now five hundred more and I can relax."

"You, relax?"

"I was just thinking about the irony of it," Granx said. "We work like hell to construct a whole new deflector shield complex then plan to blow it up when we're finished with it."

"Damn shame, but we'll do what we can, take what we can and—"

"Didn't you hear me—didn't you hear what I just said? The main reason why I called you down here is with or without that equipment, nine-thousand of our people are going to have to stay here unless we can get them onto the refugee ships . . ."

"I heard you, but this is still about your precious equipment—"

"Think what you like—"

"Alright, I'll inform General Varxbane."

"There's one more thing, Colonel." Granx began to move off. "The refugee ships that our personnel board will have to be marked, according to the Articles Of War."

Mranz reacted as if he'd taken a knee to the groin. "Damnit, I don't like where this is suddenly going. But the Pulsarians are going to shoot the hell out of those ships no matter how they're marked, no matter who is on board."

"But the refugees will have to be told and the captains flying those boats will have to be told."

"Of course they'll have to be told. I'll do it; I'll relay this to General Varxbane and from there—you know, proper channels and all that . . ." Mranz never finished his sentence and moved away from Granx. The dull ache that had been building at the base of his skull suddenly constricted the muscle fibers of his shoulders and upper back. He may've heard Granx thanking him as he began the long trek back to the BWRC, but didn't give his old friend any heed. He had plenty of unpleasant work to do and the command hospital had run out of salicylic acid weeks ago.

****

"You've got to be kidding," Leers said, as he climbed abroad the crew-compartment of the RRT-5 cargo-truck. Staff-sergeant Ringer had woken up early just so that he could pick up Leers before making one last supply run. He had just told the major the rotten news about the explosion—Major Leers who was blissfully unaware of the destruction of the DSP and thought Ringer was ribbing him, was still waiting for the punch-line that refused to come.

"Wish I was, Major," Staff-Sergeant Donrin Ringer said, gunning the engine. "This ain't ah joke, sir."

"I didn't hear anything about it—why wasn't the base alarm sounded?"

"Look Major, I'm just a sergeant remember?"

"Which is why you should know everything that happens on this base."

"Thanks for the vote of confidence there, Major." Ringer gave a shrug then added, "But maybe they didn't want to rile the refugees."

"You might be right," Leers mused. He quickly reasoned that such an alarm would more than likely travel beyond the confines of the asteroid base, all the way to the sensing probes of Pulsarian machinery—something that had to be avoided at all costs. "Man, this is gonna screw things up badly."

"You ain't ah' kidd'n," Ringer said. He slalomed around a jutting metamorphic rock out-cropping. "We got some goddamned traitor running around this base on a killing spree, leaving no forensics. And now this—he decides to blow up our only means of escape. It don't make sense, Major."

Leers didn't have an answer, not that Ringer was waiting for one.

"To my reasoning, he's got two choices," the sergeant quickly added, "get killed quickly by the Pugs, or hide out here and slowly die from starvation."

"Like I said, this is one screwed up situation. We need that deflector shield projector for our evacuation. Those refugee ships won't have a chance flying through the asteroids without shield protection."

"Not to mention our own cargo-haulers, sir."

"What a mess . . ."

"I'm not a pilot, sir, but the thought of having to evacuate without a shield—with the Pugs nipping at our heels and taking shots at us . . . I don't like it—makes me want to toss up."

"I'm sure that they'll have the DSP repaired before—"

"No, they won't because they destroyed the whole thing, sir. The whole complex is destroyed, sir. The base engineers will have to build an entirely new DSP, new generators, the dish-array—all of that stuff."

Leers braced himself as they did more swerving. "Donrin, the engineers have to have a new DSP constructed and up and running," Leers insisted. "There's just no other way—because we're all fried if they don't."

"Shit, sir, maybe you should be the on-site construction foreman."

"Not a chance in hell, I'd be totally useless," Leers said. "I'm better at blowing things up not—crap, that was the wrong thing to say."

"It's alright sir, I knew what you were *trying* to say—actually it's kinda funny."

"Hey, Sergeant, we ain't dead yet," Leers said firmly. "Let's not quit before we fight."

"I ain't thinking about quitting, sir."

"Because when the Puggies do come snooping around, we'll show'em a little something—know what I'm saying?"

I hope you're right, Major, the sergeant refused to say out loud. Instead, he focused his attention on guiding the four-ton truck through a field of feldspar and quartz. They drove into a dark tunnel a few seconds later and emerged into a cavern Leers had never seen before yesterday. He'd been stationed at the asteroid base for more than two years and had never been to this cavern; not that it was any different than any of the other subterranean caverns and canyons. He rarely strayed from his Ranger or Boulder Squadron, or even Echo, or the bombing wing that Arashi belonged to. He even stayed away from the BWRC unless he was asked to go there—and hopefully by someone with more rank than a colonel. In this cavern, the first thing he noticed were the freakish huge green and brown mushrooms just under a meter high competing vigorously with the lichens and mosses growing amongst dozens of stalagmites. The incredible sight flourishing under the harsh glare of twelve, twenty meter long lamps mounted on the high ceiling. Next, Leers' vision traveled to the irregular shapes of the refugee ships parked—no heaped up against the familiar shapes of the detestable CF-2 and CFX-7 cargo haulers.

"Yeah, I got just one more load of food to drop off and that's it," Ringer said. He held up his delivery order and read it as he drove the twelve-wheeled truck.

"What's it?"

"The food, Major," Ringer said beginning to apply the brakes. "Once we drop this off, that's all we have period. On the entire base."

"Damn, I was afraid of that."

"Which is why we need to get that new DSP operating soon and get the hell out of here or we're gonna have a lot of hungry and pissed off displaced persons breathing down our necks." Ringer began downshifting, pushing on the brake with his left and slamming on the clutch at the same time, with the same foot. Leers watched the sergeant's foot action for a few seconds then caught sight of the gathering crowds approaching them.

"Hell, who ain't hungry these days?" Leers said. "Maybe they can eat some of these mushrooms."

"Nasty," Ringer said. "I'd rather eat the ass out of a dead dinosaur than touch a freaking mushroom." Ringer pulled the truck to a halt and engaged the emergency brake. Leers was still chuckling as they both tried to get out. The refugees were already against the doors.

"Hey, hey, easy does it," Ringer shouted impatiently.

"Back away, steady now," Leers added from his side of the truck, feeling that his words were simply dancing past inattentive ears.

Someone tugged at his arm. "Hey, you, you're back."

Naturally, Leers recognized the girl from yesterday—she was in her late teens, he was sure—it wasn't easy to forget her because straining against her sweater and denim jacket were those large breasts, framed against an unusually slender frame. He'd have to be blind and stupid to forget about her, tragic since she had lost her mother during the evacuation and was solely responsible for her five-year-old brother. And where was he—there he was trying to keep his balance against the surging crowd. Leers felt for the girl and her brother. It was just too bad, the situation they were in. They were no different than the other refugees, thousands of them with their lives ripped right out beneath them; lost and hungry, fearful of the future. Yet, there was great resilience in the eye of these two and something else; something Leers indentified as hope. . . Yeah, that's what it was. It had to be hope.

"Hey, yourself," Leers greeted them as they nearly fell into him after being pushed from behind. "I told you I'd be back."

"Back at you," Her words smiled at Leers and brought a little warmth. "You forgot my name didn't you, busy man."

"No," Leers replied, clinching up and rubbing his nappy head. "How could I forget you, er, Selene."

"Yes, my name is 'er-Selene'," she said mildly. "Took you long enough."

"Like you said, I'm a busy man. I can't be in three places at once—maybe two places, but not three, my dear."

"I'm not your dear."

"Didn't say you were; merely a figure of speech."

"Whatever you say—hey!" Another brutal surge from the crowd knocked her to the ground at Leers' feet. There were about a hundred people on his side of the truck and they were all pushing, and cursing—Leers could hear the cursing now, all of it being directed at him. *Me, what did I do?* he thought as he bent to help his friend he met yesterday.

"My name is Ty," Selene's brother said before he was yanked to one side. He bounced off the forward passenger-side wheel and let out a scream.

"Hey," Leers barked at the crowd. "There's no need for that!"

Before Leers could help either Selene or Ty, he could hear Ringer on the other side of the truck, facing his own mob, yelling repeatedly, "easy does it, easy does it. We have to unload the containers first."

Selene tried to get up but was being stepped on and forced back down. Leers was trying to reach the boy as two are three men began pressing up against him. Leers began shoving back with his left hand. He too was being stepped on, his ribs being probed by sharp elbows. "Back away, back away, give us some fucking room you idiots for—"

Leers never finished as someone's knotty fist caught him across the jaw. The blow carried enough force to send him to the ground—he landed on top of Selene instead. He quickly tried to move off of her and get to his hand and knees—he had to protect her and Ty—he had to get to that kid . . . where was he? Someone began tugging at him—were they trying to help him up. Someone else was yanking at his hair; he felt his fingers being stepped on, he could hear Selene's cries of panic beneath him. He looked down; her nose was bleeding. A knee caught him on the temple—and that choking moaning noise was all around him now . . . pressing against him as he tried to shield Selene, hammering against him, where was little Ty?

Leers felt the sharp spikes of pain on his head, neck and back. In a flash, his mind tried to panic, tried to dump him back to Darmen. A blink later, it was gone, burned away by searing anger.

"Back away."

Before he could finish, the Delnalt'44 had cleared his holster and had fired. The choking noise gripping him gave way to a shriek of horror and pain. The massed bodies stepping on him, pressing against him and Selene pulled back as if by a whirlwind. Leers bounced to his feet and pointed the Delnalt at the crowd, wherever its muzzle was directed that section of the crowd receded further.

One of the refugees was lying in a smoldering heap on the ground. It was a man, a dead ruin in tattered, burnt clothing.

He gently brought Selene to her feet with his left hand and pulled her close to him. She was trembling, her eyes wild, staring right through him. She wiped the blood from her nose.

"Are you alright?"

Leers didn't get an answer as she broke away from him and raced for her brother. He was hiding underneath the truck, sobbing, scared and dirty.

Selene got to him first and began coaxing him from beneath the vehicle.

"You're okay, little man, it's over," Leers said. He reached out to help—Ringer! "Stay here," he said to Selene. "Are you sure you're fine?"

"I am—go, go."

Leers sprinted to the other side of the truck to find Sergeant Ringer lying on his back, his face torn up and bruised. He almost looked . . .

"Sergeant." Leers leaped over the man's body, dread filling his eyes. Everything seemed to stop—time frozen in violent surrealism.

Ringer coughed and slowly lifted himself up on one elbow. "I'm alright, bud, I think." The sergeant coughed again, "What the hell was all that about? What the hell is going on here?"

Ringer climbed stiffly to his feet, bracing himself against Leers. "Major, you look terrible."

"Never mind about me, how are you?"

"I said okay." Ringer looked over the hood of the truck. "You better check on girlfriend number two."

"I will."

"Say, if I look half as bad you look, I can see why you'd be concerned. . . I thought I heard a shot."

"Yeah, I," Leers couldn't finish. His head was pounding. He felt his sinuses burning.

"You shot a refugee?" Ringer began looking around frantically. The crowd, which had beat the crap out of him, wore fearful looks. "You shouldn't have done that."

"I know . . . I," still the words disappeared from his throat. Again, he'd shot an unarmed being. Shot him down, *but he could've killed me and Selene, or Ty and Ringer—he would've trampled us to death, if I hadn't done something.*

Leers moved to the other side of the truck where Selene was holding onto her sobbing brother. She was soothing him as best she could and flashed Leers a grim thank-you-for-saving-us smile. Ringer limped toward the corpse—what a mess. This whole thing didn't need to happen, the killing didn't need to happen—wait—the man was still breathing.

"Hey, he's still alive," Ringer said.

"What."

"Major, he's still alive," Ringer said examining the grotesque wound, more out of curiosity than on actually thinking up a way that it might be treated.

Leers reached into the cab and grabbed the headset to the transceiver. "Should we risk moving him or wait for the paramedics to arrive?"

"You're asking me?"

"You're right."

Leers grabbed the man by the shoulders while Ringer lifted him by the feet and together they placed him as gently as they could into the rear of the cab. Leers couldn't help looking at the man's wound. The victim's mid-section looked like a bunch of seared meat and charred, fractured bone.

How could anyone survive a wound like that? Not that Leers cared if the man survived or not.

While Ringer climbed into the driver's seat, Leers leaned close to Selene. "I think you'd better come with us."

"We're fine, Dannen."

"That's not what I meant," Leers said. "There could be trouble here if you stay," he whispered. "Anyway, I can't leave you here."

Selene clutched at her chest, uncertain what to do next.

"Don't worry, we can get you out of here on another refugee ship or a fast cargo-hauler—"

"Major, we gotta go."

Leers looked into Selene's eyes, as if pleading for her to hop in. Finally, she climbed into the forward cab sitting between himself and Ringer. Little Ty climbed on Leers' lap.

Leers ignored the cries of, "Hey, what about our food?" from the throng of recovering on-lookers.

Ringer began jamming the truck into gear.

"What about our food?" another man yelled.

"We need food."

"Are you going to shoot us too, asshole?"

Shaking with rage Leers held Selene close to him and squeezed her hand as Ringer gunned the engine.

****

"No matter how many different ways you look at it, it's still a bloody nightmare," General Dain Roim said briskly stubbing out another cigarette and fighting the urge to light another one. The commander of the 91st Omega Command Attack/Interdiction Division gripped the edge of the conference table projecting a 2D tactical map. "The Pulsarians have all of the advantages. They can hit us at any time."

General Varxbane merely grunted at the obvious and pinched a little more chewing tobacco between his cheek and left incisors. "Dain, my good friend, we already know that. I'm asking for ideas. Anything that I and my battlestaff might've overlooked."

"I'm sorry, General."

"Please stop apologizing every time I have a hint of irritation in my voice." Varxbane swallowed slowly savoring the sweetness of the tobacco that kid Leers gave him.

"General, I see what you see," Roim said quickly, glancing briefly at Guardian Jasmine and the Omega Commander. "If we were in this situation ourselves—without interference, without any burdens—we could launch ambushes and strikes against the Pulsarians for weeks and evacuate at a time of our choosing. But with the refugees here and with our supplies getting low—"

"The refugees are already on half-rations," Jasmine interjected. "They're going to go on quarter rations in a day or so."

"Exactly the point I'm making," Roim said. "Our options are limited to pure escape and survival and not 'counter tactics with ambush' in any way, shape, or form."

"Quite," Varxbane agree reluctantly. He made no secret that he'd like to take a piece out of the Pulsarians before they left.

"To do anything else would be asking for a lot of people to get killed. And I don't see the sense in harboring refugees to this point, then sacrificing them. No, general, it's simply impossible to do anything else. More than that, it's irresponsible."

Jasmine nodded silently and tilted her helm toward Varxbane. "Everything we have hinges on the deployment of your deflector shield corridor," she said. "Those refugee ships won't be able to navigate through the asteroid system without it."

"Precisely," Varxbane said. *But we already know this*, he thought.

"Once that deflector is activated," Jasmine continued, "every Pulsarian Advancer will swarm in on that signal. They might send a squadron of Advancers, or an entire task force, maybe two."

"Can you face them?" Varxbane asked.

"Yes, normally," she answered, shrugging, "but with the refugees in tow, the answer to that is no."

"One of the things that we can do with our deflector, something that you're not aware of, is we can curve it." General Varxbane paused as if sensing her slight ignorance on the subject. "When we activate the DSP, a signal will be sent out—obviously, it's pure physics; like turning on a light, the beam will travel in a certain direction. Because of the size of this asteroid system, it'll take the Pulsarians several minutes . . ."

"About twelve to fifteen," Dain interjected.

"Yes, long enough for them to detect that signal outside of the asteroid system, right? They'll deploy to intercept that signal where it breaches the asteroid system in the green zone . . . depending on where they are on the outskirts of our system, it could take them several hours at their best speed to get to that deflector exit point, right?"

"I'm with you, General."

"What we can do with this deflector corridor is bend it to a new exit point. We let it stay focused at a certain vector for several minutes, shut it down, reload it and bend it to a new exit point. We can even bend in mid-activation."

"Amazing." Jasmine was speechless. "The Pulsarians will be racing around trying to be in the right place at the wrong time."

"We hope. This little trick of ours works both ways, as you've probably already surmised."

"Yeah, you can easily outsmart yourselves with this thing," Jasmine said. "You might end up folding the shield corridor so that the exit will lead right into the heart of their fleet."

"Therein lies the danger."

"But we'll also have plenty of other decoys to keep the Pulsarians busy, as well," Dain said. "Both for the Pulsarians outside the asteroid system and the attack force already inside the system. We can't have the Pulsarians destroying the deflector complex while we're still in transit inside the shield corridor."

"No, we can't," Jasmine said. "Whom do you have in mind?"

"Colonel Piercenan has volunteered," Varxbane said.

"Is he going to . . . he's not going to stay behind is he?"

"No, Guardian Jasmine," Varxbane said reassuring her with a firm hand on her armored shoulder. "And he won't be alone either. We'll have a CFX-7 ready to pull him and his team out at the last second. Colonel Mranz will fly the CFX-7 unaided through the asteroids."

He saw Jasmine's battlehelm suddenly tilting to one side then quickly added, "Don't worry, he's a good pilot. Besides I'll be flying with him."

"No, you'll be flying with us," Jasmine hissed hotly.

"With respects, Guardian Jasmine, there'll be no further discussion on this matter."

"General Varxbane, you are responsible for this entire command. We can't risk your safety or risk having you being captured by the Pulsarians or even killed flying through those asteroids in a *cargo-hauler*."

"Guardian Jasmine, I'm not worth a bucket of spit unless I'm willing to take the same risks as the people I command."

"That's very noble of you, General, but—"

"The issue is settled."

"If you say so."

"I do."

****

Greysen could not shake the grogginess from her mind no matter how hard she tried. She stumbled toward the ready-room rather than walking with the fortitude and balance of a determined bomber pilot. With each step, she kept bumping into other pilots, navigators, non-commissioned officers and other personnel of the 22nd Omega Bombing Wing. Most ignored her, for they looked and felt as she did, a droning zombie, pushed to the limits of endurance and due diligence—others muttered mild curses, then went quickly about their business. Right now, Greysen's business was to get to a cup of coffee before the briefing. She held her empty mug tightly in her left hand and out in front of her like it was a portable sensor device; her right hand was busily checking the pockets of her flight suit—she felt as if she'd forgotten something back in her room, something damned important. The thought persisted as she made her way into the break-room and raced for the row of coffee machines immediately realizing that something was wrong. The smell of brewing coffee was absent.

"No coffee for us, Lieutenant," came a disgusted voice next to her. "We've been cleaned out."

"Terrific," Greysen said bitterly. "That's just great." Greysen tried to keep the 'whine' out of her voice. She regarded her disappointed fellow drinker with a cool glance. His smile was just as grim as hers, for he too was toting an empty mug.

"Captain Mertin Haelstrom, Photon Squadron." He held out his hand.

"Arashi Greysen," she said shaking his hand, "Ion Squadron." She didn't really need to say anything as her name and squadron patches on her flightsuit clearly revealed that information if Haelstrom cared to look . . . at her breasts, which he was trying not to do out of politeness.

"We've got plenty of hot-water," Haelstrom added, "and these packets of diet blueberry coca mix. Would you like to try some?"

"Any caffeine in it?"

"Negative."

"Maybe if we mix two packets of this diet blueberry crap together we can trick our bodies into thinking that we're getting our daily allowance of caffeine in one serving."

Haelstrom chuckled mildly. Greysen joined him and found herself staring up into his eyes, they were like blue diamonds, making her ignore his slightly off-center nose. Despite this, Greysen found that he was rather handsome, yes, but not quite her type. Something in his eyes told her that he thought she was his type.

"Where's the damn coffee?" a familiar voice behind her demanded.

Greysen turned away from Haelstrom's bold stare and greeted her navigator with a wry smile. "Hey there."

"I thought me sinuses were acting up on me again, like they normally do before a mission," Lieutenant Khardoc was saying, sniffing the air. "But we really don't have any coffee."

"No, but we have blueberry coca mix." Greysen held up a packet for him. "Diet blueberry coca mix."

Khardoc snatched it from her and grunted, "Any caffeine in this?"

Greysen started laughing and shot an upward glance at Haelstrom who was also chuckling.

"What's so damn funny?" Khardoc demanded.

"I have to go," Haelstrom said. "It was nice meeting you, Arashi."

"Nice meeting you, too," she said. "Stay sharp out there."

"Always sharp."

"Who the hell was that and what the hell am I supposed to do with this coca mix?"

"My, but aren't we full of questions today," Greysen said. "He's just some guy I met."

"Just some guy you met," Khardoc said. "I thought you'd be late for the briefing; still joined at the hip with your Omnitraus man."

"If you must know, Khardoc, we were joined at the hip last night," Greysen said absently. "But a lady doesn't discuss such things—well, at least not with the likes of you."

"Oh, I'm hurt."

"Besides, there are some things in this life more important than him."

"Such as?"

"Getting here early to grab some coffee—which it seems that I was late."

"You alright?"

Greysen blinked at the question. "Yeah, of course."

"Better be, because if you accidentally wrap us around an asteroid because of caffeine deprivation, I might have to accidently put my foot up your ass."

"Hey, you guys, look at what I have."

Greysen turned to see Hamn Yorkers, her copilot racing into the slowly clearing break-room. He was holding what looked like two packets of—

"Coffee." Greysen beamed. "Where did you find these?"

"I had them in my survival vest," Yorkers said breathlessly. "I have to take care of my pilot, right?"

"And navigator," Khardoc quickly added.

Greysen hugged Yorkers and gave him a quick kiss on the cheek.

"I didn't bring any coffee for you," Yorkers said to Khardoc, "you ugly mutt."

"I have two packets," Greysen said. "Which is better than what I had a few seconds ago. One for me and one for Khardoc, is that alright with you Hamn?"

"Thank you," Khardoc said.

"Hamn, you're a lifesaver." She gave him another quick peck.

"I know that."

Two quick chimes sounded down the hallway connecting the break-room and the ready-room with the other areas of the bombing wing.

"Briefing time gents," Greysen said, "let's go."

"I can handle anything now," Khardoc replied stirring the instant coffee mix into his cup after adding the hot water.

****

"Goddammit, Major Leers, when you step into a pile of shit you really step into it, Universe." Colonel Krandersen's voice seemed to shake the very foundations of his office. Made all the more thunderous since it was nearly empty and sealed shut. There was no escape for either Leers or Sergeant Ringer. None. They had to stand before the glowering colonel and take his fire without a word, without movement or wavering attention.

"Shooting an unarmed citizen of the Delrel Federation is a very serious matter, Major, very serious." Krandersen began pacing the room again, only this time his movements were more pronounced and determined, emphasizing his fierce displeasure. "Do either of you have anything to say about this—anything to say at all about this situation? Never mind because I don't want to hear it. Both of you are lucky not to be in the stockade and have been released to my authority."

Krandersen stopped at the wall to the right, leaned his back against it, his arms crossed and locked in front of him. "Alright, let's see what you have to say."

Ringer made a minute gesture toward Leers who remained silent, still standing at rigid attention.

"Leers, you're an Omnitraus Officer," Krandersen continued suddenly. "That makes you a cut above any pilot I ever trained with or fought beside. It makes you a cut above those special ops guys in the Strike Force. There will be an investigation into this matter. There, of course, will be a Court-martial and after the Court-martial, heads will roll—heads always roll when something like this happens. I'm not a lawyer but I can't make it any plainer than that. Word has already reached General Varxbane and Universe knows whomever else.

"Leers, you're one of the best pilots that I've ever flown with . . . I've seen you under pressure—you don't panic. You don't scare, you maintain. That's why you're leading the Ranger Squadron." Krandersen's voice suddenly took on a hint of concern. "What happened?"

As Krandersen waited for an answer, he studied their faces once again. Ringer's face, even though it'd been treated by the medical staff at the base hospital, was shredded and puffed, his left eye still swollen shut. His right arm was in a sling from a fractured collarbone. Leers' features were much better, even with a bruised jaw and cut lip—in fact he seemed to be healing before Krandersen's eyes.

"Colonel, they would've killed us," Leers said finally.

"I believe you," Krandersen acknowledged. "But will a jury at a Court-martial?"

"I lose two teeth and we're going to be Court-martialed?" Krandersen mumbled, incredulous. "I don't get it. Any fool can see that I got worked over, sir."

"There won't be a Court-martial now, but you can bet your ass there'll be one when we reach Shiborium."

"That ain't right, sir."

"Don't tell me that, Sergeant."

"But they were a crazy mob and they attacked *us*—it happened so fast."

"We can't sweep this under rug, as they say."

"I wouldn't want them to, Colonel," Leers said. "If they want to Court-martial us—or me—fine, let them. But we have more serious stuff coming our way right now."

"Yes, we do, Major Leers. Yes, we do. So you best set about getting ready for it. You're both dismissed—Mr. Leers, you're confined to the wing."

"Yes, sir."

"Sorry, but I have to note that I spoke with you and issued punishment. This incident will be issued on your official record."

"Yes, sir."

CHAPTER XXI
TREMORS

MAIKO Arashi Greysen leaned back in the uncomfortable ejection seat and rubbed her eyes. *Here we go again.* Her signs of fatigue made themselves known through the aching in her lower back, the soreness in her shoulders, and that damned itching just under her breasts. If she could only relieve the tension of her G-lock acceleration harness for just a moment, she'd feel much better. Then again, her discomfort was merely a simple reminder that her mission was nearing an end. Which was good, because having to concentrate, and stay focused on the instrument panels, the muted hued readouts, and the asteroids racing past the canopy, was taking its toll on her and her co-pilot. Returning to base meant that she could soon grab some sleep—real sleep and maybe, if she were lucky, grab a few hours of quality time with Dannen. Maybe that was asking for too much. She felt nervous, tired and quite bored—she could still perform her duties, but the hours of tedium were beginning to tax her already lagging focus. Sitting next to her in the cramped cockpit of the FB-25D Poltergeist strategic bomber was 2nd Lieutenant Hamn Yorkers, who hadn't been all too ready for his first taste of combat. Now he was more than anxious to prove to the Daughter of

Desdemona, sitting next to him, that he was made of the same righteous stuff that she was. Greysen had warned him that patience mattered as much as bravery in any fight. Being patient kept you alive.

They were in their tenth hour of patrolling the asteroid-clogged region 35,000 to 75,000 kilometers from the surface of their base. It seemed longer, since Greysen and Yorkers hadn't really said a word to each other. Flying their profile, while avoiding the asteroid storm demanded too much of their concentration. Besides, sharing the same fishing stories over and over again could get staler than the air in the cockpit.

"You know this is all *his* fault, right?" Yorkers' cloaked accusation finally broke the silence.

Greysen relaxed her grip on the control yoke then turned the bomber over and around several stadium-sized asteroids. "Who's fault?"

"That boyfriend of yours."

"Who, Dannen?"

"Geez, how many do you have?"

"What are you talking about?"

"Every time he comes back from a mission, something weird happens. We always seem to get picked to fly missions that push us to the limits. A couple of months ago, he comes back from a mission and we get sent across the galaxy to bomb some mysterious Pug experimental center. And it's always our squadron, too. Of all the squadrons in the division—we always get picked."

"How do you know its Dannen's fault, his missions are always secret."

Yorkers let a mirthful chuckle escape from his lips. "Because my dear first lieutenant Greysen, the hallway in our dorm is always quiet until he comes back from a mission—if you know what I mean?"

"Shut-up." Greysen punched him in the shoulder.

"If the shoe fits . . ." A wry smiled creased Yorkers' face.

Silence returned to the cockpit after Greysen tapped her control yoke. Yorkers took over flying duties allowing her to relax for a few moments. She pulled her facemask off and pulled a few swallows from her drinking tube.

Looking for signs of the Pulsarian invasion forces had yielded a null sighting thus far. But they were out there. Greysen knew it; just waiting to pounce on them when they were the least aware of it. That's when those bloody devils did their worst.

There were twelve FB-25 Poltergeist bombers on threat-warning patrol above the planetoid. The Poltergeist was a heavy bomber, with massive wings, four engines, and heavy armor; its usual role was that of the attacker, and not the watcher like the AWF-19 Gammatron. But unlike the Gammatron, the Poltergeist could shoot-back at any potential adversary it detected. As powerful and as versatile as the scanners and sensors were on the Gammatron, Greysen and the other bomber pilots knew that the

Poltergeist possessed equipment that the Gammatron didn't; passive warning systems like the RWP-97 and the ANQ-75A. When employed in conjunction, both devices could warn a bomber crew whenever any metallic object, flying on an intercepting trajectory, entered a defensive globe extending approximately 100 kilometers from each bomber. Additionally, when both devices were set on mode 4 proximity alert, they left no detectable residue beyond the effective range of the protective sphere. Because of this unique feature, Greysen and the others could detect trouble without alerting an enemy that they were being watched. It wasn't a perfect system by any means, sort of a passive-aggressive piece of astronics—after all, a 100 kilometer sphere of warning was absurdly small—but it was something, a gram of an advantage that General Varxbane was going to take.

Trouble was, Greysen couldn't help but feel that she was being used as bait. Her shoulders sagged slightly and she stifled a yawn. *Oh well, this wouldn't be the first time.*

****

General Varxbane paced back and forth through the crowded chaos that held the BWRC in a vice-like stranglehold. He had twelve bombers out there, patrolling more than 200,000 kilometers from the surface of the asteroid base. The bombers had to get the jump on the Pulsarians. Because if the Pulsarians attacked before they were ready to evacuate . . . the carnage that would follow—Varxbane didn't want to think about it. Once the DSP was operational, the evacuation would proceed quickly enough. But it'd be a mixed blessing. Yes, they could get the refugees out of here, but the DSP's signal would attract every Pulsarian within a parsec or more. Damn, all this conjecturing was eating his insides up. A sergeant handed him a cup of coffee that Varxbane would never drink. That's all he needed right now; while he loved the flavor, when two teaspoons of garlic salt were added—the caffeine would send him through the ceiling right now. So the general paced from station to station, looking over shoulders and hoping against all reason that the Pulsarians attacked sooner than expected; it'd go a long way toward unraveling the tight knot in his stomach. It all depended on his bombers. He knew his bomber crews had their mode 4 sensors activated, searching for the skin of a Malactite to grab onto, but most likely only getting readings from the millions of asteroids within the system. He could only imagine the strain they must be going through, having to stare into instruments while flying, looking for something hostile, such as an asteroid that moved against the gravitational tides, or one which changed direction suddenly.

"General, let me take that from you." Dargoinne appeared from nowhere and retrieved the cup of coffee from him.

"Thank you, Colonel Dargoinne."

"You didn't put any salt in it?"

"No, no salt."

"What's wrong, General?" Dargoinne took a sip.

"This whole business, Dargoinne. This whole rotten business. . ." he trailed off, frustrated because he couldn't find the words to describe the hammering in his gut. He stared at the activity in the BWRC. He sensed his gaze penetrating kilometers of rock to the activity taking place in the caves, caverns, and volcanic shoots of their hidden base. "We are sentient beings, you and I. Even the damned Pugs. We're intelligent enough not to go through with all this killing and yet here we are."

Dargoinne wanted to say something but held his silence.

"War," Varxbane said. "There has to be another way for intelligent beings to settle their differences. We have the audacity to explore the galaxy at incredible, time-bending speeds. Every biological disease we encounter, we conquer. All except war—it's like an infestation we can't control, can't get rid of." The general looked away from the colonel, perhaps ashamed. He knew that war in its crudest sense was an elemental form of extending political policy, used as a last resort. However, in a galaxy where said policy could lead to the destruction of entire worlds and the death of millions, the thought became disturbing.

"How is the work on the DSP?" Varxbane asked suddenly.

"Going along smoothly, sir. Colonel Granx reports that his crews will have it operational ahead of schedule."

"At least that's something," Varxbane's words were as heavy as the mass of a planet which had been lifted from his shoulders. "And it is good news, Dargoinne. How long does he estimate?"

"Less than half an hour, General."

"Yes, that *is* good." For an instant, a shallow wave of euphoria splashed over him. The wetness soon evaporated into a swelling fog of doubt and worry. He dismissed Dargoinne as the tactical administration staff began stripping down entire communication centers, sensor sweeping stations, computer terminals and other highly invaluable equipment that couldn't be gifted to the Pulsarians. Everything was being destroyed that wouldn't make the trip to Shiborium. Transparent plotting maps, classified documents, microsheets—everything that Varxbane and his staff didn't need to manage the imminent battle. And after the DSP was operational, the remaining systems would be destroyed also. Varxbane and his staff would then manage matters from within the belly of a CFX-2 cargo-hauler. The Pulsarians would capture an empty husk of a base.

****

Throughout the asteroid base, preparations for the attack and evacuation loading of cargo-haulers were peaking. The action was frantic as it neared completion. The refugees were already on board their ships, sharing berthing spaces with thousands of the base's non-essential personnel. Everyone on the base, even if they didn't know it, shared the same anxiety and sense of purpose that Varxbane felt. To an untrained observer, it would pass for pandemonium—but it was a controlled avalanche of emotion and activity. It was present in the minds of these individuals; there was no denying it. These people were about to die and each of them knew it—unless they could get out of here before the Pulsarians came. And yet they went about their work with a kind of calm urgency. Each knew that to beat the Pulsarians, they had to meet them at their level of combat effectiveness and then surpass them with unequaled cunning and resolve.

Colonel Blake Zears knew this well as he briefed the diligent flight crew of the Asteroid Squadron, 11th Omega Strategic Interceptor Wing. They were seated in recliners that took up most of the space in the squadron briefing room. The colonel's pilots flew the VF-97A Vision, high-speed interceptors, and were tasked to get the jump on the Pulsarians should the bomber crews give the alert. While there were other squadrons that shared this assignment, Zears hoped that they would be the first fighters to engage the Pulsarians. To Zears, it seemed everyone was thinking about running, he was thinking about fighting. No matter what anyone said, no matter what anyone felt, Colonel Blake Zears was ready. No thought, no action to the contrary could move him outside the mindset of killing those bastard Pugs.

Zears, in his intense and charismatic manner, wanted the pilots in his squadron to know exactly how he felt. Because there was a creeping sickness snaking its way through the ranks and Zears had experienced its debilitating effects before, he wanted to make sure his pilots didn't catch it. To him it felt as if everyone—it didn't matter whether they were pilots, administrators, squadron commanders, wing commanders, or even cooks—everyone was so tuned to setting up a quick and dirty evacuation that a sort of 'bug-out' fever was starting to be felt. Zears had dealt with this sort of thing at other bases and he didn't like it one bit. If left unchecked, it had the ability to completely sap one's ability to do what the uniform demanded. Suddenly you forgot about missions and your duty; all you wanted to do was run—run and be safe. Bug-out fever was worse than a retreat. With a retreat, you still fought—that is, you fought until you were out of ammunition, you fought until you were out of options . . . but you got your hits in; that was the important thing, that's what people forgot. You did whatever you could to the enemy, until you couldn't do any more. Then you got the hell out of there before you were destroyed. That's how you retreat. Bug-out fever left you unwilling to risk a fight; you avoided it altogether and fled the scene before anything happened. Zears let his pilots know that in no uncertain terms were they to let this ailment creep into their systems.

"The job of the Asteroid Squadron is attack-warning and assessment. *AWA*, people, that's what I'm talking about because we are here to fight. To fight—that's all I what you all to think about. That's the only thing I want in your heads. We have to be able to identify and eliminate any threat detected by the bombers that are now orbiting 200,000 kilometers above us." Zears paused and took in the young and not-so-young faces keying on his every word. "Right now the Tower Squadron is on stand-by, ready to support the bomber jocks in case they run into trouble early. Once this briefing is over, we'll report to our birds and we'll be on stand-by and Tower Squadron will stand down. I know the evacuation plan has been constantly changing over the last few days but that's how things stand right now."

One of his pilots raised his hand. "Colonel, what about that deflector array—do they have it fixed yet?"

"That's not our concern," Zears' stern rebuke came quickly. He felt like jumping from the lecture platform and throttling the pilot. "We're fighter pilots, not evacuees, not refugees. We get paid to fight—hell, I'd kill the Pugs for free, but there it is. When we get the alert, we launch immediately, get to attack altitude, divide into two-ships and help the bombers in blowing the living brains out of the Pugs. That's our mission—it's our only mission, our only concern. Make no mistake about it, got it?"

In the dusty, brightly lit briefing room of the Hammer Squadron, Major Allison Mann was briefing the more than eighty flight crews that flew the VF-94H Vagrants. The VF-84H, like all of the Vagrant variants, had a crew of two and the Hammer Squadron was the largest fighter squadron on the base, so she had pilots and weapon systems officers crowded into chairs, leaning against the back wall, or sitting on the floor. Also of the 11th Omega Strategic Interceptor Wing, she too wanted to make sure that no one was suffering from symptoms of bug-out fever.

"Our job, today, is to deploy a wall of Vagrants along the Kinteesen Mountain Range and protect that DSP. We'll be the base's last line of defense, and we'll stay on station until all of the evacuees are out and not a second before. We'll be flying at low altitudes relative to everyone else. But we'll coordinate our attacks with other squadrons. The bottom line is this: if the Pulsarians get past us, *they* get to the DSP and to the refugees. I will not allow that to happen. Do you understand?"

"Yes, Ma'am!" the energized response met her ears.

"Good, because I know ya'll don't want to let me down—so let's go out there and kill as many of them as we can. And then, maybe, go out and kill some more."

Colonel L'ennell Slayton was also briefing her pilots of the Echo Squadron, of the 1st Omega Tactical Fighter Wing. "It will be a target rich environment out there today. The Pulsarians are going to be all over us. But our job is the mutual support of the Ranger Squadron, which will have the task of taking out the command elements of their invasion force. We support the Rangers by keeping threats off their backs. When you see a threat, take it out. I don't want any of this handing off garbage. I don't want to hear anyone over the tactical frequencies saying they see targets two hundred kilometers downrange and then wait for someone else to come on-line and go after them. We can't afford to pass off targets today—*not today*. You see someone, you kill them! Kill them and then go after someone else to kill because there'll be plenty of them out there."

Simultaneously, Major Dannen Leers was also giving his briefing to the flight crews of the Ranger Squadron, several corridors away. "We're gonna have to hit 'em hard and fast on this one, ya'll. Ah always say, 'speed is the key', 'speed is life'." He was nervous and embarrassed at the way his voice would occasionally crack. "One Malactite carries more armament than four of our Vagrants put together. But the Puggies are slow and Malactites even slower." He paused. "Have we fought Malactites before?" He quietly asked McHellington who was standing next to him. The blonde merely shrugged. *You're a great help—we're supposed to be giving this briefing together, and I'm doing all the talking*. "What we lack in firepower we can more than make up for with our speed. We are faster than they are. We are more intelligent than they are. And we know this region better than they do. With all of these advantages, there's no way we can let these guys beat us."

Leers leaned against the lectern, scanning the faces of his crews intently. "Now there's one more thing I have to cover before we go on. I'm sure some of you have already heard the rumors and I'm sorry to say that I'm here to confirm what ya'll are already dreading. I did my best, pleaded with the wing commander, but she couldn't provide any help. So get your hemorrhoid cream ready because it's gonna be a bumpy ride friends. We have to hook-up with the cargo haulers—"

A collective wave of groans marched through the ranks of pilots and weapon system officers.

"Sorry folks, but there ain't enough fast packs to go around." Leers allowed himself a barely perceptive shrug. "Yeah, I know some of you guys were with me when we got left behind during mission A-57. But I have sworn testimony from Colonel Mranz himself that his pilots will be there for us when it's time to depart." Some of the pilots remained dubious, and Leers didn't blame them. No fighter pilot worth his or her salt trusted the likes of the cargo-hauler pilots who bolted at the first hint of trouble. Leers' role was to squash any lingering mistrust quickly. "I know how ya'll feel, but there's no other way around it, sorry. Besides which, we have permission to shoot them down if any of them try to leave us."

This brought on a small burst of nervous laughter from some of the pilots and weapon officers, while others huffed disdainfully.

"What, no sense of humor out there?" Leers said. "Then let me do the shooting—I'm in enough hot-water as it is so . . ." He let his voice trail off as his mind tried to conjure the image of the man he'd shot earlier—Leers shut it down quickly. "Now that we're finished pissing about this, let's get down to the details of our attack."

As Leers pressed on with his briefing, similar scenes were being played out from the Ranger Squadron that would be flying VF-94E Vagrants to the Aurora Squadron assigned to attack Snap-Advancers in VF-94B Vagrants, to the Caliber Squadron flying FB-25Cs, from wing to wing, from squadron to squadron—the briefings continued, plans were formulated then finalized. The fighters and bombers engaging the Pulsarians over the asteroid would maintain squadron integrity. They weren't going to merge several VF-94Fs from one squadron with VF-98As from another squadron to form independent strike packages as had been one of the favored tactics of the past. Here, unit cohesion would be maintained to keep the battle plan and the evacuation from becoming too overly complex and difficult to execute. In the swirling mass of flying stone and rock, complexity killed and these pilots knew it.

In the hangars scattered throughout the Kinteesen Range, mechanics and technicians worked themselves in a relentless but even strain. They began loading the massed array of armaments beneath the armored wings of the fighters. Fuel lines were connected to the fighters, astronics were put through last-minute diagnostic checks. It was their responsibility to make sure that every instrument and every weapon functioned perfectly. There were enough things in existence that could take the life of a flight crew that didn't have anything to do with Malactites or Spark Racers. The technicians and mechanics didn't want a faulty computer chip or fuel cell leak to lead a flight crew to their deaths.

Work was particularly keen on the Asteroid Squadron's fighters. There were thirty-two of the sleek Vision interceptors in the hangar, but only sixteen of them would be used in the strike. That was the central problem colonel Blake Zears and the other squadron commanders faced and had to solve. They wanted to have enough fighters in place to mount an organized defense, but not so many that they interfered with one another—there wasn't a whole lot of operating room within an asteroid system. Zears had a primary force of sixteen VF-97A Visions he'd utilize immediately with another eight in reserve, ready to launch once he gave the order. That left eight Visions which would be ferried to Shiborium with their pilots and five remaining pilots, without fighter seats—mostly new lieutenants fresh out of flight training—who would become passengers on the cargo haulers. And that illustrated the problem many squadron leaders faced, they simply had many more pilots and weapon officers than they had fighters and fighter-bombers. Those who weren't fighting would get to sit in their fighters for the retreat either via cargo-hauler or Warp boosters; those who weren't fighting, or actively retreating, would find themselves being taxied to Shiborium onboard the cargo-haulers themselves as passengers—and there were a lot of them. None of the fighter jocks liked it, but how else were they going to make it to Shiborium—they couldn't walk there.

The crews slated to evacuate and not fight, didn't like their role in the plan any more than the crews without ships *to* fly. To them, it was the same thing.

But if they had to retreat, many of them preferred to do it with the Warp Boosters strapped beneath the spaceframes of their particular fighter or fighter-bomber than to have a cargo-hauler ferry them to their destination. With the Warp booster pack, the flight crew had control over their fate, without it, they placed their lives on the skill—or lack thereof—of the cargo-hauler's flight crew—something no fighter jock relished. But the fast-pack wasn't without its problems and dangers. The fast-pack took up at least three of a fighter's weapon pylons which narrowed the choice of munitions a pilot could use in a fight to two instead of the preferred five or six. Another problem with the fast-pack lay in the fact that its fuel was pure unrefined anti-matter. If the fighter took a hit, it was all over. No flightcrew could eject beyond the blast radius of an anti-matter explosion. Thus, many wing commanders wanted their crews to be ferried into the combat zones with the cargo-haulers where they could go fully armed and not risk being caught up in an anti-matter explosion. The pilots flying those missions thought differently. For they'd rather take that risk; fly into the combat zone with fewer munitions; risk certain death in case their fighter was struck by an errant piece of shrapnel—than to be tethered to the cargo-haulers. It was all a matter of trust and training. The average fighter pilot received up to 1,000 hours of flight time before they were even qualified to fly their first combat mission. Cargo-hauler crews were often shoved to the front lines with barely two-hundred hours' time in the cockpit. And depending on the base, they were assigned to even less than that; sometimes they'd have to fly missions with less than forty hours of actual seat time. It couldn't be helped. Supplies and troops had to be brought to forward operation areas on an around-the-clock basis. And in the final analysis, cargo-crews ended up flying more missions than their self-righteous fighter pilot counterparts.

The second method of moving fighter crews the vast distances through Hyperspace was to allow the cargo haulers to transport them. Currently, the Star Force possessed four distinct cargo-haulers. The first and oldest from the assembly lines was the CF-2 Flanker. It could move up to 500 metric tons of cargo from the surface of a 1.5-G planet to high orbit, through deep space and then make the Warp Run through Hyperspace. It was strictly a cargo-hauler and didn't possess a fighter ferrying capability. However, many battlefield commanders thought that it could. For this to work, six retractable booms needed to be installed along its wings and the underside of its spaceframe to accommodate the transportation of combat ready fighters and fighter bombers. The CFX-2 Fearless was specifically constructed to haul both cargo and fighters along its external tractor booms in a pure combat environment. It had more armor than the CF-2 Flanker, a better array of astronics; true it was slower than the CF-2 Flanker, but it possessed a robust nature that couldn't be matched.

A fact that Colonel Mranz wanted all of his pilots to know. "Complacent. Cowardly. Cringing. Those are the words the fighter pilots are using to describe us and I for one do not blame them. We've been on dozens of missions with them, our cargo-haulers ferry them across the galaxy so that they can fight the Pulsarians and how do we repay them? By lighting our afterburners and Warping into Hyperspace the instant our scanners smell that there's a Pulsarian coming."

Colonel Mranz paced around the thick landing gear of the CF-2 Flanker and ignored the crushed grumbling of the dozen or so pilots assembled.

"What, am I incorrect in my analysis? You mean to tell me that we have pilots here brave enough to stick it out with them?"

A few of the pilots took the bait and responded with their own brand of hungry reassurance.

"I certainly hope so," Mranz said flatly, "because we've lost a lot of good pilots in this business. Flying a cargo-hauler into enemy space—with them shooting at us while we're unable to shoot back takes bravery. But the fighter jocks don't see it that way. I know we have brave crews—I'm looking at some of the bravest of the brave. But you people are being overshadowed by those complacent, cringing cowards. The whole base thinks that of the 91st. The whole fragging base. Not just the fighter jocks, or the tactical-bomber jocks, but the whole base. Cooks. Parachute makers. Commissary employees. They all think we're nothing but squirming cowards. None of them has the intelligence or skill to fly a cargo-hauler through Hyperspace but they know a coward when they see one."

"No sir, that's not true!" One of the pilots barked.

"I know it isn't true," Mranz countered. "I'd gladly trust my life to you people standing before me; anytime, anywhere. We just have to make sure that some of our brethren feel the same way on this deal. The Pulsarians are here, my friends. It's not only our reputation on the line here, today, but our very lives and the lives of those whom trust us."

****

General Preafect Sergon leaned closer to the information flashing across the young sensor officer's detection scope.

"It's no mistake," the youngster said rather fiercely, despite the powerful company he was in. "Those are faint Federation g-band emission sweeps."

"*Faint* is a non-qualifying description, boy" the Malactite keptein sneered. "Either the emission is there or it isn't."

"It's the type the enemy long-range bombers employ as part of their proximity warning suite," the weapons officer quickly added, trying his best to support the sensor lieutenant. "Highly effective, almost impossible to detect on anything other than our Advancers. But now our Command Malactites can—"

"No, no," the sensor officer interrupted, almost in a panic.

"What is it?" the keptein demanded.

"It's gone . . . it's gone." He began adjusting his instruments feverishly. "No, there it is. And another signal just popped up."

"How do you know it's the emission coming from strategic bombers?" Sergon asked the Malactite keptein. "It could be a sensor anomaly. Asteroid systems by their very nature are full of random spatial anomalies, correct?"

"Yes, General, you are indeed correct," the sensor officer said. "However, when I interrogate the signals, certain patterns begin to emerge. Those aren't anomalies ranging about haphazardly, those are military aspects moving in patterns and dedicated formations—it couldn't be anything else."

"And what if those are photon mines faking bomber signals to draw us in?" the Malactite keptein asked. "General, I smell a trap. If we go anywhere near those things, they'll explode and maybe take out half the invasion force."

"We'll just have to fly close enough until we can verify the signals' origins visually."

"Visual acquisition within an asteroid system, are you mad?"

"Not as mad as setting up a minefield within an asteroid system."

"If one of those damned things explodes—"

"It's not a minefield, keptein," Sergon interceded. "And I don't think the Delrels are spoofing emissions to manipulate our tactics. Fan out. Alert the other Malactites to stay well outside the detection radius of those emissions. Use the laser-line, not our main communications . . . low yield. We'll encircle them and kill them."

****

After grabbing another cup of mineral water, downing it in five gulps and devouring a couple high protein, high carbohydrate donuts, Leers headed for the Ranger Squadron locker room, ducking in and out of the flow of other fighter pilots and weapon system officers. Leers slid in front of his already opened locker—he never locked it—and slipped out of the utility uniform and donned his "Ranger Squadron grey" colored one-piece, fire retardant, breathable, flight suit. Originally it had long sleeves, but Leers had cut them off to just above the elbows and preferred to roll up the rest to his deltoids. There wasn't any reasoning behind this and it certainly went against all safety regulations, but who was going to ground him now because he cut his sleeves? Those sleeves would be missed if Leers' fighter was hit and there was a fire in the cockpit. But the stubborn human would say that he didn't need sleeves on his arms to pull those ejection handles, did he? And he preferred to wear the nomex gloves.

Leers pulled out his MGP-55 flight helmet and blew a fine layer of dust off it. Connected to the helmet was the AGV-28 oxygen mask with built-in communications systems and post-ejection, anti-suffocation filters and bladders; the mask was custom made to fit his face. Leers rolled up the oxygen cord and placed the entire oxygen mask assembly back into the helmet, and then placed the helmet into a black helmet bag and set it aside. Next, he fastened his anti-g suit around his abdominals and back, his thighs, and legs. With the maximum performance enhancement, the suit would protect him from the force of three to four Gs during violent combat maneuvers. Leers strapped on his survival vest, the pockets of which were jammed with emergency rations, a small first aid kit, water capsules, and other bits of survival gear. Through selected loops and fittings, he attached the PXM-88 post-ejection flare gun beneath his collar bone on the left side of his chest; a PXA-12 Personal Locator Beacon was fitted beneath the PMX-88; Leers fastened his shoulder holster and Delnalt '44 to his right, and slid extra ammunition clips below it. Last, he donned the RCR-109 Auxiliary Communications pack. Some of the gear Leers wore were standard, others weren't. Different pilots brought different items with them in the cockpit, some more, some less.

During this whole procedure, Leers kept his own counsel, occasionally mumbling a prayer, other times humming an old tune nervously. He ignored the cacophony of a dozen conversations taking place at once. At one end of the locker room, some of the pilots were singing the battle hymns of warriors long since dead and forgotten, other pilots were pacing in front of their lockers, waiting for the room to clear before they donned their gear, others patted each other on the shoulders and reassured themselves about what they were about to do.

Someone slapped him hard in the back and for a moment, the human thought about ripping the assailant's head off—

"You, all set there, Duke?" Kaltorr asked, his massive form all but blocking out the activity in the locker-room.

Leers took a deep breath. "Yes, I, ah, think so."

"You think so," Kaltorr said incredulously. "You'd better do more than think." He saw the human's worried expression then added. "Hey, I got *Versara*, the God of Victory tattooed on my neck and shoulders. We'll come out of this okay."

"Just don't wash your neck before the battle," N'ckshell Slayton chirped from her locker across the aisle. Like all Dracterians who prepared to fight a battle, whether it was in the trench, in the pill-box, or in the cockpit, she was applying blood paint to her pale face. The blood served as a symbol of dead partisans she was about to avenge. It was an ancient custom, older than written Dracterian history, and it baffled the human that an entire race still clung to ancient superstitions and tribal prejudices. Then again, Kaltorr had been talking about a lucky tattoo a few seconds ago.

"You worry about your own neck," Kaltorr snorted. "I have to look for my pilot. See you two later."

Leers gave a sharp whistle to kill the conversation in the locker-room. "Lead flight to me."

Several pilots and weapon officers gathered themselves around their leader. One of the things Leers had learned about being a combat pilot was that you always had to emphasize the basics. In an age where onboard scanning systems could lock-on and track targets several hundred-thousand kilometers away, where bandits could cover the same distance in a fraction of a minute, where fighters could put more than twenty times the force of gravity against its spaceframe while cutting those effects on the flight crew in half, it was all too easy to be overwhelmed by the sheer capability and magnitude of it all. Stressing the basics reminded a pilot that their first and last priority was flying their fighter craft—all the computer inputs, target information, distance, velocity, didn't mean crap if you couldn't handle your machine. So whenever Leers flew a mission, he'd remind himself and those he was leading that flying came first.

"Now remember," Leers began, "with these Malachite's we're going up against; they're slower and don't know this region as well as we do. But there's gonna be a lot of them, ya'll—intelligence doesn't quite know how many. But expect that for each one that we kill, two more will pop-up in its place. They have the firepower, but we have the speed. Use it."

Leers examined reactions to see if any of this was being absorbed by his pilots. It was, but for the most part it was difficult to examine the flinty stares, read what was being suppressed by the set jaws.

"Also, after bombing these targets, don't be afraid to use chaff and flares on your egress. We've got the new phase four flares that will mimic the heat signature of our Vagrants, and will even keep pace with your fighter for a few seconds. Same thing goes with the chaff. When the phase four bundle deploys, the Pugs will see a hundred Vagrants on their scanners—but only for a few seconds, so get the hell out of there."

Leers looked at his chronogram. Damn, they still had a quarter hour before they were to report to the flight-line and strap into their VF-94E Vagrants.

"Okay. Now here's something else we should—"

"Enough," Lieutenant Tomas Hall shouted, cutting Leers off. The young human stepped forward barely able to contain a grin. "Major Leers, with all past-due respect, you talk too damned much."

"Aye!" Stan McHellington boomed stepping forward as well. "The lad's right."

"Lad? I'm only a couple of years younger than you."

"Is that so?" McHellington returned.

Without warning, the two charged each other and began scuffling in front of Leers. "What the—"

In seconds, Wilson Stratamore jumped in followed by Kaltorr and Helen Lange. Soon Leers found himself in the middle of a fist and claw frenzy. He demanded that they cease—he got no response and was roughly tossed about and thrown into the air. He thought he heard singing. And laughter.

He was roughly set down. The pilots and weapon officers of Ranger

Squadron singing:

"Hooray for Dannen . . . Hooray at last . . . Hooray for Dannen, let's kick the major's ass!"

Amid the laughter, McHellington stepped up to him and said, "Congratulations on making major, sir. I salute ye."

Kaltorr congratulated him also as did N'ckshell. Tomas Hall approached and said, "we haven't got the time for a proper water drill—the Pulsarian devils won't let us. Try this for size." He threw a glass of water in Leers' face to the utter exultation of the combat crews standing around him.

Leers, trying to blow the water out of his nose while wiping at his eye, grinned and thanked them all. Thoroughly embarrassed, he hunted for a towel as the singing began around him again, just in time to hear someone say, "Hey, didn't Tomas take a leak in that water."

****

"What did you say?" Lieutenant Greysen asked, as she removed her helmet. *Egad.* Her moisture absorber had failed again. She sighed. She felt that bomber pilots got the second-hand equipment while fighter pilots were treated like royalty and issued the best. Of course, it wasn't true. It just seemed that way and gave her something to focus on other than her fatigue.

"I said that this is boring as hell. No excitement." Yorkers yawned.

"Funny, you weren't saying that the last time we were hunting for Pulsarians."

"I was scared then."

"You sound scared now."

Greysen and Yorkers exchanged glances then laughed.

"Keep your eyes focused on the task," she said.

The navigator moved up into the cramped cockpit and took his seat, positioned behind the co-pilot.

"What kept ya'?" Greysen asked.

"The bombardier needed me to input some data into his attack computer," the toothy wolf said. "He'll do fine. He's just a little nervous; he kept hitting the reset switch without noticing it."

"Yeah, there seems to be a lot of that going around," Yorkers dry response was quick.

"If he freezes, I'll kick him in the rear," the navigator, Khardoc said. The wolf began strapping himself into his ejection seat.

"Sounds good to me," Greysen said. "Tell him that I don't think we'll run into any Pulsarians today, if it'll make him feel any better."

"Hope you're right," Khardoc commented dryly. "I haven't eaten in days."

"Good luck finding food at the base, the commissary's been picked clean."

"I was thinking about eating something else," Khardoc said grinning and gave her a wink.

Greysen rolled her eyes.

A warning beep sounded on the three instrument panels. It was the proximity alarm. Greysen quickly donned her helmet. "Okay, what do we have here?"

"I got a contact in section six-two-seven," the wolf said, looking at his monitors. "No, damn it's gone."

"Are you sure, you had me worried for a moment."

"There it is," Khardoc shouted. "There it is."

"Confirmed," Yorkers said, staring wildly at his own readings. "Heading now is two-eight-zero. Speed: 17,000kpx and slowing."

"An asteroid?" Greysen asked, immediately regretting it. They had dodged and jinked past thousands in the past hour and none of them had built-in speed control.

"Speed is now 16,000. It's coming up behind us."

"Weapons, stand-by. Let's swing around for a better look," Greysen said as she gripped the steering column tightly and pulled the FB-25 around in a tight 7G arc. "Can anyone see it?"

"Speed now 15,000kpx," the wolf reported. "Getting another contact now."

Fire warning alarms blared through the cockpit.

"I see it—*My God!*"

"Malactite, closing."

"Weapons, fire on my mark—"

"Screens, screens, screens."

A nearby control panel erupted into a torrent of sparks as the first energy beams touched the bomber. The wolf shrieked as his instrument panel exploded, throwing burning metal and composites into his face.

"Ohmigod! We've been hit," Yorkers yelled as the cockpit burst into searing light and heat.

"Mayday. Mayday!" Arashi Greysen yelled; G-forces ripped and tore at her, pain belting and ripping at her insides.

CHAPTER XXII
SHOOT-OUT WITH ASTEROID LEADER

TWO FB-25 Poltergeist bombers, from the 22nd Omega Strategic Bombing Wing, exploded. Their five-member crews never knew what hit them. The count was now three. Another bomber pilot heard Lt. Arashi Greysen's frantic "Mayday!" call and immediately put his own bomber into a high-G hard turning reversal, missing death by a micro-second; lasers streaking by the bomber's space-frame. Through the canopy, the pilot could see the menacing bulk of the Malactite passing just over them, its pulse-lasers trying desperately to connect with the more agile bomber. The pilot switched on his tactical radar and wondered how in the name of the *Nine Hells of Leatweh* did those Malactites slip into their vulnerability sphere undetected! *How? My God!* And they weren't alone. With one sweep of his radar, he saw that there were five other Malactites within 1,000 kilometers of his current position. *Ohmigod! This is it! This is the invasion!*

He radioed to the others about the danger as his left wing exploded. Not a hit from a Malactite, but by an asteroid—a freaking asteroid! The bomber started to cartwheel violently, the pilot trying to maintain control so that his crew could eject. Too late—another hurtling boulder slammed into the cockpit—the bomber exploded in seconds.

Another bomber met a fiery death as it was cut in two by a Malactite's powerful energy bolts; the pilot thought that switching on the defensive screens would be the best action to take before taking any evasive move—he was wrong.

Screams for help clogged the tactical frequencies as two more bombers became burning tombs. In a straight-on, head-to-head fight, the FB-25 outclassed the Malactites by a lightyear. The bombers needed space, however—vast quantities of it—room enough to run where it could utilize its most lethal weapon it had over the Malactite—speed. But here in the dense asteroid region, the Malactites had the jump, had the edge.

Somewhere in Sector A-5, Zone 6, another bomber saw a Malactite loom up off its left wing. The pilot panicked and slammed the throttles to the stops, and the bomber plowed directly into an asteroid about the size of a house. After taking a direct hit, crews from another bomber, ejected from their exploding craft only to be incinerated in the process.

In only a matter of seconds, four FB-25s were destroyed, two more were put out of action and burning crazily. The remaining bombers, Photon Four and Ion Eight radioed back to the Asteroid base for help. None came.

****

"Ion Eight. Ion Eight—do you read?" General Varxbane yelled into the microphone of his tiny headset.

"Contact, contact, contact!" a panicked voice crackled over the communications set. "Launch the alert fighters."

"Calm down, Ion Eight," Varxbane said in an even but authoritative voice. "Can you give us any vectors? How many Malactites? What classes? Speed, heading—anything at all?"

"There's about five in our scanning area—wait a minute, wait a minute—wait! They're jamming our scanners—wide band—all frequencies and . . . it . . . looks . . . ." the pilot's voice was fighting through an angry wash of static. *"Universe! We're hit! We're hit!"*

"Ion Eight!"

"Crew eject. Crew eject!"

"I—I can't reach the handles," another voice screamed over the speakers.

"Ion Eight, are you there?" Varxbane felt helpless.

There was another tremendous wash of static, then: *"Oh Universe, we're coming apart."* Then a final wash of static as the link died.

"Damnit!" Varxbane slammed the headset down.

"They're all gone," Dargoinne confirmed looking at the data from a nearby monitor.

"This is just the beginning." Varxbane trembled slightly as he spoke. Keeping the flutter out of his voice, he ordered, "Launch control, get the

Asteroid Squadron scrambled at once, followed immediately by the others—we have to hit them while they're still in high orbit."

A youngish officer repeated the order into a nearby communication panel. Varxbane turned toward Colonel Dargoinne. "Also, I want one of our Surveillance and Warning platforms, the AWF-19s, in action immediately. We'll use it to relay vectors to the fighter squadrons. Using the bombers had been a good idea, but not good enough. Get Colonel Zimmer up there. She's the best."

"And the base's fixed scanner? With them we can get a better picture of what we're against."

"Negative," Varxbane said. "That'll lead the Pulsarians straight to us. The DSP is not operational yet. If we switch on our base's scanners, we'll have Malactites and Battlebarges breathing down our necks before we have a chance to do anything. They know they're over the right asteroid. The problem for our Pulsarian friends is that they'll have a lot of surface area to probe before they can acquire us. Besides, we can get a complete tactical picture from the AWF-19s."

"What about the bomber crews who may've ejected?" Dargoinne kept his voice even and low. "Can we get rescue teams to—"

Dargoinne never finished. Varxbane's solemn expression gave him his answer.

****

"General Sergon, we have targets moving in," a scanner officer voiced excitedly, somewhat nervously, as he stared at the bright scanner inputs rushing in. The young officer's face was pale with terror and excitement.

Sergon leaned forward in his seat. In the command section of his Malactite, the air was thick with the odor of unbathed bodies, stale food parts, lubricants and polished metal. And from the reaction of the lieutenant toward the new scanner inputs, the putrid stink of vomit might be added to the musty air.

"Gunner, stand by with the pulse-lasers," Sergon directed calmly. "Don't fire at them until they're well within range." Actually, Sergon didn't have to say anything; directing fire was the duty of the fire-control officer. Sergon's job was to monitor and manage the overall battle, not direct fire to individual targets.

"Yes, sir, pulse-lasers standing by."

"Range to their asteroid base?" Sergon asked.

"Ten-thousand megameters and closing."

"Speed?" Sergon rolled back into his seat.

"Forty-seven mmpx," another controller said.

"Targets coming into range now, zone eight," the scanner officer said.

"I'm getting transponder codes, now," another officer said. "Stand-by.

Cross-referencing now. They're Spark Racers, general. THV models. The flightleader is identifying himself on the secure tactical frequency." He placed a hand over his ear piece. "They want to know if they should hold position with us or move on ahead, General."

"What squadron are they from?"

"The R'srclan Squadron, General," a communications officer said. "All Racers are present and accounted for."

Good, Sergon thought. He now had thirty-six Spark Racer THVs on station. But where were the other two Racer squadrons: The H'reclans also flying THVs and the P'gaclans flying the superior XXRs. And most important, where was Admiral Dehyhitte and his *Shallh'Avachers*?

"Tell the R'srclan Squadron to move in and attack any targets that try to intercept us," Sergon said. "I want them to clear a path for us and the Battlebarges. Have our two ECM jamming Malactites move ahead to their pre-briefed positions ahead of us."

"Yes, sir." The comm officer turned to his panel.

"What's our ETA to the planetoid surface?"

"At current speed and course," the second-in-command said as he stared at the bright lighted codes and computations on his computer screen, "just under fifteen minutes, General."

Sergon replaced his heavy battle helmet and tightened down his acceleration straps. Fifteen minutes to target—it was going to be tight. Could they hold off Federation fighters that long? Could his crews continue to dodge these asteroids and fight that long?

There was no turning back now, they were committed. Sergon took in a gulp of the stale, musty air. As usual, the accursed fans and ventilators were inoperable . . . for him, this was the smell of battle—the dank thickness of it, its essence clinging to him like a living entity. If he died, this would be the last thing that he would remember, the sweat, the toil, the unpleasant stench of battle. Sergon smiled . . . to embrace the mistress of battle and death—he loved it so.

****

Colonel Blake Zears maneuvered his sleek VF-97A Vision through the tight, twisty tunnels that led to the *Afterburner Pit.* It bristled with offensive weapons, its booster-pack and ECM jammer pods. Following closely behind him were three other, razor sharp, ready-for-action VF-97As, crewed by even sharper pilots. And behind them were more in groups of four each, sixteen in all. This was the Asteroid squadron, veterans of the Cebossan Campaign, the Anomed Action and a dozen more bloody, brutal attacks against the driving force that wanted to enslave the galaxy, the Pulsarian Empire. Blue skinned humanoid monsters that lived for war and conquest. Savages, murderers, the rapists of the galaxy.

Colonel Zears frowned beneath his oxygen mask. *Dammit.* His squadron was supposed to coordinate a first strike against the Pulsarians *before* they reached high orbit. Curse those damned incompetent bomber crews. Real pilots flew fighters; idiots flew bombers. They should've known that the Pulsarians would figure out a way to sneak through their passive scanning modes. *Blasted idiots, damn them.* What were they thinking? Problem was, they hadn't been thinking. Once the battle is joined, you have to fight. You can't look around the cockpit for buttons to push, or scream on the radios for help. The bombers were supposed to identify the enemy, then attack them at long-range; thus allowing him and his Asteroid Squadron enough time to launch their own blow-through attacks against the invasion force. Something terrible had happened and the bomber crews had paid a terrible price for their staggering . . . incompetence.

Colonel Zears reached to turn on his gun camera; under optimal conditions it could illustrate a target up to 10,000 kilometers away. In this crazy age of high speed engagements and long-distance targeting, it helped to get a picture of what you were about to destroy so that you didn't inadvertently gun down any friendly forces. In the past, the Pulsarians had been known to emulate Delrel scanner signatures, formations and radio call signs—a visual picture of a potential adversary would help avoid any uncertainties that might exist in the vast and deadly arena of jamming and deception . . . still known to most as 'Electronic Warfare'.

"Asteroid Leader to squadron," he said into the tiny twin-coiled communicator hidden inside of the oxygen mask. "Concentrate on the lead Malactites. Push in close and get kills."

"We're with ya all the way, leader," Asteroid Senior, Jock Conrad breathed heavily into his mike. Major Conrad had attended the Bastian Academy on Minerva with Dannen Leers. He didn't know Leers until his junior year and was thrilled by the fact that he'd found someone who loved to fly as much as he did and who wasn't afraid to engage in low altitude mock knife-fights all but forbidden by the flight instructors. Hell, Conrad was once thought to be Omnitraus Officer material—a cut above the rest. But he didn't have that gift, that special knack that no one could name, that scientists always debated of its existence. Now, here he was flying Asteroid Senior. He was a damned good fighter jock, a hardware man who not only could master the VF-97A Vision, but he could out-fly, out knife-fight anyone else who flew another VF-97A against him—even the great, self-important, Omnitraus Officer Dannen Leers. A fact that he'd have to constantly remind his fellow human about—if he lived long enough.

Right now, Conrad seriously doubted that he'd make it through this mission. He wasn't as pompous or as arrogant as Blake Zears—that was probably why he was just Asteroid Senior and not the Leader. As far as Blake was concerned, they'd be the ones to knock out the Pulsarian invasion force. Everyone else's involvement in this matter was overkill—delaying actions to make sure those engineers got that DSP operating on schedule. Colonel Zears was convinced that in two days, everyone would be in the Officer's Club drinking gallons of beer and swapping stories about how they drove the Pulsarians back into the Asteroid System—at least that was the speech he gave, whether or not he actually believed it was another matter entirely.

Conrad glanced to his left and right to regard his wingmen, then forward again to catch a glimpse of Asteroid Leaders trailing flight. *Damn!* This was it. They were really going to tackle the Pulsarians on their home turf. This wasn't a deep-space hit-and-run attack, or a support mission lightyears away. This was going down now, within the asteroid system itself!

Asteroid Leader's Vision was the first to burst into the yawning mouth of the gargantuan Afterburner Pit. He pulled back on the stick and his Vision blazed up through the throat of the defunct volcano. He and his wingmen and the trailing flights sped by the thick security doors and up . . . up . . . up until they were clear of the volcano.

Asteroid Leader leveled off, rolled inverted, then pointed his fighter down toward the jagged mountain range below. His wingmen held course with him as he leveled off again, barely 10 meters above the surface—craters, gullies, boulders and rock outcroppings racing by in a dizzying blur.

"Asteroid Squadron, Asteroid check," Zears directed into his mike.

In squadron order, his wingmen, then his trailing flight reported in using the call numbers (Asteroid Two, Three, Four). Then Major Conrad reported in along with his wingmen and his trailing Flight (Asteroid Senior, Fourteen, Fifteen . . .). Technically Zears was in control of all sixteen VF-97s. However, Conrad was the so-called Senior wing leader and was in tactical control of eight of the Visions and could operate independently if the need dictated.

"We're ready to fight, Leader," Conrad called out after the last pilot in the last flight reported in.

"Whiskey-Kilo, this is Asteroid Leader checking in," Zears addressed his comm unit. "Whiskey-Kilo, how do you copy my signal?" No answer.

Zears shrugged in concern. As briefed, if he couldn't talk directly with the base, he needed to do so with an AWF-19, a flying command, surveillance, and battlefield coordination platform. The officers and technicians onboard the craft would have overall control of the upcoming battle. They would vector the different fighters and fighter-bombers into attacks with specified targets. True, the squadron already knew what targets they had to hit, but events had a habit of changing rapidly on the modern battlefield and seldom, if ever, went according to a pre-briefed plan. The crews onboard the AWF-19 had the staggering responsibility to sift through the incredible influx of target data and relay orders to friendly forces in the combat zone.

"Goddamnit." Zears looked left and right. The Pulsarians could be ready to pounce at any second and he wouldn't know from which direction they we coming. True, the VF-97 had a powerful radar/scanner of its own. It just wasn't as sophisticated as some. He could scan, but only in front and below him. Still, it was better than nothing. He ordered his pilots to switch on their scanners and to literally keep their eyes open—as if they'd do anything else. The Pulsarians were in the neighborhood, all they had to do was get a lock-on one—that's all he needed. Once they acquired one, the rest would be easy.

"Okay, here we go," Zears said after faint readings began pinging on his radar. "Let's see how many of them we can take out on the first pass."

"I've got what looks like chaff bearing about two-three-one," Asteroid Twelve, a Flight Leader reported.

"I see it. Let's—Holy Hell, my radar just turned into garbage," Zears announced.

"Confirmed," Conrad said. "They're jamming us alright. Wide band disruption. They aren't taking any chances with us."

"Can we burn through it?" a female pilot asked flying a VF-97A with Asteroid Seventeen call letters.

"That's a negative. The amplification is too strong. We'll just have to punch in closer before we can use our own fire control radars. Whiskey-Kilo, are you copying this? Do you have my signal?" Again, no answer.

"Spread to Attacking Wing."

Immediately, the Visions split up from their in-close, tight formation, to assume the 'Attacking Wing' spread. Dividing into flights of four with an eight kilometer separation between each flight. Each flight would hunt for targets as a single unit. The 'spread' command also meant that each pilot was now freed to select the 'master-arm' control enabling weapons to be primed.

Asteroid Leader, assuming that he was far enough from the main entrance to the base, pulled into the vertical; his wingmen following diligently. The Pulsarians weren't illuminating their own radars, scanners and sensors yet—all they were doing was jamming them. Zears looked at his radar screen. It was a useless white sheet of ice. He didn't need the damn thing anyway. He knew what sector the now dead FB-25s had been flying in. All he had to do was converge on that area and hopefully his radar would pick something up.

His fire warning detectors began hooting in his left ear, while his flight computer began repeating, "*Warning, Warning, Warning!*" with feminine authority in his right ear.

What the hell?

Suddenly fire control emissions cooked off all around the Visions. The signatures, though, weren't from Malactites, but from—

"Spark Racers coming in—hitting our nine!" Conrad yelled into his mike as he saw the silvery specks spiraling toward them through the computer-enhanced optics in his glare shields.

Colonel Zears looked to his left as the bandits moved in closer. He switched off his flight computer and wondered what the hell they were going to do now. His mission was supposed to take out Malactites, not to engage fighters. If he pressed on to where he was sure the Malactites were positioned, then the enemy fighters would probably get him. But if he engaged the Racers, then the damned Malactites would undoubtedly get to the surface of the asteroid base.

Damn, he wished he had considered this scenario during the tactics briefing. What to do? *What to do?* He would engage the Spark Racers. He'd let the Black Diamond, Razor and Prancer Squadrons have first crack at the Malactites. Damn. Those squadrons flew old VF-87s and 81s, they'd have a better chance at the Malactites than they would against Spark Racers.

"Bleed to the left—wingmen engage. We're going to take out those Racers," Colonel Zears said as he and his paired wingmen broke formation to fly toward the Spark Racers.

The Squadron split from the massive attacking-wing formation and into pairs. A lead and a wingman. Now they had to take on supremely agile Racers as opposed to the slow and lumbering Malactites which could mass a tremendous density ratio of firepower and throw it at them. The Spark Racer THVs had the advantage of maneuverability and firepower, while the VF-97 Visions excelled in speed.

Conrad didn't like this at all. Sure, the Spark Racers posed an immediate threat to the Asteroid Base, but their primary mission was to harass the Malactites. In less than a minute, the Razor and Black Diamond squadrons would be launching to hit the Malactites. And they definitely couldn't do it with Spark Racers in the area. But Racer suppression was the Hammer Squadron's task. Where the hell were they? More important than that, where was the AWF-19?

Five seconds from the time that Conrad made the bandits call, they had merged with the Spark Racers eighty kilometers above the surface of the planetoid surface. Within moments, the tactical frequency that the Asteroid Squadron was using became choked with sightings, vectors, warnings and cries for help.

"Tally ho, Asteroid Leader. I've got one in my sights!"

"Kill him, damnit, kill him."

"Target, target, target."

"Go for the left—I'll take the leader."

"Nail him."

"Fox One! Fox One!"

"Let's find the leader and kill him."

"My God! They're all over the place! Dozens of them!"

"Fox Two on the wingman."

"Break left, break left!"

"He got fucking nailed!"

"*OH, GOD!* I've got one on my tail. Someone get him *off* me! Someone get him *off* me!"

"Mayday, mayday!"

"Ohm'god! They got Major Davidsen!"

"Pull in, pull in, pull in—goddamnit, what the hell are you doing?"

"Fox Two, Fox Two—do you see him?"

Since the merge only seconds before, only two Spark Racers were dropped to Vision fire while five Visions went up in rippling flames. Zears knew this, frustration and disgust ripping through him; he looked left and right, above him. Now he knew why they called them Spark Racers—they looked like silvery sparks as they flashed by his canopy in this direction and that.

"Break it left. Break it left or they'll tear us to pieces," he shouted into the mike. "Whiskey-Kilo! Whiskey-Kilo, this is Asteroid Leader. Where the hell are you? We're engaged with Spark Racers. They look like THV types. They're all over the place. No Malactites in the area—repeat: there are no Malactites in the area. We need some help ASAP!"

"Stand-by . . . Asteroid . . . Can yo—" the controller's voice was lost in a fury of static.

Zears felt hope and dread wash over him at the same time. Right when he had gained contact with the Gammatron, the Pulsarians started jamming their communications. Zears turned into another frequency as a Spark Racer blurred by in front of him.

"This is Black Diamond leader, to Asteroid Leader," a voice crackled over the static, trying to burn through the intense barrage of jamming. "We're moving into position underneath you—do you copy?"

"Go to Hyper-quick, Boulder Leader," Zears said as he put his fighter into a hard turn to pursue a Spark Racer that seemed to be cartwheeling out of control. "Asteroid Squadron go to Hyper-quick immediately before our main frequency becomes a total washout."

The remaining pilots switched on their Hyper-quick transceivers. Every hundredth of a second the H-q 9000 would leap frequencies at random so that they all could talk to each other. There was no way that the Pulsarians could jam all the frequencies at once. The H-q 9000 would bounce through high-frequency settings to Sub-space channels. All of the transceivers were pre-calibrated to become active once Asteroid Leader 'went live' with his H-q 9000.

"We've got a deteriorating situation up here," Zears said as he continued to press the out-of-control THV. "I can't get ah hold of Whiskey-Kilo. You'd better press right on up to the Malactites, Black Diamond Leader. We'll try to hold 'em here."

"Copy all, Asteroid Leader—good luck, Blake."

Black Diamond Squadron's sixteen VF-87 Vampires raced above the flats beneath the spiraling knife fights above them, then pulled up sharply to rendezvous with the as yet unseen Malactites descending from high orbit. Several of the Spark Racers broke off from the nearly decimated Asteroid

Squadron to pursue fleeing VF-87s.

Zears narrowed his eyes as he concentrated again on that twisting, turning Spark Racer. How long had he been on this bandit's trail? He got an infrared lock-on to the Racer's super-hot engines. He selected laser Shards and was about to fire when his fire warning alarms sounded in his helmet. Zears looked back for the source of the attack; through enhanced optics in his lens he could see the threatening shape of the Spark Racer some thirty kilometers behind him.

"Asteroid Leader, you've got one on your six!"

"Get out of there, Blake," Conrad called. "Get out! Get out!"

Zears' left wing exploded as the first energy bolts struck his fighter. The intense energy easily burned its way through the thin shielding. *Blast!* His Vision began to tumble out of control as more energy bolts flew toward him. Zears felt rage burning his calm. He was already out of control and that sadistic Pulsarian puke was still trying to kill him. *Bastard!* Smoke began to fill the cockpit as Zears reached for the ejection handles between his legs. His fighter exploded just when the synaptic nerves in his brain had registered that he pulled the handles.

"Damnit, we just lost Asteroid Leader," Conrad shouted into his mike. "Asteroids—whoever is left, let's get the hell out of here before we all—"

"Help me—I'm hit!"

"You're coming apart."

"Punch out Asteroid Seventeen—punch out!"

"Oh, no."

"Head for the Keclid Peaks. Hit the deck—"

He was cut off as three Spark Racers zoomed in behind him and opened up with their weapons. Conrad twisted and turned, seemingly beyond the edge of control, to get away from his antagonist. The high-g maneuver worked. Two of the Racers overshot, but not the trailer. He was still on Conrad's six. Conrad slammed the throttle forward, reversed, then pulled the throttle back and pulled the speed brakes, all in a vain effort to force the bandit out in front of him. He grunted and groaned against the g-forces pulling and pushing him. The maneuver worked, but Conrad wasn't sticking around to capitalize on it. He looked around for support and saw nothing but Racers finishing off the remnants of his squadron. He was the only one left. He advanced the throttles and headed for the deck . . .

CHAPTER XXIII
HAMMERS, RAZORS, & BLACK DIAMONDS

BLACK Diamond Leader cursed into his oxygen mask; he had his hands full as the Spark Racers began to swarm all around his tactical bombing squadron. Asteroid Leader had told him to press on to the target. He said that he had everything under control at his end. What control? What target? How many Malactites; from which direction? What was their speed—were they scattered, agglomerated, or in a coherent formation? He was here to hunt them and not dodge damned Spark Racers. Obviously, the Asteroid Leader had seriously overestimated the situation. Then again, Major Reshcoan never liked Colonel Blake Zears anyway.

Black Diamond Leader was a Grizzly Aracrayderian with rich crimson and honey fur. The large flight uniform he wore threatened to burst at the seams whenever he squirmed for a better seating position in the cramped cockpit of the VF-87F Vampire. But finding a better seating position was the least of his worries now.

Major Reshcoan split his squadron in half; he was commanding the spearhead that would meet the Malactites head-on, while his senior would execute flanking and deceptive maneuvers to draw the Pulsarians' attention away from the real threat. A good plan. The only problem was those Spark

Racers buzzing around like wasps. After finding a wavelength that wasn't being severely scrambled—and even then the picture on his scanner monitor was still noisy—the bear counted twenty-nine of them. He also noted that the jamming was far too effective and selective to be coming from the noise emitters on the Spark Racers. No, the Pulsarians must have an off-station jamming platform doing this. He might have to split a flight from his attacking group to look for and take out the jammer. The jamming platform could be a MI-349A-SVR Command Shuttle or a VME-V1750 Electronic Warfare Malactite—he would have to tell his pilots to be wary, for the MI-349A-SVR was quite maneuverable and would most likely lead them on a not so merry chase, but the VME-V1750 could shoot back. Whatever the case, other attacking groups wouldn't be effective as long as it was around to disrupt their scanners.

The bear was about to give the order when two of his Vampires went down in twisting balls of flame. A third screamed for help when he too was hit—a tremendous fireball engulfing and destroying another Vampire. Within seconds, the major's plan to send a flight to take care of the jammer was erased from all tactical trains of thought. Now he realized fully what Zears had gone through. His Black Diamonds were shrinking fast. The bitter thought of breaking off the attack entered his mind when the Hammer and Razor squadrons broke onto the scene.

The sixteen VF-94H Vagrants of Hammer squadron split into pairs and pounced on the unsuspecting Spark Racers. Immediately, three Racers were destroyed, followed closely by another Vampire. Four more Racers went down to Vagrant fire before the Racer pilots finally decided to cease attacking the slow and clumsy Vampires and concentrate on the new threat.

"Thanks for taking the heat off us, Hammer Leader," the bear roared into his mike, twisting his Vampire around in a tight seven-g turn.

"No problem, Major. No problem at all," Hammer Leader responded in her raspy, authoritarian voice. "We'll take care of things here. You'd better press to the target."

"Roger that."

"We've got a lot of jamming up here," Razor Squadron Leader, Major Kiara Steirmark, said.

"We were about to remedy that situation when those fighters jumped us," Major Reshcoan said, adjusting the brightness to his HUD.

"I'll send two of my guys to take out the jammer," Razor Leader said. "The rest of us will coordinate our attack with you."

"Roger that."

"Move. We can't keep these fighters busy forever," Colonel Alison Mann, Hammer Leader, yelled as a Spark Racer blazed across the nose of her Vagrant in a barely perceptive blur.

The remnants of the Black Diamond Squadron pulled up high as eight VF-81A Vixens took up a staggered formation beneath them. Unlike the

Vampire, which was a slow—yet rugged—unwieldy, high-wing mounted tactical bomber; the Vixen was its sleek opposite. It had a crew of two, a pilot and a Bomb-Navigation Officer who sat in a side-by-side cockpit configuration; the VF-87 Vampire had a crew of one, the pilot handled flight, navigation and bombing responsibilities. In that sense, and that sense only, the VF-87 was a more complex machine to operate. The VF-81 Vixen had two Boardship & McMartin VF-200 Hyperblasting Thrust-vectoring engines instead of the one Rand & Drake VF-160XT engine which powered the Vampire. It could maintain a twelve- to fourteen-g turn and release an awesome variety of ordnance without causing undue damage to the Vixen itself. It was a sweep-winged fighter-bomber that could operate in deep-space, within the fluctuating gravity currents of high-orbit, or engage in ground-hugging maneuvers within the troposphere of a planet. It had been originally designed to supplement the strategic strike capability of the FB-25 Poltergeist and the FB-27 Phantasm; it was a tactical bomber pilot's dream. A Malactite operator's nightmare.

Razor Leader tapped the throttles and punched passed the slow Vampires. She bit her lip in disdain, trying to ignore the awful feeling of paralysis that hung around her and her pilots, clinging to all like a living entity. The Pulsarians already had the jump on them. The FB-25s had been mauled in an ambush, the Asteroid Squadron torn to pieces, there had been no coordination with any of the AWF-19 Gammatrons, and the Black Diamonds came near to being massacred. What a festering mess. She didn't like this one bit, but accepted the fact that no matter how bleak or desperate matters looked, there was always a way through it. You took your hits, took your losses, regrouped and stormed back.

"I can't see a thing with all of this jamming. Bloody Universe. Those bloody Pulsarian puke bastards," the Bomb/Nav officer, Captain Carlton Hawk, kept muttering to himself as he studied his scanning screens, adjusting modes and wavelengths.

"Well, they aren't scanning for us yet," Razor Leader, Steirmark replied. "I don't know how they plan to attack us without their scanners. But you never know with the Pulsarians. I hope they aren't testing some new scanner our sensors can't detect. That would be bad."

"I've got a fix on that jamming," the Hawk said. "The signal is strongest at heading two-eight-zero." He laughed. "You'd think these idiots would learn by now."

An asteroid crossed by in front of them. My God—there were a lot of ways to die out here. That one was close. But Razor Leader kept her cool and pressed on.

"Razor Five and Six take out that noise-maker. Everyone else stay on my wing."

One thousand kilometers above the surface of the asteroid, two Vixens broke off to intercept the jammers. The rest of the squadron continued on toward the rendezvous point where the FB-25s had been patrolling. The Malactites had to be in that area somewhere. Razor Leader was taking it slow. With the scanner jammed, she didn't want to blunder into the middle of the Pulsarian invasion force and get decimated like the FB-25s had.

Two thousand kilometers AGL. Three. Four. They must be out there somewhere. Five thousand kilometers . . . . A thousand kilometers a minute . . . slow and cautious.

"Tally ho! Tally ho! I've got two Malactite jamming platforms right in front of me," Razor Five called out. "Can't use my scanners. But the infrared primed—got it! Weapons away, weapons away."

The two Vixens fired five Harpoons apiece. The high-yield warheads could rip open the armored hide of a Malactite with the force of ten-thousand kilograms of high-explosive. Out of ten Harpoons that were fired, four of them struck asteroids, sending diamond-like fragments in every direction; but the rest scored hits on the lead VME-V1750. The big machine seemed to warp out of shape for a second before it exploded in a blinding flash of light.

The Vixens veered around a tangle of asteroids to hunt the second jamming Malactite. The battle-engine saw them coming and began to retreat, slowly—it was a mad and desperate attempt at survival—Malactites weren't built for speed. It turned its jammers to full disruptive output in a vain effort to melt the fire control equipment onboard the Vixens, clouds of chaff hurricaning away from the body. All to no avail. Eight Harpoons were launched from the swept-winged fighters and all eight scored hits. The Malactite disappeared in a bright cloud of flaming metal.

"We've got our eyes back," the Bomb/Nav said indicating the crystal clear scopes. "And I gots the invasion force painted. Sweet Universe, there's a lot of them—*Oooiee*!"

An urgent beeping sounded in their helmets as red flashing lights winked on the threat-warning control board.

"Well, if you can see them, they sure's hell can see us," Razor Leader said.

"Yeah, getting fire-control emanations sweeping the area all around us."

Razor Leader's left hand swept over the weapons select control panel. Proton weapons would take the sting out of the invasion force's stride. But it would be suicide to fire those warheads in the asteroid system. All it would take is for one to hit a stray asteroid, and the resulting explosion and shock wave would incinerate half the Vixen squadron as well as the Malactite target. So Proton-tipped weapons were out, as well as Photons. Better stick with Harpoons and Shards as she briefed and push in closer. But the temptation lingered.

"Distance: four-niner-zero and closing."

"Black Diamond Leader, you copy?"

"Yes, we copy."

"We're hitting the leading group of Malactites. You kill the ones on the left flank. Copy?"

"Copy all. Good hunting."

****

"We have eight Delrel super-attack bombers closing in on us," the scanning officer yelled over the alarms.

Sergon leaned forward, trying to read the target symbology on the monitors. There was an onslaught of conflicting information; he couldn't make sense of any of it.

"Our two jamming Malactites have been destroyed."

"Getting a null reading from them . . ."

"Yes, yes, that's a confirmation now."

"The R'srclan Squadron reports heavy losses with engagements to Federation fighters," the communications officer yelled. "Their commander says that they will break off the engagements and pull back to sector one-seven until the other squadrons arrive."

"Picking up a second group of signals moving up behind the first group of super-attack bombers."

Sergon's mind exploded as the reports came in all at once. His two VME-V1750s had been destroyed—he needed them now more than ever with the Federation bombers pressing their attack. One of the Racer Squadrons, which was meant to cover him, was flailing and losing the fight, pulling out of the action and running. And now the Delrels were attacking his invasion forces from beyond high-orbit as he had feared. The only comfort he felt was the fact that twenty-five Malactites could easily put away eight fighter-bombers—in open space. These asteroids changed matters dramatically. Sergon knew, as did the pilots of the enemy bombers, that the asteroids hampered the targeting systems on both sides. If you were hiding, fine. But if you'd been discovered and had to fight, the rocks were a nuisance. It all came down to who could get a good target-lock and fire first.

"Switch our main jammers on now," Sergon commanded. He knew that his Malactite's onboard jamming systems weren't nearly as powerful or as concentrated as the systems on the now destroyed VME-V1750s. He hoped, however, that the onboard systems would put out enough noise to render enemy scanners useless. The enemy would have to move in closer to burn through the jamming and achieve their lock-on in this swirling asteroid shower. And when they did . . .

"Counter-measures, stand-by," Sergon ordered. "Once they burn through our jamming and try to acquire us, release everything." He folded his arms. "All gunnery crews stand-by. Fire at my signal only. Let them come in closer."

****

"Fifteen seconds to optimum firing range," the Bomb/Nav officer, Captain Hawk, reported as he read the figures dancing around on his systems. "Great, they're jamming us again. Wide-band disruption. No problem. They're panicking. We can burn through it in five seconds."

A house-sized asteroid rolled slowly in front of the racing Vixen. Razor Leader jinked the fighter hard to avoid hitting the massive boulder. The Bomb/Nav officer was too busy adjusting mode and power setting to the scanners to pay much attention to the crazy scene outside of the canopy. His eyes were seemingly affixed to the scanner screens in front of him. He didn't have time to waste watching what Steirmark, the pilot, was doing. He had work to do. Looking for a hole in the onslaught of white-noise, it was static in his helmet and a blizzard on his scope. Looking for a hole to burn through. Looking . . . looking . . . there!

"We gots burn-through," he declared. He could see the fuzzy outlines of the invasion force. Every second the image would freeze then shimmer into a billion false targets. Now they're employing chaff to fool his scanning picture. *Nice try*. Too little, too late.

"Alright, let's release our warheads and get the hell out of here. The Pulsarians are trying to draw us in close," Razor Leader said.

"Send them to hell."

"Gimme a few seconds," Steirmark merely grunted. She didn't like the idea of flying through this asteroid storm to carry out a strike mission in the first place. But she knew she had no choice but to push in closer. She had to score accurate hits on the Malactites. These Malactites weren't like the jammers they had destroyed earlier, these could fight back. She had to make sure that every shot hit the target that it was meant to hit and not asteroids. But the closer the Vixens flew . . .

The Malactites fired first. Highly phased energy Dirks raced toward the speeding Razor Squadron. One Vixen took three direct hits. The first Dirk was deflected by the Vixen's powerful screens. As the deflector was momentarily warped out of phase, the second Dirk hit, causing enough phototropic distortion to allow the third Dirk to burn through. The Vixen disintegrated immediately. Its crew never knew what hit them. In a flash of light, they were gone.

"C'mon, just a couple more . . . A couple more seconds . . ."

Another Vixen was struck in the wing from the energy barrage. The Vixen flipped over and spun out of control, disappearing quickly in the swarm of drifting asteroids. The remaining Vixens held position for a few seconds longer, waiting until they were in optimal firing attitude.

Then the Vixens opened up with their own weapons. They concentrated their fire on the lead attacking group with Shards and Harpoons. Razor Leader should've moved in closer. Most of the Harpoons struck asteroids and the rest were merely swatted aside by the Malactites' shielding. The

Shards, however, punched holes through the shielding and blew apart weapon batteries that dotted Sergon's Malactite. However, one of his flanking Malactites took a lethal dosage of the Shard barrage. All scored hits on the command module, instantly incinerating the Malactite commander and his crew on the command deck. The machine began to slowly spin out of control. In a flash, the entire command center exploded, taking the lives of more than fifty Pulsarians with it.

Another barrage of Harpoons came in and obliterated the auxiliary command and control superstructure beneath Sergon's Malactite. The machine shuddered mightily with the impact. Sergon would've considered himself lucky if he believed in luck. If the Harpoons had struck the command module instead, he'd be dead. The lights in the command deck winked out and a nearby weapons control panel exploded.

"Bring defensive fire along the lateral axis now," Sergon ordered above the shouting and mayhem around him. Even as he continued shouting commands, the gunnery and engineering crews on board the number two Malactite requested Sergon's Malactite to give them cover fire while they ejected from their crippled machine. And still another swarm of Harpoons and Shards came in to connect with the number three flanking Malactite. The first Harpoon hulled the machine and took out the forward fire control section, the missile launch section, and the auxiliary command deck. Shards cut through the command module, the main engine room and a Straaka holding section. Incinerated bodies tumbled into the vacuum. The burning machine slowed, coughed flame from several sections, then exploded. Sergon's reaction was to simply spit the blood from his lacerated tongue onto the metallic deck near his boots.

Two of the Vixens didn't survive the attack, as they were torn to shreds by intense pulse-laser fire from Malactites four and five. The surviving Vixens, now joined by those that had successfully taken care of the VME-V1750s earlier, began to pull out of the combat area as the Vampires joined the fray. The Black Diamond Squadron poured it on with Harpoons and a highly explosive laser known as the Skean. The number two Malactite, which had been spinning out of control, disappeared in a titanic flash. One flight of Vampires converged on the number five Malactite as it concentrated its fire on the departing Vixens. Skeans and Harpoons exploded deck guns, sensor probes and scanner pods. Number five was hurt, but far from being out of the fight. It released a hellish storm of oblivion at the Vampires.

Black Diamond Leader cursed as his left wing was sheared away from the spaceframe. This was it! He wasn't about to give the Pulsarians the satisfaction by screaming over the frequencies. He could eject, and be captured by the Pulsarians, tortured, then murdered. *What a shame.* His Vampire exploded against a tumbling asteroid.

Two more Vampires were blown apart following their leader's death. Black Diamond Senior led the survivors away from the terrific onslaught to rejoin with the Razors. Neither Black Diamond Senior or Razor Leader expected to run into five Snap-Advancers on the return trip home.

CHAPTER XXIV
FORCE OF ARMS

"GET ready to ice up a cold one! I—*you gotta be kidding me!* I've got five Snap-Advancers in an attack formation right below us." Razor Leader's Bombardier yelled as he interrogated new inputs screaming at him on his attack radar. He had thought—had hoped that they'd make it back to the asteroid without running into any more Pulsarian surprises. He was wrong. And the sudden radar contacts made Captain Hawk ill.

"Do we have any Harpoons left?" Razor Leader asked.

"Yes, ma'am!"

"And the Shards?"

"They're almost dry. But we can manage."

"I hope so. We've got Pulsarians everywhere. And there's no sign of the Prancer or Boulder Squadrons."

"We've got five targets about two-hundred kilometers above the asteroid's surface. Looks like they're on a scanning or recon mission. They're not bombing or anything. Just hovering there for the most part. No doubt trying to find the exact location of our base for those Malactites we just hit."

"Any fighters in the area?" Razor Leader asked, pulling hard on the stick to avoid a barn-sized asteroid slicing from the left to right.

"None within my detection range."

"Well, let's not wait for them," Razor Leader barked, rolling the Vixen back into position. Her left hand danced all over the secure communications panel. "Black Diamond Leader, this is Razor Leader, you copy."

"Affirmative. 'Diamond Leader is gone, this is Senior."

Damnit! Those Pulsarian murderers. They're killing our best fighter pilots and flight leaders.

"Okay. I've got five Snap-Advancers right below us," Razor Leader declared.

"Right, my guys picked them up too."

"Well, we're gonna hit 'em on one pass and get the hell out of the area and join up with the CFX-2s. How many birds you got left?"

"Got eight all together."

"Good enough. Cover the flank and concentrate your fire on the trailer. I'm gonna hit that big metal bastard up front!"

****

Admiral Aldar Dehyhitte stormed into the Combat Control Center of the lead *Shallh'Avacher*. Anger ate at his sinews, making his stride more pronounced, determined. They were an hour late getting to the rendezvous point—Dehyhitte didn't like the situation one bit. It wasn't his fault or the fault of his crews, or even the flight capabilities of the *Shallh'Avachers*. The fault lay in the operation itself. Only a madman would conduct a battle in this swirling, chaotic mess.

His five *Shallh'Avachers* were on station some thousand kilometers above the craggy surface of a massive planetoid. His small attack force went through hell getting here. Upon entering the frenzied black-zone of the Asteroid System, Dehyhitte had ordered all of his gunnery crews to hold fire. He didn't want the Delrels to detect any explosions that might announce the approach of his *Shallh'Avachers*. So, the eight-hundred meter long manta rays had to jink, pitch, and yaw their way through the deadly barrage of criss-crossing boulders. For a time, it seemed that all of the *Shallh'Avachers* would make it to the rendezvous point unscathed. However, two of his *Shallh'Avachers* were bombarded by millions of fist and boulder-sized asteroids despite their captain's best evasion efforts. Gun turrets were put out of action, sensor pods, and comm dishes knocked out of commission; phased ECM domes, navigational beam projectors, and auxiliary power boxes made useless by the sudden onslaught of flying rock. Admiral Petti had assured the various commanders of the Invasion Force of victory against the Delrels. Victory could be made, but to put up with all of this madness . . . beforehand—before they could fire a single shot in anger? It sent ominous shudders down Dehyhitte's back. Perhaps he was mad.

Dehyhitte surveyed the frantic activity in the Combat Control Center

(CCC). All was in readiness. His smart, skilled crews eager to hear the order for attack. Reports of the current battle situation flowed in from the myriad of passive sensing equipment. At the present, absolutely no scanning beams were emanating from the planetoid below trying to acquire his battle group. No heavy defensive weapons barrage was being fired up at them. All was strangely quiet, too quiet for Dehyhitte's liking. If the Delrels were employing some sort of emissions control, this was the most disciplined use Dehyhitte had ever seen. And that begged another question, was this the right asteroid? A question easily answered because further sensor sweeps picked up dozens of weapon-scanners, along with massive amounts of short- and long-range jamming and counter-jamming emanating from some ten-thousand kilometers above Dehyhitte's orbital position.

This was a most disheartening set of circumstances because his forces in the *Shallh'Avachers* were supposed to be in position above Sergon's Malactite forces, not below them. In the three tiers of planetary invasion, he was meant to be either the second or third, not the first. The first tier was for the infantry, their tanks, mobile barrage units, Battlebarges, and Malactites. The second tier provided cover for the first in the form of Invasionbarges, Spark Racers, and *Shallh'Avachers*. The third tier consisted chiefly of Battlecruiser Advancers and other 'in-direct fight' units of the Imperial Armada. This was Imperial doctrine and had been employed in this strict manner for centuries, even before the formation of the modern Admiralty. In this asteroid campaign, the Straaka would be the first tier, the Malactites and Spark Racers the second, while he would be the third. Somehow, after arriving to the invasion point late, he'd still managed to beat Sergon's forces. Dehyhitte fumed, he was supposed to provide cover for the Straaka, not have the Straaka provide cover for him.

He gave the command to make a detailed analysis of the area above him. He could see, through quite a bit of haze and distortion, the first wave of General Sergon's invasion force. Another floating monitor revealed two different types of fighters leaving the area. That would be enemy fighters, the admiral noted calmly. Another monitor revealed the type of jamming the Malactites were using to hide themselves behind a wall of confusion, yet another displayed type of deception jammers the Delrel fighters were employing to exaggerate their numbers. A confusing picture, indeed, intense and violent, yes. But only if you let it dictate terms to you instead of thinking and working your way through it.

"Commander Pulgon, can we get General Sergon on the communicators," Dehyhitte asked, as he continued to study the brightly colored screens and displays.

A green-haired commander in full battledress with armor, helmet and breastplate, snapped to attention next to a tight knot of technicians and controllers trying their damnedest to program the computers to analyze and defeat the intense barrage of jamming.

"Negative, Admiral. All tactical frequencies are being jammed at this time. However, analysis of the jamming does indicate that most of the jamming is originating from General Sergon's Invasion Force. Our good general has seen fit to wipe out the entire spectrum."

"But, if we move closer," a controller was saying, a leftenant, "we could possibly burn through it by tapping into a few side-lobes and increasing our own power output."

"And how long will that take?"

"From thirty seconds to a minute, Admiral."

"Good. Execute immediately," Dehyhitte turned to Commander Pulgon. "How long will it take Sergon's force to reach the surface of the planetoid?"

Commander Pulgon quickly studied a nearby bank of readouts, did a bit of mental calculations, then stammered, "About five-and-a-half minutes sir, at their present speed." He paused, then added, "they seem to be operating at full combat speed now."

"Alright. Standby to release the *landt'phizers*. And ready the Straaka landing units."

Commander Pulgon's green eyebrows arched and his eyes bulged in disbelief. "Admiral, we haven't determined the exact location of their base yet. It could be anywhere on that planetoid beneath us." He gestured toward the tactical displays that had the planetoid mapped. "Sensor scans haven't picked up a hint of activity—"

"In regards to your concerns, Commander, they're duly noted. However, we're in position now to release the *landt'phizers* without Delrel obstruction."

"Yes, Admiral . . . but—"

"If we linger without taking action, the Delrels will realize what we're up to and will send forces in to investigate. And, I ask you, in a purely classroom setting of battlefield tactics—of which this is clearly not—would you release the *landt'phizers* now, while the opportunity is good. Then have our *Shallh'Avachers* loiter above them until Sergon's Malactite forces arrive. Or would you position our forces above Sergon's now, knowing full well that you'll later have to deviate from your third tier position responsibilities to position and reposition your assets as the tide of battle changes—and with that Straaka General screaming at you every five minutes?"

"The former, or course, Admiral." The commander swallowed in spite of himself. Whenever Dehyhitte used sarcasm, a reduction in rank of the individual at the receiving end usually followed.

"To answer your first question, Commander; the reason why we haven't been able to determine the exact location of their base is because our sensors are being absorbed by more than a billion tons of rock and magma displacement. This isn't Minerva. Their base is completely hidden beneath the surface . . ."

"Yes, that possibility was agreed upon during the pre-attack briefing. But how do we—"

"All of the areas that we have scanned thus far—all areas that have enabled our equipment to map the topography and, in certain cases, the subterranean features—have revealed to us one thing . . ."

Which is? Pulgon asked silently.

"An incredible amount of seismic and volcanic activity. So far, we've surveyed five continental plates all with the same results—except the one that we're flying over now." Dehyhitte indicated the readings on two of the tactical displays. "No seismic or volcanic activity on this entire plate. It's dead. And our sensor probes are getting the highest reflection rate in this very area."

"Yes, Admiral, but we haven't scanned a quarter of that planetoid—"

"The Federation has their base hidden underneath that continental plate somewhere . . . And those mountains—with the highest peaks and roughest terrain encountered. It's an ideal place to construct an underground base that has the high capability to thwart Malactite and *landt'phizer* surface attacks. The Delrels are *there*! Set everything into motion at once. We'll cover the mechanized Straaka from staggered high- to low-orbital positions until Sergon's Malactites arrive."

"Sir, we have signals moving in! Picking up short-range fighter fire control scanners sweeping our position." A harried looking controller suddenly blurted out loudly.

"Confirmed," another controller declared five seats away. "Picking up two different types of Delrel fighters with a direct bearing on us."

"Combat Control Center to Bridge," Dehyhitte said into a nearby communications set. "Release fire-control safeties. Activate all defensive screens, stand by with all counter-measures." He turned toward Pulgon. "Our little debate has completely sabotaged any hope we'd had of releasing the *landt'phizers* in a timely fashion."

****

"All hell is breaking loose beneath us, boss," Razor Leader's Bombardier-Navigator reported. "Got fire control sweeping the area right in front of us." *And they're releasing counter measures. Ha! Trying to fool my fire control computers! Too late, you Pulsarian devils.*

Razor Leader squeezed off her own chaff and flares and punched the throttle forward. They were only going to get one run at this before they called it quits. Asteroids screamed by the Vixen as it dove for the manta ray beneath it. "Standby with the Harpoons."

An instant later, bright beams of light raced toward the screaming Vixens. Most of the energy struck asteroids sending fragments in all directions. One of the Vixens was pulverized by all the flying rock and exploded. But the others, followed at some distance by the Vampires, pressed on to their assigned targets.

"Target, target, target."

"Rock One, Rock One."

"Got lock-on."

"Harpoons to the north end of the lead target."

The Federation's scrambled tactical frequencies came alive with target information and fire control orders.

"Weapons release!"

"*Oooieee!* Good hit on the Snap-Advancer."

"Good hit on their main weapons generator!"

"Ohmigod! I'm coming apart!"

The Vixens hit the lead Snap-Advancer hard, taking out communications dishes, offensive batteries, and generators. During the brief attack, one of the Vixens took a hit that knocked out one of the fighter's rear stabilizers and engines. The stricken Vixen cartwheeled passed the manta ray toward the asteroid below, the crew ejecting twenty kilometers above the pock-marked surface. With their attention drawn to the speedy Vixens, the gunnery crews forgot about the Vampires that were now slicing down on them. Harpoons and Shards cut through the phototrophic shielding on the trailing Snap-Advancer, and then cut through to the bridge. The Vampire pilots couldn't see the deadly effectiveness of their work as they blazed by in urgent disregard for their own safety—the Harpoons and Shards tore through armor bracing, computer conduits, computer consoles and the bodies of the Pulsarian bridge crew. Those that weren't torn to shreds were ripped out into the tomb of space.

"Good hit! Good hit!"

"Got two Snap-Advancers burning!"

"*Ooooiee!* Those Pug bastards."

"Good hit, Black Diamonds! Razors, this is lead. Our work is done—let's get the hell out of here," Razor Leader said into the scrambled pick-up. Steirmark suddenly felt a sickening revulsion and an intense feeling of relief. She felt like vomiting and laughing all at once. A strange mix of euphoria and disgust that wasn't new to her. Her mission was over—she'd live to fly and fight another day; many of her colleagues would not.

****

Dehyhitte was thrown against the afterward bulkhead in the CCC as the Shards and Harpoons struck his *Shallh'Avacher.* Air was forced from his lungs as a super-hot cloud of heat whipped through the CCC that was now ablaze. Control panels exploded in the faces of his best controllers. Computer imaging boards, redundant sub-system controls, conduits and nearly a dozen or more Pulsarians disappeared in an angry wash of flame. Amid the crackling bursts, he heard the screams from the seriously injured and the dying. *Pulgon!* Where was Commander Pulgon? Dehyhitte's smoke-stung eyes swept the carnage and found his commander—or what was left of him. Commander Pulgon's headless body was a gruesome, charred mass resting next to a wall of burning data boards.

Fire and medical teams rushed into the center as Dehyhitte picked himself off the deck, his exposed skin burned, his hair and uniform singed.

"Admiral, are you alright?" a fire-suited crew member asked urgently, as the fire teams sweep the CCC with flame retardant chemicals.

"I'm fine," Dehyhitte rasped, fighting off the urge to vomit. He'd been lucky. After the explosion tore through the hull, the emergency bulkheads slammed shut to keep him and other survivors from being ripped into space.

"You only have minor burns and abrasions, Admiral," a medical technician observed. "But we still have to get you to—"

"No," Dehyhitte roared. Where did this miserable *Warar* come from—suggesting that he seek help instead of fulfilling his assigned duties? He still had a battle to fight. He pushed his way past the waves of fire and medical teams busily dragging bodies out of the CCC or desperately trying to put out the blaze.

"Bridge, this is Dehyhitte, status," there was not time to concern himself with command protocol.

"Admiral Dehyhitte!"

"Status!"

"Sir, we've taken major hits on B, C, and D batteries. The emergency generator and primary communications have been destroyed. Engineers are switching to back-up systems now. Casualty reports are still coming in . . . overall the damage appears to be minor. We are cleared to navigate. Engines are aligned and operational. Lifesupport functioning."

Overall damage minor? Dehyhitte looked around at the blazing carnage, the corpses that littered the deck . . . *Minor? Imbecile.* Dehyhitte could smell the charred flesh that was brewing up around him, the acrid stench of exploding panels and melting circuitry. Through one of the tactical viewing monitors, one that still functioned, he could see his rear echelon *Shallh'Avacher* reeling in an inferno that threatened to consume the entire vehicle. In the superheated chaos, he could see escape pods ejecting from the crippled manta ray. And to his utter horror, he could see that they were launching their *landt'phizers. No!* Some of the space-tanks were vaporized instantly as they passed through the thick wall of flame. Those that survived the launch were blown to atoms from incoming fire from enemy fighters. And still those that survived the flames, the fighters, met horrifying death as they plummeted toward the surface without retro-fire control for a safe landing. None of the fifteen *landt'phizers* survived the holocaust.

Dehyhitte ran out of the CCC and down a long, crowded, smoke-filled corridor. Racing by engineers, fire teams, controllers and the wounded, he entered the confusion-choked bridge in under twenty seconds. He would have to coordinate the attack from here instead of the destroyed CCC.

Officers and controllers were at their stations frantically trying to manage the crisis before it could overwhelm them. For the time being, it seemed that the Delrel VF-94s were taking clever potshots at them and quickly darting out of range of the anti-fighter weapons. Dehyhitte ran up to his command chair, where Commander Paxtie Ormetti was seated vainly trying to communicate with the captain of the burning rear echelon *Shallh'Avacher.*

Commander Ormetti took one look at Dehyhitte and winced, only losing his military bearing for an instant. The executive officer was glad to see that the admiral was alive and quickly got out of the command chair. He wanted to know how Commander Pulgon was—

One look at Dehyhitte confirmed the worse. Without a word, Dehyhitte dropped into the just vacated command chair, his body screaming at the sudden movement.

"This is Captain Imaretti, we're taking heavy fire—"

That was the last transmission from the rear echelon *Shallh'Avacher.* Now totally enveloped in flame, it slowly spun out of control toward the massive bulk of the planetoid below.

Dehyhitte no longer felt sick, instead rage flooded him. Captain Imaretti was a good Pulsarian, his crew excellent. A grim reminder that during the trials of battle even the best could be killed.

"Commander Ormetti, the Delrel fighters are breaking off," a controller said as he looked at his monitors. He didn't know that Dehyhitte was on the bridge—no announcement was made—otherwise he would've addressed *him* and not Ormetti.

"Where are they going?" Dehyhitte demanded.

The controller made several quick adjustments on his control panel, trying to read the images through the wash of static. "All indications point to the southern edge of this main body of mountains, here."

"And not at the very heart? Are you certain?"

"Yes, Admiral."

"What is it?" Commander Ormetti asked.

"A hunch that I was forming up in the CCC—I'm convinced that the Delrel base is right beneath us. Underneath that mountain range."

"But their fighters are retreating nowhere near it. They're heading hundreds of kilometers downrange."

"So it would seem," Dehyhitte mused. "Standby to release the *landt'phizers* and the Straaka at the center of the range—where I suspect their base is—and at the location where those fighters disappeared at the edge of the range. Their base is down there somewhere."

"Sir, we have signals coming in! Just astern of us!" a Scanner Warning officer reported excitedly, his face revealing his dread. "They're fighters. Can't tell the type yet."

"Standby with the Basilisk batteries. But hold your fire. I repeat: hold your fire," Dehyhitte ordered coolly. He had to make absolutely sure that the 'fighters' weren't Racers from the Imperial Armada before he ordered his crews to destroy them. With the loss of Captain Imaretti's *Shallh'Avacher*, his crews and those on board the remaining manta rays would want to destroy everything on sight. But if they weren't careful, they would end up like Captain Imaretti's crew.

"Getting transponder codes from the signals now, Admiral," the scan officer said, pausing briefly to get new readings from equipment that seemed to be operating on the super slow training modes. "They're ours, Admiral. Transponder codes authenticated. It's the H'reclan and the P'gaclan squadron. The H'reclan Squadron Commander reports that he lost three fighters in the Asteroid System on his way in—otherwise their status is green."

Dehyhitte remained silent. He felt relieved that they were here to protect him from those flying Federation hellions. Both squadrons launched with a total of thirty-six fighters each. Minus losses, there should still be at least sixty Spark Racers in all. But where was the R'srclan Squadron? Surely they should be checking in by now; they were the first Spark Racer group to be launched.

"The flight leaders await your orders, sir."

"Tell them to proceed as briefed. Split their squadrons up. Have elements guard the *landt'phizers* on their descent and have the others provide high profile cover for us—to keep those blasted Federation fighters away from us. Get me General Sergon."

"Sir, primary communications are still out," a communications officer reported from his nearby station. "Technicians have informed me that it will take up to a quarter of an hour to by-pass destroyed systems to make transmissions possible . . . we can receive but—"

"Then address the other Snap-Advancers with the laser signaling devices. And get them to relay a comm-link with the general." Dehyhitte ordered. "We've got to establish communications with him before we're hit again. We have to coordinate our attacks. The Federation is chopping us to pieces, keeping us apart like this."

****

Hammer Leader rolled her VF-94H Vagrant around in a tight circle as she and her squadron loitered just outside the effective gunnery range of the Snap-Advancers. They were jamming the hell out of everything even with their dedicated jamming platforms gone. Ordinarily, they'd be well within the range of the Snap-Advancers point defense batteries—but the Pulsarians gunnery crews couldn't acquire them through the blizzard of jamming. Through her imagery enhanced visor, she could see that the Pulsarians were still orbiting the sector about the mountain range, now fifty kilometers above the surface of the planetoid. Too close for comfort. And now it seemed that the Snap-Advancers were being joined by fighters—two squadrons at least. More than her group could handle.

"Colonel, looks like they're starting to release space tanks," her weapons officer in the backseat reported.

"There goes the neighborhood! Shoot. Where are our damn attack birds?" Alison Mann wondered out loud. She had justification for being angry. Her job was to provide cover for the attack fighters that were supposed to be attacking Advancers and Malactites. The Pulsarians were right over their base. By all rights, they were in a perfect position to blow it all to hell. Mann bit her upper lip, her eyes frantically probing left and right. Where the hell *is* everybody?

****

General Varxbane paced about the deathly quiet BWRC as his advisors and field commanders watched him and the tactical displays nervously. They had gone to quick-quiet mode only minutes ago, when the Pulsarian sensors began to sweep the mountain range. All of the fighters scattered throughout the planetoid received their launch orders from the Fighter Operations, which in turn received orders from the BWRC. The Prancer and Boulder Squadrons were late in launching because most of the hardened communications conduits had been severed when tactical administration teams began ripping up valuable comm gear for loading onto the cargo/haulers. They hadn't realized their mistake until it was too late.

"Activate a sensor decoy in sector twelve," Varxbane whispered softly. He brought a gloved hand to his bushy chin.

"Yes, sir," Colonel Dargoinne answered.

"Those Advancers are too close to us. We have to lead them away before the main body of the Malactite force drops out of orbit."

"Yes, and they've released tanks along the eastern throat of the Kinteesen Corridor. The corridor is more than two-hundred kilometers long. But it leads straight to the site of our Deflector Shield Projector." Dargoinne shook his head slowly.

"Can we get one of our fighter groups—the Boulder Squadron, perhaps—to attack those tanks?"

"No. I don't think so. Even though we're wired hot and can get through to fighter ops. Fighter ops can't reach the attacking fighters or the AWF-19 Gammatrons for re-coordination of the attack plan. I don't know what we can do—"

"Except try, Dargoinne. You can think of something, can't you?"

Just then Colonel Piercenan moved out of the shadows to join the two, followed closely by an irritated Rook.

"General, those tanks are awfully close," Piercenan said, stating the obvious. "We have anti-tank weapons. Why don't I take some of my troops out there and ambush 'em."

"No, out of the question." Varxbane shook his head. "You and your people haven't seen action for some—"

"We know our jobs, General."

"You're base security *not* infantry."

"The Pulsarians won't be expecting it," Piercenan stated firmly. "We can take them, General. You don't need to be a special weapons expert to fire an anti-tank—"

"Colonel, you have your orders."

"Those tanks are almost on us. For all intents and purposes, they *are* on us. Once the DSP is operational, they'll know where we are." Varxbane tried to interrupt, but Piercenan pressed onward. "If they continue west down the corridor, they'll eventually run into the DSP site and I don't have to tell you what'll happen then. We must attack them with whatever forces we have and we must do it now. Fighters would be preferable if we could communicate with them. We have three Gammatrons up and we're getting nothing from them. We must use troops to attack them."

"He's right, General," Rook said, not sure if he had the status to push his way into their discussion, but doing it anyway. "We must do something. The success of the base's evacuation depends on that deflector array working."

Varxbane glared at the Omnitraus. What was he doing here? Shouldn't he be with Draystar and Jasmine?

"Alright. Take troops down to ambush those tanks. Through some miracle, we might be able to scramble fighters to support you in your task. So keep your heads down and your eyes open."

"We will."

"Good luck, Colonel."

"You don't mind if I go along, Colonel," Rook inquired briskly.

Piercenan looked him up and down, clearly not impressed. "Can you handle anti-tank weapons?"

"Yes, sir."

"Okay, try not to get yourself killed before I can use you, Omnitraus."

CHAPTER XXV
INFERNO

"WHAT the hell's the matter with you," Major Dannen Leers roared. "Those are Pulsarians out there killing our people and you're just gonna wait for some goddamned security code before you launch us? *Are you insane?*"

The launch officer took a menacing step forward, his eyes narrowing. The colonel wasn't about to take this . . . this flagrant deluge of insubordination from an inferior human—and a major no less. Who gave a damn if this hairless cub—this *purgahar*—was some sort of an exalted warrior. He would have to wait for the proper orders like everyone else. There was more to this than just launching fighters; there was security, response schedules, safety parameters, time-over-target coordination with other fighter squadrons. It was a difficult and complex task that had nothing to do with simply receiving orders and saying "launch".

"Look here, Major, we haven't received your launch order from launch control," the heavily muscled tiger snapped back.

"Idiot! What if communications from here to there have been destroyed?" Leers yelled, not backing down. Other than outranking him, Leers knew that the tiger could easily rip him apart if he was pushed too far—Aracrayderian tigers were like that—but the human wasn't going to back down—no, sir.

"We have other measures, Major," the tiger intoned threateningly, taking another menacing step forward; he was only two centimeters from the human's face now.

"Let's go," came a high pitched chime from behind Leers. Slayton was seated in the back seat of the VF-94E Vagrant, eager to get going, eager to kill Pulsarians—the way her stomach felt right now it was criminal to just keep holding them here.

Throughout the hangar, the sixteen Vagrants of the Ranger Squadron attack force were waiting for launch clearance. The pilots and weapon systems officers were already strapped in their cockpits, waiting for that elusive order that seemed would never come.

"Damnit! What are we waiting for?" Slayton shrieked again. "Let's get this shite over with."

"Look, mister, you and your back seat cohort are on real dangerous lines here," the colonel warned at closer than point blank range in Dannen's face. "I'd advise you to maintain a little discipline before you're all thrown in the stockade for insubordination."

Leers stared back at the colonel bolt for bolt. He wasn't going to back down for a second. And if the tiger thought he would, then he'd have to rethink his position—quickly. And judging from the Aracrayderian's stance, he wouldn't like it one bit.

"Look, Colonel, I'm a major in the Omnitraus Command. Don't you ever try to threaten me, or pull rank on me again, or you'll be hit so hard you'll wonder what the hell happened to you." Leers took a step toward the boarding ladder, his eyes like boiling points of lava never leaving the colonel's concrete stare. "We are launching now, Colonel. With or without clearance from launch control."

Leers climbed up the boarding ladder and gently eased himself into the cockpit. The tiger was still staring off into space, consumed in his own rage as he contemplated what he should do next. Should he get security? By that time, the Rangers could be killing Pulsarians. The ground crew finished their checks around the beastly Vagrant, while Leers and Slayton began their own interior preflight checks. Leers checked the control stick, the rudder pedals, the fuel control panel, the armament control panel, and the flaps, while Slayton checked the ECM equipment and his navigation and target computer. Leers hit the master engine start switch and plugged his g-suit connectors, as well as his oxygen mask and communications connectors, into the appropriate slots. He looked to his right and gave the hand signal for 'engine start' to his wing man parked next to him, who in turn passed the signal on down the line until all of the Vagrants began to start their own engines. Slayton and Leers quickly went over the rest of the pre-takeoff checklist—which only took fifteen seconds—and lowered and locked the canopy into place. The ground crew chief popped Dannen a snappy salute and Leers returned it with equal enthusiasm—the Rangers were on their way.

****

General Preafect Sergon's face twisted and contorted on the main tactical viewer on the ridge of Admiral Dehyhitte's Command *Shallh'Avacher*. Even though the transmission was being jammed by Delrel Electronic Warfare officers and being hampered by the *Shallh'Avacher's* own secondary communications systems, the conflagrative arguments between the two commanders continued unabated. Once the communications were established, Sergon gave Dehyhitte a SITREP, or situation report—and went on to report that he had lost two of his attack Malactites and his only two jamming VME-V1750 Electronic Warfare Malactites. The survivors of the first Federation hit and run attack were jamming all sub-space and scanner modes with their own built in Electronic Warfare devices. Sergon had already sent the landing code words to the fleet waiting outside of the Asteroid System. The second wave, commanded by Colonel Threshergon, was ten minutes from reaching high orbit. Colonel Mitragon's third wave, along with the remaining squad of fighters, was minutes behind that. Sergon indicated that he had started his landing and his force was executing operations two-thousand kilometers northwest of the admiral's current position. He needed Dehyhitte's force to provide high cover immediately, before more Delrel fighters could launch frenzied attacks against him to protect their base. That's when the argument was ignited. Dehyhitte claimed that *he* was over the Federation's base which was some twenty-five hundred kilometers *downrange* of Sergon's position to the southeast. What really got Sergon fuming was when Dehyhitte arrogantly announced that he had launched the *landt'phizers* to prove his instincts were correct.

"You fool! My crews are picking up definitive and conclusive sensor returns that indicate that the Delrel base is there." Through flickering haze of the transmission, Sergon was pointing 'off-screen'. "Two hundred kilometers to the northwest!" Sergon bit his lip and suppressed a squeal of outrage. He needed his *landt'phizers*, but to recover them could take from forty-five minutes to an hour—past the time when they would face the brunt of Delrel attacks. The only ships in the area that could recover the *landt'phizers* fast enough were the *Shallh'Avachers*. But Sergon would need them for high cover to protect his forces from attacks by Delrel fighters and attack-bombers. Yes, the Battlebarges could be employed. But they would have to alter course, fly over hostile territory relatively unprotected, pick up the *landt'phizers*, an operation that could take up to an hour, then fly back to Sergon's position to deploy them with the Volkr-Ghelk Straaka Legion . . . Insanity! Too much wasted time. The whole plan could take hours to implement and carry out. Confounded by the fact that the Spark Racers hadn't achieved superiority over the battle area yet—and probably never would. Such a wasteful operation could result in victory for the Delrels. And

Sergon wasn't about to let that happen. No, as soon as the thought had entered Sergon's mind, it was quickly dismissed.

Insanity!

A decision had to be made. Employing the Battlebarges was out of the question. Dehyhitte could do it but Sergon's forces needed protection from those damned Delrel fighters. And he was quite certain that the Delrel base was here, not where Dehyhitte was. What did the Imperial Armada puppet know about ground tactics? Nothing.

"For the last time, Admiral," Sergon warned ominously, "your forces will join on my position here and will provide high-cover for my Malactites."

"But what about the *landt'phizer* phalanx?" Dehyhitte demanded, mustering up his own hostile tones.

"It will take too long to recover and reposition them. They're on their own. This is your doing, Admiral. Your dreadful mismanagement of the situation—"

"General, I've already lost one of my *Shallh'Avachers*. I don't need—"

"Too bad—the loss was probably due to your incompetence more than anything else. Join on my position now before we waste more time and lives."

****

General Sergon eased back in his command chair. That was that. With that battle over, it was time to move on to more important matters. The incoming raid of two different attack groups would certainly be at the top of his priorities.

****

Boulder Leader took deep gulps of oxygen and switched on the Master Weapons Arm switch as his VF-94F Vagrant streaked over the craggy asteroid surface. Despite his nervousness, he smiled beneath his oxygen mask. Good, everything was going to plan. The Pulsarian invasion force had landed and was going straight for the sensor decoys in sector twelve. The Snap-Advancers were slowly moving into covering position above the Malactites—but they weren't in position yet and wouldn't be when his force of Vampires hit the invasion force. As per standard Pulsarian ground assault doctrine, the Malactites had dropped to just forty meters above the surface. Through his glare shields, the Malactites looked like vicious thunderstorm cells moving fearsomely along the desolate landscape. Commissioners of death and devastation. And the Battlebarges, looking like a cross between a scorpion and an armadillo with thick stubby wings, were in a protective pocket within those ominous clouds.

According to the scanner and surveillance controllers within the AWF-19

Gammatron, at least sixty Spark Racers—no one could give him anything more definitive than that—were flying high and low cover around the Snap-Advancers. There was a brief mention of tanks, but Boulder Leader didn't see any. That was good. But what was better was the fact that the Prancer group flying ten VF-81A Vixens were attacking the invasion force from high, while the Boulders would hit them in the opposite position from low. All Pulsarian scanners were on the Vixens, who were chaffing and flaring and lighting off their own jamming pods. In general, they were making a nuisance of themselves and attracting a lot of attention. And this was good because the Boulder Squadron was flying over the Iriaa Continent undetected; their approach was masked further by currents of jamming provided by one EWM-31 Gigadrone more than 40,000 kilometers downrange.

Boulder Leader wagged his wings to get his fighters to spread into attack formation. They were only seconds away from the right-rear flank of the invasion force. Their mission was to take out as many of the troop carrying Battlebarges as possible and if the Malactites wanted to stick their ugly noses into the fray, then take them down as well. They were in close now, close enough to turn on their fire-control scanners and burn through the Pulsarian jamming. Even with their dedicated jamming platforms destroyed, the Pulsarian Malactites still could send out a hostile barrage of deceptive and manipulative noise. The Boulder Squadron of sixteen fighters, spread over an area of more than one hundred kilometers, and attacking from three different compass points, popped up to fifty meters AGL and released a barrage of high-powered Shards and Harpoons.

The Pulsarians, taken completely by surprise, never knew what hit them. Two Battlebarges exploded in raging typhoons of greasy, acidic flame. The Pulsarians were out in the open now; no asteroids were racing around as a confusion factor. Each component of the force highlighted itself clearly. The Boulder pilots had a clear picture of everything. One Malactite swerved its command module around, training its guns on the fighters, only to be set ablaze by more fighters it did not detect. Another Malactite was put out of action as the VF-94s pressed their attack. Another Battlebarge exploded brightly, throwing metal, circuitry, Straaka and pieces of Straaka in all directions. *Five hits!* The Boulder Leader reported the victory over the tactical frequencies before he and the rest of the squadron pulled out of the area without a single loss.

Now it was time for the Vixens of the Prancer Squadron to move in. Diving down on the left flank of the invasion force, they also switched on their fire-control scanners. *This is gonna be too easy*, Prancer Leader thought as he released his own weapons. He was waiting for his wingman to do the same when he realized that his wingman no longer existed. He didn't hear the warnings coming from the AWF-19 or the frantic cries from the other element leaders. He was concentrating so intently on blasting the Malactite to atoms that he didn't even take notice of his Hostile Fire Warning Receiver blinking urgently in the red and screaming desperately in his ear. He didn't even *see* the Spark Racers slicing down on them until it was too late.

Lasers tore right through the canopy and cut into the body of his Bombardier/Navigator. Meaty chunks of gore splashed all over Prancer Leader. He only had a millisecond to register his horror before the Vixen exploded.

In only seconds, the leading elements of the Prancer Squadron had been obliterated. The four survivors broke off the attack and began jinking madly as Malactite and Battlebarge guns joined the fray. The Vixens were quick, faster than the gunners and faster than the Spark Racers, but not nearly as agile. They lit their burners and screamed out of the brutal melee flying right smack into the Snap-Advancers that were just now assuming their coverage positions.

One of the Vixens saw this and let loose with all of his weapons toward the nearest of them. The manta ray shuddered under the impact of the explosions but continued onward as if nothing had happened and slammed the offending Vixen with its own weaponry. The Vixen, along with three of its companions, was blown to oblivion.

****

Commander Terger Aragon, P'gaclan Squadron Leader, Imperial Armada, brought his venomous Spark Racer XXR around in a tight high-g turn. The weight of his armored flight suit and 'thinking helmet' increased with the steady pull of the control column. Aragon had more than 20,000 hours of flight time in the Slave Racer and nearly 12,000 hours in Spark Racers. He'd flown the CCT's, the LLR's, the fast CVT's, and the deadly XXR's. He was a megsta-ace with more than 250 Federation aero- and deep-space fighter kills, 12 Federation Starcruiser kills and fifty miscellaneous kills. A proven leader, he was highly capable and confident. He'd served in the Imperial Armada for nearly twenty years now. Killing Delrels was his job. His ambition. He was good at it. But he had grander plans after the end of the war and his retirement from service. He would finally get to develop that small plot of land on one of Ajax's ten satellites, build a home, a fortress more fitting for an admiral, with more than two hundred slaves to sow the land. He was a hero to the war effort. With victory over the Delrels, he'd be granted no less.

Right now he and his flight were on their way to kill the Delrels that had been harassing the poor Straaka trapped in those slow moving Battlebarges. Against the horizon, he could see the VF-94s pulling up and away, leaving the battle area in a big hurry. It'd be too late to catch them. But those VF-81s that were starting their dives uncontested—since most of the guns from the invasion force were focused on the withdrawing VF-87s that had just hammered them—those VF-81s, they would have to be taught a lesson.

Aragon knew that the VF-81s were fast and carried a weapons load with the potential to destroy a Cruiser Advancer if given the opportunity. He set his weapons selector to Dirks. The first Vixen he hit, a wingman, exploded. The second, the flight leader and too busy to take notice of the attack, got it through the canopy. The VF-81 flipped over and flopped around like a stricken animal before it too exploded. Commander Aragon looked around to see that his wingmen were tearing the other VF-81s to shreds. The Federationers had no chance; areas of escape were cut off. In less than a minute, the enemy VF-81 force no longer existed.

****

Rook made one last adjustment of his armored space battle suit before joining Piercenan and the twelve other soldiers, all similarly attired, at the thick blast door. The soldiers had the standard-issue Edsing 250 Blast Rifles held at the ready, while Rook carried a Hellington Standard Blast Pike. Colonel Piercenan's only weapon was a Delnalt '44, the same weapon Leers preferred.

Their space battle suits were made up of a thin kevlar and titanium material that was highly resistant to all forms of conventional rips and tears. The helmets resembled the shape of a rounded off pyramid with built in communications and a clear anti-fog face shield. An ECP-250L environment pack covered the back of the suit. Strangely, the suits weren't as bulky as Rook thought they'd be. They were light-weight and functional, and had an oxygen supply that could last up to fifty hours, with a reserve of an additional twelve. There was laser-resistant armor about the chest, arms, and legs of the spacesuit. It was adequate against small arms fire, but would do little to protect them from heavy weapons. Rook looked around for the—wait a minute. His suit didn't have a deflector system. He examined Colonel Piercenan's suit, it had no deflector system. No one had shielding capability—suicide suits.

"Pressure equalized," a tech trooper called out as she activated the thick vacuum sealed door.

The sound of stone grinding against stone accompanied the shield doors as they crawled aside. The inside of the doors looked like ordinary metal doors; the outside looked like the craggy face of a mountain side. Rook followed Piercenan and his team into the vacuum. Suddenly Rook felt very vulnerable. He was naked. He felt more at ease in a fighter flying through the vacuum—but this? This was a whole new experience for the cheetah. It was like not having fangs. Helpless.

Colonel Piercenan looked at him and smiled grimly. "Don't worry. It does take some getting used to. Don't try to force the air out. Just breathe normally." He slapped the captain reassuringly on the shoulder. "And relax."

Rook didn't comment. He only nodded and studied his surroundings. They were now in a vast canyon with towering mountain peaks along both sides of the corridor. From where they stood, it was nearly eighty meters to the canyon's floor and more than two-thousand meters to the sharp peaks above them. Boulders and rock outcroppings were everywhere along the Kinteesen Corridor.

This was Colonel Piercenan's Retainer Battalion—what remained of it—more than half his troops were either protecting the DSP, the fighter bays, fuel cells or the evacuation assembly area. In addition to the dozen soldiers in this squad, there were only about a hundred or so that remained of his fighting force to face the Pulsarian tanks.

Rook retrieved a pair of electro-enhanced binoculars and scanned *down* the corridor. No sign of any tanks, yet. They would be attacking from the east. He could see another cluster of soldiers setting up close- and long-range anti-tank weapons three-hundred meters away. Poor souls. Squad strength at best setting up equipment to take the hammer blow of a full Pulsarian tank battalion. They're not going to last ten seconds once the lasers began to fly.

The cheetah followed Piercenan and the others down the rocky slope until they came across a rock-lined, heavily reinforced bunker. Rook didn't see it until they were right on it. It looked like an ordinary rocky knoll, only this one had thin firing slits for weapons. Rook shook his head, a somewhat difficult task with the helmet on. The ingenuity that went into the construction of this base! Everything looked natural. He spotted five heavy gun towers that, at first glance, revealed themselves only as natural rock formations. But on closer inspection, he could see their organic engineering when long wicked muzzles protruded from darkened slits for a moment, then disappeared again. Incredible.

Rook stepped into the bunker when something caught his keen feline vision. *Roac' Voc Valj.* Just four-hundred meters behind the bunker, from where he was standing, to the west, was the all-important Deflector Shield Projector. He could see technicians and engineers scrambling all around the Deflector dish beneath a sensor net. And those tanks were heading straight for it. It sank in like a cold knife. All the tanks had to do was roll their way over Piercenan's forces and they could destroy the shield and effectively crush any hopes the Federation had of making an evacuation. Tanks against infantry. Infantry wearing unshielded battle suits. It was hopeless. *We're all going to be torn to pieces.*

Rook entered the crowded bunker to see Colonel Piercenan huddled over a communications tech. Piercenan turned to Rook and the others in the cramped, low-ceilinged bunker, his expression grim.

"We've got tanks, people." He pointed toward a nearby monitor. "Storm platoon reports that the leading elements of the Pulsarian advance are forty kilometers east of their position. They report the tanks will take less than fifteen minutes to reach them."

"What about fighter support?" someone asked hopefully.

What about it? "Base control and fighter ops are still having trouble communicating between themselves, let alone communicating with the AWF-19 and/or the fighters. Communications are degraded, that and the Pulsarian jamming. Things are gonna get worse from here on out. No more playing games."

"So, you're saying that we have to face these tanks alone?"

"That's exactly what I'm saying."

****

"I have you Ranger Leader at angles ninety-seven," the senior controller reported from on-board the cramped confines of the AWF-19 Gammatron. "Bandits are at two-five-niner; altitude, below one hundred meters. Good hunting."

Leers clicked his mike twice in acknowledgment and looked around his fighter. Leers knew the Gammatron was taking a risk in transmitting target data to his fighters. But weren't they all taking risks? Too bad the Gammatron couldn't shoot back. That was their problem, his was to fight. Through the imagery enhanced glare shields he could see the wingmen in his flight spread to five kilometers out on either side of him. The rest of his squadron was too far out to be picked up by an 'eyeballs' sighting at this attitude. But they were all out there. More than willing to have Dannen Leers lead them into battle. More than willing to have him lead them to their deaths.

The Pulsarians were just over the Kinteesen Ridge two-hundred kilometers away, to the east. There was another force along the flats, quickly being nibbled away into nothing, and yet another descending from high orbit some two thousand kilometers to the northwest.

There was plenty of activity along the range and the damned DSP was still inoperable. Echo Squadron was nowhere in sight. Colonel L'ennell Slayton, N'ckshell's older sister, was supposed to provide cover from Spark Racers while Dannen's fighters hit the Invasion Force. So much for plans. The good news was that there currently weren't any Spark Racers to worry about.

Major Stan McHellington, some twenty kilometers off of Leers' right shoulder, flew his flight just meters above the crusty planetoidscape. He bit his lip and adjusted the gain on his communications set. This battle wasn't going according to plan. Nothing seemed to be going right. Entire fighter squadrons had been annihilated and the Pulsarians, it would seem, had barely been touched.

Kaltorr sat in the back seat of McHellington's fighter, testing, calibrating, retesting and recalibrating his weapons and radar scanners. Like McHellington, he didn't like the way the battle was going. The bloody Pugs were *killing* them. Malactites and Snap-Advancers downing fighters. It was hard to believe—although the thought clawed at the back of his mind that Vagrants, Vixens, and Visions were all second generation fighters—rust buckets, shitcans, and pisspots standing up against the best that the Pulsarians had to offer. The observation offered little consolation for the death and carnage that was raging all around them. Kaltorr didn't know why he even considered it in the first place. But the thought persisted. Winning was highly tipped to favor the Puggies. It was no wonder they weren't getting the kills that would dictate a more realistic battle picture. Malactites, or invasion forces in general, were no match for fighters. That was the way it should be and not the other way around. They were sending their worst out against the enemy's best—throwing away a lot of lives in the process. Bloody miserable state of affairs.

Leers leaned forward in his ejection seat and glared at the onrushing mountain range. At present speed, they'd be there in less than eleven seconds. The Pulsarians were on the other side, hopefully not waiting for them.

"Ranger Squadron . . . Lead Flight, fighter check," Leers ordered, breathing heavily into his oxygen mask.

"Two."

"Three."

"Four."

The wingmen in Leers' lead flight reported in, as did the wingmen in Stan McHellington's Senior Flight and then the wingmen in the remaining two flights, commanded by Wilson Stratamore, call sign Outlaw, and Helen Lange, call sign Too Cool.

The Rangers would hit as many of the Malactites as possible, however their primary target would be the command Malactite. With it gone, the second wave invasion force would be thrown into chaotic disarray before they realized that they were on top of the Federation Base and could direct others to the area.

"Easy Aspect Two-Two, this is Ranger Leader, do you copy?"

"Go ahead Ranger Leader. We're receiving you five-by-five. This is Two-Two. Easy Aspect Two-Two."

Good! The EWM-31 Gigadrone jamming platform was still out there. Leers decided to make absolutely sure that it actually was Easy Aspect Two-Two and not Pulsarians interfering with the communications.

"Authenticate *Walker Thrallet' Psll.*"

There was a brief crackle of static over the pickup. Then "*Golf Alpha Niner.*"

"Good call, good call" Leers said briskly. "Listen, I'm gonna need ya'll to degrade all the Pug's communications within this sector—got it?" It was a completely unnecessary request, Easy Aspect knew their job. "I don't want them talking to nobody—got it?"

"Roger that, Ranger Leader. We'll do better than that—we'll make their damn ears bleed!"

"Ahh, roger."

"This is Easy Aspect Two-Two, starting music. Good hunting you guys."

Leers clicked his mike twice in acknowledgment.

Easy Aspect Two-Two would fly some four hundred kilometers downrange of Ranger Squadron. It would hit the Malactite squadron with emissions that resembled the VF-94E search radar, thus fooling them into thinking an attack was imminent in one direction when it was really coming from another.

"We're ready to fight, Duke," came McHellington's declaration.

"Up and at 'em," Leers yelled into his mike as he pulled back on the stick. "You ready back there, Niki?"

"Ready," N'ckshell Slayton said easily—all business. She turned a couple of knobs on her radar scope. "I'm painting bandits in two-five-niner." An alarm chirped in her right ear. "And I think they see us. Yes, we'll know—"

At that instant, warning hooters sounded as the Pulsarian invasion force opened up with a deluge of laser and energy weapons to greet the approaching Vagrants attacking from the high position. Green, red, blue and yellow Dirks, Javelins, Black Jacks and high-energy Gaffs filled the air around Leers' approaching flight.

Why the hell are they shooting Javelins at us, Leers' mind raged.

The Vagrants began jinking up and down, left and right, firing off chaff and flares to spoil Pulsarian targeting. Leers rolled the Vagrant once and studied the enhanced target picture through his HUD. He maneuvered to place the target receptacle, the 'piper', as it was called in the old days, onto the bloated belly of the lead Malactite.

"He's locked up," Slayton said. "You're cleared to fire. Aligning deflectors."

"Lead's in."

"Two has the target."

"Three."

"Four's in."

"Harpoon weapons selected," Slayton said. In all actuality, Leers could've selectorized any weapon his Vagrant carried—however, against a target like a Malactite, the Harpoon would prove more devastating and economical than firing off dozens of Shards.

Leers mumbled to himself as he brought the Vagrant to wings level for an instant, went inverted and dove deeper into the thick cauldron of laser fire. He found himself thinking out loud: *"Stay still you bastard. Stay still. That's it . . . . Rock One, Rock One."*

Leers squeezed the trigger and felt the Vagrant heel over as the two port-side Harpoons raced away in a dazzling fury. The other members in his flight also fired on the lead and number two Malactite while Helen's flight hit the number's three and four.

****

Colonel Mitragon was thrown savagely against the restraints of his command chair as the first Harpoons slammed into his Malactite. He had ordered full power to the shielding, but the order came too late. Through the intercom, he could hear the screams of dying crews and the *KHRUMP! Whump! Skree!* of secondary explosions. The lights in the command center flickered and died as several of the controllers' panels exploded from the far reaching blast effects of those accursed Harpoons.

"Go to emergency power," Mitragon ordered above the din as more control panels overloaded and exploded. "Gunnery crews, lay down a suppression fire with the pulse-lasers. Gaffs engage!"

"Impossible, sir," an officer yelled out. "They've got the main drive and our emergency backup systems. We're dead unless we shut down and get the fires under control."

"Bah!—Alright! Shut down! Shut everything down! Colonel Stritragon—Colonel Stritragon, you have the lead. I will transfer my command to you—" Mitragon glanced at the formation display only to realize that Colonel Stritragon in the Number Two Malactite no longer existed—the whole Malactite no longer existed. Mitragon's mouth dropped open in shock as he noted that the Number Three Malactite was burning out of control and the Number Four no longer had a command module.

"Colonel, the fire teams can't put out the fires!"

"What?"

"Sir, we must eject—get to the escape pods before—"

The officer was cut off as another explosion shook the once mighty fighting-engine. Mitragon heard more screams. It sounded like the Fire Control team commander trying to—

****

"Look at those Pug bastards burn," Slayton yelled as she looked out the back of the canopy. Without warning, the Malactite expanded in a fiery ball of superheated gases causing the Vagrant to rattle. "Now they're cooking!"

"I see it," Leers said, also looking back at the destruction his weapons had caused.

Other victory calls came over the radio.

"Guns, guns, guns—straight through their command module!"

"Ranger Three—good hit!"

"Poured Harpoons right down their throats! The flanking Malac went up like a volcano!"

"Looks like Ranger Senior is hitting them hard on the flanks!"

"Alright people, settle down," Leers advised, "settle down."

"Way to go, Too Cool—that's four Malactites out of action!"

Just as quickly as the Ranger Squadron's tactical frequency was filled with echoes of jubilation, it turned into panicked cries of fear and danger.

"Look out, Ranger Three! You've got Gaffs on your six. Get out of there, Three. Get out!"

"Break right! Break right!"

"Ohmigod! I'm hit!"

"Punch out, Ranger Three, punch out!" Slayton yelled.

"Get out of there you guys," Leers ordered. "Tomas, get out!"

Ranger Three pulled back on the control stick as alarms screamed through the cockpit, which rattled like the focus of a planet quake. The pilot, Lieutenant Tomas Hall, was busy shutting down systems, cutting fuel flow, doing everything possible to stay alive—engine fire lights were on, the flight computer was exhorting the crew to eject . . . smoke filled the cockpit . . .

Through his magnified glare shields, Leers could see the Vagrant swap ends before it disintegrated, throwing metal debris in a flaming arc fifteen kilometers long. Only seconds ago, Leers had been cheering to the ghastly deaths of hundreds of Pulsarians. But the death of two of his own, Tomas Hall and Dein Skriier, made him sick. *Damnit! Why didn't they eject? They had enough time!* He had seen this many times before. Universe, it was something he had never gotten used to, perhaps he never would.

McHellington's group pulled up and away from the three burning Malactites they had hit on the flank. Just as the Pulsarians thought they were going to extend and escape, McHellington reversed direction, faked the extension reformed for a second attack and poured it onto the Battlebarges. Two of the barges went up in a sizzling column of flame. The Vagrants hit the deck and blasted out of the area in different directions. No one in McHellington's flight took a hit.

"Excellent work, Stan," Leers commended, no longer concerning himself with the demise of Ranger Three. "Form up on my mark and standby for re-attack."

It would take the Vagrants thirty seconds to re-form, re-acquire the invasion force, activate the jamming pods beneath their wings and hit the Pulsarians again. This time though, they wouldn't have Easy Aspect Two-Two hitting the Pulsarians with deceptive radar interference. For a moment, Leers didn't want to go in like this. Then again, after the first attack, the Pulsarians might think that the Vagrants coming in with their jamming pods on was simply just another feint and would thus hold their fire and wait for the real attack. Good, let them think that, then maybe—

"Heads up, Ranger Squadron," the AWF-19 called out. "We've got eight bandits slicing down on you guys. Twenty kilometers above you and three hundred kilometers to the west."

Shit!

Everyone in the Ranger Squadron knew what to do. McHellington's group would continue to press the attack while Dannen's group would engage the fighters. If the Echo Squadron was here, they'd have the responsibility of hitting the fighters. But since they weren't—

"Tally ho! Ranger Leader, I see 'em," Helen Lange cried out as she pulled her fighter up and around to meet the threat head-on.

"Got Spark Racers over the Hargil Peaks."

"Hang-on, N'ckshell," Leers warned as he too brought his fighter around hard, the G forces slamming into them violently.

****

Commander Terger Aragon, convinced that now he was the leading Pulsarian fighter ace, grinned as he and the other Spark Racers converged on the Vagrants which had been mauling one of the Malactite groups. Good—about half of them were turning to meet his forces head on. No Vagrant was an equal match for a Spark Racer XXR. Aragon had proven that fact several times today. He didn't know how many he'd killed, but the number would be officially tallied when he returned to the Carrier Advancer. Perhaps there would be another bronze medallion for him. Just another trophy to add to his already modest collection.

Okay, he thought to himself, *let's see how many I can drop in the first pass.*

The two opposing fighter forces hit the merge and instantly began turning and burning to get behind a potential victim or to keep from becoming a victim. In only seconds, two Vagrants burst into rippling flames, while a Spark Racer blundered into a wall of Shards. Aragon twisted away from his first kill to get the Federationer that had just killed one of his own. *Good. Here's another quick kill,* Aragon thought as he quickly channeled his weapons selectors. He was about to squeeze the trigger when the Vagrant snapped into a hard 12G twisting dive. Aragon quickly turned to pursue as his armored pressure suit fought to slice the force of gravity in half. He was just about to turn on the inside of the Vagrant and execute a quick snap shot when the Federationer reversed and increased speed. *Damn!* Aragon reversed also to follow. Again, when he was about to pull off a quick snap-shot, the Vagrant reversed again popping off flares and chaff to confuse his targeting systems. Aragon watched angrily as the Vagrant powered into a climb, burners glowing red. Aragon followed, straining to breathe against the force of gravity. The Vagrant reversed again and again, Aragon turned to follow, cursing. But this time the Vagrant had chopped its throttles and had its braking flaps fully extended, and landing gear deployed. Aragon's blood froze. He was going too fast and was going to overshoot. The Vagrant reversed again, nose up, retracted the landing gear, but kept the brakes extended, slowing down even more. Aragon was forced out in front. Now he was the hunted and not the hunter. Sick with rage, Aragon dove toward the planetoid.

****

Leers retracted his speed brakes and dove to follow the Spark Racer that had been hanging on his ass for the past thirty seconds. The Racer pilot was a good stick, probably an ace, and that made him dangerous as hell. Ace or not, he was no match for an Omnitraus pilot, right? Still, the Pulsarian knew his machine and wasn't afraid to take risks, to push the envelope—that made him doubly dangerous as hell. Leers looked over his shoulders to see if he was being pursued—he wasn't. If he had, Slayton would've told him by now. Leers refocused his attention onto the Racer in front of him. Time to press the attack while he still could. If only he could keep from feeling so goddamned sick from the jinking and g-loading—negative, positive, negative, then positive.

"Hey, light'em up, N'ckshell," Leers barked as he closed the distance on the target. They were both heading for the deck at an incredible rate of speed. Sooner or later the Racer XXR would have to bleed off a little speed and pull up before he made a smoky crater in the asteroid. If Leers drove him into the dirt or smoked him with a Shard, it didn't matter. A kill was a kill and he was going to bag this guy.

"He's locked up, Duke!" She said, not at all enjoying the rough ride. "Burn him."

The Spark Racer continued to dive. Leers closed to within eight kilometers of his prey. *Universe, I'm too close!* he thought. He was about to release two starboard-side Shards when the Spark Racer executed a brilliant and beautiful—and perhaps desperate—reversal to shake him. Instead of pulling up and loading up with position G's—like he was supposed to do; like any pilot was trained to do—the Spark Racer pitched further downward, curving underneath the angle of his dive! Leers couldn't believe it. *You've got to be shitting me*, Leers thought. The Racer leveled out with its canopy just meters above the surface. *Sonofabitch! That takes guts.*

Leers' admiration for the Pulsarian pilot's desperate tactics nearly got the human killed. There was absolutely no way in the blackest pit of hell that a Vagrant could follow that maneuver. The beastly fighter would punch a hole in the ground instead. Perhaps that's what the Pulsarian wanted to happen. *Bastard!* Leers pulled back on the stick and grunted as the G's slammed down on him—his g-suit fought to keep blood from pooling in his legs; the control stick felt like a ton as he held it back.

Leers grunted again, inhaled quickly, another grunt; the terrain continued to speed up at him at an incredible rate. The control stick barely moved, he might as well have been tugging on a pillar of steel.

At the last screaming second, the Vagrant pulled up and away from the pock-scarred ground. Leers brought his fighter up and around. Sweating and sucking oxygen like crazy, Leers looked around to see if they had a bandit on their six—negative.

"Gods and Universe, what the hell was that all about?" N'ckshell demanded from the backseat.

"Nothing. Don't worry about it. Hey, Stinger, where is he," Leers asked after a slight pause to gather his senses.

"Bugging out. Zone two," Slayton said as she switched on her long-range scanner, which was useless hash. At this point, she was only guessing where their tormentor was. "If we turn zero-two-zero, we should be able to get him on max burner . . . that is if you don't decide to take another dive at the ground again—*Gods*."

Leers didn't answer. He had to find out what was happening with the rest of his group. "Hey Blondy, give me your status."

"Just finished me second attack, mate," McHellington answered. "Two more Malacs out of action—stand by one. Ah've got a little problem here. Got a Racer on me six."

"Be there in five seconds," Leers said, twisting his fighter around in a tight arc and punching the throttles.

For the first time since he had engaged the Racer pilot, Leers could hear all of the activity on the tactical frequencies.

"His nose isn't on me yet—but I'm in deep trouble," McHellington was saying.

"We've got five bandits, five hundred kilometers to the south."

"Roger that. I see him."

"Call your tally!"

"Eight has the tally."

"Got a chaff corridor one-thousand kilometers across along the Blackerton Flats," Kaltorr noted calmly. Two Dirks flashed by the canopy. "How about a little help, Ranger Eight?"

"Fox Two, Fox Two!"

"Good kill on the Racer wingman."

"Target, target."

"Watch it Ranger Leader, you've got two behind you!"

Urrgh! Leers popped off chaff and flares and rolled his fighter to the left and then yanked it savagely to the right. He and Slayton strained to catch a glimpse of their antagonists as fiery green Dirks tore the rear stabilizer from the fighter. *Damnit! We're hit!*

At that moment, Leers didn't feel fear or outrage. He felt a sheer adrenaline-charged explosion of disbelief. His Vagrant swapped ends and somersaulted twice before Leers could take corrective action. The fighter vibrated like mad. Alarms sounded in his ears. Red warning flashes screamed off his retinas. Positive and negative g-forces pulled and pushed against his body.

"Duke, you're on fire! Get out of there!" an unrecognized, unrestrained voice ordered.

"Eject, Leader, eject."

Leers pushed the stick forward and hit the astrolerons in the opposite direction of the violent spin. Spin? Hell, the fighter was tumbling, backlashing, pitching, rolling, sweeping. There was no way that he could regain control. There was no way an *ordinary* combat pilot could regain control. He was an Omnitraus Officer and tradition demanded that he not only regain control, but rejoin the fight and do so in a detached, professional manner. It went against the grain to leave a fighter without landing it first. Besides, he and Slayton would most likely eject themselves into captivity.

The Vagrant righted itself. Leers added power to the throttles to get them out of the area and away from the invasion force. But he couldn't go too fast, the fighter might not like the shock waves brought on by increased speed and return to 'departed' flight. Leers looked around him and quickly noted that the bandits that had been on him were gone—perhaps chased away by his wingmen or someone else in his squadron. But they were far from being safe. He and Slayton were now a slow, juicy target flying in a straight line. Grapes on a vine, ready to be plucked by any Pug with the gumption to do so.

"Good recovery, Dannen," Slayton said over the hooting alarms. "But we have to get out of here."

"No shit, N'ckshell."

"No, I mean eject, dumbass. Get out of this fighter."

Leers ignored her. He looked at the craggy surface racing by beneath them. "Maybe we can—maybe we should—how's the damage back there?"

"Our tail is gone. We're on fire—nothing to worry about. We have no fuel cell ruptures—all systems seem to be functional except for the transceivers and the—"

N'ckshell was cut off as the hostile threat hooters bellowed their urgent warning. *No!* A Spark Racer was blazing at them head-on. Leers pulled back on the stick and jammed the throttles forward as red Daggers burned by the left side of the canopy. The Vagrant was slow to react to his commands, but sluggishly went into the vertical. *VARP! Crack!*

"Damn! We are hit! We're hit again!" Slayton yelled out. "He hit our port engine."

Leers shut the engine down and hoped that the fire control systems were working. If not—he pulled the stick back further as the nose of the Vagrant began to dip forward. *Uh, oh.* The Vagrant began to tumble again, and despite his best efforts, Leers couldn't bring the beast under control.

"Dannen, I'm burning up back here!" Slayton yelled as the entire after section of the fighter was a mass of flames. Slayton could feel the heat licking through the canopy—she struggled to stay calm. She wasn't about to start screaming like a—not in front of Dannen. She decided that she'd wait—yes, wait for the order to eject, she wouldn't leave her friend to die alone.

"*Arrgh!* She won't recover! She won't recover," Leers reported over the bellowing alarms. *And if she does recover, what the hell are you gonna do? Continue to be a slow, fat target for some Racer rookie?*

"Passing fifty thousand AGL."

Leers wrestled with the controls some more. *I don't wanna punch out.*

"Twenty thousand."

"Eject! Eject!" Leers screamed in utter desperate futility as he reached for the black and yellow handles. *No. I don't wanna do this.*

Nothing happened.

"EJECT!"

He pulled the handles again.

The canopy finally ripped away from the crippled fighter. Slayton was the first to go, gravitation systems in the ejection seat pulled her legs in snugly against the seat as the liquid nitrogen rockets fired—this would keep the Dracterian's legs from smashing savagely against the instrument panel. An instant later, she was ripped away from the burning fighter with the force of 70G's. The ejection seat's deflector shields were activated to protect her from the effects of an explosion as well as from the friction of slicing through space at high mach speeds. A microsecond later, Leers too was exploded from the cockpit as it finally dissolved into flame. It wasn't a clean escape for Leers. His ejection seat began cartwheeling awkwardly through space. He blacked out against the tremendous onslaught of conflicting gravitational forces. He never saw the Vagrant explode.

CHAPTER XXVI
THE KINTEESEN PASS

"GENERAL, the Deflector Shield Projector is operational!" Colonel Dargoinne declared as he burst into the all-but-deserted BWRC.

General Varxbane didn't answer. He stood silently watching the last of the battle plots fade to nothing. Time to leave. And yet a small part of him was reluctant to venture away from a command he'd grown so accustomed to. His feet remained anchored to the granite as his eyes searched for the exit that was a mere fifty meters away. But the Pulsarians weren't storming the interior of the asteroid base just yet; they were still fighting for control of the space above the surface of the asteroid. It would be a matter of time before significant numbers of Straaka would be moving through the base. What concerned Varxbane, what truly gnawed at his insides, was that the DSP had to remain operational for at least four hours; the amount of time the evacuees would need to get to the outer edge of the red-zone and into the green-zone of the asteroid system. If the Pulsarians got to that DSP before then—Varxbane's mind refused to explore the nightmare that would follow.

"Final preparations for our departure are already underway."

"Security locks are opening."

"The refugee ship skippers all indicate that they are on stand-by, ready to launch on your orders, General."

"Let's get underway at once," Varxbane ordered.

Officers and enlisted personnel began moving with purpose and uneasy determination. Varxbane gave one final appraisal of the BWRC, letting a sad sigh escape from his flaring nostrils.

One of the BWRC officers ran up to him. "General, we've got mechanized Pulsarian units moving along the Kinteesen Corridor. And reports of heavy tanks and howitzers moving along the Errassii Straits."

"Our main concern is the reports coming from the Kinteesen area," Colonel Granx said gruffly chomping on a cigar. "That's where the DSP is."

"Colonel Piercenan knows what his job is," Varxbane stated flatly. *You don't need to state the obvious, Colonel.* "Question is, can we give him any help?"

"With what?" Granx said too loudly, "begging my General's pardon."

"General Varxbane, Colonel Piercenan reports heavy fighting and heavy casualties," Colonel Maxine Hightower said as the remaining 'skeleton' personnel in the BWRC began to leave.

"Can they hold?" Dargoinne demanded.

Now what the hell do you think? Rifle-arms against tanks—they haven't got a prayer, was what Hightower wanted to say. "Don't know, sir. We got one call from Piercenan: 'Engaging tanks.' That was at 04:30. We tried to get through to him and get specifics. Types, numbers, anything—but we couldn't get through—still can't. Then just seconds ago, we get another call from Piercenan: 'Heavy fighting, heavy casualties.' End transmission."

"Universe," Dargoinne breathed.

"Send whatever forces we have remaining—we still have those marines from the Stern-Strike right—well send them down to the Erassii Straits to draw the Pulsarians' attention—let the Pulsarians know that we're serious about protecting that area."

"Yes, General." Hightower moved off quickly to carry out the order.

"Marines," Dargoinne gasped. "I didn't know Admiral Walthersen lent us some of his marines."

"Yes." Colonel T'rina Dareenshar stepped up. "We can drop those Strike Force troops in—they can draw Pulsarian firepower away from the Retainers protecting the DSP. Then get them the hell out of there before it gets too hot."

"Get Piercenan some fighter support," Varxbane ordered. "It doesn't have to be an entire squadron. Two fighters would be good, a flight even better. But Colonel Piercenan will need help if he's to protect the DSP."

"At once, General," Colonel Granx said.

"Piercenan is on his own for now," Varxbane breathed. "Set up the DSP decoys in the Wvarington Heights. . . activate the main DSP then light off the decoy in the Kradium Iron Forest."

"Decoys," Dargoinne demanded. "I wasn't aware of any decoys. Why wasn't I told?"

"Because, my dear colonel, you're not the only capable officer on this base. Now, let's move out."

"Yes, General."

****

Captain Val Kirkaldy stood on the bridge of her Trieste Frigate *Helmgate*. Her officers and crew were quickly assembling themselves to their stations with the haste of seasoned veterans. This wasn't the first party that they'd attended and it wouldn't be the last—Kirkaldy just hoped that future parties she'd be forced to attend wouldn't be as desperate or as hapless as this one. Trapped inside of an asteroid base with at least a thousand puking Pulsarian pigs ready to jump them once they revealed themselves made her want to heave over on the deck of the bridge herself. Too bad there wasn't anything in her stomach besides a couple of saltine crackers and watered down skim milk. Yeah, the official word though, was that there were no more than five hundred Advancers out there hunting for them, but Kirkaldy didn't trust the military—they'd lie to you just as easily as they'd put you in front of a firing squad. Hell, the other day she heard that the base's security forces had killed a hundred refugees who were lining up for their daily water ration. A hundred people shot down for a resource the asteroid base had plenty of; then the whole thing hushed up like nothing had happened. Kirkaldy didn't know if she truly believed that though—her executive office sure did. Why go through all of this trouble to protect them from the piggy Pulsarians just to kill a hundred people over water. Tomorrow the rumor will be that the security force killed a thousand refugees over a loaf of bread.

Kirkaldy had one of the military types on her bridge right now, looking about as uncomfortable and out of place as anyone she'd ever seen. He didn't look like a killer. Just as well, because she'd have never let him on the bridge. No, he was an alien—no, non-human, a Dracterian was what they were called, although many of them didn't like that word. But he seemed reasonably calm despite the dire muck they were in. He was standing next to her and looked just as tired and as hungry as everyone else on the bridge.

"It's just that I've never been on a starship before, Captain," Lieutenant A'llen Krenner said, trying to maintain some form of decorum.

"We're finished with the jumpseat," a crewman said to Kirkaldy.

"Thank you, crewman," Kirkaldy said. "Report to your jump-station."

"Aye, mum." The Yanattiian gave a curt salute and hurried from the bridge.

"With respects, Captain," Krenner blurted, "but are we going to Warp once we're above the surface of the asteroid base—I've never heard of such a thing before."

"No, of course not." Kirkaldy allowed herself a thin smile. "Haven't you been on a freighter before?"

"No ma'am—that's what I was saying . . ."

"This is technically a freighter—or Trieste frigate since we're mounting guns—not a starship . . ."

"Is it ma'am or mum?" Krenner asked suddenly. "Your crewman called you mum."

"Which do you prefer?"

"Captain."

"That's fine, too."

"When you told him to report to his jump-station, my mind sort of froze and I thought—never mind, I'll stop babbling now."

"You're doing fine, Lieutenant," Kirkaldy said. "Try to relax. The ride will definitely be smoother than any ride on a Star Force cargo hauler."

"Captain, with respects, I can't relax," Krenner stated. "I don't even know what I'm doing here. I don't know a thing about freighters. I didn't know you guys were Warp capable until a few minutes ago. I don't know why I'm here—I'm just an astronics tech for the Star Force."

"Lieutenant, you're here *because* you're in the Star Force." A crewman stepped up to her and handed her a data-slate to sign. She quickly scribbled her name with the stylus then handed the slate back.

"What, you mean like a spy?"

"If it'll make you feel any better, Lieutenant, when we arrived here at this base—after retreating from Yanattii—I had a thousand metric tons of tritium ore in my cargo holds along with about two hundred refugees we picked up from the Arcbane shipping docks. Now, several weeks later, I still have my cargo, we still have the personnel from the loading docks, but I find myself being allocated with a hundred more refugees and fifty of you Star Force people. So no, you're not a spy, you're more like a representative of the military and we're all going to have to get along for our trip to Shiborium. No one likes this, but we'll just have to work outside of our comfort zones for a little while. Is that okay with you, Lieutenant?"

"Quite clear, Captain."

"Why don't you have a seat; there's no need for you to stand next to me at attention like some midshipman under review."

"Yes, Captain." Krenner stiffened, slightly. He'd never been so subtly chastised like that—yes, he had, but not in front of a dozen people he had never met before. The bridge crew were all professional, as he could see, for the most part—but every once in a while they would look at him—like he didn't belong there, and worse, that he wasn't welcome.

Krenner took his jumpseat which had been hastily power sealed to the metallic deck of the bridge, and positioned to the left of the captain's command chair. He looked around the bridge at the merchant officers, all uniformed, their manner keen. Some of the equipment they powered up he recognized; some of it looked obsolete, other components looked fresh out of the box. Through the forward viewports, he could see the elongated forward deck of the *Helmgate—what a name for a freighter*, he thought. *A better name would be* Junkgate, *or how about* Junkyard? But he also noted the modern phased-array communications domes, the spindly sensor probes, the scanner pods, and the forward mast. What he couldn't see were the mammoth engines, the cargo compartments or the four Thorium deckguns. All of those were obviously out of the viewing angle of the forward ports. He wondered if they had the tech to project a floating image so that he could see the other parts of the ship. Probably not.

Kirkaldy activated a device on the left sleeve of her uniform and donned a headset. She adjusted the mouthpiece.

"This is the Captain, give me a 'go', 'no-go' for launch," she said. "Engines?"

"Go," the helmsman answered from his station a couple of meters in front of the captain.

"APU?"

The chief engineer replied, "go." Krenner couldn't see her. She wasn't on the bridge and was keyed into the bridge comm system from her station in the engineering department. The Auxiliary Power Unit was ready to engage if for some reason the primary drive system failed.

"EPU?" Kirkaldy asked, continuing with the launch checklist she had memorized.

"Go."

Again, Krenner didn't see the assistant chief of engineering clearing the Emergency Power Unit safe for space travel. Krenner knew enough about engines to know that if the primary drive failed and the auxiliary crapped out on them, then the emergency power unit would be the only item that could get them to a safe port. He also knew that if they had to rely on the EPU, then things would be very bad . . . very bad for them indeed.

"Cabin pressure?"

"Go."

"Life support?"

"The light is green."

"Hull plating?"

"Go."

"Deflector grid?" Kirkaldy asked glancing to her left.

"We are go," said an officer less than a meter from Krenner.

"Deflector auxiliary?"

"Good to go."

"Gravitational field?"

"Go."

"Vertical climbers?"

"We're go, Captain," the executive and chief of navigation said.

"Helmsman, bring the main engines on-line," Kirkaldy ordered, finally taking her seat. "Stand-by with the vertical climbers."

"I don't think we'll need them," the executive officers said off-handedly.

"Thanks for having so much confidence in our engines," Kirkaldy returned. "But let's not scare our guest too much in case the ride gets bumpy." She patted Krenner gently on the thigh. Both the helmsman and exec laughed mildly from their stations.

Krenner didn't think it was funny. Let's see how much they chuckle when the Pulsarians turn the heat up on them. Krenner swallowed—actually he didn't want to find out how they'd react after all.

****

A tremendous wall of flame tore apart one of the pulse-laser gun nests. Rook watched in horror as Colonel Piercenan Retainers and pieces of Delrel Retainers were thrown out of the nest as ammunition canisters and energy generators exploded with the blast. Rook and several others ducked behind a rock outcropping as more tank blasts ripped apart the ground in the deadly arena.

How long had it been since the Pulsarian tanks first made contact with the entrenched Delrel battalion? For Rook, there was no way to measure something as elemental as time—it seemed to freeze when the first lasers cut through the void, then time began racing along furiously as explosions began dancing along the valley floor, then as people died, that elemental sensation began hauling itself down to a bloody and terrifying slowness. There was no way to recognize it, to contain it, to make it all stop. Rook had seen individuals literally ripped apart as enemy laser fire hit them. The sight was so grotesque in its surreal execution that Rook had a difficult time comprehending what he was actually seeing. When he flew his VF-95C Valkyrie—death was a fantastic blur—the horror concealed by distance and staggering speeds. You never knew that people were being killed unless you settled down and really thought about it—something considered an obscene luxury while flying a high-performance fighter during a battle in deep space. Now however, on the surface of the moon, this bloated asteroid, things moved much slower, the visual impact stark and relentlessly horrifying; for it was happening all around him at a pace his mind could dissect, yet his eyes didn't appreciate.

Inside of his spacesuit, he was well protected from the vacuum; with the suit's armor plating, his fully in-closed armored helmet, he could withstand near misses. However, a direct burst would rip him apart like some of the others. His visor was reinforced with thin armored mesh and thin deflector screening which meant that he could repeatedly slam it into the ground without worrying about it cracking. The natural reaction for any sentient being wearing a spacesuit would be to do the exact opposite, to make sure their actions didn't harm the suit. The Accent Technologies A1-E1 tactical environment suit could take the punishment and then some. Rook still didn't want to risk it, ignoring the grim fact that to survive in a battle you had to take a dive, you had to find cover. Rook wondered why, in the name of the

Lord, he had placed himself in this twisted situation—naturally because he wanted to do something. Beyond being duty bound, he had to fight; he had to lend his support and skill where it was needed. It was one thing to fight tanks. It was another thing to fight tanks alongside personnel who had no more experience at fighting tanks on the ground than he did, no more experience than what a tactical simulator had taught them. And it took nothing short of raw nerve to do this on the surface of the asteroid, surrounded by vacuum. Adding to the mayhem within Rook's mind was being in a total vacuum while still having gravity . . . that aspect made what he was seeing, what he was experiencing . . . it was almost too much to comprehend. So he did his best to keep his head down, listen to the orders crackling on his helmet's internal speakers and follow Piercenan's plan—even as things seemed to be falling apart.

The colonel's plan was effective, at first. When a column of tanks approached, you just didn't open up on them, you had to wait them out until you couldn't stand it, then you waited some more. Then you hit them from all sides all at once. The plan had its merits, even Rook knew this. It would be suicidal to have launched an attack against tanks head-on with only a few Pulse-laser cannons, rifles, an assortment of side arms, and only two dedicated anti-tank weapons which had been uncrated less than fifteen minutes ago. A sane plan would allow Pulsarian armor to roll over the tops of the concealed bunkers and the subterranean service corridors that connected them. Piercenan's personnel would stay put, keeping communications and other emissions to null levels. No target radars would be used, no infrared trackers would be switched on, no threat emitters would be utilized. He wanted the entire valley, the Kinteesen Corridor, to appear dead. The bunkers, although hidden by sight, were constructed of the same sensor absorbing material that went into the general construction of the base. A scanner search, or a quick communications check would only alert the Pulsarian tankers to their presence, waiting to ambush them. The plan was to make the Pulsarians think that nothing of interest was in the corridor, maybe lull them into a false sense of security, then he'd hit them from all sides. If done quickly, coldly and accurately, Piercenan could create enough chaos within their ranks to insure a small measure of success—that is, until the Malactites and Battlebarges joined the party. If that happened . . . Rook knew he didn't have to think like a human to know what would happen to them then.

For now, they only had to deal with tanks. Piercenan was sure that his battalion could handle them. Rook wasn't quite as confident. But the cheetah had to admit that when the first shots were fired, it looked as if the colonel's crazy plan might work.

Still, it would be a formidable task when one considered the Pulsarian tank, the *landt'phizer*—there were at least a dozen different types of these Pulsarian weapons—Rook was too busy to remember them all, but most were between ten and fifteen meters long and three to five meters wide. All were built with a revolving command top-turret mounted on top of the primary drive housing. Four gunnery sergeants were used to operate and control the two-pronged principle barrage cannon that was more than nine meters long. Other tank personnel included scanning and radar operators, a countermeasures operator, anti-personnel gunner, space-track and anti-fighter controllers, two drivers, an engineer and, of course, the tank commander, usually the rank of leftenant. Pulsarian armor could race over most planetary terrain at near supersonic speeds if given enough room. It could demolish ninety-story skyscrapers with a blast from its barrage cannon and bulldoze the rumble with its thick frontal armor. Its reputation as a murderous machine that pulverized everything in its path from machinery, reinforced concrete, to steel and flesh was well deserved and ruthlessly executed every time the Pulsarians went into action. Piercenan and his battalion—of which Rook was now a member—much to the cheetah's chagrin—would have their work cut out for them just to survive. Forget about 'a small level of success'.

After the opening volley, Rook could see that Piercenan's plan was working. After the initial contact, the tanks were thrown into chaos. The tanks at the front of the profile were hit first, followed by attacks against the rear of their formation. Piercenan's Retainers burst from the hidden bunker and opened up with heavy weapons, and concentrated bursts from pulse lasers. The three leading tanks were put out of action immediately. The fourth tank came to a complete stop as laser beams either tore long gashes in the thick armor or bounced off like lead pellets. Panicking, the driver put the tank into reverse and it crashed into the tank immediately behind it. Delrel guns plastered both of the mammoth machines at close range; there was no way they could miss. Fanatically, other tanks swerved around the wreckage and began blasting away blindly with their cannons in a manner that ran contrary to the disciplined practice of shoot and maneuver. Their poorly executed tactics only added to the maddening confusion that rocked the Kinteesen Corridor.

The tanks at the rear echelon suffered the same deadly surprise as those in the leading element. Two of them were put out of action outright; a third took several dozen rounds directly into the command module. Burning crew members, in twisted contortions of agony, ejected from the burning module or burst out of hatches and tried to run for cover. In escaping the flaming horror, all were mercilessly mowed down by Delrel lasers.

The Pulsarians were stunned. They were used to attacking in formation, spread out on the battlefield for several kilometers—they didn't have that. They were used to having long-range artillery support from Malactites and Battlebarges—they didn't have that. Finally, if they weren't granted close-weapons-support, or low-orbital support; at the very least they should have APC's and Straaka jogging alongside the armor—they didn't have either of those. The only thing for them to do was shoot at anything that signified a hostile signal return, which at this point, signal returns seemed to be pinging all around them.

The Pulsarians at the rear of the armored column recovered quickly. Dorsal mounted anti-personnel napalm guns went to work on suspected Delrel positions. Computerized sensor sweeps began to pin-point the zealous attackers. Small computerized, motion-directed, pulse-laser guns joined the roiling devastation being wrought by the flame guns. Within seconds, dozens of Delrels were eaten up by murderous fire as bunkers were obliterated, gun emplacements destroyed, ammunition and energy stores brewing up. Several Retainers began struggling vainly to pull themselves from flaming wreckage or molten rubble, were cut down by the motion tracking pulse-lasers with the same merciless edge that the Federationers had granted them just moments earlier. With the threat at the rear cleared at last, the *landt'phizers* began to direct their main fire toward their flanks, while secondary defensive weapons went to work smashing bunkers and enemy positions virtually underneath them. The Delrel defenders began to catch hell. Within seconds, twelve bunkers were destroyed, along with nearly a hundred retainers. Then the Pulsarians began to hit targets 'up' the corridor.

Colonel Piercenan's bunker took a near miss, the shockwave bounding and rebounding through the tight chamber. Rook felt his feet rattle in his boots before he and several others were thrown against a far wall. The sensation lasted only a second, but he knew he'd never forget how he lost control of his body and was tossed aside like a doll. His visor hit a processing panel with such force he thought it would crack. It didn't, but he could see his panicked breathing fogging the clear plate before his eyes.

"Everyone out of the bunker," Piercenan ordered. "Get out, get out now!"

Another blast hit the bunker drowning out the colonel's orders. Rook bounded up, an invisible hand shoved him through the opening, his legs kicking through the vacuum. He felt himself spinning up, over, around; he could see the blackness of space, the surface of the asteroid, space—*crack!* he hit the ground. Gods, it hurt, spittle hitting the inside of his face plate. Working to get a glance at the approaching tanks—someone landed on top of him, knocking him back onto the hard surface.

"Sorry," the human female said, rolling off of him.

A staccato burst of pulse laser fire tore up the ground mere meters in front of him. Rook stared at it, eyes blinking against the blinding crackles of superheated flame.

"C'mon, Omnitraus," Colonel Piercenan yelled. "Find some cover before you get your ass killed!" He and several others raced past the startled cheetah, Pulsarian lasers searing the space around them.

Rook finally sprang to his feet and found cover behind a rock outcropping with the colonel, almost arriving ahead of the humans. Rook looked behind him and winced. He saw several soldiers being cut down by

Pulsarian armor more than forty meters away. He managed to drag two slow-moving humans behind the massive rock formation, much to their gratitude. A communications officer crouched next to the colonel wearing one of the portable communications packs. Before he could take another breath, Piercenan plugged himself into the set and struggled vainly to listen to the urgent message trying to break through the static.

A voice stated calmly that the Deflector Shield Projector was up and operational.

What? Piercenan felt an amazing surge of relief. He gave everyone a thumbs up and activated his own built-in transceiver to communicate with the rest of what was left of his Retainer Group.

"Hey, hey, everyone listen up," Piercenan barked into the microphone as a green and blue laser shrieked overhead. "They got the DSP operating, along with the decoy modules too. We've got to hit these bastards until all the evacuees are away."

"Yeah, I'm getting a confirmation that the evacuation is underway," one of Piercenan's officer said.

"The authentication is coming through loud and clear," another officer shouted.

The *landt'phizers* rumbled closer, Pulse-lasers cutting down Retainers like they were so many scattering insects. Rook felt disgusted. Suddenly, blue beams of intense light screamed overhead or clipped off large chunks of rock that he and the others were hiding behind. One soldier was struck dead in the chest. The beams went right through him, meaty chunks of red gore exploding from his back. Horrified and enraged, Rook stared blankly across the carnage of the battlefield. A bunker was burning here, a gun emplacement went up like a miniature, exploding volcano there, fleeing troops were torn apart further up the valley. Those that weren't ripped apart by the fire storm were squashed to a bloody pulp under the tremendous steel treads of the tanks.

Angrily, Rook brought his Hellington Standard Power Rifle up and aimed it at the nearest tank some two hundred meters down the corridor. He fired twice, and to his surprise, the armored vehicle exploded. What? The power rifle wasn't that puissant. He saw two distinct blurs streaking overhead. *Fighters?*

"This is Astra Ten rolling in on a three-two-niner," a voice crackled over his and everyone else's helmet transceivers. "Colonel Piercenan, do you copy my transmission. How are ya'll doing down there?"

"I copy, Astra Ten," Piercenan barked. "Give me an authentication, please."

"Sorry, no time for that Colonel, we're a little busy up here."

Yeah, I don't doubt that, Rook thought.

"Advise you take cover," Astra Ten said. "I'm gonna make another pass with a couple of Maces . . . standby."

"Copy that, Astra Ten," Piercenan acknowledged. "You're cleared hot." *For what it's worth.*

"Roger. Be there in five seconds."

"Take cover, take cover; grab some dirt," Piercenan ordered, diving at the ground himself.

Rook could feel the explosions crashing through the valley. He bounced up, clawed at the vacuum then hit the ground again with a solid thud. Rook had fired a Mace or two when he flew his Valkyrie, but he'd never been this close to the receiving end of one detonating and he didn't like it at all. The pressure wave hitting him felt like the hand of God. When his senses rebounded, he looked up as Piercenan thanked Astra Ten for his support. Bunkers smoldered in flames being fueled by energy canisters and ammunition packs. The dead and the wounded from both sides littered the blood-stained planetoid surface. Rook could see fifteen tanks smoldering.

"Hey, there's still about three of them out there," one of the Retainers said pointing down the valley frantically.

"Crap, we're gonna have to finish them the hard way, Colonel," said another.

"Omnitraus, you're with me now, move your ass," Piercenan shouted, as he and seven others charged the nearest *landt'phizers,* brandishing their weapons, "Hurry up, you're going to miss it!" Galvanized into action, Rook sprinted to join the colonel as other troops further down the valley struggled to assemble an anti-tank weapon. Rook fired the Power Rifle from the hip as if it were a Sub-Pulse Gun. He concentrated on taking out the menacing war machine's anti-personnel weapons as it turned to face the scurrying ants that were trying to destroy it.

"Hurry with that gun or we're dead!" Piercenan yelled at the technicians struggling to assemble the small, squat, bazooka-like weapon.

"Finished!"

"Fire, fire, fire!" Piercenan roared.

An angry green bolt of high-yield energy, comparable to the blast yield of the Harpoons used by fighters, screamed away from the anti-tank weapon and hit the tank's superstructure. Flames leaped from the threads but the armored behemoth rumbled on and moved straight toward them. *My Lord, what did it take to stop these monsters?* It'd be several seconds before the techs could recharge the weapon and fire again. An eternity. Rook thought frantically as his heart began to race. He could feel death staring him straight in the face—he stood there frozen in place, gritting his teeth and cussing in several different languages, brandishing his weapon in a sort of crazed rage. The monster rumbled closer now, within one hundred meters, bringing its anti-personnel weapons into play. Another fire team, further down the hill and to the tank's left, began to unload grenade launchers and Power Rifles onto the tank's steely sides. It ignored them and concentrated on Piercenan's group. A Retainer standing next to Rook was firing his Edsing 250 Blast

Rifle one second, and in the next second, his upper torso took the full force of an energy bolt. Rook was showered with bright red gore. The man's arms were blown in this direction and that, his head disappeared in a sheet of flame. What was left of the soldier's body fell on top of Rook.

As Rook struggled to pull himself out from under the grisly corpse, the anti-tank technicians fired their weapon again with a full charge. The blast should be enough to knock the tank back into orbit, too bad the technicians didn't take an extra second to aim the weapon. Yes, too bad. The second blast just glanced off the side of the command module—or so it would seem. However, it caused a big enough explosion, the full force of which traveled down conduits and optic leads to explode weapon system control boards, circuit breakers, and drive systems. The tank rumbled slowly to a halt only two meters in front of Rook—fires began to spread throughout the module as crews began to pop hatches to egress from their stricken machine. If Rook was horrified by the soldier exploding next to him, what he saw next would live with him forever. Space-suited Pulsarian tank crews, their faces contorted in agony, their mouths agape in some eerie muted screams, their bodies being eaten raw by invisible and bright red-orange flames, struggled to get out of the burning monster. Rook wanted to race up and help those poor murderous bastards—they had lost, the battle was over, the fight yanked out of their souls. But instead, he, like Piercenan and the others, began to open up on the helpless and unarmed soldiers. He could almost hear them scream as their bodies withered at the impact of the death beams. Rook couldn't stop killing and killing and killing. He began shaking. *What am I doing?* Rook threw his weapon down and dropped to his knees, sick. He clawed at the unyielding rock . . . his vision faded, failed . . . then came back with violent clarity. The ground seemed to be moving, far away objects closing in on him like shadowy monsters.

Rook felt his stomach heaving and pulsing, he hoped that his helmet had some sort of drainage filter as the bile came up.

****

Draystar examined the data on monitors to his left and right, then focused his full attention on the power readings of the Deflector Shield Corridor on the main viewer. The flight deck rang with the chatter coming from the refugee ships. Some of the skippers piloting those rigs were captains in name only—holding tight formations and maintaining speed with a Gladatraus warship required skill many of them just didn't have. Draystar wasn't too bothered by the ceaseless comm traffic; it made him focus on his duties more. He quickly entered an updated schematic of the evacuation forces for what must have been the tenth time in two hours while studying the deflector readings.

Damned if Colonel Granx and his engineers hadn't done it—the deflector shield corridor was pouring out more power than it had several weeks ago when he had first delivered the refugees here. The work they had accomplished under the most adverse circumstances was phenomenal. It wasn't a simple matter of adding parts to a functional DSP; they had to construct the whole network by scratch: the DSP, the array, the generation complex, the whole thing. Not only was the colonel responsible for the DSP's complete reconstruction, he'd also allocated technicians and mechanics from the base's fighter squadrons and set them to work making sure that every ship in the evacuation force was spaceworthy. When the ships were cleared technically, he had to make sure that they could endure the rigors of Hyperspace travel—not an easy thing to do since not one of the ships was permitted to fly, let alone light up their cores for testing. It was extremely dangerous for any ship to perform that function while twelve to twenty kilometers underground. And to do so would send out a signal that the Pulsarians would've easily traced back to the base. Instead, Granx and his technicians had come up with ways to simulate launch, maneuverable spaceflight, Hyperspace transit, and Warp deceleration without tipping off the Pulsarians. Granx did all of that, coordinated the evacuation, while making sure everything was squared away properly—no wonder the walrus was suffering from staggering mood-swings and violent outbursts.

While Draystar busied himself with admiring Colonel Granx's superb work, Jasmine keep both hands on the steering yoke; calmly guiding the *Mekadore Traveler* through the shielded vortex.

"*Golden Commodore*," Jasmine said through the open ship-to-ship evacuation frequencies. "Close it up please, close it up."

She could see a blue icon drifting out of position. *What was that man doing back there? How difficult is it to stay in formation?*

"*Emerald Queen*, this is the *Mekadore Traveler*," Jasmine barked into the channel. "Why are you scanning me? If you *have* to calibrate your scanner, please focus your directional beams toward the port edge of the formation. If you can't do that, shut your systems down completely."

"*Condor*," it was Draystar's turn to bark into the channel. "Close it up. This isn't a race, maintain interval and speed with the galleon in front of you, *The Musketeer*—don't worry . . . hold your position."

"*Emerald Queen*, if you don't shut that damn scanner down, I'll shut it down for you." Jasmine was angry now. "Awesome work, *Emerald Queen*, thank you—I knew you could do it."

"You weren't really going to fire at them, Jasmine?" Draystar asked.

Jasmine ignored him.

The evacuation plan called for the base's evacuees and the refugees from Yanattii to move out in five distinct waves. General Varxbane had ordered that the Gladatraus be the vanguard of the first wave. The *Mekadore Traveler* would punch a hole through any intercepting Pulsarians Advancers and nothing more. The evacuation order detailed explicit diagrams and instructions to get the Yanattiian refugees to safety; the *Mekadore Traveler* would be utilized solely to destroy any immediate threat preventing those refugee ships from making their Warp Runs—all contingencies regarding how the Gladatraus engage and destroy Pulsarian war materiel were rescinded.

Draystar had backed himself into a corner. He made a promise—no, it was more than that. It was his *mandate* to see those refugees safely to Shiborium. Otherwise, what was the use in being a Gladatraus Guardian? He was also under the mandate to obey every order delivered to him by Gladatraus Supreme—a mandate he and Jasmine violated. The refugee situation had burned on Draystar's mind for more than three days—he couldn't drop it. What was going to happen to him and Jasmine when the made it to Shiborium? When Gladatraus Supreme gave you an order, you took action and had the job done before she finished speaking. Right now he'd rather go toe-to-toe with a Pulsarian Battlecruiser Advancer than to face Gladatraus Supreme.

Draystar brought his thoughts back to the schematic of the five evacuation waves again. There were more than a hundred of the Yanattiian refugees flying an odd collection of Warp-capable vehicles from galleons massing 3,000 metric tons of spatial displacement to the small, fifteen metric ton feluccas; sleek high-speed starliners that could barely squeeze more than four hundred people within its spaceframe to the hulking 8,000 metric ton luxury liners that could hold ten-thousand; not mentioning the beaten up merchant marine freighters, rusty star-sweepers, orbital barges, tramp launches, and cutters. However, only seventy or so of the Yanattiian refugee ships would be making their escape with this first wave. The others, mostly merchant marines, with professional crews and captains possessing decades of experience, were flying formations among the remaining waves.

As much as he and Jasmine had argued that they stay behind until all five evacuation waves were clear, General Varxbane made it abundantly clear that they leave with the first wave. They had to get the mission data the Omnitraus stole to Shiborium. They were already three days behind. If they refused to go . . . Draystar didn't want his brain to travel over that well-worn ground again.

"Contact, target ahead," Nancy stated calmly.

Draystar wasn't alarmed, this was to be expected. Like all deflection screens and shields, the DSP was invisible and prevented the dense rain of asteroids on the outside from penetrating its shell. Vehicles and vessels could easily move from the inside out, but not vice-versa. Draystar nodded to himself as thousands of asteroids in the distance, of different shapes and mass, were being reflected back into the storm once they touched the powerful practical shielding. The shielding on his Gladatraus warship couldn't generate a practical shield a tenth as strong as the one protecting them now. Every once in a while, a boulder traveling at the right speed, with an acute angle of attack, would manage to sneak through the shielding.

"By the *Gods of Avbriltar—Golden Star*, increase speed or you'll be left behind," Jasmine raged into her communications set.

"We're doing our best, Gladatraus," came an almost insolent reply.

"Do you want us to deploy the tractor beam?"

"Negative."

"Do you wish to declare an emergency?"

"Negative." Came the *Golden Star's* panicked reply.

"Then keep up!" Jasmine fire back.

"Ease your inputs, Jasmine," Draystar said soothingly. "Easy does it."

The proximity alarm sounded.

"Section four-eight-seven," the flight computer read the coordinates and fed more information into the tactical display in front of Jasmine.

"I see it Nancy," Jasmine said calmly, as her fingers tapped lightly on the weapons console. "Stray asteroid, magnitude five, bearing two-niner-oh-three, six by six."

An asteroid as big as the *Mekadore Traveler* itself burst into a brilliant ball of flame, split neatly in half by Jasmine's gunnery. She paused, flexed her fingers then turned the remaining halves into luminescent dust.

"Good shooting," Draystar calmly noted, disregarding his flight systems to add, "you seem more anxious than what I would consider normal, Jasmine. What's wrong—"

"Draystar, we have to get out of here."

"That's what we're doing."

"Draystar, I've seen it," she said. "I've seen what the Pulsarians are going to unleash on us."

"Here?"

"No—that intel those Omnitraus stole. I know what the Pulsarians are planning to do to us—it's horrible, Derek, just horrible."

Draystar felt his spine tingle. She never called him Derek unless there was something truly rotten. . . "Well, we still have to get these civvies out of here, okay." He gave her a reassuring squeeze on her shoulder. "Let's concentrate on that, then once we're in Hyperspace, you and I can . . ." Draystar trailed off as the proximity alarm sounded again. Jasmine quickly dispatched the rock with the warship's weapons. He didn't know what it was Jasmine had seen or how big of a threat it was. All he knew was that it had her shaken and it had his own mind wondering about what lay ahead. Too bad he couldn't give it more thought, with the proximity alarm seemingly sounding about once every thirty seconds and refugee ships flying erratically, he had more pressing matters to focus on now.

****

Rook hefted the wounded soldier over his shoulder and ran for the wasp-shaped CFX-7 some two-hundred meters away. The Retainer had taken a piece of flaming shrapnel in the hip when a nearby gun tower exploded. The integrity of her armored space battle-suit had been breached for a few terrifying moments, but it then sealed itself around the still hot piece of metal and kept her suit from de-pressurizing. The human female screamed at the excruciating pain. It was the same female that had fallen on him earlier when the bunker blew up.

"You're okay, Love," Rook reassured her. "We're almost there. A few more strides and I can set you down and a medic can have a look at you."

"It hurts," she screamed. "It hurts so much."

"I know . . . but you are going to be fine. Trust me."

Suddenly, she stopped screaming. "You better not be lying to me, sir."

Rook chuckled. "We're *both* doing good, Love."

All of the Pulsarian armor had been destroyed in the Kinteesen Corridor. Colonel Piercenan and his Retainers had paid a terrible cost. Of the more than five-hundred souls that had fought against the Pulsarians, only four dozen or so remained to race for the CFX-7 or were wounded and had to be carried to it.

The battle had taken a tremendous toll on him and his Retainers. They were emotionally, physically and spiritually exhausted. It would take months to snap the survivors out of their shock. Months before any of them would be mentally fit to see combat again. Most would be ready, but others would never have the frame of mind to pick up a weapon and point it at another living being ever again, no matter how rotten and filthy the Pulsarians were. Rook felt as if he was drifting toward the latter. It was one thing to be in a Valkyrie, quite another to see the madness this close. Omnitraus Officer status be damned, he was going to do his best to make sure his next combat assignment was in the cockpit and not on the ground. Fighting on the ground was insanity magnified.

Rook ran up the ramp of the CFX-7, through the thin phototropic screening, and into the crowded hold, where he gently set the woman down and called for medics to help her. As Rook ran back out to assist other soldiers onboard, medical personnel converged on the twisted bodies of the dying and wounded. The field doctors removed charred helmets and cut into crusty spacesuits, eager to aid them, yet appalled by the nightmarish wounds inflicted by modern weapons. Nonetheless, they went to work in earnest, busy to save their suffering comrades.

Rook helped a bloodied and confused Dracterian onboard and watched as a woman carried a massive lion onboard.

The survivors were pouring in. But it didn't seem fast or urgent enough. Everyone acted as if the CFX-7 was some sort of sanctuary when it was nothing of the sort. They'd be safe only when they were in Hyperspace and not before. They still had to run a Pulsarian gauntlet. And in case no one noticed, they were still parked on an asteroid that was being overrun by a tenacious enemy. Sanctuary? Not a chance. They'd better hurry.

What—Something caught Rook's keen eyes. *No!*

A Battlebarge was approaching from down the corridor. Gods, it just burst out of nowhere. And the wounded were still limping up the ramp as if they had all the time in the universe. Rook's blood froze. *Hurry up, you fools!*

"Battlebarge!" someone yelled.

Fresh explosions sprang around the battlefield as the barge's 100mmx and 200mmx laser guns opened up on the wasp-like CFX-7. Some of the Retainers reacted by swearing and grabbing their weapons to return fire.

Everyone on the CFX-7 knew that they were dead. The cargo/hauler had no offensive weapons. And its shields and screens were more geared toward providing the flightcrews with a sense of heightened morale than on actually protecting them from hostile fire.

Rook and a dozen others were thrown to the deck as an explosion crackled against the shielding, sending sparks and ionic shards cycling up into the midnight sky.

Damn. To come this far to have it end like this.

Another explosion rocked the CFX-7, the Retainers fired at the barge knowing that their weapons could do nothing to stop it. Another explosion crackled through the wasp. Its effects ripped through the shields to fast-fry two unlucky Retainers who shrieked at the bite of death.

And still another explosion slammed into the cargo/hauler, and another. They wouldn't be able to take more of this. Damn.

A second Battlebarge joined the first. Rook knew he would die in seconds.

Then the two Battlebarges ceased their fire. Weapons spit flame upward. Something was attacking the barges. But what? Rook strained to look skyward and saw nothing. What was it? Then he caught a glimpse of fast moving metal. A brick with wings. A Vagrant. The warbird rolled in on the barges and lit them up with concentrated fire from its railgun. Bits and pieces of metal popped from the Battlebarges along with large slabs of armor plating. One Battlebarge slowed to a stop, heaved to the left and exploded, flaming solids ripping into the second barge.

"This is Ranger Senior," a harsh voice crackled over Rook's comm unit in his helmet. "Ye'er all clear for right now. Get that damned hauler out of here. Malactites are converging on this area. Now move!"

Rook thought he'd never be so happy to hear Stan McHellington's voice.

"Ah'll try to cover for ye until ye reach altitude. But it won't be easy. Ah only have me gun."

"Affirmative, Ranger Senior," the pilot of the CFX-7 acknowledged. "Launching now."

"Good. Say, listen. Ah, missed me hookup, like ah bleeding rookie. Ye wouldn't mind if ah hooked up to ye before ye make the Warp Run?"

"Of course not, Ranger Senior, of course not."

Rook and the other Retainers ran into the cargo hold as the main ramp closed and sealed behind them. In a few moments, he could hear the engines rumble to full power and feel the vibration they caused. They were clawing for altitude twenty seconds later.

Rook leaned against a metal beam and unfastened his helmet. He'd forgotten how much it stank, dried vomit and mucus was crusted all along the inner lining. He exhaled loudly and wiped dried vomit away from his snot and cleaned his whiskers. He hoped that Dannen and N'ckshell had made it safely away from this carnage and desolation. He thought about asking, but would McHellington even know? If he knew Stan, the human would've said something by now if he had any information. During a battle, it was all too easy to become separated from your friends. He exhaled slowly, batting his eyes to hold back the moisture. He'd already seen enough death and mayhem in the last few hours to last him a lifetime. He just hoped his friends had made it, but he was too tired to calculate their chances. All he wanted to do right now was find a place on the deck that wasn't covered in blood or filth and rest.

Before Rook could settle himself in, Colonel Piercenan knelt beside him and handed him a cigarette.

"You did good out there, Omnitraus," Piercenan said, lighting Rook's smoke, then his own. "Real good. You should join my Retainers."

"My name is Rook, sir." He took a drag from the cigarette and almost started coughing when the smoke entered his lungs.

"Yeah, whatever."

"Are we allowed to smoke on this flight, sir?"

"I'm a colonel, no one's gonna say anything to me."

Rook chuckled lightly and took another drag. He felt the euphoria washing over him, the nicotine relaxing him. "I wonder who—"

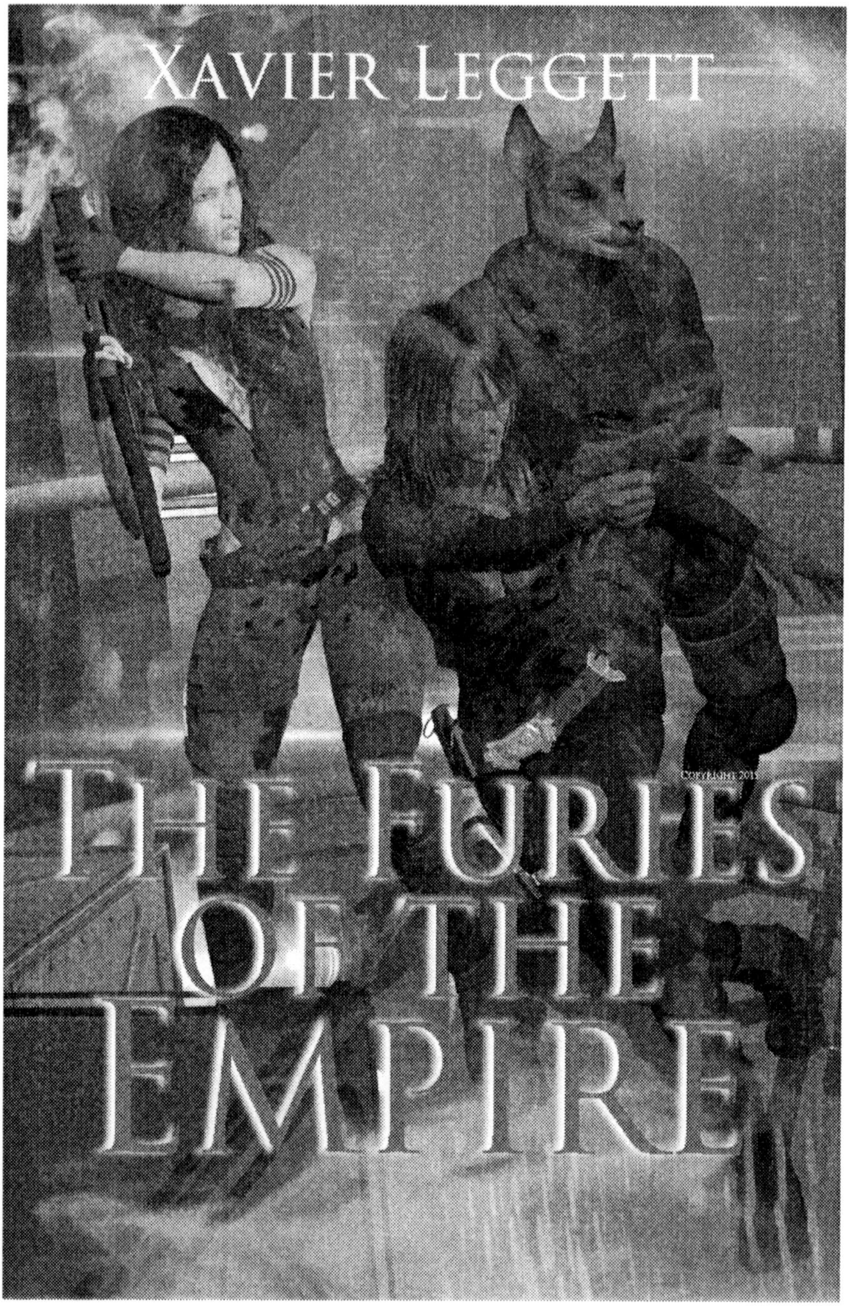
XAVIER LEGGETT
THE FURIES OF THE EMPIRE